SHAME

SHAME

Bergljot Hobæk Haff

Translated from the Norwegian by
Sverre Lyngstad

HARVILL PRESS
LONDON

First published by Gyldendal Norsk Forlag in 1996
with the title *Skammen*

This edition first published in 1999 by
The Harvill Press,
2 Aztec Row, Berners Road
London N1 0PW

www.harvill-press.com

1 3 5 7 9 8 6 4 2

Copyright © Gyldendal Norsk Forlag, Oslo, 1996
English translation copyright © Sverre Lyngstad, 1999

Bergljot Hobæk Haff asserts the moral right to be
identified as the author of this work

A CIP catalogue record for this title is
available from the British Library

This translation has been published
with the financial support of NORLA

ISBN 1 86046 531 5

Designed and typeset in Minion at
Libanus Press, Marlborough, Wiltshire

Printed and bound in Great Britain by Butler & Tanner Ltd
at Selwood Printing, Burgess Hill

To the Memory of
Alexandra H. Lyngstad

S. L.

I

A Lively Fellow

1

Once again I've been committed. This time to the clinical section of the prison-like asylum where I'm placed from time to time when I lose control of myself and succumb to my old desire to roam.

My fellow patients are almost all senile or profoundly deranged and up to several decades older than I, who will turn fifty-seven come spring, if I should live that long. They drift about the corridors like the lost souls in Dante's *Inferno*, mumbling unintelligibly, raising their arms beseechingly toward the ceiling, laughing ecstatically or bursting into childish sobs with their heads in their hands; or they sit for hours on end in the same position, rocking back and forth.

Apart from the loss of freedom, which was very trying the first few days, I have no complaints; the place feels almost like home. I have my own room, larger and lighter than the cramped maid's room that has been my permanent address for the last thirteen years (when I haven't been committed or on the road). I can spend the day pretty much as I please, thanks to my benevolent twin sister, the psychologist and media queen Thrinebeth Sand, who has a Ph.D. in split personality and identity disorders. It's her private eyes that track me down when I wander aimlessly about town, rummaging in the trash cans, getting a fix when offered, or sleeping on a bench at the Central Station with one of my bags for a pillow.

The medical director is a loveable elderly man who is almost never to be seen, but who knows how to make himself popular when he finally makes an appearance. He pops up now and then on Sundays; looking like a rubicund Santa Claus, he pats us on the cheek, hands out chocolate bars and bags of sweets, and utters a few encouraging words at random before beating a hasty retreat.

"Dear friends, you will pardon me, won't you?" he says with a smile as he backs out the door, waving like an old film star, his arm outstretched.

The haste of the assistant physician is of a different sort when he rushes through the ward on his way to the clinic for neuroses, where he rides his hobbyhorse: group therapy. What business does he have here, where he encounters nothing but old age, decline, and hopeless cases? His every movement reveals his discomfort among these human wrecks and that he regards this ward as a transit point. He consults his watch all the time, rustles his papers vigorously, and is careful not to meet anyone's eye. The charge nurse follows faithfully at his heels, relieving the patients' disappointment with a few kind words. But being a part of the system, she sees to it that nobody clings to his white coat or poses inopportune questions that may hinder his sprint through the ward.

Because I am a new patient, he is obliged to put his head in at my door and cast a glance at the case-sheet that the nurse shows him. He is about to go when she says something to him that makes him stop and turn round.

"I hear you have requested pencil and paper," he says, with a sceptical look. "You intend to write your memoirs, perhaps?"

Embarrassed, I shake my head in shame, but he is feeling benevolent and assures me that I can have all the paper I want.

"Didn't you, as a matter of fact, publish a book once?" he says, his voice revealing all too clearly that he considers my writings a mere caprice.

"Nine," I reply, with a certain firmness. "Six novels, two collections of poems, and one play."

"Is that possible?" he says theatrically, rolling his eyes. "Then you're almost a writer of sorts! Who knows, maybe some day you will surprise us with a whole family chronicle."

Soon he is gone, and I put my head out the door just in time to see him disappear into the office of the charge nurse. I steal on tiptoe along the hallway and listen outside the half-open door. It is me they are talking about in there.

"Go ahead, let her have all the paper she wants," the assistant physician repeats in a low, resigned voice. "That'll keep her occupied for a while. Anyway, judging by the case sheet treatment is out of the question. But she has to make the time pass, of course, and it probably won't do any harm if she scribbles a little. Just in case, keep an eye on the wastepaper basket, and have one of the interns check whether there might be anything of psychiatric interest. And one more thing: see to it that she is under constant surveillance outside the hospital grounds. She can't be trusted, and we'd rather not have any repetition of what happened last month."

I quickly withdraw and hurry into the toilet, so that no one will discover I have been eavesdropping. The fact that I am under surveillance soothes me, despite its being insulting. It can only mean that they will grant me leave once in a while, so that I can go for a walk in the town and shake off my torpor.

What happened one evening last month – and this had better not be repeated – is that I was in town on my own and disappeared.

One morning around mid-September I was summoned to the head nurse's office to discover that I was going to the cinema that evening, the early show. The ticket had been bought without anyone bothering to ask me what film I'd like to see. It was a test, said the head nurse, handing me the ticket and a fare card for the tram. If I was back in time and showed myself worthy of the confidence placed in me, I might have hopes of being discharged.

The film was quite impossible, needless to say, sweet as saccharine and full of improbable situations. Half way through I had had enough and left the cinema feeling strangely weightless, which ought to have warned me of what was to come. I paused in the street to look at the poster for a film I would like to have seen but that no doubt was considered too real for a hollow soul like mine. I still had an hour and a half to kill before I had to go back to the hospital. I shivered in the chill evening air and didn't know what to do. Suddenly a darkness seemed to descend on that part of my brain that watches over me and guides my steps – something like what happens when the light goes out in the cinema and another reality appears on the screen. I walked with hurried, restless steps, not knowing what was driving me or where I was headed.

When they found me, I had kept going for six days and nights and employed all sorts of ruses to shake off the narcotics agents. I had picked up quite a few fixes, partly by selling my bracelet and chain, partly by dipping into my last savings.

I was now sitting at the very edge of the Aker Quayside, basking in the radiance from the Akershus Fortress. I had been given a fix for free by some young men who were too high to care about the money. Coming by, they asked if the old lady would like a trip, and I held out my arm and got an adder's bite so gorgeous that I screamed. I was beyond all pain by the time the gang waved goodbye and disappeared into the consumer paradise that has risen on the ruins of the old machine factory. I sat dangling my legs over the water, staring in fascination across the bay. The sombre fortress was enveloped in light like a huge halo, and however much I looked I couldn't get enough. It's always like that when the drug starts working – the world expands and takes on a greater luminosity. Everything that weighs me down falls away, the gates of heaven open, and I'm lifted up and borne into celestial bliss.

But as I sat there swimming in ecstasy, something embarrassing happened which brought me back to reality. I had to pee, but considering the state I was in I couldn't possibly look for a toilet in the consumer paradise. Besides I was completely broke – I didn't have even the one krone necessary to make the door to the privy fly open. As I sat pondering the situation, I grew more and more desperate and realized that time was precious. Looking over my shoulder, I made certain there wasn't a soul to be seen. I staggered to my feet, raised my skirt, pulled down my panties and squatted so far out on the edge of the pier that my little yellow jet was immediately swallowed up by the grey waves. I breathed a deep sigh of relief and continued sitting there, comfortably rocking, long after the warm jet had ceased. Everybody is familiar with this situation, though few are shameless enough to admit it. To urinate in an emergency gives a sensation of pleasure greater than any tax relief. It's like being born again or saved from imminent danger.

I was brought back to my senses when I heard footsteps approaching. Turning my head, I saw a small group of about six people stop nearby, posing for effect. It must have been quite late in the evening, they had probably been dining in one of the many quayside restaurants, celebrating something special or holding a company banquet. At first they seemed to take offence, unable to believe their eyes, but when they realized the situation they bent forward and inspected me inquisitively. I still had my panties round my ankles, and however much I struggled to stand, I couldn't make it.

The last thing I remember before I lost my balance and fell into the water was a woman's voice raised in outcry, and the shadow of a man who rushed back to the consumer paradise, most likely to call the police. I seemed to hear, far away in the distance, a heavy splash, before an icy cold pierced me. As I lost my breath and sank down through all the chambers and corridors of the kingdom of the dead, the thought flashed through my head: Now it's over, now you're drowning!

Fortunately I was spared all the fuss with police and ambulances that usually precedes an admission. When I awoke, I was lying in a sparkling-white sickbed, not in the loony bin but in a quite ordinary medical ward.

I lay there sporting a mass of tubes and cannulas, which kept my biological processes going while I myself was practically dead. It took some time before I recovered my body again, and resigned myself to the awesome thought that I had been raised from the dead.

I lay dozing in that white bed for nearly three weeks, partly to recover after death by drowning, partly to get detoxed. First my body was pumped for water and mud from the Oslo Fjord, and later for more insidious, unmentionable substances. I lay on my back gasping for some relief day and night, my skin reduced to a huge bandage of pain and all my mucous membranes, including my cracked lips, invaded by an unbearable drought. In the meantime my indefatigable twin sister had procured a place for me in the loony bin's darkest corner, where I'm now devoting myself to the scribbling that the assistant physician has prescribed.

On the very day when, having thrown a glance at my case sheet, the assistant physician declared me incurable, the charge nurse enters my room and places six green pencils and a box of writing paper on my night table, beside the glass of water and the vase with dried flowers.

"Five hundred sheets of bond paper, what do you say to that?" she asks, smiling with her big, white teeth. "It should last for a while, unless you surpass yourself and have a volcanic eruption. You can safely write whatever you like," she adds in a slightly lower voice. "Just give me the sheets as you go along, and I'll see to it that the interns don't get hold of them."

I give her a wavering look, overwhelmed by the thought that so much sympathy and thoughtfulness can be found inside a white nurse's uniform. She is supposed to be new to this place, and is so unlike the Good Samaritans I've had to deal with so far that I can hardly believe my luck.

"Let me give you a good piece of advice," she continues, "don't let what the assistant doctor says get to you. He has his own sense of humour and often says things that may hurt. But he is kind enough and means no harm by it."

"It doesn't hurt me to be told that I am a completely unknown author," I answer, turning to gaze vacantly out of the window. "It's been almost seven years now since I published a book. And besides, I have always striven to make myself invisible."

"I know," she says, with a mischievous smile. "After all, every one of your books deals with people who have lost their identity."

"What do you know about my books?" I say, almost shouting. "They were pulped, rubbed out, a long time ago. Nobody remembers what they were about any more."

"Don't say that, don't say that," she smiles, shaking her finger at me. "The mortality rate among books is very high, heaven knows, a hospital can barely keep up. But not every reader was born yesterday."

My face feels hot. I am weighed down by the strange sense of shame that always comes over me when someone mentions my books. It's as if they point to a defect that I have, or touch an incurable wound I'm hiding somewhere under my clothes. I instantly seek cover, and in my momentary embarrassment I'm ready to deny, and to recall, every single word I've written.

The ream of paper is left intact for a long time, even though the charge nurse has arranged everything and brought a table and chair for me. For the first couple of weeks I seem stunned, unable to shape a clear thought. My body is still in revolt after the withdrawal, thirsting for stimulants and writhing in the most dreadful abstinence. When the pain occasionally eases off, I prowl around on the floor as if fighting shy of something, full of a restlessness not unlike that which takes over just before I abandon my permanent home and take to wandering.

I often catch myself missing Unit B – the last continent of normality before I absconded and stepped out into empty space. There, too, I was committed, it cannot be denied, but under much more relaxed and open conditions. The last five months in Unit B were full of deprivation and restrictions, but I still found myself on the right side of the fence, among ordinary yearning, suffering people. They might be depressed, rebellious, anxious, panicky, but they still had something to look forward to. They had retained their hopes and possibilities and hadn't gone so far off the tracks that there was no way back again.

Why didn't I stick it out, torn by restlessness though I was and my feet hankering for asphalt and cobblestones. What did I get out of my rash escape, other than hopelessness and aggravated circumstances?

How do you teach yourself to live without hope, nakedly and without prospects like an animal in a cage? Where does a human being turn when her wandering is over and all roads are closed, except for those that lead backward in time and space? Is my memory strong and vivid enough to sustain me, or do I resemble "that most unhappy one" in Søren Kierkegaard, who lives now in his memories without having anything to remember, now in his hopes without having anything to hope for?

One thing is certain: in my present condition I won't be able to concentrate on anything for any length of time. Occasionally I experience flashes of insight and a certain *joie de vivre*, but these happy moments never last long. Before I know it I've lost the thread of my thoughts and I slide back into no man's land or emigrate to the realm of distraction. It was really quite risky of me to ask for pencil and paper, even though I am, in the words of the assistant physician, "a sort of writer". If I succeed in putting anything on paper at all, it will no doubt be just as incoherent and unfinished as my life.

To avoid drowning in my own life history, I have to distance myself from it and tackle the subject as I did when I went to school and had to write a composition on an assigned topic. Only by keeping my scribblings within a strict, almost impersonal framework can I hope to capture a material that is constantly vanishing, evading my grasp. To submit to a course of events dictated by fate, by a superior power, by chance, suits me better than ever; in fact, it has become my refuge and the only way I can relate to anything.

At school it didn't much matter what the assignment was. After pondering a while, with my hand pressed to my forehead, I stepped out of myself and into the topic, until the borderlines were erased between me and my subject. In my happier moments I still believe the subject is just a pretext and that I am capable of working my way into practically any material. People who are not clearly defined persons sometimes have the gift of being able to crawl into almost any existence and make it their own.

But what about inspiration? I can hear the aesthetes sighing. What about personality, identity and the other spiritual requisites that should guide the hand of a writer? To that I have to answer once again that I have no identity, and that at the age of fifty-six I have only a faint inkling of who I am.

For the time being I visualize a story in five or six parts, which can be filled out here and there with scattered remarks on my present condition and a few glimpses of recollection that cannot be worked into a chronological presentation. It will be a writing exercise that differs radically from those short, compact plots so characteristic of my previous books. Whew, I can already see the reviewers knit their brows and arm themselves with their most damning formulas. At one time it was wrong that my books were so taut and stylized, now the complaint will be that I'm not in control of my material, but allow it to spread into an account with neither head nor tail.

I'll have to accept that risk, sink or swim. I take solace from the fact that literary reviewers are people like myself, with clear-sightedness and limitations, wishes, expectations and irremediable disappointments. Sitting here on the stumps of my wasted life I cannot pay any attention to what they might regard as good or bad literature. I can only listen to my inner voice and try to hold on to the pictures that in fugitive moments light up on the horizon of recollection.

When I lie half-awake at night the past comes alive again, drifting like huge clouds above my head or popping out of the corners like vague shadows. I breathe a deep sigh of homesickness and drowsily travel back through time and space, until the world opens up and receives me. After a delay of thirty, forty, fifty years, the memory-pictures rush in upon me, so vivid and fresh I have to sit up in bed and rub my eyes.

I can see every tiny flicker in my father's indignant face and notice how the atmosphere becomes charged and throws off sparks, until the devil breaks loose and the fit of rage comes upon him. I can see him lying full-length in bed during his long illness, one side paralyzed, throwing himself angrily here and there and shooting brilliant, half-crazy sentences from one corner of his mouth, while his young daughter takes down the document that he calls his apologia. I can hear his singing voice float sonorously through the bays of the church, a sound so rich and renowned that it even summons the ungodly to God's house. I can see my mother, head held high and her mouth pinched, after she has once more won the argument and makes a victorious exit. From my hiding place I can see her twist and turn before the mirror, puff out her bosom and admire herself from every conceivable angle, until she is certain that nobody could resist her beauty. In the middle of the war, she stands in the hallway putting on her new fur coat and taking it off again, the coat she has received as a present from the enemy, uncertain whether she dares to wear it in the street. I see her pouting underlip when something goes wrong, hear her light footsteps on the stairs and her happy girlish laughter when the workaday world has loosened its grip and something new and exciting is around the corner.

And thus the stream flows on from the blood bank of my memory. At one moment I stand small and dwarfish on a street corner tearing down one of the Nazi posters, stamping on it and casting frightened glances in every direction. At the next I am my own double and follow hard on the heels of myself during my first flight from home, which was to become the prelude to so much homelessness and so many long wanderings. Then a shiver passes through me, and I feel the fidgets of the seven-year-old as she sits on the lap of the SS officer, aware of the magic that radiates from the death's-head on his collar. The next moment I climb the steep stairs to the attic of Grandfather's house and see the little Jewish boy sitting curled up in there, his dark eyes wide with fright as he makes mute signs to me not to betray him.

Then the wind of time sweeps across land and sea and I feel the ship rocking beneath me during my first voyage to Denmark, at a time when I had signed some strange documents and was on my way to a foreign coast to give birth to my child in secret. I see myself roaming about in the provincial Danish town many years later, in search of the child that can no longer be found. I see fleeting visions of myself wandering through Europe's small towns and big cities, perhaps still in search of something too precious to be lost. Then I am home again, middle-aged, my spirit broken; I find myself a temporary place to stay and become gradually inured to hopelessness. Mother's vanity is gone, along with her beauty, and she seeks compensation in a narrow-minded Christianity. Grandpa is ailing and preparing to do penance. And horror of horrors: there I see him walk with firm steps up to the podium in the meeting house, bow his head in silent prayer and make that fatal confession, which will ruin his good name and turn him into a target for the malicious gossip of our small town.

When the night nurse hears me moaning, she sticks her head round the door and asks if I would like an injection. The cold turkey is not yet over, and some nights I'm so exhausted that I let it happen. But my resolution grows in secret, and I know that the day is approaching when I shall be strong enough to bear the pain.

The first chapter I have in mind to write I've called "A Lively Fellow". It will deal with how my maternal grandfather rose in the world, from being an ordinary seaman and a devil-may-care chap to become a ship owner, entrepreneur and head of the town's strictest congregation.

All that relates to his accomplishments before my time I have from his own vivid accounts and from the tear-choked confession he made to me during the three weeks I was watching over him on his deathbed. Otherwise I have picked up a little of everything from members of our large family, from the employees of the shipping company and the barracks industry, from small farmers that he ruined and, not least, from those belonging to his religious congregation, the so-called Ark.

I hope my account will show that Grandfather was not simply a hypocrite and petty swindler, who eventually developed into a big swindler and a heaven-inspired spiritual castigator. This complex man was also a warm and innocent human being with a modest, but genuine poetic vein and an honest will to serve God and man. That he didn't always succeed was due to the other side of his nature, what he used to call "the old Adam", which time and again made him buckle under to the devil and to the world's temptations.

Viewed in retrospect, despite his strictness and his patriarchal outlook, he appears a lively and amusing man. The fact that he never hit it off with my father will surprise no one, considering the old man's evangelical views and his ineradicable hatred of everything that smacked of liberal theology.

Just as I'm about to begin my first chapter, there arrives a letter from my twin sister, a document so cold and heartless that it completely paralyzes me for several days. Only afterwards, when the paper no longer trembled as I picked it up, was I able to gloat over the lack of self-knowledge it displayed, despite the condescending tone. The letter went as follows:

Dear Josefine Charlotte (or Idun, which I believe you prefer to call yourself),

Now that you have been committed once again, I send you a last warning, which I hope you will take note of. With your latest antics you have made yourself completely impossible and once and for all betrayed the trust of the hospital and the family. Accordingly we have no recourse but to hospitalize you for good and see to it that you are declared incompetent.

I suppose I don't have to tell you how embarrassing it is for me, your twin sister, that you are at large and getting up to all sorts of trouble and shenanigans. Even though we are not identical twins, there is unfortunately a certain physical resemblance between us, and I must make sure that my clients and viewers won't run into you and think it is I who stagger about in a groggy state, rummaging in the trash cans for empty bottles, seeking the company of street-walkers and obeying the call of nature in public. As for your other feats of shamelessness, they do not even bear to be mentioned. But, after mature deliberation, I have taken precautions. My patience is exhausted, and I won't tolerate my work being ruined by a sister who looks like a hideous and malicious caricature of myself.

As I've said, we shall see to it that you are declared incompetent, physically as well as financially, and that you will no longer be free to indulge in your lunacies. But we do not wish to punish you, and if you behave yourself we will take care that you have certain advantages which your fellow patients do not enjoy. As you can see, you have been given your own room, you do not have to go for treatment, and you can spend your day as you please.

Stay as well as you possibly can, considering what you have let yourself in for. In a few days an attorney will call and present some papers for your signature.

Your grieved and deeply disappointed sister,
Kathrine Elisabeth

The following day the attorney showed up with the documents, which were composed in cryptic words and opaque turns of phrase. A stroke of the pen, and I would be stripped of property, self-determination and personal freedom.

He first queried why I called myself Idun Hov, when the name Idun was not to be found in my baptismal certificate and both my siblings had Sand as their family name. Was I using a pen name, perhaps, or how come I was trying to hide my true identity?

I told him that it was a bit complicated, but not difficult to clear up. Hov was my father's name and therefore my correct name, and Idun was one of the three Christian names to be found in my original baptismal certifi-cate. But after the war my mother had begun to be ashamed of being called Hov, and as soon as my father died in 1951, she took the name Sand for herself and her three children. At the same time she decided to get rid of the baptismal names of Norse origin which my father had entered in the church register without her consent.

I was only fourteen when this happened, and nobody paid any attention to my protests. But as soon as I came of age, I took the matter into my own hands and filed an application with the government to have my real name back. It was granted, and I was given a new baptismal certificate, the third of its kind, with everything as it had been from the beginning.

My father had been convicted of treason and had served five years of his sentence when he was released on account of failing health shortly before his death. I did not defend his attitude during the Occupation, I explained, it was far too ambiguous and careless, though it was never conclusively established that he was a Nazi. Nevertheless I didn't want to let him down by disowning his name and rejecting the additional name he had given me. I was the only one of his children who had been attached to him, and I wanted to show my loyalty by openly acknowledging myself as his daughter.

The attorney said nothing, but shook his head slightly as if to show that he gave no importance to my explanation. Then he began to explain his errand in a pedantic and over-simplified language, as though talking to a child or an imbecile. I would lose my right of inheritance, he said, and when my mother died I would not be consulted during the settlement of the estate. But I would be taken care of in the best possible way; I would have two guardians, and a small monthly sum at my disposal. Unfortunately he couldn't promise me that I would ever again regain my freedom. I had been put to the test more than once, but had shown time after time that I was unable to look after myself.

When he had finished he pushed the papers to my side of the table and pointed to where I was to sign my name. I hesitated a little, and he assured me once more that the arrangement was for my own good and that everything had been done to give me kind and right-minded guardians. I nodded, but refrained from asking the names of my new superiors. The mere fact that they had expressed their willingness to step into that role sufficed to make me distrust them and want none of their beneficences.

As I got ready to sign, it struck me as odd that a person considered mentally incompetent was required to confirm her own incompetence. I glanced at the attorney and hinted something to the effect that my signature was probably self-contradictory, but he didn't seem to understand what I meant, and, after briefly practising my ballpoint on the corner of a newspaper, I swallowed my objections and signed my name where it was supposed to be.

The next moment the attorney slipped through the door with his prize, and I was left behind, humiliated and stripped to the skin. The fee he received for erasing me from the ranks of the living and transforming me into an imaginary quantity, must have been anything but a modest one.

After I had sat a while pondering my new status, I shrugged my shoulders and said to myself that it did, after all, agree quite well with my actual situation as a clinical patient and incurable lunatic. At the thought of having been eliminated, a sort of gaiety rose within me – I could now spend the rest of my time as a free hitter in the great ball game of life. From now on I could pull out all the stops, the crazier the better, and nobody would be surprised or attribute any significance to it.

I paced the floor, drying the tears that came to my eyes. Then I took a sheet of paper out of the box and jotted down a brief letter, which I immediately rejected and threw straight into the waste-paper basket.

Dear Urd (also called Kathrine Elisabeth, or Thrinebeth, in what seems to be your preferred jargon),

I have just had a visit from your hired assassin, who carried out his mission and twisted his knife in the wound for good measure. Don't worry, I'm annihilated, and you have nothing to fear from your clients and viewers. You may appear on the screen on Fridays, speaking instructively to thousands of homes about repressions and unconscious reactions, while your evil genius is behind bars. Good luck with your Friday therapy in public! I do admit it is more seemly than my own evacuations at the Aker Quayside. Whether it has greater social utility is perhaps a moot point.

Your twin sister Idun
(also called Josefine Charlotte, or Finelotte, if you really insist)

P.S. Pardon my asking, but could it be that Mother is seriously ill? If not, I would be surprised at your being in such a hurry to have me declared incompetent and exclude me from the settlement of the estate.

15

2

Grandfather's original name was Andreas Sandane, and it was only when he had settled down as the town's mightiest man that he changed his name to Sand.

He was the next eldest son on a small windy farm far out by the mouth of a fjord, and like so many younger sons in those parts he had gone to sea immediately after confirmation. He had sailed the seas for eight years and worked his way up to ordinary seaman when, on a spring day in 1914, he went ashore to sign off. One stormy night something had happened to him that he was unable to forget afterwards, when the seas finally calmed down. He had been alarmed by a premonition, a half-waking dream or what he later called a "revelation", which warned him of a coming catastrophe. Now he was on his way uptown to have a serious talk with the ship owner, and to advise him to call his fleet home before it was destroyed.

Andreas Sandane was a lissom young man of barely twenty-three, not particularly tall, but with broad shoulders and an athletic physique. His face was handsome, with a blond mop of hair, a delicately curved nose and radiant blue eyes. When he smiled, as he often did, he displayed a set of sparkling white teeth, untouched by the decay that usually rewarded his contemporaries with a set of artificial teeth as a confirmation gift.

As he walks from the harbour with his duffel bag on his shoulder, he steps lightly, making a little jump now and then out of a zest for life or simply to show that the bag is no big deal. There is an abundance of strength in his body that must find an outlet, a strange joy presses upon his lips and is released into the air in the form of a cheery, trembling whistle. He whisks the cap from his head and drops greetings right and left, to acquaintances and strangers alike. Being particular is not for him, he has always taken the wider view and lets his sun shine on the righteous and the unrighteous alike. From time to time his eyes take on a remote look and he hums a couple of verses of a song to the ship *Quietude* that he has composed himself, an ode of thirteen stanzas written in calligraphic script on grey packing paper and framed and glazed as a present for the ship owner.

As a poet he doesn't exactly chart unexplored seas, but his metre is correct, the rhyme is always in the right place and the rhythm is regular enough. He has already written many poems, mostly on biblical themes, although he knows how to help himself to the goods of life and is by no means a killjoy. So far the highpoint of his poetic art is an epic about the apostle Peter, the fisherman, and if we are to believe what he himself relates, it has been read aloud many times in the seamen's churches all around to endless applause. Young Andreas is not someone who hides his light under a bushel, he is generous with praise and doesn't draw a very clear line between praise and self-praise.

He pauses outside the shipping office and lets his eyes wander along the high flight of stairs with the wrought-iron railing. He appraises the many steps, which suggest a Jacob's ladder, and nods approvingly at the heavy oak door, which Saint Peter could not have constructed more ingeniously. But when his glance reaches higher, he becomes more reserved. He heaves a deep sigh and shakes his head at the firm's name, which in his eyes is too modest and has failed to keep up with the times. *Skipper Torjussen's Boat Crew*, it reads, as it has for several generations, in old, crooked lettering from the middle of the last century. He thinks it is about time to remind the skipper that he is no longer fiddling with fishing smacks and coastal steamers. Doesn't he sit there like Neptune himself, ruling the waves, with steamships sailing to foreign ports!

He puts his bag on the sidewalk, passes his hand over his forehead and thinks things over. He will gladly drop a few words about the firm's name, that's clear as day and ought to have been done long ago. He knows that Markus Torjussen is not a stick-in-the-mud, even if he is of the old school and shuns anything that looks like pushiness and *braggadocio*. As everyone knows, the skipper is proud of his life's work, he oozes prosperity and loves his vessels as if they were his children. Who else would have hit upon the idea of calling a transatlantic steamer *Quietude*, with all the storms it would have to ride out and all the spindrift it would have to plough through? Does he imagine, maybe, that the Atlantic is the Sea of Galilee and the ship's mate a Son of Man with power to subdue the winds?

It will be trickier to reveal his real business there, to put on the right face and find the right words. How can he get the skipper to understand that the universe is in revolt and it is high time to take certain precautions? It's a question of life and death, and it is incumbent on the messenger to present his message so that no doubt is possible. He stands for a moment practising his words, muttering in a low voice; then he knows his course and that he will be heard.

He shoulders his bag and is already halfway up Jacob's ladder, when he suddenly remembers something and climbs down again. Markus Torjussen is known to be an extremely pious man, and people say that he never employs anyone in the shipping company without first asking him if he is a believer. Fortunately the sailor has already thought of this obstacle: when he visited the seamen's church in Brooklyn, he took the trouble of providing himself with an admission ticket. Stealing into the shadow of the stairs, he glances around before fishing out a little gold crucifix from his breast pocket and fastening it to his lapel. It's not sheer hypocrisy, no, "far from it", as the apostle Paul is in the habit of saying when he has an occasional close call. Young Sandane believes in the Father, the Son and the Holy Ghost, but he carries his piety lightly and is not one to refer to the Trinity unless strictly necessary.

In the anteroom he is attended to by a lovely young woman, who usually sits withdrawn at the other end of the room, while the secretary sees to the sailors and pays out their wages. But today this distant beauty is alone in the room and is forced to rise from her chair and come up to the counter. Andreas knows it is Torjussen's daughter and that she has a damaged hip. Nevertheless he is startled when he sees her waddling across the floor. His compassion is easily evoked, tears spring to his eyes, and he has to bend down and fuss with his duffel bag to regain his composure. How could the Lord have the heart for it? he wonders, on the verge of calling the Almighty to account. Just think, to create such a fine, seductive woman from her topknot to her middle and then to make such a sloppy job of the chassis that the effect is ruined as soon as she takes a few steps! How old can she be, anyway? Not exactly a spring chicken, for sure, but not an old maid either. Maybe twenty-seven or twenty-eight or a little more, but definitely not a day over thirty.

She blushes as though she has read his thoughts, and for a moment they stand in silence on opposite sides of the counter, until the sailor finally composes himself and says he must absolutely have a word with "the boss". She casts an uncertain glance at the door to the inner sanctum, smiles sympathetically and says that she will go in and find out if her father is receiving. She lets go of the counter and makes her way across the floor in the same heart-rending way as before.

He stands there following her with his eyes, shaking his head sadly as she disappears into the office. "Poor, poor pretty little woman," he mumbles, seeing her in his mind's eye besieged by an entire host of suitors, who change their minds as soon as they discover what is wrong with her. "Yes, poor, poor thing," he sighs, choking with compassion. And she's Torjussen's one and only lamb, who will inherit everything, lock, stock and barrel, when he passes away. "It's just too bad," he whispers, making a threatening gesture with his fist. "Do you hear, you up there, who created heaven and earth? I say it's just too bad!"

The woman is away for a long time, during which the sailor allows his imagination to wander, anticipating the course of events by several months. He closes his eyes and pictures to himself what will happen when the suitors have taken flight and there is only one left. And, lo and behold, all ends well: she can walk up the aisle as a bride dressed in white. She barely limps, and her long veil hides her awkward build and the fact that the chassis doesn't quite measure up to the slender back and the fine, long swan's neck. And by the altar stands the bridegroom all spruced up, waiting anxiously and agonizingly. It's not easy to see who it is with the mind's eye, but there's something very familiar about him, there certainly is, by George.

The seaman sighs and regrets all of his frivolous adventures in foreign ports. "You are a mangy dog!" he says to himself, thumping his breast with his fist. "A miserable sniffer and snooper who loses all control as soon as you catch the scent of a skirt. You should be ashamed of yourself, you damn cur! What business do you have imagining pure maidens in white bridal gowns, you who are so filthy and defiled they can smell you a mile away?

"Jesus," he mumbles, crushed, fumbling for the crucifix on his lapel, "you are the only one who can save me and liberate me, and if things turn out the way I hope, I'll turn over a new leaf. I shall go down on my knees and sing your praises, no mistake, and never again lead a dissolute life, wallowing in the gutter."

When the door opens and she calls him in, he doesn't dare look at her, but hurries past with the bag in his hand. Before he steps through the door, he straightens up and brushes back his mop of hair, and it is as though, with this quick movement, he puts behind him his early youth. An almost sedate dignity comes over him, and it is a fine, dependable fellow who enters the room and holds out his hand in greeting.

Markus Torjussen takes his hand between both of his and shakes it emphatically, but does not get up from his chair. He sits enthroned behind a large writing table, nothing more than his torso showing, as though he too has an embarrassing defect that prevents him from rising to his feet. He is a sallow, elderly man with a huge walrus moustache, which he habitually twists when pondering a question, be it religious or secular. His face is good-natured, but it has a suffering expression, and who knows whether there isn't truth in the rumour that he is afflicted with a mortal illness. He breathes heavily, and there is a decrepit air about his stooped figure that gives the young sailor something to think about. Poor fellow, listing badly already, he thinks, knowing from experience that this means a shipwreck is imminent.

He sits on the visitor's chair in front of the writing table and doesn't refuse the quid of tobacco the skipper offers him. It will give him something to chew on should it be wise to wait with his answer, and if the taste leaves something to be desired, there is a spittoon at a suitable distance. He finds it advisable to put off his message a moment, and to gain time he bends down and quietly loosens the string of his duffel bag.

"Well, imagine you here," the skipper begins in his usual affable tone. "What does the compass say, my dear Sandane? Are you taking another trip across the Atlantic, or have you decided on the mate's school in the autumn?"

Andreas mulls it over, then sends a long, brown jet in the direction of the spittoon. A moment later he bends to remove a flat parcel from his bag, pushes it to the other side of the table and asks the boss to accept it. It's nothing special, he says, at once modest and boastful. But it is something that comes from the heart, of that he is certain.

The old man unpacks the things and looks at them. In no hurry, he unfolds the wrapping paper fussily, twirling the string around his fingers. While he is busy with the wrapper, he steals a glance at the contents: a showpiece of a house tablet, which will turn increasingly yellow hanging on the wall of the shipping office for more than forty years, until it is eventually torn down in grief and shame. The pen-and-ink drawing of *Quietude* is an awkward business, the skipper is used to seeing that sort of thing framed and glazed. But the thirteen verses are wonderful and something that an old salt doesn't see every day. My, oh my, how prettily they are arranged, with six larboard and six starboard stanzas, and an extra stanza stretched out beneath the keel, like the Pacific Ocean. Markus Torjussen is full of wonderment and stammers his way through the first stanza, before pushing the hymn over to its originator and asking him to read it aloud.

Young Sandane doesn't wait to be asked twice. He inhales deeply and tries out his voice until he finds the special chest tone that has proved so successful in the seamen's churches round about. He rides the metre on a wave of euphony, strengthening the effect with long theatrical pauses and eloquent gestures. Like a modern Demosthenes he recites with kelp and seaweed in his mouth, until he has overcome his obvious flaws. (Whether the "Ode to *Quietude*" is good or not, or downright ludicrous, will have to wait until a subsequent appraisal, being at the moment immaterial and impossible to decide.)

Old Torjussen is speechless during this recital. He has never heard anything like it. Now he sighs as though entranced, now he nods his head, his moustache trembling with emotion. The fact that he places his elbows on the table and begins to twist the two ends of his moustache is a sure sign that some thought is in the offing. It will be some time before it takes concrete form as an offer, but there can be no doubt that the young sailor has been a success. And when the reader lowers his voice, the skipper's brown eyes light up; he lets moustaches be moustaches, claps his hands together and utters these memorable words: "But my dear Sandane, you have a gift from God, no doubt about it!"

After this it doesn't take long for the sailor to get started. He lets his tongue wag more than he has planned to and holds forth about the strange vision he had when *Quietude* was in mid-voyage outbound, pitching in high seas, just north of the fiftieth parallel. It was night, and he stood watch on the upper deck; the waves reared up as tall as houses, and for a long time the fog was so thick one couldn't see a thing on the troubled waters. Suddenly the darkness seemed to recede and a blinding light fell upon the desolate sea. And, holy smoke, at once there were vessels everywhere, as if all the world's shipping had gathered at this particular position. But what his eyes beheld was anything but a pleasure cruise. Every single ship was in distress – one was listing, another was sending out SOS signals, a third was already sinking. Intermittently loud crashes were heard, which could only mean that the ships were inside a minefield. He wanted to sound the alarm and call the crew on deck, but noticed to his horror that he was rooted to the spot and unable to budge. He screamed as loudly as he could, but his voice was small and thin like a bird's and was drowned out by the roar of the storm and the crash of exploding ships. Gradually his body seemed to wither away, and all that remained was a pair of eyes that looked and looked with a sight that expanded until it encompassed the entire universe. The whole thing lasted a mere moment, a few seconds perhaps, then he was himself again and all was well. But he was never the same afterwards; he was full of terror and dread and realized that he had received a warning of something that was still hidden from everyone else. He knew that some terrible things would come to pass, things that would shake heaven and earth and turn the world's oceans into craters of death and destruction. That was why he went ashore with the intention of asking for his discharge. Now the message had been delivered and the case presented in the right place. If the skipper loved his fleet, he would call it home and let it be laid up until the times became more reassuring and God's punishment was past.

"Well, after something like that you have probably had enough of the sea for a while," Torjussen says thoughtfully. "That's no problem, Sandane, my boy; come autumn, just start at the mate's school."

"I received a warning and I have presented it in the right place," the young sailor repeats, rather more stubbornly. "I'll never again set foot on a ship's deck, that's for sure! And God strike the skipper dead if he turns a deaf ear and doesn't watch out while there's still time."

"Am I to understand, Sandane, that you are a believer?" Torjussen says, when he has pondered the sailor's speech for a while. "Holy smoke," "God strike the skipper dead" – what kind of language was that? It sounded undeniably rather strong, well, one could almost call it cursing and swearing. But thank the Lord for that little crucifix on his lapel, which not only changes water into wine but also profane language into striking pieties.

Andreas Sandane nods meaningfully, but doesn't answer the question directly. For a while the two men sit in silence sizing each other up, showing their teeth so to speak, a trial of strength that is rather one-sided, since the skipper has dentures while the sailor's teeth are strong, with an excellent bite.

At last the old man has had time to reflect and begins speaking in his paternal manner.

"Listen to me, Sandane," he says, suddenly raising his head. "If you really mean to turn yourself into a landlubber, I may have a post to offer you that could be every bit as promising as the mate's school. I know you have a knack for book learning, I could tell that much from the papers and testimonials I saw when you were hired as a deck hand. Your conduct on board *Quietude* has always been exemplary, many can testify to that. With what you have accomplished in the poetic vein, you are someone quite unique and could be a great blessing for the boat company. And since you openly confess that you have been saved and born again through the precious blood of Jesus, I can see no obstacle to . . . "

Markus Torjussen twists his moustaches and is in no hurry to reveal what his offer entails. Approaching the matter with caution, he begins by complaining of his poor health, which lately has caused the burden of work to weigh more heavily than usual. The kidneys are no longer doing their duty, and his heart isn't what it used to be either. He has for long needed a trustworthy man who could serve the enterprise in the right spirit and perhaps some day become his successor. And Augusta, that poor little daughter of his, has her failings as well, of course, and might need some support. Could Sandane perhaps entertain the thought . . . ? Well, he doesn't have to be in a rush and give his answer out of hand. He can think it over in his closet and lay it all before God in his hours of prayer.

The sailor is all ears, and a faint smile appears on his face when the daughter's name is mentioned. But he doesn't need any time to think it over, he can tell him without a detour to his closet.

"If you mean to ask me whether I could see myself as your right hand, then I close with you and say thank you many times over. To tell the truth, I have myself thought of looking for some work that could be considered a calling. Oh, I can assure you I'll put my shoulder to the wheel and fill my place, if you have no qualms about trusting me. I'll carry out your wishes from morning till night and run at your slightest hint till my legs give out."

"Then we are agreed," replies Torjussen, so deeply moved by the solemnity of the moment that he finds the strength to get on his feet and show the Crown prince out. "You'll begin tomorrow morning and will have your place here, in the office; I myself shall withdraw upstairs to a private room. And we'll find something in the way of lodging too, if you aren't too particular. I have an empty room in the attic that I think might do. It's not exactly a throne room, but you will have a roof over your head right here and be able to see the whole town from your window."

The rest of the day is spent in a holiday spirit, with big purchases in town and dinner at the skipper's table. Andreas Sandane makes deep inroads in his bank book, where he has regularly deposited his wages, saving up money for the mate's school. But now his prospects have become so bright that all scrimping and saving must end. He buys himself two suits in the latest fashion, one light, one dark, two dress shirts, and two pairs of shoes. And, just in case, a winter coat, a topcoat and two hats, one tall and awe-inspiring, another a bit roguish. In his transport of joy he gambles on pairs in a big way, and who knows if he doesn't have something sweet and pleasant in mind that will be his crowning achievement and the pair above all pairs.

Only when he enters his attic room in the evening does he remember that he forgot to say anything about the name of the firm. But, he tells himself, there is no hurry, maybe it's wiser to wait and see what it all comes to. A shipping company is not something you establish every day, you'd better proceed by small steps and let things take their time.

Before he goes to sleep he kneels by his bed and thanks the Lord humbly for all the profit that this day has yielded him. He gives thanks with great seriousness, not a single false note steals into his devotions. He promises to walk God's unsearchable ways from this day and hour, to keep a steady course and never make the least detour. And as the practical man that he is, he enters into a mutual contract with the Most High, no less promising and binding than the one he has just entered into with Markus Torjussen. On the one hand the Lord commits himself to keeping a watchful eye on A. S. and giving him as much success and earthly happiness as is at all possible. On the other hand, Andreas Sandane commits himself to a *quid pro quo* in the form of a devout and blameless life. The contract is binding on both sides and can be nullified by one party if the conditions are not met.

When the transaction has been concluded and properly formulated, Andreas Sandane goes to bed and sleeps soundly and dreamlessly for a good nine hours. For once it can be said about him that he is home and dry and sleeps the sleep of the just. After a chaotic and stormy youth he has finally cast anchor and finds himself on *terra firma*.

3

Since these pages have no ambition to become a family chronicle, I won't dwell very long on Grandfather's time as a male Cinderella before he won the princess and the whole boat company.

Once he has equipped himself and placed his relationship to God within a set framework, he goes all the way and joins Torjussen's congregation. It's a rather melancholy and aged group of people, one that might cause more long-suffering fellows than Sandane to turn away at the door. But fortunately Bethel has a section for juniors, where young men and women can meet on Wednesday nights and even the score. As soon as the devotions are over, they kick in with skits and forfeits and whatever nonsense they bring with them. Laughter comes easily and jokes fly through the air, including the so-called Bible jokes that blend playfulness with seriousness in a meaningful way. This innocent amusement has its spirited moments, but they are never so elated that they don't at once fold their hands when the chairman rises and summons them to concentrate on the one thing needful.

April and May go by, and suddenly the white nights of summer have arrived, with boat trips along the coast and outings to the islets and skerries. Even on the outermost point of land can be found a small meadow where the young people can play games and romp. Outdoor games are a gift of God, as long as they do not become so wild that they switch to three-four time. "Napoleon and his army" may pass muster, "Hawk and dove" be warmly recommended, and "Thief, thief" is also acceptable, despite clammy hands and shaking breasts. The mating instinct must be kept in check, but cannot be completely banned, and it passes muster as long as it merely finds an outlet in a bit of hoopla and innocent capers.

Andreas Sandane is a hawk who swoops down on his prey with sure aim, and as the evening wears on he reveals himself as a master thief who steals hearts as easily as others steal a hand or an arm. But no sooner have the hearts begun to throb and the doves' bosoms to flutter than he bows out and goes to sit on the rug with Augusta Torjussen. He has in vain tried to make her join in the game – on that point she is insistent, refusing to parade her infirmity. She sits there looking on with the invalid's mild self-denial, and takes care to be useful by setting out the cake trays and keeping the coffee pot warm on the Primus stove.

Exhausted, Andreas sinks down on the rug beside her, snatches a doughnut from the cake tray and twirls the golden ring teasingly around his forefinger before swallowing it in one mouthful. A moment later he pretends he's sitting on a stone and moves closer so that he can squeeze her hand. He has to do it secretly, because nothing must yet be revealed, though the matter is pretty much decided. Augusta will be thirty-two at the end of August and is named after this late summer month, which also promises to be her wedding month. Markus Torjussen has begun to exert a cautious pressure, eager to see his daughter well in port before he goes to his rest in the graveyard. How about the twenty-ninth of August, when she has her birthday? Why not have a double celebration? Andreas in no way declines, but makes a point of holding back and not showing himself to be too keen. Augusta is nine years older than he, and he both shudders and laughs at the thought of what the gossips will make of it. He will become the talk of the town and be envied through and through, that he knows very well. They will call him a seducer and a fortune hunter and many worse things, and no living soul will believe that he is taking her out of love.

But in this the gossips are wrong. He certainly has no objection to bringing down the bird with the pot of gold, far from it, but he is not a pure gambler either. A genuine warmth spreads through him when he sits beside her, and her invalidism is almost an advantage. Feeling doubly competent, he likes to help and support her, and to guide her with a gentle hand through life's ups and downs. As she sits there on the rug she is without flaw, and the very one he has always dreamed of. Why should she bother to aim for the vertical, when she is so seductive in all other positions? He has never met a woman with such a gentle look in her eyes and such a sweet, sad expression about her mouth.

At first the name Augusta is a little difficult to accept; in his difficult childhood by the mouth of the fjord it belonged only to old biddies and shrews. But, but – he has a knack for making the best of everything. Anyway, would it have been any better if she were born a few weeks earlier and was called Julie? "Augusta Sandane," he whispers, believing in the combination; soon the name has complied with his wishes and merged with his light and playful mood. My beloved Augusta, he thinks, so loudly that she can almost hear it, Augusta the only one, little sweet baby Augusta! Just wait, my little autumn flower, and you will know what it means to get married in the hottest month of the year. I'll bring you down from your august position, he threatens, but with a twinkle in his eye that suggests it is rather a promise. I'll take you by storm, hug you till you swoon and lose your breath – Augusta, I'll bust ya! Ah, the twenty-ninth of August will be an august day, I say no more, but you'd better be prepared for anything . . .

4

In the midst of all the wedding preparations came the war, which for a long time was an ordinary war and was only promoted to a world war when it approached its end.

For four years Torjussen's fleet continued to ply the seven seas, since he couldn't decide to call it home. When the peace came all his largest ships had been lost, and only the Danish boat and a few minor coastal routes were still intact. Fortunately the skipper didn't live to know that his dearest ship, *Quietude*, went down, almost exactly at the fiftieth parallel and under circumstances that uncannily resembled those Andreas Sandane had foreseen in his nocturnal vision. When it occurred in March 1918, the old man had already died and could no more shed tears over the shipwreck than be grieved that none of his boats were properly insured.

It was Andreas Sandane who had to bear the loss, and he learned his lesson thoroughly. He realized that thrift no doubt was a virtue, but that it often brought its own punishment in the turmoil of life. It was much better to think big, and then to reap a double profit when the time came. He became a warm advocate of insurance at full value, not only as far as spiritual matters were concerned but also in more immediate things like marine insurance.

He entered the post-war period almost empty-handed and had to build everything up again from scratch. The coastal steamers had to be replaced, and the Danish ferry was an old rusty hulk that took in water and could barely crawl across the Skagerrak. But Andreas Sandane had the courage to push forward and didn't shut his eyes to the most dizzying prospects.

In order to set himself a visible goal and to strengthen his self-respect, he had the front of his house renovated and a new name for the firm engraved in the area above the entrance door. He vacillated a long time in regard to the wording and was in at least seven minds, ambition battling against superstition, misgivings and an inherited feeling of respect. At first he had thought of following local custom and calling the shipping company *Late Markus Torjussen & Co.*, but after mature deliberation he found it insufficiently challenging. He let the space remain open for a while, making sure the boat company observed a decent period of mourning. Then he swept all scruples aside and got the town's most able coppersmith to deliver a slab with the somewhat anticipatory legend: *Andreas Sand. Brokerage, Shipping and Entrepreneur Company.* Many years had yet to elapse before this point was reached, and the name change was only granted in 1931. But his striving spirit never flagged and he always took care to be one step ahead of events.

To keep going while he established this new and modern fleet, he distributed the risk and staked what capital he had on several enterprises. If one of these failed, he reasoned, another might yield all the greater return, an argument that perfectly matched his flexible expectations. He went in for construction, gradually began to speculate in shipping shares, and lent money to farmers and fishermen who were in financial straits. His reputation for helpfulness spread far and wide and induced skippers and smallholders to bite off more than they could chew. When they struggled with the instalments, Sandane was someone they could talk to, and at the last moment it was always possible to reach a settlement.

But since the ship owner was not Providence in person, there were limits to his forbearance, and sooner or later he had to let the hammer fall. I don't think he lied when he expressed sorrow at having to drive a debtor to foreclosure. Even in the darkest recesses of his businessman's soul there was a bright area where not everything was reckoned in profit and loss. When he brought his own childhood home to bankruptcy and drove his elder brother from his farm, he cried bitterly in private but still preserved enough firmness and sound common sense to let everything take its course. He was cut to the quick by the imminent foreclosure and by his brother coming cap in hand to ask for mercy. His family feeling and good will flinched, and he had to turn away and wipe his tears before he could bring himself to make his offer. He would buy the farm at the auction himself, he said, to save the ancestral soil, and his brother could stay there as steward for the rest of his life. But he would have to listen to good advice about modernization and see to it that his sons didn't associate their future with the place.

From start to finish, the settlement had the appearance of an agreement between brothers: neither of the parties made a fuss or even raised his voice. When the rightful heir said goodbye, not a harsh word had been uttered, and everything seemed to have been arranged to the satisfaction of both. The humiliation was all but invisible, and the younger brother was greatly surprised later the same year when his elder brother broke up from the old family farm and emigrated to America with two sisters, his wife and four sons. He could only see it as a bad omen. Besides, other things had happened which threw doubts on his image of himself as one of the Lord's chosen.

During the war, Augusta had borne him three children with less than a year's interval between them. First a healthy and well-formed daughter who was the spitting image of her father, later two sons that took after the other side of the family and were of a more dubious quality. The two little boys were sickly from birth and wouldn't survive. Nor had Augusta herself got through her three pregnancies scot-free; her poor hips had suffered irreparable damage, and that highly praised torso also began to show signs of weakness. When she got up after her last childbed, she had stitches in her chest, and gradually she succumbed to such an enervating cough during the night that her husband didn't get the sleep he required. A stay at a sanatorium was already being discussed when the Spanish flu came, bringing about a more drastic solution to their problem. Father and daughter were only lightly affected, but in the case of the mother and the two little sons the sickness struck inward and carried them off in the first week of the epidemic.

Andreas Sandane took the loss hard and could see these misfortunes in no other way than as a sign from above. Here at last came the punishment for his frivolity, his forgery with the crucifix and all of his youthful debauchery. He went into his closet and reasoned with the Lord, laying before Him every single lapse and submitting it to judgement. When he came out again, he had accepted his punishment and sentenced himself to sexual abstinence for life. He must have known that he thereby put himself to an almost impossible test, for lust was an integral part of his healthy, hot-blooded nature. But precisely for that reason, celibacy was necessary so that he could be born again, purified and cleansed of his sinful proclivities. How his self-discipline fared as the years went by will not be reported here, but will be thoroughly treated in due course. Let me simply reveal that the "old Adam" never gave him peace, and that he fought a lifelong and hopeless battle with his rebellious drives until the day when he finally broke down and made his notorious confession.

To a pious temperament like his, fornication was the sin above all others; indeed, when you got right down to it, it was the only sin a Christian soul could fall prey to. By denying himself this earthly pleasure he won a spiritual victory over himself that made him feel he was practically free from sin. When he so diligently sowed his seed in other fields, he viewed it as a divine blessing and a reward for otherwise keeping such a firm hand on himself. In this way his abstinence was not only a self-discipline but also a boost to a higher and more abstract principle. Above all it became an economic stimulus, which helped him accumulate a fortune that before long made him into the wealthiest man in the region.

Early in the boom period someone had whispered in his ear that there was no need at all to have ready cash in order to deal in shipping shares. One could borrow the shares in a Dutch bank and sell them in a hurry on the Amsterdam stock exchange while the freight rates were still high. At first he couldn't believe his own ears and almost lost his temper at this attempt to cram him full of such un-Christian nonsense. Still, the information had taken root, and for some time he went around with such a strange, faraway look in his eyes that his fellow believers thought that he was wrestling with some religious problem.

But no more than before did his closet prove to be a permanent refuge for him. He made an appointment to meet with the bank manager, who had hitherto helped him out of many difficulties. But the meeting was regrettably short and yielded no tangible result. He had to seek advice from higher authorities, and already the next morning the ship owner was on the train on his way to the capital to speed things up.

By the following year he had made his big coup, and money poured in in such fantastic quantities that he occasionally became doubtful and asked himself whether God's blessings weren't coming his way in greater abundance than was desirable. Once more the spectres emerged from the corners, and omens suddenly appeared out of nowhere. But since being hung up on soul-searching was not one of his vices, he weathered the crisis this time as well, his head held high and his grandiose plans intact.

Not long thereafter the news was known all over town: Andreas Sandane had given up his membership in the religious assembly of Torjussen of blessed memory and intended to establish a congregation that was more upbeat and in tune with the times. When he aired his plans, he made no secret of the fact that he had received a prophetic inspiration, not unlike the one that years back had enabled him to predict the Great War. Verily, he had received a command from God to build an Ark that would save the Elect from a coming Flood. The congregation would for the time being have to use leased premises, but he could promise those who were prepared to follow him that the Ark would be ready for use on 29 August, 1924. By this memorable date, both the birthday of his deceased wife and the tenth anniversary of his earthly wedding, everything should have panned out, so that the brothers and sisters could intone their hosannas and get a foretaste of the heavenly wedding.

After her death, Augusta had become increasingly glorified in his memory from year to year, until she had attained a status that was not of this world. Remote and motionless, she was a shining light behind all his many enterprises, as if he had been lucky enough to smuggle a saint into his Protestant faith. Well before the Ark was ready in the summer of 1924, he had called in a local painter and commissioned him to paint an altar-piece on the theme of "Madonna and Child". When the painter hesitated, not seeming to know what a madonna was, it looked bleak for a while, but before long the newly fledged director came up with a remedy. He took down from the wall a yellowed photograph of Augusta with her firstborn and asked the painter to look at that if he needed something to go by. It probably didn't occur to him that the man might take his instructions literally. But what is a faithful naturalist, of a pious disposition and inca-pable of abstracting from his model, supposed to do? When the altarpiece was in place, there was no mistaking its subject, and it became the target of coarse derision from the town's godless mob. But the brothers and sisters found it to be a comfort to the eye and an eternally valid interpretation of the sacred mystery that even Michelangelo couldn't have improved on.

The inauguration was held around St Olaf's Day, 29 July, and Andreas Sandane didn't content himself with just climbing up to the roof-tree and hanging a huge wreath of flowers around the chimney. When this feat had been accomplished, he flexed his knees tentatively for a moment, as if he meant to take off and leap straight into heavenly bliss. And, praise God, while the congregation broke the silence and intoned a sacred song for their home, he flipped over and suddenly did a handstand up there, his head turned humbly downward and his polished shoes kicking at the blue sky. The congregation was so terror-stricken that the hymn broke off in the middle of the refrain, but since the acrobat, with God's help, kept his balance and even had the strength to walk on his bare hands along the roof-tree, jubi-lation broke out. What other than sweet blessings would ever visit a house whose director could perform such religious exercises between heaven and earth? Who could wish for more signs and hints? Wasn't it clear to everybody that the answer was on the way and that there was power in folded hands?

The event became a milestone in evangelical history and attracted such a huge following to the newly established congregation that Bethel had to close, making Torjussen of blessed memory turn in his grave. The Ark was filled with a diversity of human animals, representing every species and mutation endowed with an ability to stand on two legs and give testimony before the Lord, prostrate themselves at the penance bench, and in brighter moments play stringed instruments and piano accordions till the music verged on dance rhythms.

Andreas Sandane rose to the occasion and emerged as a rousing preacher who, in a brisk and bold manner, would threaten them with hell fire and eternal damnation. He had at his disposal a repertoire of jokes and eloquent anecdotes, which he worked into his fulminations in such an ingenious way that the audience would sit there laughing in the midst of eternal torment. High-church people ground their teeth and were terribly annoyed, but couldn't deny that they felt a certain reluctant respect for this vigorous man who had just as good connections in the next world as in all the nooks and crannies of this vale of tears. Positions of trust were showered upon his strong shoulders, not only such commissions that could clearly be kept separate from his spiritual activities, but also posts that shuffled the cards in a disquieting way. Before anyone had time to protest, Andreas Sandane was chairman of the parish council and had the decisive word in the nomination of the town's clergymen. With this, the high- and low-church townspeople had given one another a forbearing hand. But there had also occurred a confusion of preaching and enthusiasm that wasn't easy to grasp.

In his daily conduct the ship owner was dignified and modest, though he dressed in the latest fashion and liked to show off his divine physique. That his obvious vanity had its secret opposite was known to very few. But anyone who had seen him thrust a hand into his waistcoat pocket to consult his watch was well informed about it. Judging by the heavy gold fob across his stomach, the watch should be correspondingly solid and of the purest gold. But it was really "far from it". From his pocket the ship owner pulled to everyone's amazement a cheap nickel watch he had at one time received as a confirmation present and since then held on to with an almost super-stitious veneration. What was wrong with a nickel watch? Had it not followed him to the top through thick and thin and faithfully measured the time for him behind its dented cover? Did gold watches keep better time? And anyway, what did he want with an eighteen-carat timepiece hidden away in his pocket, with not a single soul being able to enjoy the sight of it?

And this is how it was in so many things to do with this unpredictable man. In the midst of all success and advancement he remained loyal to that stratum of the population from which he had come and did not mix with the smart set, unless it was for the purpose of business or as a spokesman. When he walked through town, he dropped greetings left and right, as in his youthful years, the sole difference being that now it was a rakish hat and not a cap that he doffed. He often stopped on the way to engage people in conversation, not only fellow believers and business friends, but just as readily market women, milk carriers, street sweepers, sextons, drunks and wanton women. By the time he donned his hat and said goodbye, each and everyone had received a Christian admonition, which was well meant and well received, despite the fact that it was gruff and spoken straight from the shoulder.

But in more select circles he had a reputation for being uncouth and unmannerly, ignorant of the difference between a fish knife and an ordinary one, and incapable of using either correctly. He cut up his steak like a butcher, and then wolfed it down as though it were a matter of life and death. He was said to smack his lips so loudly that all who knew better grew pale and looked at their plates. But once, during a big dinner, the young son of the host thought it was a bit much and, momentarily forgetting that silence is golden, succumbed to his talent for cheek. Having considered the phenomenon from every point of view, he couldn't restrain himself any longer but bent across the table and asked: "Pardon me, Mr Sandane. Does it really taste as good as it sounds?" The question, which was phrased ever so politely, acquired as long a life among the small-town gossips as the ship owner's quick and good-humoured reply: "Yes, young man, it really does – and praise God for that!"

Thus the dinner was saved, and forbearance and high spirits could again descend upon the damask tablecloth. Andreas Sandane was reported all over town as the undisputed victor in the situation and could rejoice in the general applause. When he shortly thereafter performed the trick of driving his host to bankruptcy, thereby spoiling the succession of an unappetizing smart aleck, he was not the only one who gloated and laughed on the sly.

But despite his unassuming manner he was no egalitarian; he knew his own worth and believed in a natural distinction between high and low. The labour movement was from the very first a thorn in his flesh, and if someone dared mention the words "class struggle", he would snort and quote Holy Writ to prove that there had to be masters and servants. What would otherwise happen to charity? he asked with righteous indignation. If there were no longer any poor people – God forbid! – how would it be possible for someone who lived in abundance to bend down to the needy and do good? All kindheartedness and all higher renunciation would disappear, and everybody would be equally greedy and insatiable. With age he became more and more inclined to such jeremiads, always knowing how to avoid becoming personally involved. It was quite obvious that he didn't attribute any greed to himself, but that he had only the Almighty to thank for his luck in life.

With his particular outlook on the distribution of the good things in life, it is no wonder that he became the town's – well, perhaps the whole country's – greatest private benefactor. Every year he donated considerable sums to good and public-spirited ends, always making sure it was done publicly and in his name. The begging letters poured in, but it was one of his peculiarities that he gave nothing away in secret. I once heard him observe that this would have been money down the drain, and he was full of contempt for the old saying that the left hand should not know what the right hand is doing. If the gifts were to come from heaven, then they really *had* to come from heaven, he said, seizing his chance to make a genuine Bible joke. That he got his "gifts" back in the form of tax relief occurred to nobody, and his reputation for unselfishness would no doubt have lasted till his dying day if an unpleasant tax suit hadn't come his way. By means of good connections he managed to hush the matter up and convince the authorities that he had been in good faith. But his infallibility had been stained, and a moral mildew spread beneath the surface until the decay corroded him from within, causing him to end his days in shame and humiliation.

He loved his only child with a tender and excessive love, but he was strict and chastened her betimes, as is written. When he discovered the first signs of vanity in her, he quickly intervened, so that the sins of the fathers should not be visited upon the children. As she grew up, she increasingly became a mirror image of his own faults and shortcomings; just looking at her filled him with a vague despondency. The first time he used the birch was when he caught her in front of the mirror at the age of five, dancing back and forth before her own idol, while chanting and singing to her heart's content: "Oh, I'm so happy about my beauty, oh so happy, so happy

34

am I!" Severe and painful remedies were called for, there was not a moment of doubt in his tender father's heart on that score. Unfortunately, he was frequently obliged to fetch the birch from its place behind the mirror as the years went by, not least for the sake of his own self-discipline. After the punishment he took her on his lap and explained to her that the birch had been sent from heaven and hurt him as much as it did her. Then they would cry bitterly, cheek to cheek, and make up in torrents of repentance and contrition. Only when they had both kneeled down and begged forgiveness from the Most High, could all be forgotten and the time come for the bag of goodies, the picture Bible, and all the saved-up caresses.

But little Mary wasn't always inclined to let it end with kneeling and reconciliation. If she happened to fight back and refused to crawl to the Cross, Andreas Sandane was not someone to joke with. Then his bright face would darken, and he assumed the figure of the thundering demigod his granddaughter would come to know several decades later. Mary was dragged to the scaffold one more time and then shut in the closet underneath the stairs to sit and think things over. After a while her father opened the door a crack to see if the darkness and the incarceration had softened her. Usually she asked forgiveness in a thin voice and was freed and forgiven immediately. But once in a while she held her own and sat there hardening herself, until she was overtaken by convulsive sobs and her father had to give in. Then it was he who had to crawl to the Cross, and he begged forgiveness in such heart-rending words that the child swallowed her tears and threw her arms about his neck.

I have never been able to understand the complex nature of my grandfather, in which warmth and cold, tenderness and Old Testament wrath existed side by side without any apparent conflict. Did he continue all his life to be the simple young sailor, someone who was governed by sudden impulses and had strange visions of the destruction of the world? Or was he, on the contrary, a clever, cunning soul who knew how to negotiate his way through difficulties and turn everything to his own advantage? In his changeability, was he now one and now the other, or both things at once? I don't know. At this point in my scribbling I can give no explanation for his duality, but maybe later events will come to my aid and provide us with an answer.

II

Our Town Gets a Controversial
Parish Pastor and Mary Executes
the Only Daring Act of Her Life

1

I was not mistaken, Mother has been seriously ill for a long time and was at death's door the day the family attorney was here to disinherit me. She died in early December, I don't know on what day exactly, because nobody found it worthwhile to notify me.

On the other hand, I know she was buried on 9 December, because someone was thoughtful enough to put the funeral hymns in an envelope and post them to me. I sit leafing through the little printed sheet. The first page is artfully done, with Gothic lettering on quality paper edged in black all round. *At the Bier of Mary Sand*, it says, and I must admit that I felt quite a jolt when I pulled the paper out of the envelope. I had of course had my suspicions and was by no means unprepared, but it's something else suddenly to see it in black and white.

However unbelievable it may seem, I haven't seen Mother in almost nineteen years. Year by year she has moved further and further away, receding in time and space until her once so desired figure has drifted into the realm of the unreal. I have gradually come to terms with her absence, have thought about her less and less often, and have almost forgotten the wild and hopeless love I felt for her in my childhood.

Since 1976 I have been hospitalized six times, all in all, but she has never dropped me a word or come to see me. Nor did I expect she would after what happened between us in the early seventies. At that time she didn't mince her words, but sent me one letter after another reproaching me for my conduct and for my "incomprehensible and destructive" books. With all that I knew about her, I probably should have controlled myself and swallowed the bitter pill in silence. But since she attacked me again and again, not leaving me alone for a moment, I just couldn't help myself.

I grabbed my pen and answered back that I was unable to see how she could decide that my books were destructive when it was impossible to understand them. Compared to Theresa Charles and Monica Dickens, Runa and *The Family at Skaugum*, they were perhaps not so easy to fathom. But there was more than one kind of reader, and I had never thought that my books had anything to say to those closest to me.

It couldn't really surprise her, I wrote, that my books were the way they were. From my earliest childhood I had been the black sheep of the family, and she who is repudiated and lives in exile doesn't write Pollyanna stories. And as far as my conduct was concerned, it was chiefly my own problem. Our family was known to be close-knit and intimate, but I had never been part of that closeness. There had been times when I was weak and vulnerable and could have done with someone's shoulder to lean on. One particular time, six members of the family were gathered while I pleaded for mercy, crying aloud for help, but not one of them was capable of hearing my cry of distress. After that I was a person who belonged nowhere, and leaving and saying goodbye became my only true actions.

I never heard again from Mother after that. Feeling aggrieved, she withdrew and used my twin sister as her mouthpiece. The reproaches continued to pour in, but now in Kathrine Elisabeth's neat handwriting, so suspiciously like Mother's that it was like reading an accusation written with someone else holding the pen. I continued to be a freak and a blot on the family's honour, with the sole difference that from now on they were determined to render me harmless.

I turn the pages of the printed sheet and read the funeral hymns. There are only three, printed in ordinary type. They are the familiar tunes that are sung at all funerals, first "Always fearless where you walk", then "Blessed, blessed", and finally "To live is to love". Though I have a lump in my throat, I cannot help smiling at the thought of the funeral guests, forced to bite their tongues and twist and turn their lips on account of that hateful New Norwegian. The family swears by Dano-Norwegian, one and all, and if they ever tried to live and love, it certainly didn't occur in that jaw-breaking lingo. In her later years, Mother was so fired up that she used every opportunity to show how she felt. She would stand in the post office with a long queue behind her and stick to her point, tossing her head snootily as she refused to accept a stamp with the New Norwegian spelling, "Noreg", for Norway. Without heeding the impatience of those behind her in the queue, she turned the place into a battleground of language and wouldn't desist until the clerk divided the postage into uncontaminated five- and ten-øre stamps.

But the irony of life caught up with her in the end. She had to keep quiet and refrain from raising her voice, while they sang "Ancient 'Noreg', all-time northland" over her dead body. And because of the emotional nature of the occasion, the funeral guests were able to take a broad view and "long for richer goals" as they strode behind the flower-decked coffin. Whether they also attained to "truth in all their dealings" shall remain unsaid – I wasn't present, and therefore couldn't see what secrets were hidden behind their solemn expressions. But when the last verse had been sung and "all wrongs and lies laid to rest", there were no doubt many who cleared their throats and sighed with relief.

The curious thing is that while I harden my heart and mock my mother's funeral, something is happening to me. My eyes feel heavy, there is a tightness in my throat, and some strange, deep sobs force their way out. When I raise my head, a strange light, mild and soft, falls upon my darkness. And suddenly I see something I haven't seen for a very long time. A vague, faraway figure takes form and moves into my field of vision, coming closer and closer, growing in clarity until I recognize it. It is my young mother, deeply loved and unattainable, at whose heels I always followed, but who pushed me gently aside, telling me not to cling to her. I can see her blond hair and innocent blue eyes, and the sparkling smile that was always directed toward others, not me. How did it happen that this divine figure was lost to me, leaving me so bitterly alone and lacking in joy? Where did things begin to go wrong? There had to be a turning point, a critical moment, a blow of the axe that separated my life from hers forever. I had, after all, been carried in her womb at one time, suckled at her breast, was cradled in her arms, and learned to walk with my outstretched hands securely held in hers. Am I wrong to attribute so much absence and indifference to her? Wasn't it, in reality, me who kept aloof, filled with an insatiable need for possession that refused to share her love with anyone else?

This morning, four days after the letter with the funeral hymns, one of the male nurses from the men's wing comes into my room, dragging a big carton that he chucks on the floor. "Look here," he says, straightening up to catch his breath. "A surprise package for you!

"Well, you'll have to excuse us, we were obliged to open it," he continues when he sees me staring at the broken tape and the half-open flaps of the top. "Regulations. No patient gets packages distributed before we have checked whether they contain something that might hurt them."

"What's lying there, on top?" I ask, though I can easily see what it is.

"A picture of King Olav as a child," he says, taking it out of the box and holding it at arm's length. "I'm afraid we've had to remove the glass and put in a piece of plastic instead. But it looks quite nice, don't you think, though it may seem to shine a bit too much. If you wish I can hang it up right away, I've brought a hook and a screwdriver."

"No, thanks, I don't think so," I say, after glancing at the old picture for a moment. It used to hang in the dining room at home, above Mother's sewing table. A little round prince in knee-length trousers and a sailor's blouse, with a sailor hat the size of a millwheel.

"Now, don't be angry that we've replaced the glass," he says, as though that were the problem.

"Just take it away, find out if someone else would like to have it," I say when I have managed to compose myself a little.

"As you wish," he replies in the same quiet tone, but I notice his surprise and his puzzled glances. "If that's what you really want," he says. "I can assure you there are plenty of others who will be glad to have it on their walls, both in the men's and in the women's wing."

"No doubt," I say, without raising my voice. "Just hang it up some place where it can spread joy and loyalty to the King."

As soon as he is gone I walk over to my bed and sit down with my hands squeezed between my knees. Although I know the package contains nothing but perfectly innocent things, I'm afraid to touch it. I sense a lurking danger, as if I can't put my hands into it without burning my fingers.

The evening is wearing on and the night nurse has already dropped by with my sleeping pills when I finally take courage and walk with firm steps over to the big box in the corner by the door. First I read the letter that one of my guardians has placed on top. "By rights you shouldn't have been part of the settlement of the estate," writes my mother's cousin, Signe Alcott, a dry and well-meaning old maid about my own age, "but we haven't forgotten that you are fond of books, and so we agreed you should have your mother's library. We hope you will take good care of it and read the books over and over again, as your mother did to the very last. May God bless you, my poor Josefine Charlotte, and may the books help you and give you strength, so that you can recover from your mental illness and find the right way at last."

I take the books out one by one and stack them on top of each other in a tall swaying tower that reaches from the floor midway to the ceiling. Aunt Signe is right – they have allowed me to be part of the settlement of the estate, which has made me the owner of a library for the first time in my life. Devotional books on top of hefty best sellers, missionary tales and honest travel accounts squeezed flat between horoscopes, incense, the laying-on of hands and faith healing. Theresa Charles, Monica Dickens, Runa and Margit Söderholm in illicit intercourse with Billy Graham, Bo Giertz, Lars Rustbøle and Karsten Isachsen. No petty discrimination, a hodgepodge of this, that and the other, gush and godliness, vice and virtue all mixed up. But on the whole recognized and altogether harmless literature that Mother didn't have to put away when a sister from one of the many mission societies dropped by. On the contrary, she could read aloud from them when it was her turn to host the Seamen's Mission, the Parsonage Mission, the Church Circle, or the Israel Mission.

At the very bottom of the box are some dust-covered, musty collections of sermons by Hallesby and Wisløff that haven't been opened for the last half century. I take one of the books into my hand and am about to dust it off when I notice the cover has some ugly scratches on it. A shiver runs through me, something thrusts itself forward and wants to cross the threshold of consciousness. I try to resist, but the pressure increases and keeps growing stronger, until I can no longer defend myself. And all at once it comes over me, with such overwhelming power that I have to step back and lean on the wall to stay on my feet. My forgetfulness is broken, like a deep nocturnal darkness illuminated by dazzling flashes of lightning, and I see a vision, compressed and condensed, as though viewed through a pair of magical binoculars. A book is thrown on the floor by an invisible hand, and a boot, covered with greyish-brown leggings, kicks and kicks it from one end of the room to the other. "Rubbish!" shrieks a voice I know very well, but now risen to a falsetto and completely distorted by rage. "Rubbish! Rubbish!" And far away, at the edge of the picture, someone covers her face with her hands, while a quiet sniffle gives way to loud sobs, which in turn become a convulsive weeping. But the boot neither sees nor hears, the leggings remain unaffected, and the book darts across the room, colliding with chair legs and getting battered, and finally comes to rest in a corner, its pages turned inside out. "Rubbish! Rubbish! Rubbish!"

No sooner have I placed the book on top of my tower than I feel dizzy, struck by another lightning bolt. This time what I see is more obscure and enigmatic, as in a nightmarish dream. In the middle of the picture there is an abyss or a gulf or perhaps a furnace, half hidden by flames and smoke rising up from the depths. It's like the end of the world, and two strange, swift-footed creatures like little devils dart back and forth, their arms full of books that they throw into the gulf. At the other end of the room a bigger devil is ripping books out of a bookcase, so that she can have a fresh load ready for the little devils when they return empty-handed.

In my mind's eye, it is an event beyond time and space, although deep down I can easily fix it in time and remember the place. It is a few months after Father's funeral. Grandpa has restored us to favour after six years of banishment and we are going to move from our Oslo apartment back to his big, small-town house. The move is already in full swing, and down on the pavement stands a rubbish truck we have rented to get rid of piles of trash and odds and ends. The mattress Father lay on when dying has already been carried down, as well as the pillow, the feather quilt, his clothes, his stick without the silver handle, and all the medicine vials. My two siblings, appointed angels of death (or devils), are continually running down the stairs with things that have been condemned, while I have been assigned to wash the cabinets and the shelves as they are cleared. At a certain point I turn my head and see the two angels of death rush past me with another pile of rubbish. I give a start and rise to my feet, unable to believe my eyes. But they don't deceive me: it is now the turn of Father's library, which is to be exterminated to the last volume. Brother and sister come up from the street with empty hands, and over by the bookcase stands Mother, her brows knitted, looking like a furious avenging angel as she fills their arms with more books. Suddenly a shrill voice cuts through the room, so wild and strange that it's difficult to believe it is my own. "You are a pack of devils to throw away Dad's books!" the voice cries. "You are a pack of devils, pack of devils, devils . . ." The words become fewer and fewer, and the voice thinner and weaker, until finally it fades away and disappears into nothingness.

I stand observing the wavering tower of books for a moment. Then, with a start, I perceive a light nudge against my foot, and an avalanche of books crashes in upon me and hits the floor with an earsplitting noise. I feel deaf and blind and cannot grasp what has happened, until the night nurse opens the door and thrusts a frightened face inside to see what's up.

"Oh, it's only your books that have fallen on the floor," she says, obviously relieved that it's nothing worse, like, for example, that the patient has become restless and has had an attack of destructive fury. "Why are you up and messing around at this time of night?" she says reproachfully. "Why haven't you taken your sleeping pill and settled down for the night?"

I explain to her what she very well knows, that I always keep the sleeping pill for later in the night, when I wake up for the second, third or fourth time. If I were to begin swallowing pills already at bedtime, I would have polished off an entire pharmacy before all my waking hours and occasional dozes were over.

She puts a finger to her lips to remind me that I'm talking too loud and disturbing the other patients. When she has tidied up the avalanche of books and replaced everything in the box, she gently but firmly grasps my elbow and takes me over to the bed. She folds back the quilt, shakes the pillow, and does not leave until I have gone to bed and solemnly promised to be quiet.

I lie half-awake far into the night, tossing and turning while my mind burns and refuses to be at rest. It's like a mill that has run wild, grinding out whims, dreams, anxieties and memories without order or meaning. I consider calling the night nurse to ask for a shot, but recall that I'm no longer on detox and that the sleeping pill is my only recourse. I do not take it, because I know that, once I find myself in such an alert and open-eared state, stronger stuff is needed to turn off the stream of thought. I hear the big clock in the belfry strike one hour after another and send a sympathetic thought to the little woman over in the six-bed ward who becomes completely frantic every time she hears the clock in the tower strike. For some reason she thinks it is a passing bell, and that the strokes mean that someone is coming to get her. I have heard her beg and plead for the clock to be stopped, so that she can stay alive. But the physicians and nurses just laugh and pat her reassuringly on the shoulder. "It's impossible to stop the passage of time," they say, hurrying on to the next ward, where the inmates are more conventionally crazy and do not try their patience unnecessarily.

My churning thoughts grow weary and concentrate more and more on one single question: Did the book tower fall on the floor entirely by itself, or did I kick it? If it fell by itself, everything was as it should be and I could safely lie down to sleep. But what if I inadvertently gave it a kick? Wouldn't that have to mean something more than that the mere sight of the books made me frantic, so I let them fall? Didn't it have to imply another and deeper aversion, a rejection of her who owned them and who was so absorbed

45

by them that she read them over and over again? If it was as I feared, didn't it really mean that I had given my mother a kick and annihilated her a second time, after she was already dead and gone? Didn't it mean that I had become doubly motherless and was left completely alone in the world? Released from my wild and inordinate need for love, but at the same time stripped of origin, of attachments, tenderness and a life-giving warmth?

How could I make it all come alive again? I ask myself. What do I have to do to restore that which once was and put it into its proper context? How to raise her from the dead, not in the form of the careworn old lady I haven't seen for nineteen years, but as the fair and radiant young woman I was once so enthralled by? She who was so sad, so sad and so vulnerable at heart, but still sang at the top of her voice as she ran up and down the stairs, privately practised dance steps on the floor, poured out her troubles, abandoned herself to sudden merriment over nothing and laughed uproariously with her hand over her mouth. She who was lavish with smiles and promising glances, only to withdraw them the next minute. Who folded her hands in prayer while she was secretly on the lookout for excitement and change, turned and twisted herself before her own image in the mirror, stamped her foot and made vicious, cutting remarks which she immediately regretted and withdrew. My frivolous young mama, who pretended to be melancholy, and perhaps was, deep down, for all I know.

You have tried detoxing and diversion long enough, I say to myself in a whisper. Been on the run, a wanderer, long enough, seeking the shadows and the deceptive half-light. What if you went back to the fountainhead of all things to see what could be found there?

2

In the late autumn of 1933 the parish pastor in our town retired, and when the application period had expired the parish council met to nominate his successor.

The parish council was composed rather evenly of high- and low-church members, with slightly more from the latter. As chairman, Andreas Sand had used his influence to promote his own favourites, and he took great pains to explain each and every applicant's merits and religious position. But he was intelligent and pragmatic enough to understand that the candidates who favoured an extreme pietism were excluded. He controlled the gathering with a practised hand, and after a tug-of-war he succeeded in consolidating the majority around two applicants, both confessional theologians and good, traditional preachers. Since they were nominated as Number One and Number Two, a concession was made to the minority by choosing a liberal theologian as the third candidate. This candidate was dubious, but impossible to ignore, since his qualifications far exceeded those of the others. Besides his university degree in theology, he had a doctorate in theology from the University of Oslo and a Ph.D. in philosophy from the University of Freiburg. A minority had long insisted that with these superior qualifications he ought to be nominated as Number One, but they began to give way when it turned out that the majority was more disposed to exclude him altogether. After long discussions and arguments the meeting agreed to nominate him as Number Three, at the bottom of the list, after the two confessional theologians.

With that the minority felt their voices had been heard, and the majority thought that they had secured themselves against getting a dubious spiritual leader. The man's name was Vemund Hov, a peasant's son of modest background, the same age as the century. He obviously wasn't cut out to be a pastor, but had envisioned an academic career for himself. He had resided in Germany for four years, the last period as a *Privatdozent* at the University of Freiburg. But a doubtful rumour had it that during the summer he had hastened home to Telemark to be at his mother's deathbed, where he had promised to return to Norway and seek a living.

The appointment took place in the late winter of 1934, and to everyone's surprise the Department had turned the list of nominees upside down and appointed the dubious third man as parish pastor in our town. Andreas Sand called an emergency meeting of the parish council and proposed to appeal against the appointment. But when the meeting came to vote on his proposal, it turned out that he no longer had the majority on his side. It was stated that the Department was not bound by the ranking order of the nominations. Candidates One, Two, and Three were all on the list and must therefore enjoy the congregation's complete confidence. If the council deemed one of the applicants unsuitable, it ought to have made this clear by not nominating him in the first place.

Vemund Hov had announced that he would arrive on the fourth Sunday of Lent, around two o'clock in the afternoon. A reception committee was formed, and since a train arrived in town at exactly this time, everybody assumed that he would be on it.

Well before the train was due to arrive, a small group of men in black rushed to the station with Andreas Sand at their head. To be on the safe side, he had procured a photograph of the pastor, and when the passengers alighted from the train, every male of appropriate age was inspected from top to toe. But no one answered to the description, and soon the last traveller had alighted and the platform was empty.

Disappointed, the men in black looked at each other and were about to depart when the verger came into view with every sign of being in a hurry. The little man had run so fast and was so flustered that at first he couldn't utter a word. But once he had recovered his breath and calmed down a little, he could relate that a stranger was waiting in a convertible in front of the church. It had to be the new pastor, though he seemed foreign and looked almost like a tourist.

The reception committee rallied itself and reached the church in no time, with Andreas Sand's supple figure a good distance ahead of the rest. It was Vemund Hov all right, and when he learned that the parish council had taken a fruitless trip to the station, he was generous enough to apologize for not remembering to mention that he would be arriving in his private car. His voice was deep and resonant, so sonorous, in fact, that the men in black involuntarily raised their heads and listened, as if it were a rare and precious music.

A tall man, burly rather than stately, the pastor stepped out of the Ford and shook hands in an abrupt and bashful manner. He was scarcely ignorant of the fact that he had only been ranked third and no doubt sensed that the men who had shown up were dissatisfied, even though they didn't let on. His face was bold and fine without being handsome; his large nose resembled an improved potato, his forehead was high and clear, surmounted by brownish, curly hair that receded above the temples. His mouth looked resolute, with a somewhat protruding lower lip (a trait that was eventually to be inherited by one of his two daughters). Still, it was the eyes that dominated the entire face; they were of an indeterminate blue with brown flecks and had an expression, at once intense and thoughtful, that would shift to melancholy when he occasionally forgot himself.

48

All in all the man would have given a solid and trustworthy impression if it hadn't been for his attire, which instantly caused the men in black to take offence. How could a man of the cloth arrive in this fashion, dressed in a suit that was a cross between a uniform and a hunting outfit, with trousers that bagged below the knee and were followed by leggings and heavy army boots? Before the stranger stepped out of his car and bared his head, he had sat behind the wheel in a sort of visored cap pulled down over his eyes, a headgear that none of the four townsmen had ever seen the likes of before. They averted their eyes, taking pains not to betray their indignation. But during the sparse exchanges that ensued they observed the newcomer surreptitiously, casting meaningful glances out of the corners of their eyes.

To Andreas Sand's great relief the new parson spoke standard Norwegian, although his phraseology was unusual and bore traces of dialect. The ship owner was sensitive to linguistic peculiarities and prided himself on his ability to determine a speaker's origin within a dozen miles or so after an exchange of only a few minutes. And since he had himself purged his speech of rural expressions, he had also become very particular about the speech of others, and he would have been aggravated if the town had been forced to listen to sermons in peasant brogue.

The pastor left his vehicle in front of the church, took a rucksack from the boot, threw it over his shoulder and prepared to go on foot the few hundred metres to the parsonage. The Ford was already surrounded by little boys and, while the pastor was still waiting, they had taken turns jumping onto the running board to ask if they could sound the horn. Before abandoning his vehicle, the pastor strode toward the flock of boys and half-jestingly threatened that there would be hell to pay if anyone touched his car while he was away. He probably wasn't in the habit of joking, for his words seemed unnecessarily harsh and didn't exactly give the impression that they came from someone who liked children. Frightened, the boys withdrew behind the cemetery wall, and only the most courageous of them peeked out at the marvel between the bars of the gate.

The small company headed toward the parsonage, where a banquet awaited them, the pastor lost in his own thoughts, though willingly answering several practical questions. No, unfortunately, he was not married; he hadn't yet found anyone who would have him, he added with a little laugh. Did he want the housekeeper to stay on, after she had served the old parson for more than twenty years? Hm, he didn't quite know, having up to now lived in a small apartment with no need of a servant. Well, yes, certainly, now that he had an entire parsonage to maintain, perhaps he had better let the housekeeper stay on. Could he undertake the instruction of the confirmation class? The old parson was willing to prepare the group if he felt it was too troublesome to take over. What was that? Oh, the confirmation class? No, he didn't find it troublesome, but if the old parson would prefer to handle the confirmation, that was quite in order. Could he possibly host the Parsonage Mission twice a month, as his predecessor had done; it might be a bit difficult, since he didn't have a wife? The Parsonage Mission, what could that be? Was it, perhaps, what went elsewhere by the name of the Mission for the Heathen? Hm, that could wait, couldn't it, until he'd had time to consider and get to know the town's heathens? A parson's wife? No, as he'd said, not for the time being or so far. Anyway, what did that have to do with his duties? As far as he knew, parsons' wives were not appointed by royal authority and did not receive any salary of their own.

As the five men walked beside the cemetery wall, they attracted great but respectful attention. Despite the time of day, the usual dinner hour, the short stretch of road was packed with people in their Sunday best who greeted them, while casting quick, sidelong glances at the newcomer. The men in black tipped their hats and returned the greetings, letting fall some casual words in passing. Pastor Hov appeared rather pained, forging ahead with such long strides that the others almost had to trot to keep up with him. Maybe it had finally dawned on him that his attire was arousing indignation, and that he ought to have thought of this beforehand.

Two young ladies were standing at the corner of Parsonage Avenue, seemingly quite by chance; they were so engrossed in idle chatter that they didn't seem to notice the pastor and his companions. But no sooner had the men passed by than they tossed their heads, drew a deep breath with a little squeal and, giggling, fell on each others' necks. For a while they stood motionless, staring up the avenue as if unable to believe their eyes. Then they squeezed their bucket hats firmly on their heads and ran toward the centre of town to tell their friends what they had seen.

But while all these people were milling about, keeping a lookout, putting their heads together and crowding the streets, young Mary Sand was left high and dry, away from it all. Alone at home, in the large house on Strand Street, she was staring out of the window at the grey afternoon, looking abandoned. Before her father had left for the station, he had forbidden her to go outside and threatened to ground her for the next two Sundays if she was depraved enough to defy his order. Foresighted as he was, he knew all there was to know about the curiosity of the young townswomen and didn't want his daughter falling over herself to catch a glimpse of the new pastor.

Opening the curtain slightly and peeping cautiously down the quiet Sunday street, Mary is ready to withdraw in an instant if someone she knows should come by. She is despondent, and her fresh young face has a sullen, self-pitying expression. Now and then she passes a hand over her forehead, wondering how best to circumvent her father's prohibition. What if she locked the door to her room and climbed through the window, which she sometimes did when she had to? The pear tree by the wall is easy to climb down, leaving her best dress without a scratch. Poor stupid Papa who is so easily fooled, especially when he thinks everything is out of harm's way. He will assume that she has locked herself in to sulk, and simply wait for her to come out and apologize.

No, she mustn't do anything that might bring its own punishment! It will never do to show herself in town on a day like this; every entranceway is a trap, and she may run into her father or one of his spies on the first street corner. Better to possess one's soul in patience, then it will all work out. In any case, her father couldn't very well forbid her to go to church next Sunday, for that would be tantamount to preventing her from hearing the gospel. But Papa's gullibility is of an unpredictable sort; once he has become suspicious, you never know. No, no, forget about climbing through the window! No misfortune could be worse than house arrest. What would the organist say? After all, she sings in the church choir. Her voice makes all the others sound like yowls and caterwauling. Oh, next Sunday she will sing at the top of her voice, with all her soul and all her heart, so that the new parson will be obliged to lift his head in the midst of the litany and look up at the gallery in astonishment. Does he know how to chant, or will he reel off the *Kyrie* in a dry creaking voice just like the old pastor? And next Sunday is the day of the Annunciation, how strange! It had to be fate or at least providence that willed him to hold his first religious service on exactly that day. The day of the Annunciation, Mary's day. What message would then pass from him to her, or from her to him? But that joy could wait till the time came. How thrilling, though, to discover whether something unexpected would come to pass that day!

Mary wipes away her tears, which are mostly crocodile tears, and suddenly feels quite animated. According to what she could relate a generation later, she had heard the hour of fate strike, a curtain had been pulled aside, giving her a glimpse of something that would give her life an entirely new direction. Something alluring and dangerous, which she was unable to resist, nor wanted to resist for all the world. For in such matters you had no will of your own, you were bred and predestined like a fatted calf and couldn't do anything one way or the other.

She heaves a deep, pleasurable sigh and abandons herself to thoughts and anticipations not unlike those that marked the path for Andreas Sandane twenty years earlier. She is not the apple of his eye and legitimate daughter for nothing. Like her originator, she is equipped with a vivid imagination and a desire to forge her own happiness. A long shudder steals through her, an almost prophetic chill that not only promises happiness and good fortune, but also presages heartbreak and undreamed-of torments.

But soon afterward she straightens up and bursts into brief, fearless laughter. Thirty-four years old already, if it was really true that he was the same age as the century! Almost an old man, fifteen years older than someone who hadn't yet turned nineteen. But pooh, why bother about that, hadn't she always had an eye for things that others didn't think went together, like green and blue, butter on top of lard, sugar with blood pudding, and Christmas Eve and an old woman? She would simply laugh, yes laugh, if someone should really be so petty as to mention the age difference.

No, stop – small steps now, over again and slowly, as the music teacher used to say. What if he shouldn't be a bachelor, but came to town dragging a wife in tow? Or what if he looked like a weakling, with hollow chest, a dripping nose, and clammy clergyman's hands? No, thank goodness, she didn't have to worry about that, she had carefully examined the photograph of him lying uppermost in her father's desk drawer. In fact, he looked splendid, like a real heir to the throne. But easy now, easy, don't go overboard! Mary, you have to get rid of your habit of thinking out loud and walking around with a face like an open book. You must learn not to let on, to look the other way, avoid blushing at the wrong moments. You had better proceed cautiously and cold-shoulder him at first. If only it wasn't so difficult to be someone other than you are. But pooh, she would find a way. Ha ha, it would certainly be fun to see their faces when every obstacle had been cleared away and the inconceivable had taken place.

Vemund Hov's arrival in town was not a success, and the banquet at the parsonage did not improve matters. From the very first moment he acquired a reputation as a learned barbarian who despised received custom and did his best to offend. Many years later, when everything about him was an open book, this Simnel-Sunday was remembered and noted as a bad omen.

But he evened the score the following Sunday, the day of the Annunciation, when he gave his first High Mass. The church was filled to the last pew, not only by regular churchgoers but also by people who usually didn't set foot in the house of God. A so-called society lady was supposed to have groaned aloud as she elbowed her way in, cursing all those regulars who couldn't stay away just once so that others might get a look-in.

That Sunday the pastor observed every possible propriety, letting the unholy car stay at home and walking across the churchyard on foot wearing his vestments. His clergyman's gown was an excellent fit; indeed, it did real wonders for his queer, controversial figure. People who had seen him the previous Sunday could scarcely believe it was the same man. He didn't go around by the sacristy, which was customary, but kept out of sight in some unknown place, waiting for the congregation to stream into the church and take their seats. Only when the bells had rung for the third time and the introductory prayer had been read, did he enter by the main door and walk up the aisle with firm steps, carried forward by the prelude, to which, on this particular Sunday, the organist managed to give the air of a fanfare. When he kneeled at the altar in silent prayer, a hush fell in the crowded church. All present held their breaths, and the atmosphere was charged with a suspense that could vent itself in anything whatsoever – relief, wonder, indignation, sensation, or perhaps outright scandal.

But nothing sensational happened, apart from the fact that after the prayer the pastor turned to the congregation and sang a solo hymn, without musical accompaniment and with such feeling that he made a deep impression. The sermon was rather short, the rituals had a larger place than usual, and the litany developed into an unusual antiphonal singing between the altar and the gallery. Not surprisingly for anyone who had heard the pastor's speaking voice, he had a mighty baritone that filled the entire church and received a response from a clear soprano that surpassed itself this Sunday and attained truly divine heights. The congregation sat as though dumbstruck, while the two voices rose and sank and mysteriously mingled, as if conducting a secret conversation in the midst of the organ peal. Later there were many who said that they had immediately realized what was taking place between the pastor and the young warbler.

3

But let this be enough from my hand about an event that is so remote that there is hardly a living person who can recall it. Let us instead hear what the pastor himself has to say in one of the diaries his young daughter managed to save from the rubbish truck.

For most of his adult life, until his right hand was paralyzed, Vemund Hov wrote brief, or not so brief, reflections on the way of the world, not daily or even regularly, but by fits and starts whenever he felt the need. These notes might be limited to a line or two, but were often more extensive, written in a dense scrawl right across the dates of his almanac, or on some blank sheets he inserted at different places in the book. His scribblings are in no way remarkable, but the presentation reveals great sincerity and has at times an emotional richness that deserves to be remembered.

On Simnel-Sunday, 1934, for example, he writes:

Arrived at my new living today, Sunday, 11 March, at two o'clock. Had calculated the time to a hair, looked at my watch when I got there and congratulated myself on my punctuality. Mild, almost springtime weather, no sun to be seen but long catkins on the willows and birdsong in the air. Noticed suddenly that a weight had dropped off my back, my soul was singing, expectation and joy shooting through me. But how long was Adam in paradise? Sat waiting outside the church for almost half an hour, thinking it must be the right place. No mortals to be seen anywhere, sounded my horn discreetly, but only succeeded in attracting a flock of boys. When I was finally discovered and identified, everything had gone awry and I was met with studied coldness. My cheerful mood vanished, I felt unsure of myself and very bewildered. Only afterwards, when I had had time to think it over, did I realize that my misfortune was to some extent of my own making.

Faux pas No. 1: I had forgotten to give notice that I was arriving in my own car, so that the four gentlemen from the parish council had first made a fruitless trip to the railway station. When we finally met, they were so surly that I was immediately infected by their bad humour. Stepping out of my car, I missed my footing, and when we finally shook hands it was done in a hesitant, half-hearted way. As always happens when I get confused, my sound judgement deserted me; I withdrew into myself and became as sombre and unapproachable as a troglodyte. I knew, after all, what the situation was and that, on the whole, I was unwelcome in this town. A mere moment sufficed to make me lose all hope of our finding a civilized way of dealing with one another. A blind urge for survival welled up in me, as in my earliest youth when my existence was threatened from every quarter. Happened to remember a passage in Heidegger and found comfort in the thought that the mere fact of being alive is a great blessing.

Faux pas No. 2: My clothing, again my own stupidity! I left Siljan in the usual uniform that I use when driving. God help my thoughtlessness. I was in good faith and had no inkling that there was anything wrong with my attire. At the university in Freiburg that sort of thing wasn't given a moment's thought, everybody dressed more or less carelessly, even the Rector, Professor Heidegger. But here one is inspected and damned from top to toe – jacket, trousers, leggings, boots, not to mention the cap I was obliged to take off and carry under my arm. Ran the gauntlet through the streets and grew more and more sensitive and gloomy. To my horror I noticed violence rise within me; one of my hands twitched as if preparing to strike. Fortunately I have sufficient control over my impulses to prevent anything drastic from happening.

The Day of the Annunciation, 18 March.

Rose early and took a walk in the woods to meditate on my sermon, which I wanted to make pure and clear, without too much exegesis. As far as my preaching is concerned, I'm determined to stick to the text and let it speak for itself. No sermon can ever be superior to the gospel, so shame on anyone who adds or subtracts anything.

Saw tracks of hare and fox at the edge of the forest, and a little farther the distinct imprints of the hooves of Brother Moose. We are equally shy, he and I, and are on our guard. But maybe our paths will cross sometime in the fall, when the moose hunt begins.

Practised the *Kyrie* a while and did fairly well, even if I say so myself. The birds rose, the air was crystal-clear and gave a rare resonance. But suddenly, without any perceptible reason, I lost courage and fell to brooding.

What would become of me? I thought, sitting down on a rock with my elbows on my knees and leaning my forehead on my hands. What did I wish to return to Norway for, and what in the world was I doing in a place like this? I who had always felt terrified by the many-headed monster that is called a congregation. How was it possible to return home when one didn't have any place one could call home, to settle down when one was a fugitive, to be weighed and measured when one was so slippery and without specific gravity? God in heaven, what had I let myself in for, I who had sworn I would never stand in a pulpit? To be sure, there was my promise to Mother, given in an unguarded moment by a runaway cotter's son who wanted to embellish his betrayal and make up for something.

No, I had no business in the pulpit, that was clear. But had I anything more to offer in other places, when all was said and done? An academic career? No thanks! First, I was neither a thinker nor a theologian, despite two doctorates. His highness *Ratio* and I were irreconcilable quantities that could never agree. I was a person with strong hunches and intuitions, which would occasionally give me insight into things that were not entirely self-evident. But I would never be a man of reason, I was irrational through and through, and my knowledge was nothing more than approximations and loose conjectures.

And besides, it was open to question whether fine arts like theology and philosophy had anything whatsoever to do with reality. Who knows, I thought, perhaps I was a greater charlatan behind the lectern in Freiburg than I'll risk being here in the town pulpit. My awful brother, Balder, is surely on to something when he makes fun of my German doctorate, maintaining it's something you can take while the train is waiting: *Freiburg nächstmal. Absteigen bitte, Doktorgrad nehmen!*

The Sunday in church did not begin well, and I thank those spirits of light that caused it to end so happily.

When I was putting on my gown I couldn't find the ruff anywhere. Rummaged high and low, hearing to my despair the church bells ringing. Suddenly remembered that I had pushed the box with that miserable priest's noose under the front seat of my car. Rushed out and got hold of it and managed to get ready at the last moment. I had beforehand dirtied

56

my black shoes in a rather embarrassing manner. I had put them out in front of my bed beside the chamber pot, and when I stepped out on the floor at daybreak, I chanced to bump into the punch bowl, giving my shoes a proper dousing.

But it all panned out, and by taking a short cut across the churchyard I arrived just as the bells started ringing the second time. The church trail was completely black with people, and my old dread of crowds almost unmanned me for a moment. I stopped short, my chest contracting and the ruff feeling like a millstone round my neck. I thought I'd better make a detour and take cover behind the church until the congestion had passed. As I walked up the aisle I got the idea of singing a hymn for the congregation right after the silent prayer. It proved to be a happy thought. I immediately noticed that the mood changed and that their good will was flowing towards me. I sang:

> Mary she was a virgin fair,
> May God bestow his grace.
> She bore a son without compare,
> Him let us laud and praise.

The organist must have understood that it was my way of calling upon the congregation, for he let the manuals and pedals rest while the old Mary ballad spread through the vaults of the church. When I had come to the end of the last verse, I felt strengthened and restored to favour, and I saw myself capable of carrying through the High Mass according to the established pattern.

While I stood singing before the altar, I had no ulterior motives and was unaware of what poignant consequences my choice of hymn was to have. I had let the Christian calendar make the decision and had no idea that Mary happened to be the name of a young woman who sang in the church choir. Only during the litany did the situation develop in a manner that shook me out of my devotions and forced me to lift my eyes toward the gallery.

A single female voice suddenly broke out of the choral singing and met my masculine voice in such a way that I was almost dumbfounded. It was a voice just as high and clear as mine was deep and dark, and they found each other in an intimacy that seemed to say they had been meant for one another from the beginning of time. For a short while the congregation sang along with the litany; then it grew quiet in the stalls and the antiphonal singing was left to me and the young woman in the gallery. It was truly a sacred hour, so high and pure that it will never fade from my memory. "*Kyrie eleison*, Lord, have mercy upon us. *Christe eleison*, Christ have mercy upon us." The words fell like a gentle spring rain on my lacerated soul and gave me a profound peace. However incredible it may seem, I had never until that day and hour thought about what the word mercy implied, it was a word that had long ago become ritualized and which my musical spirit had converted to purely tonal values: F-G-A-A-G-A-A, *Kyrie eleison*, A-A-G-G-G-F sharp-G, Lord, have mercy upon us. Now the old Gregorian chant came to me as a gift from heaven, and I felt like one of the Elect when it was my turn to give the response.

When the service was over I feigned an errand to the organ loft to arrange something with the organist. Met the singers in the church choir on the stairs, but didn't see the one I should have liked to thank for having graced my Sunday. When I got all the way up I realized she had been delayed, she had her back to me and was collecting her things. When she noticed me, she grew flaming red and turned away rather brusquely. Then she was in a hurry to get going, but still turned around midway and gave me a lingering look. She refused to listen to the organist, who asked if she might like to meet me, let out a brief snort and hurried on in her oddly hesitant and irresolute manner. She stopped on the landing, giving a last backward glance before withdrawing her eyes and rushing down the stairs with a commotion that made the organist and me look at one another and smile understandingly.

I've been thinking about her ever since and given her the name "Furiosa", after the musical designation for wildness. Maybe I ought to give her the nickname "Vivacia", for liveliness and movement, and "Adagia" for something lingering and tender in the midst of it all. Several names could be discussed, like "Formosa", as an expression of her beauty and loveliness.

Tuesday, 20 March. The weather completely changed, snowfall and frost. The woodshed in the basement quite empty, so I have had to order a cord of birchwood, kr. 15.40; 10 sacks of coal, kr. 17.00; and 10 hl. coke II, kr. 22.00. The housekeeper nags me about getting an electric stove in the kitchen. Gladly as far as I am concerned, but I wonder what the authorities have to say in such times of crisis.

Yesterday had a letter from Vidkun Quisling, son of my benefactor, Dean

Quisling at Gjerpen. He welcomed me back home to Norway, reminded me of our lessons during the summer of 1917 and 1918, and invited me to become a member of his newly formed party, *Nasjonal Samling* (NS), National Union.

I replied and thanked him, but asked him to wait and have a bit of patience with me. I had no head for politics, I wrote, I simply didn't understand that sort of thing and had never been able to decide to vote for any party. But I thanked him once more for all that his father and he himself had done for me, at a time when I was a down-and-out cotter's son with two empty hands and an insatiable thirst for knowledge. Without the help and support I had received at the parsonage in Gjerpen, I would most likely have continued to eke out a living as a farm hand up in Telemark somewhere. If, that is, I hadn't gone completely to the dogs and ended up on the road, as happened to a couple of my uncles on my father's side.

When I had sent the letter I felt relieved, but an obscure sense of guilt was gnawing at me on the quiet. How could I repay the debt I owed to the Quisling family, which had virtually dug me out of the dirt and made me? I recalled my blatant admiration for young Quisling (Vidkun) when he was home on holiday and undertook to give me extra lessons in German and mathematics. Thirteen years my senior, he was already a captain on the General Staff and so learned that I was all agog as soon as he opened his mouth. He stayed up all night to work at a vast philosophy of life that he called "Universism", and talked to me in an abstract and fantastic language that was way over my head. I thought in my simplicity that it was the proper language of learning, and as soon as he was out of sight I made haste to scratch his words of wisdom down on a piece of paper. Does he still continue to engross himself in that kind of obscure talk, I wonder? Today, I suppose, I should be able to sift it and find out whether it was worth listening to.

Wednesday, 21 March. Had this morning another meeting with the organist, whom I'm already getting along with very well. Together, we have conceived a magnificent plan of performing Verdi's *Requiem* during Easter Week. Time is very short, only a little over a week. But the organist is confident that the church choir will be able to rehearse its part before the four holy days arrive. The choir has sung some of the parts before, but since the service sets strict liturgical limits, there has never been a question of performing them in church.

The programme looks as follows: Maundy Thursday, *Requiem* and *Kyrie*. Good Friday, *Dies Irae* and *Lacrymosa*. First day of Easter, *Agnus Dei* and *Lux aeterna*. Second day of Easter, *Sanctus* and *Libera me*.

The performance will thus alternate between choral song, organ fugues, and solo parts for young Mary Sand and myself. The organist has already begun to instruct the choir, which is very much to his credit. He became sincerely glad when I told him that it could compete with the best chamber choirs I had heard in Germany. We will have the first general rehearsal Friday evening. The performance will obviously have certain shortcomings – we have to manage without an orchestra, and the organ will be responsible for the entire musical accompaniment. Fortunately, the church organ is an incredibly rich instrument, having incorporated a number of other instruments, from flute to *viola dolce*.

The only question is whether my own baritone will be adequate, able to span the entire scale from bass to tenor. Nevertheless I'm exhilarated and filled with happy expectations. *Sanctus, Sanctus, Sanctus!* The roof of the church will rise and a strip of heaven become visible!

N.B. Must try to be careful in my association with Mary Sand. Have met her quite by chance a few times since Sunday. Lovely, lovely, but hard to figure out. No sooner has she given me a dazzling smile than she takes it back, looking as if I have annoyed her in some way.

Friday, 23 March, four p.m. Cold continues, 9° C this morning when I got up. Practised *Lux aeterna* before going down for breakfast. Notice that my voice easily gets strained when it has to do both high and low parts. But after a few unsuccessful tries I did get it right and ended up quite satisfied. All I do these days is in the spirit of the *Requiem*; I catch myself humming and intoning in the most unexpected places. *Sanctus!* Looking forward to the rehearsal this evening as if it were a wedding party!

The housekeeper, whose name I'm constantly forgetting, came suddenly barging in on me in the middle of my office hours to ask if we shouldn't hire help, so that we could do a spring clean before Easter. Was annoyed at being disturbed, and my answer was not entirely nice. As far as I can see, the house is already shining from attic to basement, so why should we have a domestic doomsday in the middle of Holy Week? And how can the *Requiem* survive in me if they produce a draught and set the whole house on end?

I was on the point of answering her that she ought instead to do a spring clean on herself and leave the house alone. Her body odours are not good, and I've wondered why it never occurs to her to extend the cleanliness to her own person. When I go to the kitchen in the morning to fetch a tub of warm water and carry it down to the laundry room in the basement, she becomes just as pop-eyed with amazement (or indignation?) as the morning before. This morning bath has for many years been my fixed and indispensable ritual, despite the fact that I grew up in conditions approaching animal filth. The laundry room in this house is a real bonanza, with a long pivoting tap which I can duck my head under when I have washed myself clean in the warm water. Wonder how I have become such a bathing buff, whether it isn't one of the many ways I have of distancing myself from my origin, or what. I scent bad body odours at a distance of a hundred metres and would rather dispense with the Lord's Prayer than with my warm and cold baths. The first morning, my housekeeper (Guri Moen?) seemed to think that I was going to use the tub to wash clothes, for suddenly there she was in the basement, letting out a loud scream as she saw me sit stark naked under the cold tap. God be with her, she is a good country wife who doesn't spare herself. She's just slightly mistaken about her human worth, thinking it is to be found in the parsonage's windows and panels.

Must remember to dress decently this evening, so that nobody will make faces and consider me a queer fish. Fortunately I have a practically new pepper-and-salt suit which nobody can find fault with. If only my voice holds out, and puts up with being stretched from low G to high F sharp.

Thursday, 5 April. Have done four services with the *Requiem*, the result above all expectations. The church was so full, especially the two days of Easter, that people stood jampacked in the aisle all the way to the vestibule. My voice held out, I don't think I've ever sung better! After the High Mass I was surrounded by elegant ladies who lauded me to the skies and thought it was a shame that I hadn't gone to the opera instead. Oh well, that is one way of looking at it, no doubt, although it doesn't exactly strengthen my position as pastor. The dinner invitations poured in – I folded my hands over the hymnal and said thanks sort of casually. Cannot really say I'm dying to be at table with merchants and ship brokers. But we'll see – if someone among them should happen to be musical, it might be bearable.

Was filled with gratitude when Easter was past and every good fortune had stood by us. Mary Sand's singing voice is marvellous, it seems to dwell like a waif in a young woman who otherwise doesn't distinguish herself by any great spiritual gifts. I cannot help wondering about the spirit of music, which is so sensual and lives like a young cuckoo in the nests of perfect strangers.

Unfortunately I feel unfree towards her and become virtually dumb as soon as we do not communicate with each other through music. When I thanked her after our last test of endurance, she at first looked seriously at me, then began to giggle with her hand over her mouth. And when I asked her what was wrong, she burst out laughing and told me that my suit was three sizes too small! I couldn't help joining in her laughter, she'd uttered the words so nicely, and I felt too cheerful and happy to take the criticism to heart. I went about singing the entire rest of the day, walking from room to room in the almost empty parsonage and listening half dreamily to my own voice, which knew nothing of unfreedom but bounced powerfully back from walls and roof. And like a distant-sounding echo I could hear her response, full of abandonment and youthful joy.

The backlash came yesterday, Wednesday, in the form of a letter of censure from the parish council. The house of God was no concert hall, it said in the letter, and this had to be the last time that I violated the liturgy and introduced new ceremonies without permission from the bishop. Many churchgoers had been disappointed that the message of Easter was drowned in music and that Christ's passion and death were pushed aside in favour of ambitious singing accomplishments. The sermon was much too brief, and its form suggested that the congregation was in no need of any instruction but could freely make their own reflections on the text. Nor could it be tolerated that I offered solos during the service, as I had done at my induction on 18 March. True, the Mary ballad was to be found in Landstad's hymnal, but it was practically never sung and was almost to be considered as a leftover from the Catholic period. Altogether, there were several misplaced elements in my service, things that couldn't be said to belong in the Lutheran Evangelical Church. These excrescences had to go; they were liturgically indefensible and would not be tolerated in the future. The letter was signed by Andreas Sand, chairman of the parish council. Hm, hm, I thought, as I made a mental note of the matter. I couldn't help asking myself whether the man had occult powers, and what other warnings I could draw from this petty and highly unmusical dressing down.

* *

Sunday, 22 April. My incumbency in this town is now entering its seventh week, and there's not much news to record. Beautiful spring weather, the buds on the trees ready to burst, and a touch of green on the grass in the garden. Had expected that my housekeeper would give notice and skip out on moving day, 17 April, she's dissatisfied with nearly everything and is constantly asking if I won't soon purchase furniture for the empty rooms. But the moving day came and went and she didn't say a word.

Yesterday I went to a Saturday dinner party at Consul W., together with a number of the local big shots. Four courses, so overloaded with trimmings and garnish that I hadn't the faintest idea what I was putting away. Did my best, but scarcely found the correct strategy in this clutter of knives and forks, tall and low glasses, plates on top of other plates, and mischievously splashing fingerbowls. After-dinner speeches welcoming me into the circle, as if I had already been bought and paid for. Coffee in such tiny little cups that I made the mistake of emptying mine in a single mouthful.

After the coffee, fuss over wanting to hear my singing voice, but preferably in something slightly more cheerful than what I had on the program during Easter Week. Tried as long as possible to excuse myself, but wasn't let off the hook until I had sung some snatches from *Rigoletto* and *The Bartered Bride*. Big applause and fresh laments that I hadn't gone on the opera stage. Had to give an extra number from *Carmen* before I was finally left alone.

Afterwards half-educated conversation and boredom as thick as the smoke from the gentlemen's cigars. Sat looking at my watch on the sly, wondering when I could leave without offending my hosts. Fresh glasses on the table, tall and low and almost ball-shaped; nodded and mumbled cryptically when I was offered a choice between three kinds of drinks. I'd rather be in some Freiburg pub, where you can quench your thirst without being an expert on fine flavours and on smacking your lips. The conversation dragged on, until one of the ladies mentioned the name of Adolf Hitler. The women began to cackle and wave their arms, just like the chickens in the Hov henhouse when they lifted their inert wings and flew up to a higher perch. Gawd, what a stylish gentleman, what with that side parting and those eyes and that sweet little moustache under his nose! A pure artist from top to toe. And that voice of his, which knew what it wanted and went straight for your subconscious, if not further still.

The gentlemen joined in and praised the Führer's iron will and his incomparable grasp of the German national psyche. Not to mention his desire for law and order – now the trains would run on time and all strikes be called off. And just wait, he would be dead certain to keep his promise of crushing world communism. The Weimar Republic had failed, it was nothing but sheer chaos and scattered skirmishes anyway, worse luck. The die was cast – after fifteen years of humiliation and misunderstood democracy, Germany was retaliating.

I sat in silence without taking part in the conversation, until the consul made a pause in his instructive talk and wanted to know what the pastor thought. I hemmed and hawed and excused myself as usual by saying that I had no head for politics. But this time I didn't escape so lightly; soon they came at me from every quarter, refusing to let me wriggle out of it.

Taking the plunge, I mumbled something to the effect that it wasn't easy to understand a phenomenon like Nazism. Maybe it was nothing but an episode that would disappear from history without a trace, just as it had appeared. Or perhaps it was a horse cure that Germany had to go through in order to survive as a nation.

"Horse cure, did you hear? The pastor said 'horse cure'!" the ladies yelled, and one of them stretched out her hand to pat my cheek, but instead scratched my forehead with those long barnyard claws of hers.

"We have to remember," said the consul to placate them, "Pastor Hov is the son of a peasant. When he speaks about a horse cure, he no doubt means the same as we do when we think of tested remedies."

"A toast to tested remedies!" cried the medical director of the county hospital, raising his glass. He is a specialist in surgery and known for getting at the root of any evil.

"Allow me to abstain," I said, not picking up my glass. "We cannot all speak like those two surgeons who stood bent over a patient considering how to treat the case: 'Shall we operate, or shall we let him survive?'"

The company exploded with laughter, and the bad feeling dissolved in general merriment. Made haste to get on my feet and leave while the going was good. Felt utterly downcast and at odds with myself. Drove like a madman through town and nearly ran into an oncoming biker without a light at a curve in the road. Decided to forget about Vidkun Quisling's overture and keep ever so far away from National Union!

When I got home it was nearly two o'clock, and I was so wound up that I realized it was useless to try and sleep. Warmed the coffeepot in the kitchen and went into my study to get out my German doctoral dissertation with the rather pretentious title, *Das vor-sokratische Denken im Vergleich mit dem hebräisch-christlichen* (A Comparison Between Pre-Socratic and Hebraic-Christian Thought). Became lost in thought as I leafed through it, reading a little here and there. Put it aside and sank, as so often before, into an obscure despondency.

How had I chosen precisely that subject for my dissertation? I asked myself. No doubt for obvious reasons, because it was about survival. From the time when I was a tiny tot I had had to summon all my fighting spirit, so that nobody would walk over me and steal my life. No wonder that self-preservation had become my way of life and that it ended up determining all my thinking. Poorly equipped as I was, indeed almost naked, I had been thrown into a world governed by the law of survival and the war of all against all. Barely escaping going under, how often had I experienced the truth of good old Heraclitus's words that strife is the father of all things!

Morning, four o'clock. The day is dawning, the spruces at the edge of the forest look like black shadows against a nearly white sky. Quiet, quiet, not a breath of wind in the air. *Warte nur, balde –*

Tuesday, 24 April. Weighed and measured myself this morning. Height: 187 cm; weight: 74 kg. Have lost four kilos since my arrival in town, which says something about what hardships I have undergone to preserve my spiritual and physical equilibrium.

Have forgotten to mention in these pages that last week I went to Oslo briefly for a check-up at the National Hospital. It could take place in full discretion, since an old acquaintance from my student days is assistant physician in the medical department. When the tests had been taken and analyzed, he assured me that I was completely sound, and that my spinal fluid didn't contain any of those nasty little spiral animals. I could marry and father children without any risk whatsoever, he said. My relief was indescribable. Since my first trip to Germany in 1924, when I came to grief, I've feared the worst and never dared believe in the physicians' assurances that the sickness had been stopped at a sufficiently early stage. At that time I was just an impoverished student who couldn't spend any money on doctors, but had to turn to a clinic for common folk. Have always felt uncertain whether I showed up in time and received the correct treatment.

* *

Wednesday, 25 April. To my surprise I have no problem with the sick calls, where I thought I would fail completely. Was extremely helpless at the outset and considered the parish nurse's offer to relieve me. In fact, I made an agreement with her that she was to do her rounds as usual and only send for me if somebody wanted the sacrament.

Fortunately I thought better of it and discovered to my great delight that I have a way with the old and the sick. They don't regard me with suspicion or look for my weaknesses, and they never try to trip me up verbally. Everything takes its usual course: I read a piece of Scripture, listen to their complaints and sometimes place my hand on the affected spot while saying a silent prayer. Here as everywhere else I'm well received by people in boundary situations; our extremes find each other and reach a tacit understanding. Perhaps it shows on me that I'm someone who has been through a little of everything in life and is no stranger to their troubles.

It's an experience that almost takes the form of a rule, namely, that high up and deep down are my true places. On the other hand I lack bourgeois instincts and don't know how to handle the sort of people who have settled down comfortably in the middle.

Friday, 27 April. Again came to think of Martin Heidegger and one of the philosophical conversations we had in his Schwarzwald hunting cabin last autumn.

I hadn't appreciated his inauguration speech and had asked him whether he wasn't getting too deeply involved with the new powers that be. For a moment he let go of the wood grouse he was plucking and looked musingly at me. Then he laughed briefly and said that this was an odd criticism from someone who had just defended a doctoral dissertation about survival.

"My young friend, let's not think so much," he said. "We Germans have always had the great fault that we work out systems, while we bury our heads in the sand and fail to act. Let us liquidate idealism and pure reason. As we know, man is something that must be overcome! Let us follow Friedrich Nietzsche and invoke the laughing lion who is not ashamed of its existence. I do not have to tell you, do I, that 'die blonde Bestie' has nothing to do with blood and descent, but with affirming oneself and saying 'Yes' to one's destiny. Remember, existence always precedes essence! Just give the new brooms a chance to sweep for a while, until the dust settles and we'll see what comes of it. Let that lout Adolf Hitler go over the institutions and overthrow everything that has no right to life. Then maybe Germany will appear at a higher level and survive on its own terms."

I demurred that it might be an expensive experiment, one that could result in the death and annihilation of all familiar forms of life. "All right, and so what?" he replied, raising his knife and beheading the bird with a quick cut. "Everything arises from nothing, and death always precedes life."

Tuesday, 2 May. Thank God, the day of the labour movement is over! Shut myself up in my office when the duty service had been delivered; just can't stand this day with its clenched fists, posters and cheap slogans. Heard the mass procession pass by – I hunched up and covered my ears with my hands to muffle the shouting and screaming. What was it all supposed to be good for? I thought. Before the day was over the bubble would have burst, the apostles of justice be dead drunk, and the streets look like a garbage dump.

Today I'm a little more soberminded and ask myself why I object so strongly to this parade. I don't know, I just realize that I react far more strongly than the occasion justifies. Do I want everybody else to choose my own path and reach toward the light with a nearly superhuman strength of will? Shall nobody have distinct rights but gain their human worth in a lonely life-and-death struggle? Do I want everyone to suffer my torment and have my troubles, my drive, my abilities and my luck in finding good helpers?

By the way, on this one point, oddly enough, Andreas Sand and I are in agreement, however great the gulf is between us otherwise. We both think we are self-made men, and that God only helps those who help themselves.

Friday, 5 May. Keep running into Mary Sand, whatever the reason may be. She sits in the office of her father's shipping firm, but is constantly in town on some errand or other. She hurries off as soon as she sees me, but there is always an air of reluctance about her haste. A moment after she has gone by, she stops to smooth her hair or flick a pebble from her shoe, and then she turns her head on the sly and looks back.

True, I must also turn around to discover that she does, so perhaps we come out even.

Monday, 8 May. Yesterday visited the Ark, after numerous invitations from the head of the meeting house, Andreas Sand. Came through without suffering any harm, but not exactly with an olive branch in my mouth. It's incredible how Sand, a ship owner and a through and through ungodly man, can mount the platform and act like a crony of the Lord. Has the gift of the gab, but speaks in an insufferable jargon and doesn't refrain from any vulgarity. He does big business as a fisher of men, with all the quartering and cleaning out of the innards that entails. Felt completely nauseous at the end, as if he had his lengthened index finger deep down my throat. Alas, what easy victims he finds, a hall crammed with sighing and groaning souls. And up on the podium he has a penance bench, where those people whose souls cannot be washed clean through the Word alone are put through their paces.

The only extenuating element was the choir, where Mary Sand sang her banal songs with exactly the same fervour as she put into Verdi's *Requiem*. What am I to think of her? Is she completely devoid of discrimination, or can it be that for a singing angel the repertoire doesn't matter? Everything rises to a higher sphere, masterpieces and mere trash issue from the same lips. I have to admit that I was moved, even when she sang awful tear-jerkers like "When Jesus set the soul free" and "Where will you be when your hour has come, / Inside the gate or outside?" It wasn't easy to tell by her face what she herself was feeling, her eyes were just as clear and her cheeks as flushed as when she sang *Lacrymosa*.

Either she is a shallow nature, or she is so musical that she extracts beauty out of the poorest melody.

Thursday, 11 May. Yesterday something unexpected happened to me, something that looks so much like a dream that I still feel dizzy and clutch my head.

During my office hours between eleven and twelve there was a gentle knock on the door; so gentle, in fact, that I believed at first that it was a twig hitting the wall. After I had called "come in" twice, there was still a moment's delay before the door opened and the visitor ventured to cross the threshold. It was Mary Sand, flaming red and embarrassed, but tossing her head to show that she came on legitimate business.

When I asked what she wanted, she bit her lip and turned half away, fumbling with the buttons of her coat. After another toss of her head, she stared obliquely out of the window and asked what was going to happen to the Parsonage Mission. The old parson had held meetings every second week, and many were wondering whether there wouldn't soon be a meeting, or whether they were to end for good.

I couldn't help smiling, but hastened to compose my face. She didn't exactly look like a mission wife, and it wasn't difficult to see that there was something else behind it. I answered rather vaguely that the summer was around the corner, but we would see what we could think up in the autumn.

"Think up!" she said – and now it was her turn to smile. "You, a pastor, speak as if the mission should be something new and exciting. Something quite unheard-of, which has never before existed in this town."

We looked at one another and laughed, and at the same moment we were released from our bonds and chains. Suddenly we were just as close to each other as in church, where we attained the seventh heaven through our song. I pointed to a chair and asked if she wouldn't sit down, but she shook her head and explained that she was "dreadfully" busy. Well, I knew, didn't I, that she worked in the office of her father's shipping firm? When she went out before noon, it was solely to mail letters and take care of important business.

I was on the point of taking her at her word and asking if her visit to the pastor's office was important business, but I watched my step. She seemed to be on the point of leaving at any moment, and I realized that she might easily get frightened and rush headlong out the door.

When we had talked a bit about this and that I showed her out, and we stood on the stairs a moment, delaying our goodbye.

"Why don't you ever wear the suit you had on your first day anymore?" she asked all of a sudden. "I have heard so much talk about it, and I'm about the only one who hasn't seen it."

"It's nothing much to look at," I replied. "That was how I used to dress in Germany, where they aren't that particular about one's attire. It didn't occur to me that it might attract attention around the town."

She knitted her brows and threw a critical glance at my new workaday suit, the one she had told me was three sizes too small for me. Then she turned her back and took a few rapid steps over the gravel. I was fairly certain that this didn't mean goodbye, for she made haste very slowly and dragged her feet, making the pebbles fly. And sure enough, on her way to the gate she caught sight of something that forced her to stop short, her eyes popping.

"What a lovely car you've got," she said, sneaking over to the Ford, which was parked in front of the woodshed. After walking around it and inspecting it, she cautiously brushed the back fender, as if patting a sweet, somewhat exotic animal.

"Do you know," she said, withdrawing her hand and heaving a deep sigh, "I'll soon turn nineteen and still haven't sat in a car."

I suggested we might take a drive some evening, so that she wouldn't enter her twentieth year completely inexperienced. But that, evidently, was something I shouldn't have said. She tossed her head back and stared at me as if I had made an indecent proposition. "Take a drive," she mimicked, haughtily. Ha! Little I knew her father, if I thought he would ever give his permission for that. Then she seemed to get lost in thought, helplessly biting her lip and kicking up gravel with her foot. I stood there in a sort of dream listening to the jingling sound, which went on and on and became a windless storm in my ears.

"The only way we could do it would be in secret," she said at length. "I go to business school at night, but could probably get away with cutting class for once. We could meet at the other end of the woods and take a quick drive out to Sandane, which is about three miles north. Then I could show you the place where Father was born. The house is empty most of the year, and it would be nice if someone checked on it."

The same day, 9 p.m. Tomorrow, tomorrow it will happen. I feel hot and cold by turns, scarcely daring to believe it's true.

Wednesday, 9 August. Had a strange letter today from a certain Rolf J. Fuglesang, a.k.a. "Birdsong", apparently the new general secretary of the National Union party. He had been asked to send greetings from Vidkun Quisling and thank me for my letter, and for my positive attitude toward his great idea. My allegiance had now been assured, it said, and "the movement" had the honour of enrolling me as a member.

I flared up for a moment and wanted to grab my pen, but told myself it was a trifle that had no claim on my zeal. National Union was, after all, just a small quixotic sect that would never have any political significance. If it hadn't been for the fact that Vidkun Quisling was its founder, I would never have taken the trouble to reply to the query. Just let them put me on the membership list, I said to myself, they need a few names for fear the whole enterprise will otherwise look like an *idée fixe*. Personally I prefer authentic birdsong to the general secretary of the NS. But as long as this world is a false and disharmonious place, all must be allowed to sing with their allotted beaks.

Fine! At last I'll have the experience of being a member of a political party, even if it's all a misunderstanding or sheer trickery. Congratulations, Vemund Hov, you incorrigible old separatist! You who have always gone your own way and fallen between two stools any number of times. Soon you will probably receive a solar cross in the mail. But remember: it must never appear on your lapel! First, it would be a lie, and for the rest it would be rather too reminiscent of the sign of salvation that Andreas Sand is displaying on his breast.

4

My parents, Vemund and Mary, were married on 2 October, 1934, in the little white rural church of the neighbouring parish a third of a mile outside town.

The wedding took place on the quiet and was later only spoken of in mysterious hints and allusions. No guests had been invited, no rice was scattered, not even a wedding picture was taken. What reckonings and familial quakes preceded the ceremony has never been clearly revealed. But to an observer who at the time was a mere speck in cosmic space, the course of events appears roughly as follows:

One day just before Midsummer Eve Mary is summoned into the inner office, where her father slaps a letter on the table in front of her. It is from the principal of the business school, who writes that Mary will not be promoted to the second level of the evening course. Since the middle of May she has been more absent than present, and is now so far behind that she will have to take the first year over again.

Andreas Sand roars like a good-sized lion and wants to know where his daughter has spent those evenings on which she was not in class. Mary presses her lips together and at first refuses to give an explanation, but soon realizes that this time it's no use being obstinate.

"I've had a headache," she lies at random. "Papa, I simply cannot stand sitting inside all day, first seven hours in the office and then three hours at school. So sometimes I take my bike and go for a ride."

"So, you go for a ride, do you?" her father says in a tone of voice which may mean anything. As the practised tactician that he is, he is in no hurry to expose her; he adroitly encircles her and acts as if nothing were the matter, though he knows better. "You just need a bit of fresh air, is that it?"

Mary nods, but she too is a bit of a tactician, and she has already caught something ominous in her father's voice.

"Perhaps you could tell me where you go biking, since you manage to be away for several hours. North or south, upcountry or out to the ocean, let me hear."

"I prefer to bike upcountry," Mary replies, trying to change the subject from the particular to the general. "It's so nice to see the cattle being put out to pasture in the spring."

"There wouldn't be someone else put out to pasture, too, would there now?" the father says as he slowly pulls out his desk drawer and places another letter on the table.

"Why do you always have to distrust me?" Mary cries, on the verge of tears. "I'm nineteen years old, and you watch over me as if I were a child."

"When young, unruly heifers are let out in the spring, they need to be watched," the father says, waxing allegorical. "But in this instance it looks as if the watchman has neglected his duty."

"If you want something of me, then tell me straight out, so I can understand what you mean," she replies obstinately. "I'm no good at solving riddles."

"As you wish," says Andreas Sand, taking letter number two out of the envelope. He holds it in his hands for a moment, rustling it ominously before folding it out on the table with inordinately slow gestures.

"I have this very day had a letter from Aslak Nodeland, our neighbour out at Sandane. He relates that during the last several weeks something strange has been going on in our house out there. In mid-evening the light in the kitchen is turned on, but when he walks over and knocks, nobody opens. He walks over to check again later in the evening, but then the light is turned off. This has happened not only once but many times, so he thought he'd better give warning, since he's looking after the house. And that's not all. The very same evenings his son has seen a car parked over at the bend by the quarry. The boy thought it was the car of the new town pastor, but that couldn't be, could it? What would Pastor Hov have to do at Sandane late in the evening, and so far outside his own parish?

"Well, that's what Aslak Nodeland writes," her father concludes, letting fall the hand in which he holds the letter. "He doesn't know what Pastor Hov can have to do in those parts, but maybe someone else does. What do you say, Mary? There wouldn't be a connection, would there, between your absences at the business school, the car at the bend of the road, and the light that is turned on and off in the house at Sandane?"

"Papa, that's enough!" Mary cries, assuming an air of self-righteousness. "I won't put up with your constant suspicion!"

"Good! Then you'll have to think it over more carefully," her father says, abruptly rising from his chair. "I'm going to lock you up, and I won't let you out till you have confessed before God what sort of trickery you've let yourself in for."

And with that he grabs his daughter's arm and leads her away to her lockup, which is no longer the closet underneath the stairs but the almost equally dark archive behind the office. It is a room without windows, full of dusty chests of drawers and with a lamp-light that can only be turned on and off from the outside.

"It's now ten past eleven," he says, looking at his watch. "I'll be back again around six o'clock, after I've had dinner, and then I hope you'll have something better than cooked-up stories to tell me. If you continue to harden your heart, I shall be forced to keep you locked up overnight, and you won't get any food until you've made a full confession."

Mary offers no resistance, but merely bows her head and groans like a wounded animal as he pushes her through the door. But he is thoroughly mistaken if he believes that seven hours of confinement can make her change her mind. When he returns toward evening, she is far from softened up; on the contrary, she has gathered strength and wears a defiant and injured face.

But Andreas Sand knows his daughter's disposition as well as his own, she can be obstinate and a hard nut to crack. However, if he just holds out and remains unbending, the crack-up will come sooner or later.

And sure enough, when he lets her out the following morning she is completely crushed; she has vomited on the floor, is shaken by sobs, and throws herself imploringly around his neck.

"Dear, sweet Papa, don't be angry with me! I'll do what you want and tell the truth!"

Oh yes, Vemund Hov had driven her out to the farm a few times, that was so. Not many times by any means, perhaps three or four, or at any rate not more than six or seven. She had only shown him the house and the locality, they had walked around awhile and looked the place over inside and out, and nothing more had happened, that she could swear to. All right, no swearing then, if that meant taking God's name in vain. But he must please believe her, she had only wanted to find out how it felt to ride in a car, and wasn't it about time for someone who had turned nineteen? And now she had told him everything as it was, cross her heart. Kneel? Oh, but sweet Papa, in all that dust, and on such a rough floor! Oh well, if she had to, so. If God really wanted her to make herself dirty and have splinters in her knees.

But Andreas Sand is not someone who lets himself be fooled; he is no novice in the art of explaining things away and knows to the full every dodge used by the soul before it finally humbles itself. He has himself wandered down trackless paths and knows all there is to know about the shameful traffic that has been taking place at Sandane, from the time the light was turned on until it was turned out again. Disgust wells up in him, and he takes God to witness that he won't set eyes on the place again until all the sinful exhalations have been aired out.

Having cursed his daughter and consigned her to house arrest, he decided to take his holidays in town and rent Sandane out to summer guests. With this decision he punished himself more than anyone else, for he was attached to his childhood home with the tenderest bonds and didn't deny himself any poetic excesses when singing its praises. During his mad rush to build an empire on land and sea, Sandane had been his place of relaxation, the only place where he could find rest.

The summer grew warm, and while the thunder rolled and the air stood still in the large house, Mary was carrying a secret that was too big and sweet to make her want to share it with anyone. Occasionally a desire for revenge arose in her, and she promised herself that she would remain silent until her father grew suitably subdued and ate humble pie. Oh, she would wait and stand firm, until time began to run out and he came and begged her to get it over with.

But mostly she was in a tender and languishing mood, dreaming about the knight who was going to come and carry her off. Not the knight on the white horse armed cap-a-pie, but the one in a Ford convertible with a visored cap, leggings and tall boots. He had promised to love her for better or worse, just like before the altar in church. And now the worse was upon her, and she didn't doubt him for a moment. One day he would come and set her free, in the nick of time and at a speed of at least thirty miles an hour.

Andreas Sand had his visions as well, and certainly didn't let time run away from him. He sat down and wrote a letter to the bishop, in which he presented the matter in all its abomination and demanded to have the pastor dismissed. After a couple of weeks had gone by, the bishop replied that he had spoken with Vemund Hov, who declared his love for Mary Sand and would like nothing better than to lead her to the altar. As the matter stood, there was no reason to make any uproar. True, the pastor had been too hasty and had shown a poor example, but he had committed no fault that could be called dereliction of duty. The bishop advised the ship owner to hold the wedding as soon as possible, and to forgive his future son-in-law that he had taken the law into his own hands.

"Never in all my life!" Andreas Sand cried, clenching his fist and swinging it in the air as he used to in his youth, while letting fly a few of his old juicy phrases. "I'll be jiggered, what a swine of a parson! If he ever should get away with living in sin and, on top of it all, be rewarded for his fornication, I'm a dead duck! He won't get Mary even if he comes crawling on his knees, by golly, he won't!" He would give him a piece of his mind all right, brand him for all time, for eternity. "Do you hear that, you son of Leviathan? Here it won't help you to ask for forgiveness. I'll lambaste you and send you packing, turn you out in the cold so your courting will freeze to ice on your depraved lips!"

This was where the barometer stood in late August when the ship owner's housekeeper one day stepped into his office and asked to have a few words with him in confidence. She was wondering whether something could be the matter with Mary, the young lady felt nauseous in the morning and hadn't had her period since sometime in early May. Sure, she had tried to talk with her more than once, but the child had become so strangely remote, as if she didn't hear what was said to her. There couldn't be anything seriously wrong with her, could there, she had always been in such good health. But something wasn't the way it should be, so in her quandary she came to consult the ship owner.

Fresh interrogations of Mary and fresh evasions and denials, until she finally gave in and broke down in tears and self-accusations. Alas, no, she was not the one they all believed she was, she had thrown herself away and was a wasted and worm-eaten soul that deserved nothing but contempt.

75

She had sneaked away from home to live in sin, not just once, but evening after evening. And now she was ruined, and punishment had caught up with her. Vemund Hov wouldn't have her anymore, he hadn't dropped her a word since before Midsummer Day, nor had she seen a glimpse of him. Ay-ay, what grief and nuisance, having to bear the shame all by herself and put up with being the laughingstock of the whole town. But it served her right, she had only herself to blame and could expect nothing else considering the predicament she'd got herself in.

Her father listened to her, sighing deeply – he finally had the confession he wanted and couldn't have wished for a greater repentance. But when the chips were down, he flinched and pushed the cup away from him. As soon as he had heard her lament to the end and soundly castigated his daughter, he put on his hat and coat and went over to the pastor's office. What took place there, history doesn't tell, but to all appearances he had to bargain and speak in a low voice. At any rate, he came out very much bowed down, didn't swing his hat as was his custom, and sneaked home by the most deserted back alleys. The only thing he could boast of was that he had speeded things up, so that already the following Sunday the banns were read for the two sinners, in the town church by Pastor Hov himself and in the rural church by the neighbouring pastor.

The wedding was set for ten o'clock the first Tuesday in October, on a miserable workday and at a time intended to attract as little attention as possible. Nor was there any great gathering of people, though every one of the town gossips appeared and, crowded together, made up a wall of curiosity in the two front rows. Afterwards they could affirm with certainty that the ship owner's Mary was "in the family way", though she tried to hide her condition in a specially made bridal gown and slyly held her bouquet in front of her belly. The ship owner had looked angry and careworn, but he did his paternal duty and led his daughter to the altar as was meet and proper.

The bridal couple themselves didn't seem to be particularly unnerved; they both answered loud and clear that they would have one another and exchanged rings before the altar as though it was no shame at all that there hadn't been an engagement. To do them justice, they made an attractive couple and looked very happy and solemn as they walked down the aisle. Too bad, though, that they wouldn't be given a wedding party, but had to part from good old Sand on the church trail and go home to the parsonage alone. Nor, most likely, could there be much of a wedding night, since they had been so reckless as to take it all in advance.

Thus far the gossips, who trekked from house to house with their reports and gave a fillip to the dwindling church attendance. On the following Sundays the pews in the town church were as fully occupied as during those memorable days of Easter. Many liked to see how a pastor looked when he had been caught fornicating and had to get married head over heels in another parish. But Vemund Hov was his usual self, with his semi-Catholic rituals, his operatic chanting and his all too brief sermons. The new clergyman's wife was not to be seen; she didn't accompany her husband to High Mass, and her place in the church choir had remained empty since some time around Whitsuntide. That was something anyhow – that at least one of them had a sense of shame!

Finally a few words from the before-mentioned observer, who thinks that she knows something, though she was a mere speck in cosmic space at the time.

Even if the bridal couple kept up their courage and didn't seem to miss the wedding party, it must nonetheless have lingered in the memory of one of them like a gnawing injustice. It would come up as a subject of controversy between my parents for a long time to come, giving rise to endless bitter complaints on the wife's part. As soon as my mother felt let down by her spouse, she would rattle on and on about the wedding he had deprived her of, which she had had such lovely dreams about as a young girl and looked forward to with such expectations. If he hadn't led her on and seduced her, she could have entered the state of matrimony as spotless as her friends, and the great day when everybody made a fuss over her would have been hers to remember. Instead, she had had to sneak up to the altar like a criminal, while the gossips fixed her with their evil eyes and caused the child she was carrying to be an idiot.

My father would mostly turn away, refusing to dignify that sort of wild talk with an answer. But once in a while he lost his patience, and then he pulled no punches. Aha! So now he was to blame for having seduced her, too! Some honor that was, for sure. He was the nasty tempter who had ambushed her and led her down the primrose path. Ha ha, that was a good one, that was a good one all right! Who was it who so itched for adventure that she couldn't wait until someone presented himself? Who had shown up in the pastor's office on a faked errand and arranged the trips out to Sandane? Who had set her snares, tempting and leading him on, so that a poor fellow couldn't help being trapped? He didn't regret anything, she mustn't think that, he would do the same over again if she came and offered herself to him. But there had to be a limit to female hypocrisy, he would have none of that whimpering tone of seduced innocence in which she played the victim. Was that clear?

I can still see my mother vividly before me during these disputes, how she first provoked and attacked, then grew sullen and more and more pale in the face, until she started at the words "Is that clear?" and marched out of the room, her head held high. And how Father stayed behind, foaming with rage, opening and closing his fists and stamping his foot. In my early childhood I always sided with Mother and was ready to defend her tooth and nail. Sometimes I was even bold enough to run up and poke at Father, bite his hand or try to kick him.

Later I came to look at it with different eyes and to distribute blame more evenly between them. Today I'm convinced that he was the more vulnerable of the two, and the one who suffered the most. It fell to him to go about brooding over insults that she quite simply forgot or shrugged off. He was the deeper of the two, and maybe the more appalling as well. But she was able to do more damage and drove him to despair with her frivolity and forgetfulness.

When Mother had left the scene and withdrawn to one of the side rooms, Father soon followed, sometimes so indignant that he was ready to fly at her and throw her from wall to wall. At other times so hesitant and helpless that you could read his remorse in his every movement. We, the children, were left behind, scared out of our wits and expecting the end of the world; drawing together into a knot, we became a trinity with six listening ears. But the wild screams we were expecting never came. On the contrary, it became strangely quiet in there, and shortly afterwards Father came out and said with a strange note in his voice that we should go out and play. He followed us right up to the door and locked it behind us, and while we crept together on the steps and whispered about death and mutilation, the great reconciliation took place inside. When the door was opened to us after an hour or so, Father and Mother received us locked in an embrace, kissing all the time and unable to keep their eyes off one another. Soon the house re-echoed with song and music, and what had looked like the end of time had turned into something that resembled a miracle and a salvation beyond our comprehension. The parson and the parson's wife had had another fit, as the housekeeper called it, and it would carry them through the next few days, their feet barely touching the ground, while three gaping kids were made invisible and transformed into thin air . . .

But enough of annunciations and anticipatory quantum leaps, everything will come to light at the proper time, when my account gets to that point. Let us remember that for the moment the year is 1934, though the narrator is no slave to the calendar and cannot promise that her elucidations will always be chronological.

So let us stop the wheel of time and cast a last glance at the newlyweds as they climb into that unholy car and set off for home. Vemund sounds the horn, greeting the day with a triumphant fanfare; then they gather speed, and Mary's veil flares out to form a white wing behind her, while the gossips skip aside like grey cats and slink away in shame. There can be no doubt that the bridal couple are keeping up their courage amid all the slander, and despite the ban of the bride's father.

For in the morning the very same day something had happened that Mary barely managed to whisper to Vemund before they stepped into the car after the wedding. Just as she was about to put on her bridal gown, her father had entered the room and informed her that he could no longer regard her as his daughter. He would go as far as to accompany her up the aisle, but afterwards everything must be over between them. She had rebelled against him and forced a son-in-law upon him who was the last person he himself would have chosen for her. All right, then, they would go their separate ways for the rest of their lives. It cut his father's heart to the quick, she must understand, but he could no longer acknowledge a daughter who had been so grossly disobedient and cast so much shame and disgrace upon his house. At the next meeting in the Ark he would announce the anathema from the rostrum and ask the congregation to shun her and consider her as dead and lost for ever. It went without saying that from now on she must never attempt to set foot either in the meeting house or in her childhood home, but accept the consequences of her rebellion and keep to the husband she had chosen.

III

That Crazy Family at Nether Hov

1

"Idun Hov, you've done something stupid," the charge nurse says to me one day in December. "You know we agreed that you shouldn't throw anything in the waste-paper basket unless I had first seen what it was. Today at our orientation meeting a letter was presented that you had written to your twin sister sometime last month. And now the physicians have made the diagnosis they hitherto had left open, and you can no longer entertain any hopes of being discharged."

I'm having violent palpitations, but pull myself together and try to act as though nothing is the matter.

"Well, and so what?" I reply. "I feel comfortable where I am and have no wish to go anywhere else."

"Oh, come now, you can't mean that," she says reproachfully. "If you don't have any wish to be discharged, it must mean that you've given up on life altogether."

"Maybe I have," I reply, shrugging my shoulders. "I'm fifty-six years old and have long been a physical and mental wreck. I have nothing more I can expect from what you all call life and may as well remain here among these shards of human beings and the living dead."

When she has thought things over for a moment the nurse replies, "Maybe you can recall what was in that letter?"

"Quite frankly, no," I reply. "I scrunched it up as soon as it was written and dropped it in the wastebasket."

"Then I'll have to remind you of it. You wrote about a hired assassin that your sister was supposed to have sent here to bump you off."

"That's true, now I remember. I wrote that he had carried out his mission and twisted his knife in the wound for good measure."

"You have to admit that this is rather strong stuff?" she says, giving me a troubled look.

"I thought that people with an M.D. would understand figurative language," I say, raising my voice. "But no, they obviously don't."

"There, there, don't fly off the handle. I just wanted to let you know that the diagnosis has been made and that from now on you will be considered a hopeless case."

"Listen to me," I say when I have calmed down a little and cleared my thoughts. "The letter was found in the wastebasket, wasn't it? That is to say, I was critical of it and decided to discard it. It would've been something else if I had put the letter in an envelope in all seriousness and asked you to mail it."

"You have a point there, you certainly have a point there," she mutters, giving me a brighter look. "I should have thought of that a short while ago, shouldn't I, when we were discussing your case?"

"Anyway, the diagnosis has been made, hasn't it?" I say, keeping at it. "Perhaps you could tell me what it is?"

"According to the new regulations you have the right to review your medical record," she replies, hemming and hawing. "But before I say anything more I would ask you to remember that a diagnosis is an artificial product. It's a kind of learned gibberish that can't very easily be translated into ordinary human language."

"Out with it," I say, feeling my courage grow. I'm now remarkably calm, and an almost clinical coldness has come over me that enables me to face my trouble without fear.

"Wait a bit and we'll see," she says, leafing back and forth in her folder. "Yes, here it is. If you give a glance this way you'll see it's written 'paranoia' where I'm holding my finger. That's a diagnosis than can mean any number of things, but simplifying a bit we can say that you suffer from persecution mania. Your inner demon has broken loose and set up house in a person outside yourself."

I have become quite elated and can't help laughing. "No trifles, to be sure," I say. "And this medical science has concluded simply by pulling a discarded letter out of a waste-paper basket?"

"The letter is only one thing," she says, and now she appears almost stern. "During the seventeen years that have gone by since you were first committed, your record has grown quite substantial. Among other things, material has been collected that shows that several individuals in your father's family have been psychologically deviant."

"Quite, that's probably correct. By contrast, my whole mother's family is supernormal, so it may come out even."

"Then there's this inclination you have to go wandering. Since no real reason can be demonstrated, the physicians think it may be due to persecution mania."

"Why, just imagine," I cry, indignant. "So it has finally been cleared up! My homelessness has no natural causes, but is one long flight away from imaginary enemies and persecutors!"

"What do you propose yourself?" she asks, giving me a searching look. "What do you think is the reason for your vagabond tendencies?"

"If I only knew," I say despondently. "It suddenly comes over me and I must start off."

"So many things come over us," she says, a gentle look in her eyes. "But it's up to ourselves whether we give in to our impulses."

"You mean perhaps that I'm not capable of distinguishing between fiction and reality?"

"Yes, maybe something of the sort. You're no longer satisfied with transforming life into literature, as you used to. You've chosen a more dangerous path and are going all out turning literature into life."

"Rather tell me straight out," I cry. "Do you regard me as insane, or what's your real opinion of me?"

"I guess I can't call you altogether normal," she says with a little smile at the corner of her mouth. "But when I read what you write I can't see there's anything wrong with your sanity."

"You shouldn't take those scribblings all too seriously," I say. "In the last bunch you got there isn't much that I invented myself. Most of it is copied straight out of one of my father's diaries."

"Your father's diaries?" she says, surprised. "I haven't set eyes on any diaries, though I've gone through your things with a fine-tooth comb."

"Didn't I tell you about the time I rescued Father's diaries from the rubbish truck? Not all of them, but three, one for 1917, one for 1934, and finally one for 1944. I've taken care to stash them well away, so that no one in this place can get hold of them."

"Are you really sure of this?" she asks, looking sceptically at me. "Isn't it rather that you read them sometime long ago and recall them as you write?"

"Think what you like," I reply, realizing that this is something I don't want to go into any further. "It's one of those things that will probably never be cleared up. I can only tell you that when I used the diary for 1934 I did not just have it in my head. I could hear Father's voice rise from the old pages, I saw every single character before me, and when I finished the chapter about his first period in our town, it was just as if I were writing from dictation."

2

The Hov farm was situated at a freshwater lake in Lower Telemark, midway between Skien and Siljan. The place had been a cotter's plot under the Fossum estate, but at the turn of the century, the same year my father was born, Grandfather had managed to scrape together the 3,000 kroner necessary to buy out the farm.

Grandfather had been employed at the ironworks in his first youth, and afterwards continued at the sawmill when the ironworks closed down. He was born as far back as 1853 and is supposed to have been a handsome young man. But an early disability sneaked up on him, and already in his sixties he was so crippled by arthritis that he could barely drag himself forward with the help of two sticks. Still he lived till past ninety, and I can remember him from my first childhood as an old man, bent and irascible, who thought so much faster than his body could keep up with him that he was on the point of bursting with impatience. He probably overtaxed himself in his youth, for in his mature years his vigour declined so quickly that it couldn't all have been due to the arthritis. As the end of the century was approaching, there wasn't much left of the strikingly handsome Thormod Hov, a dance enthusiast who could work for sixteen hours a day and still have the energy to drop by the threshing floors here and there and do a hambo or a roundel.

Before becoming altogether infirm, he managed to distinguish himself in many ways, and at an early age acquired a reputation for being something of a prodigy. Already as a schoolboy he had his permanent corner in the public library, where he would sit as though bewitched, with such far vistas into remote lands and kingdoms that he jumped up like a sleepwalker when told the library was closing. Often he would come and ask for books that the librarian had never heard of and had to be ordered separately from the main library in Oslo.

86

At school he was so terribly smart that the schoolmaster clutched his head and prayed the good Lord to have mercy. Every once in a while he would dream up arithmetical problems that the teacher thought were unsolvable, but which Grandfather easily worked out on the blackboard by means of two mysterious quantities that he called "nix" and "gnome". The boy didn't know about equations with two unknowns any more than the teacher did. But he had the solution at the back of his head and let the nix and the gnome fetch it out, while the teacher stared and the pupils lay flat on top of their desks, laughing. Right up to extreme old age Thormod Hov was a wizard with numbers; he could "see" the solution before him and complete long calculations in his head before his two educated sons got as far as putting the problem down on paper.

The first time he appeared before people at large was on confirmation day, when he made such an unprecedented mark for himself that there was a piece about him in the town paper the following Monday. As a cotter's son, his place was supposed to be at the end of the aisle, but the pastor was so impressed by his knowledge of the Bible that he felt justified in disregarding accepted practice. The examination was lengthy and took the form of a complicated debate between the pastor and the confirmand, while the rest of the class stood tongue-tied and the congregation sat agape listening. The pastor rubbed his hands and set his traps, leading the confirmand a dance through the law and the prophets, while dropping by the evangelists and the Acts of the Apostles; nor did he forget Ecclesiastes or Revelation. The cotter's son would scratch his head for a moment and think it over, and then the answer came, as clear and exhaustive as if read from a book. When the pastor gave the cue "the writing on the wall," the confirmand was immediately fired up and held forth about the prophet Daniel's visions during the Babylonian captivity. When the pastor smiled slyly and said "Cherethites and Pelethites", the confirmand knew that it had to do with the Cretans and the Philistines in David's bodyguard. The boy didn't hesitate to name the gospel of Mark as the oldest of the three synoptic gospels, and the one that was closest to the oral tradition. Synopsis, what was that? – Oh yes, just a moment, that meant one could demonstrate agreement when one put the text of the three gospels side by side. Luke? Well, he was a physician by profession and Paul's companion on his missionary travels. And the same Paul had initially persecuted the Christians before he suddenly saw the light one day and had his Damascus experience.

Intermittently Thormod Hov kept himself modestly in the background and let the others answer questions that he found it beneath his dignity to bother with, such as the Ten Commandments, the Lord's Prayer, and Luther's explanation to the three articles of faith. But there he was again with the information that Jesus' words on the cross, "My God, my God, why hast thou forsaken me?", were not simply the lament of the crucified one, but a strong and self-fulfilling quotation from David's twenty-second psalm. Towards the end of the examination he discussed in detail the prophecies in Revelation, such as the millennium, Anti-Christ, the Last Judgement, and the glory of paradise. But now the congregation had just about had enough, and it breathed a sigh of relief when the prodigy rounded off Revelation by declaring that the number of the beast was six hundred three score and six, and that this mysterious number probably pointed forward to the Roman emperor Nero.

After this feat the pastor couldn't accept the thought that such brilliant intellectual talents were to be wasted. Young Hov had to be rescued from the swamp of ignorance, and in the spring the pastor went from one farm to the next and persuaded the community's big shots to help the boy get ahead. But to everybody's chagrin, Thormod Hov rejected the offer and replied that he was capable of helping himself. Barely fourteen years old, he had set himself a goal that eclipsed all other future prospects, namely, to scrape together enough money to settle accounts with the landowner and buy out the farm.

During the next three decades he worked like crazy to realize his plans; he worked at home on the farm from four to six in the morning, went on foot a mile and a half to show up at the sawmill at seven, and continued his work on the farm well into the evening, until he dropped into bed. He never observed Sunday, despite his knowledge of the Law of Moses, but went off to the woods to gather berries, drain bogs, or do the necessary tree felling. Besides the baskets with berries, he often brought home a hare or a grouse, and went straight to the proprietor at Fossum to convert the goods into ready cash.

When he finally was so near his goal that it couldn't go wrong, he proposed to a farmer's daughter who was well off but remarkable neither for great intelligence nor beauty. A letter she wrote to her fiancé in 1898 has been preserved; it shows that she was practically illiterate, despite the fact that she had had better schooling than her betrothed. However, she had a gentle and patient nature and a strong, beautiful singing voice, which mostly vented itself in lullabies, cattle calls, and spinning songs.

When the wedding took place the bridegroom was well up in his forties and the bride a middle-aged girl of thirty-six. In the course of the following eight years she gave birth to five children, first two sons and a daughter, then after a break of three years another son and daughter. None of the children inherited the father's conspicuous good looks, but some received his intelligence, his unbending will and his eccentricity.

The eldest son, Vemund, went his own way early on, often fell into a brown study at work, and always had a book in his pocket that he read on the sly when his father's back was turned. At confirmation he made himself noted in a quieter way than his father and didn't try to edge out anyone. Once having got by the pastor, he infuriated his mother's family by returning his confirmation presents, because, as he said, he didn't want to begin his adult life by owing a debt of gratitude to anyone. From his father's family there came no presents, and for good reasons: two of Thormod Hov's brothers had by this time vanished without a trace in America, and two others had joined a company of navvies and tramps and taken to the road.

As the flock of children grew, Knuthilde Hov's patience came in handy. All three sons were touchy, hot-headed types unable to get along with their irascible and incapacitated father. Vemund, the heir to the farm, was the most thoughtful of the three, but once in a while, when he lost his temper, he would go berserk, roaring like a savage and flinging tools and pots and pans from wall to wall. He made no attempt to hide the fact that he disliked the farm work, did what he could to dodge it, and dragged his feet to the day's chores. Nevertheless it came like a bolt from the blue when he slung his bundle over his shoulder one day and made off, abandoning his native soil, his patrimony and property. His father made no attempt to bring him back, but cursed him in Old Testament locutions and didn't rest until he had called down every sort of punishment on the head of the runaway.

Son number two, Balder, had many of Vemund's eccentricities, but was a far more dubious case. He too had a good head for books, but he lacked steadiness and couldn't stick at anything for any length of time. That he eventually managed to become a teacher in secondary school, was due to his being so bright and, not least, to his cleverness. When he was in the right mood he could be quite a wit, and though he preferably poked fun at others, he didn't spare himself either. During World War Two, when he had settled in our town, he often joked about the fact that there were good reasons why he had such a great knack for discovering cheating at school. He was himself a crack cheat better than any, having smuggled in secret material at all his exams, even during his final university examination. "Take note of this, you people," he would say, laughing brazenly, "the burglar becomes the best policeman, the liar the best witness to truth, and the swindler the best defender of law and order."

He would cultivate this special form of moral cynicism only at a mature age, when the world situation was such as to invite it. But there were traces of it early on. Already as a teenager he made his parents' hair turn grey with his cunning, his mendacity, and his reluctance to distinguish between yours and mine. Not yet fifteen, he was caught poaching and cutting timber on the landowner's domain, and he was spared prosecution only because of his tender age. The landowner had the boy brought in, gave him a good flogging, and threatened to have him sent to reform school if his scandalous behaviour was repeated. After that Balder took pains not to get too close to the landowner. Still, the lesson was not so great that it prevented him, a few weeks later, from being caught in the act at the milk ramp, while he was pouring milk from the well-filled pail of Upper Hov over into the half-empty pail of Nether Hov. At first the boy tried to get around it by being glib, but hard pressed he finally confessed that it was a traffic he had carried on for a long time. With that a riddle was solved, and at long last the farmer at Upper Hov had an explanation why his own account didn't tally with the dairy's statement.

Upper Hov was a medium-sized farm that had never been a cotter's plot, with twelve milking cows, by contrast to Nether Hov's three. With its vast forest areas and its fine sandy soil, the farm was a mockery of the neighbour's stubborn bog holes and fields of sedge grass. The farmhouse dominated the landscape from where it sat high up the mountainside; by its situation alone it was a thorn in the flesh of the troglodytes down in the hollow. Envious glances darted through the underbrush up to the model farmstead on the heights, which had a mowing machine and a separator and a harmonium that no poor devil up there knew how to play. In this regard, many sharp and pungent remarks escaped the lips of the musical and witty sons of Thormod.

The children at Nether Hov were the same age as those at Upper Hov, and though they went out of each other's way at all other times, they were forced to sit side by side at school. And here the ranking order was wisely turned upside down, as it was the cotter children who enjoyed intellectual gifts, while the louts from the farm barely managed to stay in school till they graduated.

Up to now it had been the folks at Nether Hov who swaggered and cocked their noses in the air, so that the revelation about the milk ramp was a burning humiliation. The matter was arranged amicably by old man Hov, who stuck his hand into his coffer and paid his way out of it. But the family had made itself a target of the community's distrust and was never completely forgiven. Between his sixteenth and his nineteenth year, Balder rambled from one farm to another and managed to perpetrate quite a good amount of trickery, until he followed his brother's example and left Nether Hov. By then he was so disliked by everybody that it began to be too much even for an extreme misanthrope like him. Before he took to the road, he clenched his fist at his native hamlet, spewed it out of his mouth and promised to wreak a thorough revenge when the time was ripe.

With the brothers' departure the youngest son, Steingrim, became bound to his father's farm, something he put up with without great protest. He was a dark, melancholy, physically vigorous boy who struggled with the sour soil throughout long work periods without exchanging an angry word with his demanding and cantankerous father. But suddenly one day he had had enough, a smouldering glow flared up into a bright flame, and he had to see fire. If his sisters didn't look out and watch his steps, he would run off with matches in his pocket and set fire to a haystack or a dried-up spruce. The farmhouse and the cow barn were always spared, for in the midst of his intoxication with fire he retained a deep awe towards living things. When he had found a release for his urge, he at once ran home and revealed what he had done, so his obsession never caused any great damage. The first few times the arsonist was picked up by the sheriff and taken into custody, but he was soon let out again, with solemn promises that it would be the last time. As he grew to man's estate, the attacks occurred less and less frequently and found a more natural outlet in burning brush, straw and potato grass. But nobody dared be completely confident of him. With his smouldering inclination he was not to be trusted, and joined the other sons of Thormod as someone of whom anything could be expected.

While the sons were small, their father had punished them severely and at times almost beat them to death when his temper flared up. But year by year they grew beyond him, and the strength ratio was no longer in the old man's favour. One day when he was letting down the trousers of sixteen-year-old Balder, the boy fought back and threw off his tormentor.

"Enough is enough!" he yelled, knocking his father down with his clenched fist. "Do you hear that, you old creep! If you so much as touch me with your little finger from now on, it will be the worse for you. Then I'll give you such a roughing-up that you'll need five sticks to help you crawl across the yard."

When the old man got to his feet, he sized up the situation and decided the wise thing would be to resign himself. His father's dominion was broken, and for the rest of his life his hot temper vented itself in fixed ideas and a muffled squealing. Fortunately he had just at that time found a new cause to devote his life to. Nether Hov had by its natural situation the ill fortune of lying so low that water from the lake sometimes overflowed large areas of the flat fields. If only he could get someone to lower the water level in the Hov Lake one or two metres, the flooded grounds would dry out and the waterlogged fields overgrown with sedge grass would be transformed into fine rich soil.

As always when Tormod Hov had an ingenious idea, he was quick to implement it. He sat down at his long table, got out pen and paper and wrote a letter that would become the introduction to a complicated correspondence between Nether Hov and the authorities. First he tried his luck with the local administration, but when they merely hemmed and hawed in response to his request, he realized that he had aimed too low and had to move on to a loftier terrain. For a while his pride at corresponding with the government was so great that he was satisfied by vague and promising replies, which he would run around the hamlet with and show to everyone who crossed his path. His own letters were written in an old man's scrawl and couched in a high, archaic style that surely must have amused the addressee in the capital. The geographical conditions were meticulously described, with measures of length and cubic metres of water, and the enclosed drawings were so intricate and detailed that one had to know the terrain to make sense of them. The replies that came back were concise and, in a way, just as inscrutable. Nearly two years went by before he realized that something was wrong, that his counterpart was fobbing him off with talk and regarded him as an old idiot, or was simply making a fool of him. As time wore on it had become difficult for him to hold his pen, and with his last strength he composed an ultimatum to the government authorities, demanding that they speed up the matter. No answer ever came to his own address, but one autumn day in 1918 he was visited by the sheriff, who earnestly advised him to drop the matter. After all, Norway was full of fresh water that spread over cultivated land, and if the government were to undertake the job of lowering all those lakes, it wouldn't be able to do anything else. It was really too bad that the fine fields at Nether Hov were flooded as soon as there came a fairly long period of rain. But the Lord himself had made it that way, so there must be some meaning behind it. And besides, sedge grass was good fodder too, even if it was a bit hard to digest and tended to give the cows tympanites.

Thormod Hov saw that the battle was lost, and while the farming muddled along he gave himself over more and more to quiet brooding. What could the explanation be, he sighed, that everything went wrong, and that he who had so faithfully made the most of his talents should be punished with such disobedient and vicious offspring? His complaint was not without foundation in reality, because Nether Hov fell into decay inside and out and soon looked more wretched than when he began his life's work. At this point one of his daughters had also fled, and the emigration from Nether Hov began to assume threatening dimensions.

The eldest daughter, Svallaug, was the most balanced of the children, and the one who most resembled the mother both physically and mentally. A quiet, strong, and good-natured girl, she managed to remedy many of her brothers' offences by her level-headed behaviour. Nevertheless she must have had a flaw or weakness in her character, since she gave up halfway and ended her life in great shame and degradation.

But in 1918 there was yet no cloud on the horizon. Svallaug was in her seventeenth year and was a mirthful and happy young girl who didn't allow herself to be infected by the sombre atmosphere at Nether Hov. She was the only one in that shy flock of siblings who felt a need for friends, and she kept her good reputation in the parish even after the episode with the milk ramp. In her early youth she often went dancing and had just got herself a sweetheart when Balder, her brother, intervened and killed the burgeoning love affair with his jealousy and his venomous tongue. Incestuous as he was by both inclination and conviction, he held that tender

93

feelings had to remain within the family and shouldn't benefit those who were unworthy of them. Long before he openly declared himself a Nazi, xenophobia was second nature to him, preventing him from tolerating any rival or intruder. Svallaug's sweetheart had a trifling and not particularly damaging physical defect, which her brother was able to magnify to the point of the grotesque by his cruel wit. For a while he contented himself with giving his rival comical nicknames, before he went one step further and began drawing caricatures of him in places where they couldn't avoid catching one's glance. On fences and telephone poles, on barn doors and house walls, chalk drawings popped up that with diabolic perspicacity exposed the youth's lopsided shoulders and slightly rounded back. Under the caricature there was usually some joke that was at once apt and malicious and could only aggravate an already bad situation. The drawings were erased as soon as they appeared, for Svallaug was faithful and went for a walk on the main road with a washrag in her pocket every evening. But in the long run she wasn't able to stave it off; her efforts worked against her and stuck to the face of the hamlet like a mocking smile. Finally she couldn't take it any longer, and one late autumn day in 1918, about the same time as her father was visited by the sheriff, she broke her engagement and took a maid's job in Skien.

There are many indications that, when Balder finally pulled himself together and left home, it was to chase his sister and prevent her from liberating herself. A vague rumour has it that every evening for a whole week he positioned himself in front of the house where she was in service, throwing pebbles up at the window after catching a glimpse of her. For several days Svallaug didn't dare go out, and in the end she was so desperate that she broke down and cried and asked the man of the house for help. She didn't dare reveal that the tormentor was her own brother, but let the family think that the man in the entranceway was a rejected suitor. After that Balder disappeared and didn't show himself anymore. Unsure as he was of himself, he was as easily frightened as he was intrusive, and reluctant to risk a direct defeat. His advances and retreats were two sides of the same coin, and when he found the courage to be aggressive it was because he had provided for a way of escape.

But he refused to let go of his sister. He continued to pester her for years with letters and requests, in which prayers and pet names were mixed with a good dose of threats. The collection of letters was only found when the war was over and the sibling pair had evaded prosecution for treason by choosing to die together. In these letters Balder betrays a bond to his sister that must have been deeply felt and may have been the only form of tenderness this warped man was capable of harbouring for another human being. From one line to the next the tone would shift from coarse threats to declarations of love with clearly sexual undertones. This is not the place to explore their enigmatic life together, and the drastic end to which it came. That will all be presented in the proper place, with all the conclusions that can possibly be drawn from their fateful connection.

Nor would the youngest child, Kjellfrid, get to be old at Nether Hov, although she was the one of the siblings who held out the longest. A peculiar, incommunicative soul with a hidden life, she was profoundly musical and had a gift for languages, but she could never find the right words to her tunes, or the tunes to her words. She would slip away for hours at a time to desolate places, where she spoke to herself in a muffled voice, let out choked screams or sang snatches from some inward song. She had been very bright at school and was the only one of the siblings who could compete with Vemund as far as intelligence was concerned. After confirmation she cautiously suggested that she would like to go to a folk high school, but her parents were already old and saw no way they could dispense with her. So she complied and never again said a word about going away to school. She had a gentle disposition and bore her troubles quietly – so quietly, in fact, that many confused her meekness with contentment. She only dared to let herself go when she was out herding cattle, and occasionally the neighbours would hear such a strange sound coming from the edge of the forest that they believed it was the fairies singing. That it was Kjellfrid bemoaning and lamenting her unhappiness wasn't easy to apprehend, for now the voice sounded like a cattle call, now like laughter, hooting, animal cries or the wailing of a mourner.

When she was not out-of-doors with the cattle, she was dull and unenterprising, looking about her with squinting, semi-blind eyes and shuttling back and forth between the farm house and the outbuildings like a sleepwalker. Nether Hov had never been a model of order and cleanliness, but as the old people grew tired the housekeeping on the farm deteriorated to the point of sordidness. Word was spreading about the uncleanliness of the family; it was said that the stench in the farmhouse at Nether Hov was worse than that in the cow barn and the pigsty elsewhere.

And Kjellfrid walked back and forth as though aware of nothing, as though it were all just a dream. One autumn day in the last year of the war she disappeared into a hole in the floating sod that formed a footbridge between the farm and the plots on the other side of the lake. She was only found several weeks later, bloated beyond recognition, her hands so tightly closed around the tree roots underneath the sod that there could be no doubt she had thrown herself into the hole on purpose. At that point she was alone with her hoary old father, who was no longer clear-headed and had to be guarded like a child to protect him from harming himself or others.

One would be hard put to find any brotherly or sisterly love among the children at Nether Hov. They were prisoners languishing in the same prison, chained to one another night and day, with no other thought than their own survival. At times some fine threads of feeling might be spun between two of them, between one sister and the other, between one of them and Vemund, between the eldest and youngest brother. But these threads were like a late summer spider's web that shines so alluringly in the sunshine but breaks at the slightest touch. All the lovely songs that have been composed in celebration of family life, the solidarity, the togetherness, were never sung at Nether Hov; the place was too narrow and the breathing space too suffocating for so many greedy throats. They all had their own troubles to contend with, dreamed their own dreams, sang their own laments and sought liberation on their own hunting grounds.

Not even music could keep this musical family together. The tone they used with one another was hoarse and jarring; a scream was always lurking in their vocal chords and could rise to shrill heights without any perceptible reason. Only under the open sky did the prisoners find freedom, and from the plots, the pastures, the thickets you could occasionally hear some promising notes. They mostly took the form of monotonous glides and leaps along the scale, singing experiments with triads, melodic intervals and chromatic ascents and descents. But now and then there might be the beginnings of antiphonal singing, questions that were rewarded with answers, a message echoing from mouth to mouth. And once in a great while the song would rise to a unisonous jubilation, a concord of voices that betokened reconciliation and ascended to heaven in the purest hymns and madrigals.

3

And with this the family at Nether Hov should have been described to the extent necessary, and it is about time to open the diary for 1917 and see what Vemund writes about his escape from home, where it led him and what were its consequences. Whether this diary actually exists and is available will have to remain uncertain, since the charge nurse hasn't set eyes on it and is very much in doubt about its existence.

To reassure other doubters I can inform them that the book is reddish brown, has a flap that is closed with a snap button, and a number indicating the year imprinted in gold letters on the front cover. Inside, the pages have a calendar on one side and space for memos on the other, and it was in the latter that Vemund wrote down his reflections. At the end of the book there is a number of blank pages that Vemund augmented by sewing in some loose leaves, and since Vemund's handwriting is minuscule, he could without difficulty find room for the notes that are here reproduced, and many more.

New Year's Day, 1917. Left Nether Hov yesterday, the last day of the year, and won't let myself be taken back. Remember that, Vemund, not at any price! Stick firmly to your decision, whether the old man rages or makes his voice ever so thin. Today you're turning seventeen, and you have had enough. Now the important thing must simply be to survive!

The reason for Father's divine rage was also this time a trifle. I had fed the cows with hay meant for the horse because it was New Year's Eve; I thought it was mean to have them munching sedge grass. I knew of course that the horse feed was sacred and inviolable, and that it was blasphemous to dispatch it into the four stomachs of the chewers of cud. But as I've said, it was New Year's Eve, and maybe the cows should also get to taste banqueting fare once in a while.

Balder saw what I was doing and wasted no time in telling the old man, who summoned me from the cow barn and started taking down my trousers. He was so furious that he couldn't control himself, but struck out blindly without caring where the blows fell. The fact that I stood there accepting them without a sound made him even more worked up. Fortunately he hasn't very much strength, so his arm soon grew tired of swinging. I waited till he had calmed down and was taking his after-dinner nap. Then I went upstairs to pack my bundle and saw my chance to steal off.

I set out in the direction of Luksefjell, without a clear idea where I was going. Maybe I intended to take refuge with my maternal uncle, Nikolai, I don't know. But about midway I suddenly stopped and came to remember something. I had, after all, returned that nickel watch he gave me for confirmation, telling him straight out that he could keep it for himself. I didn't want to start my adult life owing anybody a debt of gratitude, I wrote to him. I could tell by the sun what time it was, as I had always done, and buy myself a gold watch once I was able to afford it.

I felt the chills running down my spine when I realized that the road to Luksefjell was closed. Now I was homeless! I stood there shivering like a stray dog, and the slight desolation I have always felt expanded into a desert inside me. I had no kin I could turn to, but was completely alone in the world with the bundle in my hand.

Turning round, I began to walk south at random; I walked and walked till the day waned and dusk crept up on me. The snow was falling steadily, I was tramping in heavy, wet snow and was already soaked. God in heaven, what would become of me? Would I have to swallow my shame and go back to Hov, dropping to my knees and begging for mercy? Never! Rather get lost in no man's land and perish in a snowdrift. I was blubbering like a little kid, blowing my nose on my fingers and thinking of my two paternal uncles, who had gone so thoroughly astray that they ended up as tramps and navvies. The wind blew so hard that I walked almost doubled-up, the tears gushing and mingling with the ice-cold driving snow that was lashing my face without a break. Never, Vemund! Never as long as you live!

I cannot say how long I had been struggling ahead on the unbroken trail when I caught sight of a church tower and, slightly to the side, behind some tall trees, a long house with light in all the windows. What sort of place was this? I stood still a moment, my hand pressed against my forehead, totally disoriented about the direction I had been walking. Then I understood that the church must be the Gjerpen Church and the house the parsonage. Did I dare go up and knock on the door? I had heard that Dean Quisling was as hospitable as he was learned, and that no poor devil went empty-handed away from his house. I hesitated before the house for a long while, taking a few steps forward and then again withdrawing, while my pride and my desolation fought like two wild beasts inside me.

Then I rushed up the front steps, dropped my bundle and hammered away at the entrance door with both fists.

Second Day of the New Year. I began to write in this book yesterday and continue today in a slightly calmer state of mind. It is the first almanac I have ever owned, the Dean gave it to me yesterday when he heard it was my birthday.

When I came here the day before yesterday, he was in bed with a fever, and a servant girl was about to slam the door in my face when the Dean's son came into the hallway and asked what sort of errand I came on. His name is Vidkun, an odd name, as if he had decided at his baptism to become someone great and famous. A tall, erect ramrod of a man, rather gruff in manner, with eyes like lightning and a whitish-yellow mop of hair that is constantly falling over his eyes.

He towered before me like a runestone, and at first I was so scared that I couldn't utter a word. But suddenly a tiny smile flitted across his face, and he became altogether different. I summoned up my courage and explained that I was a runaway peasant boy with a love of books who wanted to make something of himself. I could take on any work whatsoever, I said, cart manure, quarry stone, fell trees or whatever it might be, if only the Dean would give me a few lessons when he had the time.

I could see that young Quisling was bewildered; now he thoughtfully stroked his chin, now he straightened up with a start and scrutinized me mercilessly with those intense eyes of his. Again that little odd smile that seems to steal briefly across his face. Then he told me quite simply that he was only home on holiday and couldn't take a stand on my inquiry. But I could stay in the parsonage over the holidays, and if the Dean was free of fever the next day, I would have a chance to talk to him.

"Gunhild!" he called in a voice that echoed off the walls. Shortly the same maid who had tried to chase me off appeared. "Take this fellow into the kitchen, give him something to eat and see to it that his clothes are dried. The hired man is off during the New Year holidays, isn't he? Fine. Then let this boy stay in the servants' quarters and keep Even's bed warm for him."

His voice was still gruff, and his words crackled like firings on the drill grounds. For a while he stood at strict attention observing me, I scarcely dared breathe, afraid that he might change his mind and send me away. But gradually his attitude grew less stern, and that strange smile again flickered on his lips. I glanced cautiously up at him, but he didn't return my look; he had become absorbed in thought and gave an impression of being far away. But suddenly he took a step forward, placed his hand on the nape of my neck and let it rest there a long while, as though he charged me with a secret mission or gave me an initiation.

The next day (that is, yesterday) I was summoned to the Dean, who had recovered his strength sufficiently to be able to get up. His clothes gave him an odd appearance, being very loose and made up of a mixture of different things. His nightshirt stuck out from under his robe, his chest was bundled up in a woman's shawl, and on his head, perched at a sharp angle, sat something that could be either a nightcap or a skullcap, I wasn't able to tell which. The grey furry wrist warmers he had on his hands made them look like an animal's paws; the fingers sticking out were so crooked that they made you think of claws. I had never before seen such a quaint getup and hastily looked away in order not to burst out laughing.

When I had presented my errand he told me that he was getting old and frail and couldn't undertake to give me any regular instruction. The family had lost a daughter the previous autumn, which had taken much out of him. In a year or two he would retire as a clergyman and move to Fyresdal, so I couldn't count on his being able to prepare me for a degree of any kind. And the parsonage had no need of an additional hired man, the tillage was not large, so one farm hand was quite adequate. But he would make inquiries with the farmers round about, whether there might be a job for me some place or other.

As far as intellectual pursuits were concerned, he said, he first had to examine me in order to decide whether I should devote myself to book learning in the first place. I mustn't mind that, he said, with an almost humble air, as if he were the young hopeful and I the immensely learned old man. But if I wasn't too exhausted after yesterday's exertions, he might as well put some questions to me right away, questions I must do him the favour of answering as exactly as possible. (Do him the favour – yes, imagine, that's what he said!) If the test came out to my advantage, he would do something for me and take on my instruction as long as he remained in Gjerpen. He had been a teacher in his youth, he told me, and had always been interested in the fund of intelligence that lay hidden in the common people.

The first thing he did was to reach for the hymnal, a gem of a book with gilt edges and thin leaves that lay in front of him on the table. When he had sat a while fumbling with the leaves, which he wasn't able to separate, he pushed the book over to me and asked me to look up the hymn I liked the most and read it aloud to him. It didn't take me long to make up my mind; I found my favourite hymn and greatly surprised him by singing it at the top of my voice:

> No man will win eternal peace,
> who shies away from battle pangs.
> The soul must persevere and seize,
> the faith on which salvation hangs.

The song must have made a strong impression on him, for he sat with closed eyes and listened long after I had finished. When he finally turned his head and looked at me, he had tears in his eyes. But it didn't have to mean anything, I told myself, it could be due to the fever, or the mere fact that he was old. A long time passed without his saying a word, and I began to feel a little ashamed that I had taken the liberty of singing. Finally he seemed to wake up from his absent-mindedness and come to his senses. "But my sweet fellow," he said in a warm voice, "you sing like a cherub."

I didn't know exactly what a cherub was, but thought it must be some celestial being or other. If that was the case, maybe I didn't have to feel ashamed that I had sung, but rather be proud. And right enough, after sitting for a moment absorbed in thought, slowly rocking his head, he asked me if I would give him the pleasure of singing another hymn. It didn't take me long to make up my mind this time either. I hummed a bit up and down until I found the correct register, which is still a bit uncertain after my voice change. Then I sang, "In heaven, in heaven" to the old Norwegian folk tune, with many flourishes and grace notes, as I had heard Mother sing it to me when I was so small I was still in my cradle.

Afterwards he put me through my paces in the four basic arithmetical operations and let me have a crack at ready reckoning, where I had to pull myself together and think really hard. Although I'm not a wizard like Father, I did very well – so well, in fact, that sometimes it was the Dean who got mixed up and lost his bearings. I also did better than expected in knowledge of the Bible, grammar and spelling, I don't think I made a single mistake. At any rate, the upshot was that the Dean asked me about my future plans, and how many years I thought would be needed to prepare for my *artium* degree.

"Two and a half years," I said without blinking, because I had already made up my mind and explored how it could be done. In the spring of 1919 I would sit for the degree as an external student at the Skien Latin School, sink or swim.

Wednesday, 3 January. The instruction has begun, and for the time being it is young Quisling who pounds learning into my head. But he will be leaving for Kristiania one of these days, and then the Dean will take over.

Even, the hired man, came back last night and was a bit annoyed when he heard that he had to share his bed with me. But it will be only for a few nights, then I begin working for Ola Gardatun nearby. It will be sad to leave the parsonage. I'll miss the library, where I have been sitting for hours gorging myself on books. How nice, though, that the Dean has found a job for me near the parsonage, so that I can occasionally make a flying visit over here in the evening.

Young Quisling is strict, but just; never praises me, but pipes up mightily when he discovers that I am an ignoramus, as he calls it. Don't quite know what he means by it, must remember to look it up in the big dictionary in the library. (Twelve thick volumes, and even then it seems a new, expanded edition will soon appear.)

Quisling says that my situation is precisely as he had expected: high points and peaks of real ingenuity, and corresponding abysses of ignorance. What has to be done, he says, is not to undertake a levelling, so that I will have the usual average intelligence. The high points must be preserved, even though they are a bit skewed, and the abysses must be filled in and raised, so that they too emerge in the terrain. Whew, I really wonder what sort of blastings and fillings he intends to undertake before he gets my intellectual landscape in shape.

What he will do to begin with, he says, is to give me a quick course in the elements. (That is to say, the fundamentals, essentially what has to do with the four elements, earth, water, air, and fire.) At the same time he will survey my abilities and take careful notes on a piece of paper, so it won't be too difficult for the Dean to take over.

Latin will be the toughest, there I haven't got a crumb in my bag. Mathematics is promising, he says, I have a knack for thinking abstractly. (The abstract – that is something artful, a figment of the brain, something that is not tangible.) For example, to do computations with x and y instead of with actual numbers. In that way the operation can be done once and for all, and the numerical values can be inserted as they are needed. Or not inserted at all, so that the equation will remain a shining light to thought, like Aladdin's palace in the desert.

Wonder if it wasn't something like this that Father had in mind as a boy, when he did sums with nix and gnome. I have no illusions of being as smart as he, I need more time and very seldom have brilliant ideas or revelations. On the other hand, I have been endowed with a good portion of sound common sense, which he lacks. I hope that this thoughtfulness will be helpful to me and save me from becoming the kind of eccentric Thormod Hov has been all of his life.

Sunday, 7 January. Vidkun Quisling has gone to Kristiania. Yesterday evening he gave me the last lesson, which stretched out and became a double lesson, and more.

Its lasting so long was due to the fact that he had brought a big bunch of papers that he wanted to show me. It said *Universism* in big Gothic letters on the first page. It was his life's work, he told me, a philosophical treatise that he had begun already when he was my age. Many a time he had thought that now he was on the point of concluding the work, but fresh thoughts were constantly turning up and had to be co-ordinated with the old ones. Gradually he had come to understand that it was a work that couldn't be completed, but that he had to carry with him and continue to elaborate throughout his life.

He turned a few leaves of the bundle, going back and forth, and was soon so engrossed that he wasn't aware of my presence. I sat wide-eyed beside him; the sheets were so embroidered with insertions and additions that I couldn't understand how he was able to keep track of his argument. But that didn't seem to be any problem to him. As I sat there looking on, he repeatedly grabbed his pen and made a parenthesis, or he wrote something crosswise in the margin and fitted it into the context by means of a long arrow.

He continued scribbling on the sheets for quite a while, until they looked like verbal labyrinths; then he suddenly woke up and came to his senses. He explained to me quite soberly and matter-of-factly what the document was about and what its purpose was. I cannot say I understood very much of what he said, but nevertheless (or perhaps just because of that) I was completely bewitched. I thought that if there was anything great in the world, it must obviously be way beyond me. Being just a poor peasant boy of seventeen, who had practically no schooling. If I had understood the line of thought in his life's work, I said to myself, then it must be something extremely mediocre and obvious, which each and everyone could grasp.

Thus concluded my first meeting with Vidkun Quisling, and it probably won't be the last. When he got up and collected his papers, he said he had come to take an interest in me and would check on my progress when he occasionally returned to Gjerpen for the holidays. When I was ready for it, he would introduce me to Universism, and maybe someday we would reach the point where we could discuss it on an equal footing.

Universism seems to mean two things: first, the intention and the governing idea that inform his work, and second, the title of the big pile of papers that to my humble intelligence seem to be without any order or coherence.

Monday, 15 January. (Midwinter.) Began this morning at half-past four as a farm hand at Gardatun. The Dean accompanied me here yesterday afternoon and discussed the conditions with the farmer. I had to acquit myself well and do an honest day's work, but my master mustn't drive me too hard, so that I could also find time for my books. It took a while before they agreed on the pay, but in the end the farmer accepted the Dean's proposal to the effect that I would have half the pay of a full-grown hired man.

The Dean's wife had seen to it that my clothes were washed and mended, and besides she had given me some discarded garments and a pair of unpatched boots, a hand-me-down from their son, Arne, who is a few years older than I. My old boots were ready for the scrapheap – Even guffawed when he saw the gaping holes at the toe. They looked like a pair of hungry badgers, he said.

The Dean has given me all of the books I need for the first year, besides pen and ink, pencils and notebooks. (I have no idea what he will say about it, but I have removed a few sheets in the middle of one notebook, cut them to size and sewed them into the almanac, so I'll have a little more space for my jottings.)

In the evening the same day, written as well as it can be done in the light from the cow barn lantern.

Was so excited about opening my books this morning that I could hardly wait until my agreed-upon free time between twelve and two. But it was pitch-black in the servants' quarters when I got up and no use thinking about books. The room has no lamp, and I could barely get into my clothes.

While I was milking the cows, I could think of nothing else but those two free hours, and I had to give myself a talking-to before I got the right hold on the teats. Suddenly my master turned up and kept standing on the threshold to make sure that I knew the trick. Feeling I was getting shaky, I nearly made a mess of it and fell out of rhythm, though I have been milking cows since I was eleven.

But everything went as it should, the milk made music in the pail, and the cows quietened down and quickly got used to the strange hands. I usually find a song to milk by, a melody that has a sufficiently strong beat to make everything seem like a game. Cows must be musical animals, for they like the rhythm and literally rock back and forth while they let go of the milk.

As I sat there humming softly, I could see over my shoulder how the master went sniffing about the stalls to make sure I had mucked and spread straw properly. But he found nothing to complain about and almost looked cheated as he ducked his head in the doorway and disappeared.

Strange, incidentally, that the owner of a big farm hasn't long ago taken care to make the door to the cow barn higher. I, by no means a giant, have already managed to bump my head several times. But not a word has escaped my lips! As always, I accept the conditions, taking them as a sign: You will have to duck your head, Vemund, both in one way and another.

Was ravenously hungry when I was called in for breakfast shortly after six. The master and mistress had already eaten, and I shared the table with the two maids, the grandfather, the parish pauper, the hired man and the kids, who were already in full swing shovelling it in. The table looked like a battlefield, with milk and spilled coffee and breadcrumbs all over the tabletop. Couldn't help thinking of Father when I saw the old man with his beard full of food scraps. (And not only scraps from this year, but from last year and the year before that!)

My porridge must have been dished up at an unearthly hour, for it was completely cold and had a skin that had stiffened to a crust. The two thick slices of bread with pork drippings were so hard and lumpy that I almost had to crack my jaw to get the better of them. I tried to take them as a joke, calling them "the horse's birthday" to myself. With it all, a cup of overboiled coffee and a small bowl of blue-and-sour skimmed milk with a dead fly in it. I took what I got and said nothing, but made a mental note of the fact that the fare on this big farm was almost more wretched than on the small place where I came from.

The hired man and I were in the woods felling trees all morning; one hour went by after another, and I began to worry what would happen to my spare time. When we got back home it was a quarter to one, and by the time we had unharnessed the horses and swallowed our food it was almost half-past one. The master cleared his throat and said it was our business to watch the clock, reminding us, to be on the safe side, that the meal break was part of the two free hours.

There was a thick fog and evening darkness, and when I mentioned that there was no lamp in the servants' quarters, the master burst out laughing and asked if I had poor eyesight. Young eyes should be able to see by daylight, he thought. I realized I might as well forget about it and sneaked quietly down to the servants' quarters.

Nor is there any heat in the tiny room I share with the hired man; the farmer probably thinks that two bodies can make up for a stove, even at midwinter and in biting frost. I felt freezing cold in the draught from the window, and my fingers were so stiff that I had difficulty holding my pencil. My companion snored to shake the walls, and every once in a while there also came some other sounds, which spread an awful stench in the room. The air was pretty thick beforehand, what with wet clothes, sweat and chewing tobacco. Dear me, how am I going to endure all these exhalations? I sit in filth up to my neck and have only exchanged one pigsty for another.

But I won't say a word to the Dean, not so much as a sigh! Let come what may until summer, when I can take my books out with me. For the time being I will have to take refuge in the cow barn and try to read on the sly under the lantern over there. If I rise at half-past three, I should have about an hour's time to myself before I have to begin mucking.

Hm, the story of my life is beginning to look suspiciously like my father's. I certainly have to look out so that I don't walk in the old man's footsteps and end my days as an ill-tempered, yelling curmudgeon!

Wednesday, 31 January. Everything is taking its usual course, so there's not much news to write about. In the forest all morning with a crust of bread in my pocket, the hired man dragging his feet and unwilling to listen when I tell him we should be home at twelve o'clock sharp. We won't get to the table until close to one in any case, he says, and he is right about that of course.

The noon rest period goes by as usual, my companion snoring and spreading a bad smell while I cram Latin words or try to solve an equation. In the afternoon to the forest once more, then milking, mucking, and feeding the animals, big and small. After that, shovelling snow and incidental chores until supper.

Then the time should be my own if the agreement were kept. At first I fetched my books and began working with them under the kitchen lamp. But no, not a moment's peace to be had! No sooner have I started with my declensions than the master comes with a tool that has to be repaired, or a stool that needs a new leg. Suddenly he has come up with the idea that I have to learn to sole boots, naturally not my own, which have nothing wrong with them, but his own and those of the whole family. With that the matter is settled, and I know how I can make my evenings pass for the remainder of the winter.

God in heaven, help me, help me! Soon I won't be able to control myself and let fly at my tormentors.

Tuesday, 6 February. My books are already beginning to smell of the cow barn; I hope the Dean won't notice and ask how that can be.

While I sit and read under the cow barn lantern, I'm scared to death that my master may show up and see what I'm doing. The cows have already become used to my studies; they lie quietly in their stalls, merely turning their heads now and then and looking at me with their mild animal eyes. When the clock is approaching half-past four, they start mooing a bit, reminding me that it's about time to begin my morning chores.

The master stays away most of the time now, after assuring himself that I keep the cow barn in impeccable order. But he does make spot checks, and who knows whether he won't catch me red-handed some day as I sit on the milking stool with a lighted lamp out of season.

For the sake of change I have begun to decline words when I milk the cows. "*Amo, amas, amat, amamus, amatis, amant,*" I chant, my head resting against the bovine bellies as I lovingly pull on the teats of Dagros and Rosa and Rødlin. But they dislike Latin verbs, even when they deal with love. They swipe their tails contemptuously and don't behave until I drop the Latin and begin to sing.

Thursday, 22 February. My studies are coming along much too slowly, and I notice that the Dean is dissatisfied with the progress I'm making. I hope he won't lose patience and conclude that he has overestimated my abilities. I won't tell him anything about how my days are passed at Gardatun, never in the world! If the Dean doesn't find out that something is wrong by himself, my lips will be sealed.

I scarcely manage to get away the two evenings a week I have lessons at the parsonage. The master snorts and takes a long spit when I make ready to go, obviously appraising my brain at the size of a hazelnut. But he has a cringing respect for the Dean and doesn't dare violate the agreement in a too obvious way.

What will become of me, tell me that, you omniscient one, what will become of me? What have I gained by running away from home, other than to exchange one slave driver for another? Help me, God, if it's true that you exist. I'm only seventeen years old, and it can't be possible, can it, that my life is already over?

Monday, 25 February. Today the sun appeared for the first time above the roof of the barn, and it immediately made me a little more cheerful. I have promised myself that I will acquiesce and accept the conditions, as long as there is no other way. Even the apostle Paul realized, after all, that it was no use kicking against the pricks. The Dean touched on that yesterday in his Sunday sermon, and it was a message that went straight to my heart.

My maxim from now on must be: Suffer all, bow to the inevitable, be satisfied with simply surviving. But never lose courage, never be so cowed that I lose sight of my goal. It won't be easy to carry through, but I will, I will, I will do it!

I have come up with a remedy that usually helps when everything goes wrong and I can't take it any longer. I flop down, empty myself of all longings and desires and lie motionless, as though dead, on the floor of the outbuilding. Nothing touches me, nothing interests me, nor is there anything that can hurt me in this lifeless condition. I lie like this for a few minutes, completely still and invulnerable, until I perceive that something eases off and a fresh power of resistance springs forth within me. I don't always get it right, and sometimes I jump up in an impotent rage and bang the wall with my fist. But my rage merely saps my strength, while the other way protects and preserves me, until I am strong enough to take life into my own hands.

This is something I can never confide to a living soul, not even the Dean, who no doubt would think that my reconciliation is not of the right sort. Only here, on this white paper, can I reveal myself and take counsel with myself about how to survive.

Friday, 1 March. It worries me that I haven't heard anything from Mother. I have written five letters to her since I left home, and I haven't heard a sound!

I have resigned myself as long as possible, consoling myself with the thought that silence doesn't necessarily mean anything. Mother is no letter writer, I have told myself. She has her own ways, and as far as I know she hasn't touched a pen since she wrote that helpless engagement letter to Father almost twenty years ago.

But it isn't like her to leave me without a reply, and little by little a suspicion has awakened in me and grown bigger and bigger: could it be that Father has snapped up the letters in order to punish me and push me out into utter darkness?

Since that thought arose in me, I haven't had a moment's peace. I can see Balder sneaking into the living room with the mail, making signs to Father and taking him aside. My younger brother is always ready to play into the hands of the enemy; I haven't been able to keep track of all the times he has ingratiated himself with Father by stabbing the rest of us in the back. He can spit in the old man's face like no one else, but the next moment he curls up and goes over to playing the role of a lickspittle.

No, there's nothing for it, I shall have to take a trip home to Hov shortly. If only I weren't so tied hand and foot, and hadn't abandoned my whole past. I've taken a step that has alienated me from my family and origin once and for all, hurling me into a place where I haven't gained a foothold. How shall I be able to retrace that step without losing myself, plunging into the great nothingness?

Shall – shall not, shall not – shall!

Weekdays it won't be possible to get away, needless to say. But if my master won't fool me like last time, I should be having a Sunday off soon, when I don't have to do the morning chores in the cow barn. I should use the day for study, of course, and I'm constantly arguing back and forth. Yes, I have to take a trip home and see Mother! No, I must get to my books and make up for lost time! Desire and duty tear at me, and I'm often so confused that I don't know which is which.

One thing is certain, however: I can't settle down to anything until I've seen Mother again. But it must take place in deep secrecy, so that the old man, who keeps his eyes peeled, won't notice the footprints of the prodigal son.

Sunday, 10 March. Today I did it! I sprang up from my bedstraw already at a quarter to three and told myself: Now or never!

The weather was fine, almost no snow and a light crust, so I could reduce the distance by taking short cuts across the fields. I had planned it all very carefully and knew I had to be early if I wanted to see Mother alone. Sunday is Seven Sleepers' Day at Nether Hov; none of the men open their eyelids until eight, at the earliest. Only Mother gets up at her usual time and goes to the cow barn around half-past four, and while she milks the girls get on their legs to stir the morning porridge and set the table.

As I've said, the weather was fine this second Sunday in March, with stars in the sky and a big, bright moon that leaned kindly down and showed me the way. I crossed fields, jumped ditches, forged my way through brushwood and climbed fences; everything was working out fine, and I fairly danced over the crunching crusted snow.

When I approached Nether Hov and saw the tiny farmhouse squatting down in the hollow, I made an abrupt stop and caught at my chest. I had violent palpitations, my thoughts stood still, and it was as though an unfamiliar sorrow shot through me. I remained standing on top of the hill for a long time, squinting down at the yard with those miserable, sunken houses. It was the first time I saw my childhood home with those eyes, as though from the outside and at a great, great distance.

I can't say how long the spell lasted, standing there as if rooted to the ground and staring into another world, mild and infinitely transfigured, as if it didn't know what evil was. It was paradise itself down there, veiled in a mirage that no bad memories were capable of dissolving. Could it really have been here that I had suffered so much for seventeen years, slaving out of necessity, dreaming my dizzying dreams and planning my treason? Could this be the place I had moved away from step by step, first in thought and spirit, later more and more resolutely, until my betrayal was ripe and had to have visible consequences?

I placed my hand over my eyes until I came back to my senses; then I stole down the slope, around the barn bridge and into the woodshed. The door to the cow barn was ajar, and I could see there was a light in there. A wild, engulfing longing for Mother came over me. I whispered her name many times over and had to restrain myself in order not to rush in and throw my arms around her, let go of all that was me and mine, throw myself on her breast and lose myself in the sweet smell of milk that enveloped her. Half dreaming, I could hear the sound of the milk singing in her pail, that accustomed sound that I ought to know inside out but that now was touching my inner ear and took on another, more enchanting resonance.

When I started back two hours later, I had a little of everything to think about. I was glad and relieved that I had seen Mother and been reassured that everything was the same as ever between us. The tray of food she brought from the kitchen was full of goodies, and it felt so homey to be having one's morning coffee in the hay. At the end my sisters, too, came stealing along to share in my clandestine visit.

But before we parted I said more than I had meant to and gave mother a promise that I'm not certain I can keep. I promised her I would study for the ministry and choose the only career that in the eyes of my parents can justify my flight from Nether Hov. I have no idea how it happened – she may have fretted a little about Father having bought out the farm and sacrificed his health and life to no purpose.

I could have answered as so often before that Father's choice was not mine, that unlike him I was not tied to Hov. His dream was not my dream, and besides I didn't have the stuff in me that farmers were made of.

Instead I blurted out that I wanted to become a pastor, which had never entered my mind before. And Mother heaved a deep sigh and said that, if that was how matters stood, I had to follow the call in God's name.

How to explain to her that I hadn't received any call and had never given a thought to any profession? That I was just thirsting for light and beauty, and for satisfying my insatiable appetite for knowledge?

Now I'm caught in the trap. A word is a word, and I just cannot break my promise to her.

Wednesday, 20 March. Last night the Dean's wife detained me before letting me into the study, and after eyeing me for a moment she asked if I got enough food and sleep. I had become so thin, she said, and she didn't like my hollow cheeks and the dark circles under my eyes.

I replied that she didn't need to worry, everything was as it should be with me. Still, she must have had her doubts, for when the lesson was over she brought me a glass of milk and three huge pieces of malt loaf with a thick layer of butter. I thanked her politely and said that she shouldn't have, but became so carried away by the good smell of cake that I threw myself forward and ate it all in one swallow.

I noticed that the two old people looked at one another and exchanged nods, as if a suspicion they had long harboured was confirmed. Before the wife withdrew she patted my cheek and said I need not be embarrassed by my ravenous appetite. Having had growing boys herself, she knew what quantities of food they could tuck away.

That was an interpretation I could share, and I was relieved that they left it at that. I have firmly decided to remain mum about the conditions of life at Gardatun; they are my own business and may be a good schooling for someone who knows that he must fight his way ahead in life against big obstacles, and with many renunciations.

I remained at the parsonage till late in the evening, sitting alone in the library and helping myself greedily to the books. Finished Shakespeare's *Tempest* and began a strange book by someone named Erasmus of Rotterdam. The book is called *In Praise of Folly*, which is a translation of the Latin title *Laus Stultitiae*.

Sat a long while examining the picture of the man on the jacket, while wondering what the title might mean. Could it really be possible that Erasmus praised folly, or did he merely wish to show that it had its price? I scratched my head and weighed the pros and cons, until it suddenly dawned on me that the book was a satire.

There is much in it that I don't understand, and I have only reached page twenty-seven. But it promises to be a powerful mockery of stupidity, which appears at the lectern in a professor's gown in order to extol itself. Quite a sly fox, this Erasmus, who hides behind Madame Stultitia and manages to tell his contemporaries some bitter truths without anyone being able to make him responsible for them. Ha-ha, it's Stupidity alone that speaks, after all, the man who holds the pen is completely innocent and cannot answer for her mistakes. Censorship must surely have been in a predicament when the book came out at the beginning of the sixteenth century. Should it be condemned and placed on the index, or should it slip through the eye of the needle with the blessing of the church?

And now I ask: Is an author raised above his work or, when all is said and done, is he responsible for what his characters say and do? How can he be certain that the readers see the joke and join in on it? What if they misunderstand it, as I did at first, and take it all in dead seriousness?

NB! Must absolutely discuss this with the Dean the next time I go there and find out what he thinks!

The picture on the jacket made almost the greatest impression on me. Erasmus is standing at his desk, totally engrossed in his scribbling – perhaps he's writing *In Praise of Folly*. He has a shawl over his shoulders and a big fur cap on his head; maybe it's just as cold in his monastic cell as it is in my servants' quarters. The expression of his drawn face is utterly concentrated and tense, as if it's a matter of life and death to get a couple of lines down on paper before somebody disturbs him, summoning him to Mass, asking him to accept a distinguished visitor or give a lecture. Who knows, perhaps it wasn't all that easy in the fifteen hundreds either to find the peace and quiet necessary to collect one's thoughts?

Saturday, 23 March. The Dean thinks I'm doing better in Latin, which till now has been the big stumbling block. I have swallowed the grammar and assimilated it, just as the prophet Ezekiel swallowed the sacred book that God gave him to eat. As I hope to be saved, I have chewed and swallowed it to the last crumb, "and it was in my mouth as honey for sweetness!"

Fortunately, the hired man has become used to my eccentricities, he no longer looks so distrustfully at me when I go about mumbling things. He himself belongs to the quiet sort and doesn't exactly let his tongue run away with him.

When he finally says something, it is *à propos* of nothing and simply to make what is happening clearer to himself. "Now we'll see if it won't soon fall," he says as we stand at opposite ends of the crosscut saw and the pressure increases on the spruce trunk. "Now we'd better harness the horse," he says with great emphasis, spreading the harness on the back of the horse. "Now you'll see some ploughing, all right," he cries in the midst of the driving snow as we walk doubled-up between the farmhouse and the outbuildings pulling the plough.

I won't deny that I like his simple way of communicating. His words create what they name, as the Dean is in the habit of saying; what's more, they almost become a kind of magic formula. Fancy having to keep company with someone who never let his tongue rest for a moment all day! What would then have become of *per ardua ad astra, pax vobiscum, humanum est errare,* and all those other mottoes I have learned by heart and made my own?

Incidentally, the other day I made a terrible blunder with one of them. When the Dean uses an aphorism in Latin, I hurry to take it down; later I use it in my written exercises to please him and show that I have been attentive. Remember *humanu mesterare,* I had jotted down in my notebook, in the naive belief that it concerned becoming a master in something or other. The Dean had a good laugh when I later served it up to him in my neatest calligraphy; I blushed to the roots of my hair when he explained to me what my misunderstanding had been.

But, but – *humanum est errare,* to make mistakes is human. I managed at least to take wisdom at its word and confirm it with my stupidity (*Stultitia*).

Palm Sunday, 1 April. My master has forbidden me to sing during work hours, he says it frightens the cows and that nobody can do his best work with song on his lips.

He caught me in the act (*in flagranti*) yesterday morning as I was singing scales at the top of my voice. I was in high spirits and running up and down the gamut like an archangel, while Rødlin was swaying in a trance and the milk squirting into the pail. He was so angry that he darted over and gave me a blow on the neck, and afterwards he took me aside and read me the riot act, forward and backward. To sing was something one did in church on Sundays, couldn't I get that into my noodle? All other places it was an absurdity that took away one's capacity for work and lowered the milk production.

Now afterwards I don't know whether to laugh or cry, but I think I choose to laugh. *Nil desperandum,* never despair, I wrote in my notebook yesterday, underscoring it with a fat line. But I do have my heavy moments, when it is almost impossible to look at Madame Stultitia from the playful side.

What will become of me when I'm deprived of song and I cannot find an outlet for my deepest joy? My master has said that if he catches me "bellow-ing" one more time, I'm finished around here; then I can pick up my bundle and take to the road. There I can do as I like, he says, throw my lot in with gypsies and dark-skinned trash and praise idleness from morning till night.

Nil desperandum, Vemund, *nil desperandum*!

Oh well, Latin sayings are all right, they sound so infallible that they almost elevate you into another world. But how can I manage to survive? It will be two years and two months until I have my *artium* degree, if I don't give up and drop by the wayside before that time.

Maybe it is a defect, after all, that I am so patient. I keep holding things in, and God help me the day I've had enough and something snaps.

A rope is hanging from a beam in the hay barn. I often peek up at it and quickly withdraw my glance.

God, if you exist somewhere in the universe, help me so I won't lose courage and give up.

4

But Vemund Hov did not give up. Through all his hardships he managed to fight the good fight, complete the race and preserve his faith that a better life was awaiting him.

In the spring of 1919 he entered for the *artium* examination as an external candidate at Skien Latin School and did brilliantly. It had been his secret goal to do as well as his model, Vidkun Quisling, and he succeeded. When the results were announced, it turned out that he had surpassed both himself and his teacher. And this despite the fact that during the last year he was left to himself and had to struggle through most of the material by means of private study.

It was a great loss to him when the Quisling family moved to Fyresdal in the autumn of 1918. Not only did he lose the guidance given in the study and the happy moments in the library, but also the moral support that had helped him keep his spirits up. But the Dean had taken care to provide for him before leaving, releasing him from the slavery at Gardatun and renting a room for him in town, not very far from the Latin School, where he was able to attend classes as a visiting student during the last few months.

Many years afterward, when Vemund Hov was dictating his so-called *Apology* to his thirteen-year-old daughter during his long illness, he would occasionally lose the thread of his defence and come to a dead stop. In the middle of a brilliant train of thought he would suddenly drift off and sink into a sort of eclipse. His face stiffened to a grimace, his head fell back on the pillow, his lips refused to serve him any longer and distorted his speech to an indistinct mumble.

"Idun, wait a little – how far had we got – what was it I wanted to say?" he stammered in his ruined voice, which had once been so strong and sonorous. "Why, who would believe it, I think I lost it."

He made a last effort to raise his head, as if to make sure that the escape route was clear and that no outsider was present in the room. Then he lifted his withered hand with difficulty and made a gesture in the direction of the bookcase in the chimney corner. "We'll take a break," he whispered, "and instead look at those other things you know about for a moment."

And Idun knew very well what could lift her father's spirits when he had his fits of melancholy and hopelessness. She jumped up from her chair, put the writing materials away, and hastened to fetch the worn oilcloth folder hidden in the drawer under the bookcase.

She was just as eager as the sick person and could barely wait while she opened the two clasps and placed the contents on the bedspread. Having learned her lesson, she was careful to put the documents in the lower part of the bed, so that her father couldn't stretch out his hand and get hold of them in a fit of destructive rage. She held back a certain envelope with a sombre and menacing content, letting it lie untouched in a special pocket of the folder. That was the sentence for treason, a document that her father insisted on keeping but couldn't bear the sight of without going into a fit of rage.

She had done it many times before, and her hands quickly finished their job of arranging and sorting. Here they were all of them, one after the other, the visible proofs that Vemund Hov had existed and left traces after him in the world. When everything was in place, the documents formed a veritable pyramid, which widened downward with increasingly weighty and honourable material.

At the very top of the pyramid was the yellowed baptismal certificate from Siljan Church, so worn at the folds that it had been pasted together with adhesive tape. Next, the slightly lighter confirmation certificate and the elementary school diploma with almost nothing but firsts. And then the documents followed blow by blow, on more and more stiff and choice paper, decorated with seals and stamps and royal crowns. *Artium* degree from Skien Latin School 1919, honours. Discharge papers from the military after doing his compulsory service 1920, with laudatory remarks and a recommendation for the Military Academy. Qualifying examination in philosophy at The Royal Frederik University the same year, result: 1.7. Preparatory courses in Greek and Hebrew 1922, both 1.5. Divinity degree 1926 from the University of Oslo, newly so called because of the name-change of the city, *laudabilis*. Ph.D. in theology 1929 from the same university, with a dissertation on the Old Testament subject *The Tree of Life*, printed in a little volume with the picture of a wide-branching tree on the front cover. A grant in 1930 for study at the University of Freiburg im Breisgau; the following year *Privatdozent* in the same place. German doctorate of philosophy in the spring of 1933, on the subject *Das vor-sokratische Denken im Vergleich mit dem hebräisch-christlichen*. That too in the form of a book, to all appearance strictly scientific and without a trace of pleasure for the eye.

All this was what her father jokingly used to call his achievements, a word he turned on his tongue, clearly indicating that it had more than one meaning. Only in his weak, hopeless moments did he take them altogether seriously, otherwise he was in the habit of making fun of them and calling the documents in the folder pulp and padding. As long as his health lasted, he never stopped insisting that they were nothing to boast of, they were mere delusion and window dressing, while life's true nourishment was to be found in altogether different places.

But during his last year of life, after his release from prison, he could no longer take such a broad view of it. As he lay there, defeated and disarmed, squinting at the heap of documents, they rose before his mind's eye as the only fixed points left in his fugitive life history. At his whispered order his daughter had to take now one, now another document in her hand and read it aloud to him. She had learned them by heart long ago and knew which passages in *The Tree of Life* he was particularly proud of and liked to hear over and over again. She had even taught herself to read German so fluently that she had no great difficulty mastering *Der Vergleich*, which – for the sake of convenience – they called "the dissertation with the drawn-out title".

As her voice rose and sank, the sick man lay motionless, following the reading as if in a trance. But he was listening attentively, because here and there he would interrupt with a correction, an indeterminate sigh or a snort of dissatisfaction. The moment he made a sign to her, she lost no time taking a pencil and crossing out a sentence, correcting a printer's error, or replacing a not very felicitous expression with a more precise formulation.

All the same she somehow was on tenterhooks all the time, barely able to hold back her tears. She knew that this quibbling wasn't worthy of her father, and that he would soon realize it and turn about. She knew better than anyone else those changes of mood that would overwhelm him almost without warning, transforming him from a dear friend into a screaming savage. As she turned the pages of *Der Vergleich*, she already felt uneasy, afraid lest a misreading should irritate him and awaken his slumbering rage.

And true enough, without any perceptible reason his cheerful mood vanished and the spirit of rejection came over him. Shaken by a long tremor, the paralyzed figure raised his head with a jerk and ordered her to tear the bundle of papers to pieces and burn it in the stove.

"Away with it!" he screamed. "Do you hear? Burn it all up! The *Apology*, too, then we're through with it!"

"No, no!" she cried, leaning forward over the documents like a frightened hen protecting her chicks. "I won't, I won't! You have said yourself that I must look after your papers, so they won't get lost."

"Yes, I remember," he said, in that murderous tone that she feared more than anything else. "I was stupid enough to make an ignorant child into an archivist. But enough is enough, and you must do as I say!"

"No, no," she sobbed, and as she bent over the documents she tried to push them so far toward the foot of the bed that her father couldn't get at them. "You'll ask for them tomorrow, and then there'll be nothing but dust and ashes."

"Tell me, by the way, wasn't there one more paper, one we forgot to read?" he suddenly asked with a sly gleam in his eye. "What have you done with it, stupid brat that you are? Don't ever get the idea that you can conceal any of my achievements!

"Find it!" he cried, letting out a devilish laugh. "Let us hear what the punishment is for betraying a fatherland one has never had!"

"No, no, I won't do it, I won't do it," she whimpered. She could see from under her raised arm that he had managed to get up into a sitting position; he sat there strangely erect, as if the rage had given him back his strength.

And before she knew how to defend herself, he raised his healthy arm and let it fall like a sledgehammer, heavily and rhythmically, over her thin back.

"Do as I say, you serpent, you basilisk, you little disgusting reptile! Do as I say, do as I say, do as I say!"

But no sooner had the evil spirit left him than he burst into deep sobs, praised her for her courage and thanked her in the tenderest words and expressions. At such times he repeated over and over again that she was his only child, the only one who cared about him and treated him like someone still alive.

And she wiped his tears and answered him in the same heart-rending tones. While she shook out his pillow and helped him to settle down, she vehemently professed her love, assuring him that she had never for a moment been ashamed of him, and that she would always defend him and stand by his side. She grasped the hand that had just hit her and squeezed it tightly in hers, as if she couldn't ever make herself let go of it.

"I'll never, never let you down," she whispered, "don't be afraid, I'll answer them back when they say nasty things about you. And when I grow up some day I'll write a book about you, a new *Apologia* as big and thick as *The Tree of Life* and *Der Vergleich* together."

Her father nodded wearily, and afterward they kept sitting together for a long time hand in hand, until an intimacy grew up between them that helped them overcome their shyness and loosen their tongues. Mostly it didn't take long before her father deserted her and withdrew into himself. But once in a while she succeeded in holding on to him in a conversation that was not merely evasion and a waste of time.

It was a conversation that was always new, different from all previous and later ones, and yet ran through and contained all of them. As it is reproduced here, it has been pieced together from the many questions and answers that took place between father and daughter during the four months he was bedridden.

"Dad, I have often wondered," she might take it into her head to Δ122ask, "how did you feel when you started at Skien Latin School? It couldn't have been very easy for you to start going to school again."

"No, my child, it certainly wasn't easy, believe me. But, you know, I was used to making the best of things, so it worked out in a fashion."

"Did they make fun of you?" she asked suddenly, giving him a searching glance.

"Make fun, how can you think that? What should they make fun of?"

"Oh, I don't know. But I remember you said once that you went through the gate of Skien Latin School like a visitor from another planet."

"Yes, I believe I said something like that once. You see, I had been so much alone, I thought aloud and had developed the bad habit of talking to myself. My clothes smelled of the stable and the barn, so they shunned me and held their noses when I got too close. And as soon as I opened my mouth during class, they fell forward on their desks laughing."

"Was it because you gave the wrong answers to the teachers' questions?"

"No, not exactly wrong, but surprising and a bit off the point, as often happens with autodidacts. And then there was my peasant speech, which they never grew tired of mimicking. Several of them were themselves farm boys who had recently taught themselves urban speech and urban manners. But you know, nobody is a more merciless critic than someone who himself suffers from the same weakness."

"Did you never strike back when someone went after you?"

"No, I stayed clear of that. Already as a youth it was like this with me that, once I gave in to my anger, I was no longer able to control myself."

"Then you probably didn't have any friends the five months you went to the Skien Latin School?"

"No, little Idun, I didn't have any friends, not a single one. I guess I was too proud and refused to forgive them when they began to turn around."

"But wasn't it sad to be by yourself during the recess and to sit alone in your furnished room at night?"

"Oh, there were enough people in my room. There I had Balder to contend with most of the time."

"What, you shared a room with Uncle Balder? I never heard about that before."

"No, nor was it a happy arrangement. He appeared at the end of the winter and forced himself on me, pretending not to hear when I said I couldn't let him stay. From February to May he made himself at home in my bed, so that I could hardly sleep a wink."

"Yes, but how could he do that? After all, you were older than he. It was your room, and you were studying for your final examination."

"Bosh, what do you think Balder cared about that?"

"Was it because he was bigger and stronger than you?"

"He *was* bigger and stronger, but that was not the decisive factor. He had a greater will to power, that was it. Once he'd taken something into his head, he always knew how to force it through. Straight ways and roundabout ways, he knew them all equally well."

"But he must have noticed that he wasn't welcome, and that you wished he were at the back of beyond?"

"Of course he noticed, he wasn't stupid. But, you know, Balder was made in such a way that he always acted in a strangely perverse manner. If you told him no, he turned it into a yes; if he met an obstacle, he took it as an encouragement; if he understood he was not welcome, he became even more determined."

"He went after Aunt Svallaug, didn't he?"

"Oh yes, God help me, he seemed to be obsessed with her and ready to swallow her whole. I quickly realized, of course, that he had come to town to go after her, to prevent her from breaking free. He would stand in front of her window evening after evening, spying on her half the night. But Svallaug was in service with some good people, and the end result was that they intervened and told him to get lost."

"What are you saying, was he chased away like a Peeping Tom? I imagine he must've felt pretty bad about that, since he was forced to give up for once."

"He didn't give up, don't you believe it. He was down in the mouth for a couple of weeks, licking his wounds. Then he was sitting pretty again and cocky as never before. Within the end of the month he had racked his brains and come up with a new strategy, which he wanted me to join him in."

"Oh, no, Dad, now you almost frighten me. You didn't let yourself be – "

"No, don't worry, I didn't let myself be persuaded, although he kicked up a terrible row and accused me of having no family feeling. Finally he must have realized that he wouldn't get anywhere with me. For suddenly one day he vanished, and I had no news from him for several months. It then turned out – "

"Yes, what then? Hurry up and tell me before you lose it!"

"There, there, my child, not too fast. You must remember I've had a stroke, and that my brain stands completely still sometimes. What was it I wanted to say? Oh yes, Balder who suddenly made himself invisible."

"You said that when you finally heard from him, it turned out that – "

"Yes, that's true, now I remember. It turned out that he had taken a trip to Fyresdal and looked up Dean Quisling. He settled down for the whole

121

summer up there, not budging till the Dean had collected money for him so he could go to a rural gymnasium. For thanks he stole two valuable books from the Dean's library and later sold them at a good profit. The theft was never discovered, for the Dean was old and feeble, and his library was so large that no one in the family knew it altogether. Later the thief made merry over his robbery, using it as an example of how early he had been drawn to the world of books."

"But Aunt Svallaug, what happened to her? She ended up getting together with him anyway, didn't she?"

"Dear me, yes, that's what happened. She held out for more than twenty years, but Balder had stamina and time to wait. One day her resistance was broken – life had treated her so badly that she was ripe for his stranglehold."

"And now they're all gone," Idun whispered, with a faraway look. "Both Balder and Svallaug and Steingrim and Kjellfrid."

"Yes, little Idun," her father repeated with a nearly imperceptible change of words. "Now we're all gone."

His voice sounded strangely remote and alien and faded away in a long sigh as he released her hand. A moment later his head fell back on the pillow and his eyes closed, and when the daughter bent over him she couldn't decide whether he had fallen asleep or had merely sunk into one of his many moments of preoccupation. Unless he had . . .

She suddenly got up and began to collect the documents, while keeping a watchful eye on the patient. When she had replaced the folder in the drawer, she turned around and gave the man in the bed a last uneasy look, before stealing quietly out of the room.

IV

Treason

1

I have not yet related a surprising thing that happened to me last autumn, more specifically during those six days when I was at large before I fell into the Oslo Fjord.

The third or fourth day, just as I was hurrying from one hiding place to the next, I suddenly stopped dead and came back to my senses. The flight demon let go of me, my thoughts cleared, and I no longer gloated over playing a cat and mouse game with my superiors.

"Now listen, Idun, my old furtive friend," I said to myself. "What if you climbed out of your underworld and quite simply took a walk in town? Strolled briskly and boldly up and down Karl Johan Street just like anyone else, waiting to see what would happen? All your ideas about being persecuted would then be tested, and in all likelihood they would turn out to be nothing but idle fantasies and nightmarish visions. You wouldn't need to sneak like a thief along the walls of the houses anymore, but could go along with the crowd and turn the corners as if nothing were the matter. Should someone come and place a heavy hand on your shoulder, well, it was a risk worth taking. Then there would be an end to your dissipation, and you'd just have to go along and let yourself be put in storage again."

I stayed in hiding until darkness came on, then stole by fits and starts up to the furnished room in Homansbyen that I still keep as my permanent abode in this world. The hospital has the key, and in their great wisdom my benefactors believe that it is the only one. It is a maid's room with a tiny toilet that at one time was part of a large residence, but was separated from it when the apartment changed owners. Since then, the room can be entered only through the courtyard, and she who lives there has to climb five floors of back stairs before she is home. It is her well-kept secret that the doorstep is loose and that she can get hold of an extra key by raising it and sticking her hand in.

Neither in the courtyard nor on the back stairs did I meet anyone, and I let myself in without any problem. The room was stuffy after my long absence, and I opened the window a crack to get some fresh air. I didn't dare turn on the light, but groped my way noiselessly up to the bed and threw myself on it fully dressed. The purpose of my visit was to get a good night's sleep before setting out on my new adventure. I wanted to wash and groom myself after three days' filth and get out some clothes from the closet that didn't tally with my description. In this new, transfigured guise I would then descend from on high, cut across Palace Park and mingle with the throng on Karl Johan Street.

Everything went as it should. It felt good to stretch out in one's own bed after three sleepless nights; I slept so soundly that the day was well advanced before I awoke. Unfortunately there was only cold water in the shower, but at least I was able to wash my hair and rinse off most of the odours of vagrancy. Having eaten some stale crackers and taken a few mouthfuls of water with them, I made ready to go out. I took a look at myself in the mirror one last time, passed a comb through my hair and bedizened myself with whatever jewellery I had, among other things the gold chain with the rubies my maternal grandfather gave me on his deathbed. But after thinking it over, I took it off again to keep it for some other time. Suddenly I remembered that I needed some money, and before replacing my secret bank box in the mousehole behind the panel, I helped myself to a spanking new thousand-krone note and a few crumpled hundred-krone notes.

Nothing sensational happened on Karl Johan Street. I was in my element as a stranger among strangers and joined the crowd so imperceptibly that it was almost disappointing. I wandered back and forth between Palace Place and Railway Square as many as four times without attracting the least attention. In my self-assurance I even tried to tempt fate and make some small deviations from the straight path. At regular intervals I asked somebody what time it was, stopped and listened to street musicians, bent down and patted toddlers and dogs, and crossed the street against a red light at the Storting, barely escaping being run over.

Later I slipped through the door of the Grand Café without first stopping at the checkroom, and walked straight through the room past the service counter, pretending I was just looking for someone. Before finding my way out again, I stopped before the large painting on the back wall, contemplating it with the air of a connoisseur and losing myself in speculations. I wondered about all those Kristiania Bohemians who walked in and out on the canvas – could they conceivably have had the same errand in the café as myself? Suddenly it was perfectly clear to me that my excursion in the city had a double purpose: I was split in two and wanted at once to be seen and to make myself invisible, to hunt and be hunted.

And that was perhaps the way it was with most people in this place, living and dead. How about that avatar of Henrik Ibsen, for example, who at this very moment entered from the street? Would he shun human society and shuffle over to the corner to have his whisky and soda, or would he seek out a window seat, where he could sit and act entirely unaffected while displaying his splendid isolation?

I must have looked quite convincing as I stood absorbed in thought before the painting, for not a single waiter batted an eye before I quickly turned and left the place with gracious nods all around. A strange mood had come over me, I was so elated that I virtually floated during my next walk down to Railway Square and back again. To celebrate the day I bought myself a triple ice, a regular ice torch in green, yellow and pink which I raised triumphantly into the air like some goddess of liberty as I crossed the street to sit on a bench under the falling leaves of the Students' Promenade.

That was the moment when the surprise occurred. As I sat there on the bench lapping up ice cream and sun in turn, a man suddenly stopped in front of me on the pavement and sent me a determined, but still considerate glance. I started when I caught sight of him – my first thought was that it must be one of my sister's private eyes and that I was rapidly heading for storage and locked doors.

But when I had taken a closer look at the person, my dread abated somewhat. The man lacked the smooth, disinfected appearance characteristic of the lackeys of the health service, and looked rather like a slightly absent-minded professor. He was dressed in correct but comfortable clothes and was carrying an old prehistoric briefcase, which struck me as almost touching after all the attaché cases I had passed on my walk. I didn't dare look directly at him, but a few quick glances told me that I was in the vicinity of a human being, a quiet man in his forties with a grizzled full beard, high forehead, and gentle eyes behind a pair of big horn-rimmed glasses.

It looked as though he was considering sitting down on the bench but didn't quite know how it could be done, since I was making myself at home in the middle of it, with my things strewn around on both sides. I stammered forth an excuse and was just about to move aside, when he signalled with his hand that I could take it easy.

"Tell me, aren't you the author Idun Hov?" he asked, taking a step towards me.

I became so frightened that everything went black, and I sat completely motionless a long while, staring down at the tips of my shoes. I could see that the ice cream was trickling down my hand and into the sleeve of the nice little suit jacket I once, in another life, had inherited from my landlady. The author Idun Hov, what kind of curious phantom was that? Could it be possible that she was still alive, and that somebody addressed himself to her without trying to console her or make fun of her? I had preserved a remote recollection of her, and it was that which gave me the strength to stay afloat from one day to the next. But it was so endlessly long since anybody had called me an author that it sounded like a slip of the tongue or a poor joke.

"Pardon me for intruding," he said, after clearing his throat. "But I was just this moment trying to figure out how I could arrange a meeting with you. And then I find you here, in the middle of Karl Johan Street, having an ice!"

I realized that he must be well informed about my social status and knew all there was to know about me. I turned away and gave a long look in the direction of the Palace, feeling a blush of shame burning my cheeks. Would I never again feel confident and on an equal footing before another human being, but always have to contend with a life history that turned me into a doubtful case?

"Pardon me, but you *are* the author Idun Hov, aren't you?" he said, somewhat more diffidently and speaking formally. "Perhaps I am mistaken and confuse you with someone else."

I noticed that he had withdrawn a little and realized that he would soon go away if I didn't reveal who I was. I looked at him and nodded vaguely, but clearly enough to leave no doubt that I acknowledged my identity.

That did it. He took a long step forward, held out his hand and, waiting until I had wiped my own, introduced himself as the new editor at my publisher's. Yes, of all things, he really said "your publisher", as if I owned the whole shop and could order the personnel around to my heart's content.

I bit my lip and tried to remember, and for a moment there was something that didn't tally. Then it dawned on me: I realized that he must have replaced that little squirt with the fisheyes I'd had so many run-ins with at one time. Of course, of course, I thought to myself, with an instructive tap on my forehead. Time passes and new brooms start sweeping, even in a dusty old publishing house like yours. Thousands of books have been opened and closed since your time, people come and go, and what is more natural than that one editor takes the place of another?

I squinted at the man with the shabby case, which was suspended from his hand like some mysterious appendage. With a bit of imagination I made it look like a bird's wing, and at the same moment the entire figure changed, turning into a spring swallow that descended on Karl Johan Street in the middle of September and harbingered better times. Mr Fisheye had yielded his place to Mr Chirpety-Chirp, and I could already hear new trills in the air. But what in the world did this harbinger of luck want with me? What sort of flute tones did he wish to whistle into the ear of an author who was a psychiatric patient and hadn't published a book for ages?

When he had explained his business and reassured me that he was in earnest, I followed him to his office, where I remained for over two hours, until it was near closing time. He fetched food and drink from the canteen and placed it in front of me, as if he had no suspicion at all that I had been roaming around for three days and nights, eating leftovers from the trash baskets. What we talked about for such a long time is not quite clear to me, and afterwards I have often come to question the experience, fearing that it was all nothing but a dream and wishful thinking.

What he wanted to talk to me about was, incredibly, a new edition of three of my books. During his summer vacation he had quite by chance happened to read the little bittersweet story of mistaken identity, *The Papessa*, and it had made an indelible impression on him. He didn't hesitate to call it a classic and a gem of narrative art, and he had been surprised that such a rare book could be altogether forgotten after fourteen years.

"Oh, that can't be very much of a surprise," I chuckled, helping myself to a mouthful of coffee. "It was forgotten from the moment it was displayed in the bookstores. As far as I recall, only thirty-seven copies were sold, though the publisher had surpassed himself and placed an ad as big as a good-sized stamp."

"I read it breathlessly and at a single sitting," he said with warmth in his voice. "And afterward I got hold of your other books and was not disappointed. I promised myself that I would do something to promote your work, and persuade the publisher to reprint three of your books. That I've done, and I can only congratulate you! To begin with, *The Papessa* will appear in our classics series, it's already included in our spring catalogue and will be available sometime in early June. Then two other books will follow. I'm thinking of your modern Oedipus drama *Jocasta's Revenge* and the little psycho-philosophical thriller *The Angel and the Monster*."

Before we parted we agreed that he would send for me some day at the end of May, so that we could write a contract and agree upon everything regarding royalties and complimentary copies. When he mentioned royalties, a thought suddenly crossed my mind, and I asked if I could possibly have the money in cash when I came to sign the contract. It was just a whim on my part, and when I asked I wasn't aware of having any ulterior motives. Only afterwards has it occurred to me that my impulses are ahead of my thoughts, and that already in September I was busy with plans that could have great and sweeping consequences.

As I was leaving, groping my way through the labyrinth of the publishing house, I came past the door that at one time led to Fisheye's office. I had nearly passed by when I noticed that the corridor was completely deserted and that a bunch of keys was in the door. I stopped short and, to be on the safe side, looked around in all directions before pulling the jingling chain out of the lock and slipping it into my shoulder bag. I immediately felt violent palpitations, both because it was a brash thing to do and because I had a presentiment of what I would use the keys for.

For a few seconds I was as though spellbound, not knowing which way to turn. Then my thoughts cleared up, and I hurried on through the publishing labyrinth, down flights of stairs and around corners and to the end of the last corridor, through the glass door, past the sales desk, out through yet another door and down the stairs to the basement floor. It was seven minutes to four, the entire building was closing down, but not a soul could be seen anywhere. The checkroom was still full of street clothes, invisible feet were on their way, doors banged and voices buzzed far away, but I managed to escape into the toilet without being noticed by anyone. There I sat down on the bowl with my elbows on my knees, trying to figure out what I had in mind to do, and whether it was wise of me to make up that sort of adventure within the walls of "my own publishing house". I again laughed at the expression, which in a way gave me extensive authority and turned my enterprise into something that was quite legal. I sat a long while on the seat, listening to the noise from the floor above, near voices and faraway voices, light footsteps, dragging footsteps, firm footsteps, all of which receded more and more as the hand on my watch approached half-past four. At one moment someone took hold of the door to my hiding place, but went on to the other toilet when she realized it was occupied. A little later I heard her come out again and wash her hands; the door banged shut behind her, the hand on my watch suddenly made a big jump, and a profound stillness descended on the deserted building.

From something Chirpety-Chirp had said when I happened to drop my milk glass on the floor, I had understood that the cleaning personnel would only show up at six o'clock the following morning. That meant that for twelve hours I had the place to myself and could steal into Fisheye's office and use it for my overnight lodging. If I wasn't mistaken, there was a sofa by one wall, not exactly a dream bed but a cosy nest where I could curl up as in the womb and slumber sweetly till daybreak.

I was not mistaken. The sofa was where it should be, though otherwise the room looked very much changed, with hard, cold surfaces and seven years of expansion of human omnipotence. I sneaked about in my stocking feet, touching all the equipment before I could believe my own eyes. And when I got to the very altar, the sacrosanct PC, I nearly fell on my knees and prayed a silent prayer to the deity of estrangement.

When I had finished looking around, I peeked into the refrigerator, where I found what I hadn't expected but very badly needed. The little flat whisky bottle was nearly full, and I put it to my lips and drank till I had to stop to catch my breath. Then I curled up on the small round sofa and took another swig from the bottle; I sensed that my spirits were rising and that I felt like laughing. Suddenly I was reconciled with all and everything, I ascended into the heavens and could observe the miseries of life from an elevated plane. I waved three frivolous fingers in the air, wishing Mr Fisheye a pleasant journey as his finicky spirit left the house and went elsewhere. He was now head of public relations to one of the oil companies, according to what Chirpety-Chirp had told me. Look at that! I thought, taking another swig from the bottle, finally he had landed in the right place. He no longer had to struggle with any overwhelming linguistic riches, but had a manageable vocabulary and a simple syntax before his eyes. No quaint or unusual expressions would make him open his eyes wide, no pun disturb his peace of mind, no imagination outfly his understanding, and no ingenuity provoke his pedantry.

I laughed aloud when I recalled my controversies with him, until I suddenly had a start and pressed my hand against my lips. It was not simply that this horselaugh could betray me and attract attention to my taking the law into my own hands. It dawned on me that it did not spring from any natural gaiety but was a kind of uncanny echo of a grief I would never be able to liberate myself from.

When all was still again and I raised my head of a sudden, I noticed that I had acquired a new sensitivity to sound. Not the kind of sensitivity that immediately picks up what someone else is saying, but a delayed sense of hearing that recalls fragments of a conversation concluded long ago. My recollection raced ahead like a defective tape recording, where long parts had been destroyed and erased. At the same time space was expanded and I began to hear voices, a sure sign that my susceptibility had reached breaking point and mental derangement was imminent.

As in a waking dream I heard Chirpety-Chirp ask why I had stopped writing, and whether I couldn't see myself picking up the thread again and continuing where I left off. My own answer was vague, but not so reserved that it couldn't be interpreted as promising. Like every other writer with glowing irons in the fire, I made myself mysterious and replied that we would wait and see – well, I believe I actually hinted that I had great plans and was already under way. What I was working on, I naturally refused to say. But the work was getting on smoothly, I said, and the manuscript was accumulating into a sizeable pile.

He looked kindly at me and nodded his agreement, but a deep, vertical wrinkle that I didn't like formed on his brow. We sat talking back and forth about my new manuscript for a while, with me feeling more and more ahead of the game, so much so that in the end I was generous enough to promise that the book would be ready the following autumn. But there was throughout an all too airy quality to our conversation, and the place was strangely indeterminate, as if I had been given a sort of supernatural apti-tude for being in many places at once. Now I was sitting in the corridor of the loony bin, mumbling to myself in a low voice, now I found myself proud and cocky in Chirpety-Chirp's office, now I was lying curled up in a semi-slumber on dear Fisheye's sofa. As evening turned into night, my head began buzzing ominously – a long, intrusive, painful singing note that cut into my auditory passages like a glass splinter and made me sit up in the sofa.

"Tomfoolery!" I said to myself; or rather, I shouted it so loudly that I started and put my hand to my lips. "The idea of you writing?" I said contemptuously to myself. "You who no longer know what it means to hope and live your life from hand to mouth, without any prospect. You who have lost your future and thereby the ability to transport yourself in imagination and have taken to doing fiction with your body. The only novel you can write is another physical adventure where you let yourself go, getting messed up in all sorts of impossible situations. Your legs are your only writing tool, streets and alleyways are the hard, insensitive pages that receive your imprints and erase them as soon as you round the next corner."

When I had looked at my watch, I sank back in the sofa and began to wonder how I could be lying in someone else's office at night without anyone seeming to have discovered my break-in. How could it be, I asked myself, that no one had become suspicious when the bunch of keys disappeared? Was I sitting here caught in my own trap, or was the occupant of the office just as absent-minded as myself, who could never remember where I put things? Yes, that must be the explanation. While I was lurking in the toilet biding my time, a person of unknown sex – but in all likelihood a male – had been running around in the publishing maze like a rat in a lab experiment, having a thousand confused thoughts about where he could have forgotten his keys. Finally he had procured himself a key from the janitor, soundly locked the door and pushed the problem aside till the next day. And presto, hocus pocus, abracadabra, tomorrow morning he would surely be in for a surprise, plus a big headache, when he came to the scene of the crime and found the keys in the door. I had a fresh attack of laughter at the mere thought and wondered how soon he would discover that someone had raided his refrigerator and emptied his whisky bottle.

I must have slept intermittently, but during the hours before daybreak I was mostly awake and lay thinking about the book that had been rediscovered and would come out again in the spring. As always when I am lucky, my critical spirit revived, a spirit of doubt and rejection not unlike the one that had plagued my poor father during his final days.

Was the book really as good as Chirpety-Chirp had said? I asked myself. Had he read it carefully enough, and could I trust his words – if, that is, he had said anything about it at all? What if it was all just nonsense, a fabrication of my overwrought brain, which had run idle for so long it was apt to produce anything whatsoever? What if I wasn't lying on the sofa in Fisheye's deserted office at all but in my bed at the loony bin, where everything under the sun was possible: my imagination running riot, nightmares erupting, divisions and doublings occurring, and all kinds of self-glorifying wishes coming true?

I raised my head and looked about me but couldn't get a clear idea of the place; the night rushed spectrally through the room, and only a faint glimmer of light fell in through the window. Jumping onto the floor, I once more went around and touched every article in the room to reassure myself that they were really there. Yes, they were all there, my hands stroked and patted the hard surfaces with tenderness, as if caressing friendly living creatures. Thank God, my imagination was not tricking me, I didn't find myself in the loony bin, but perhaps in a place that was just as bad, a place of lawlessness, break-in and thievishness that I could only leave when the cleaning women came and shut off the alarm.

In the morning I quieted down and experienced a few moments of remarkable clearsightedness, during which I neither overestimated nor belittled myself but found peace in a self-respect all my own, one that was not awarded me by some outside authority. Suddenly I knew that *The Papessa* was a fine, rare book that I needn't feel ashamed of. And what's more, it was one of those passionate narratives that can be elevated and expanded by the imagination but that only personal experience can fill and make credible.

But with all its fervour and empathy, it was nonetheless so strange that the Zeitgeist couldn't be expected to accept it. It indulged in religious meditations in a soulless world, had the audacity to be ambiguous, was full of smut and filth, depicted insanity and possession, mixed the holy with the profane, employed humour in improper places, and imbued myth with honour and dignity in an age when the word "myth" was equated with lies and falsification of reality. Maybe it wasn't so strange that the reception was lukewarm or downright condescending, and that no more than thirty-seven copies of the book were sold.

I closed my eyes and saw before me those thirty-seven uncowed readers whom, in the year of Our Lord 1979, had defied all arbiters of taste and bought the book. In order to make the group more concrete, I arranged it in two long rows, with eighteen persons in each row and one extra person standing in front like a sort of Virgil in Dante's comedy. What sort of talk was it that said the book had not caught on and that it lacked readers? I laid my head back and reviewed the small gathering like a conjurer, until it grew before my mind's eye and became an enormous crowd of good readers, fairly evenly divided between the two genders, although the author was a woman and ought to write litanies for her sisters only. Those thirty-seven readers were people who didn't belong to any definite stratum of the population, they were neither exclusive nor omnivorous, didn't go along with the crowd or speak with one voice, didn't profess any established creed or conviction. They were searching and unadjusted individuals who were still growing and wandering, often lonely, sad and alienated in a world where the *esprit de corps* was winning out and quality was synonymous with quantity.

I let my head rest peacefully against the soft back of the sofa, and for the first time in a long while I dared to accept my years of wandering, with all the distress and delusions they entailed. That was in the days when the Zeitgeist had a knife between its teeth, when there was a war of all against all, and my sisters barricaded themselves in the castle of the bourgeoisie, unless they marched forward in a body with a rose sticking out of a clenched fist. By contrast to these red and blue amazons I was really unpropertied and, in every sense of the word, unprotected. A long exhausting previous history had separated me from family and fatherland; I was beyond every creed, released from all belonging, and inclined to roam about for as long as my legs would carry me. Over a number of dizzying years I was wearing out my soles on the highways of the Continent, except when I settled somewhere for an indefinite time to earn a shilling to keep body and soul together. Wherever I went I took whatever work was available, harvesting grapes, raking leaves, digging root crops and cleaning latrines; or I did some innocent clowning in the street, in order to be able to winter in one of the big cities and play the role of a carefree tourist. That is how I chanced to be in Rome on just that winter day in 1976 when I met my Papessa and got the idea of writing a book about her.

The meeting took place on a bitterly cold day in February, just after I had shivered my way through the winter on the outskirts of the city. It was my last year of wandering before I was sent home at the expense of the consulate; I was nearly forty years old and had reached an age when wandering at large was no longer a sign of a youthful desire to see the world, but of physical and psychological misery. I had had a late abortion, during the fifth month, was nearly penniless, and lived wretchedly in a basement, on condition I sweep the yard and run errands for the landlord. Innumerable small and big misfortunes had conspired against me. I was still bleeding a little after the abortion and was plagued by a deep cough, which I neglected in the hope that the warm weather would soon arrive and clear it up. I was emaciated beyond recognition from malnutrition and illness, had practically stopped grooming myself and looked worse than the streetwalkers, for one of which I was often mistaken and approached as I stole through the district at dusk. My condition was so well known in that part of the Eternal City that I attracted little attention, but merged with the faceless stream of down-at-heel characters who had a worse time of it than I did, having neither house nor home and being forced to sleep under the city's bridges and viaducts.

But I still retained a remnant of dignity and tried as best as I could to give an appearance of being simply a slightly shabby tourist who let things slide of her own free will. I washed myself from top to toe under the faucet in the basement at least once a week, put on what respectable clothes I had, and set out for the heart of the city to look around and to disappear in the crowd.

One day I was on my way out to the Aventine Hill when I suddenly felt like dropping by the Fortuna Virilis temple to look at the frescoes there. Passing by the Bocca della Verità, like most tourists I couldn't resist the temptation to put my hand into the Mouth of Truth and sound out my momentary fate. It struck me as being uncertain, but not directly threatening, so I withdrew my hand, shrugged my shoulders and continued *dolce far niente* up the stairs to the temple.

As I entered the portal, I saw that someone was squatting before the entrance, his back half turned towards me. At first I thought it was a pilgrim kneeling at prayer, but when I got a little closer I realized that it must be a homeless person, sleeping with his head against the wall. As I walked by, the figure turned abruptly and opened his eyes. I then saw that it was a woman, not many years older than myself. She emitted a stench that made me back away and catch my breath, but the woman looked robust and gave no impression of squalor. Her face was fresh and ruddy, her eyes lively, and her whole figure strong and in fine shape. She had protected herself from thecold with good clothes and a tight-fitting crocheted hood that revealed only the contours of her face. Her hands were bare and seemed strangely emaciated against her coarse clothes, and as homeless people are in the habit of doing, she had her feet in a plastic bag to keep them warm.

I was about to walk on when she raised a crooked finger and motioned me to come closer. As I advanced hesitantly, she pulled a small pillow from one of her bags, tossed it over to me and invited me to be seated. When she saw that I was reluctant to do so, she broke into a low, hoarse laughter and snapped her fingers in the air to make me decide. To persuade me that I ought to sit down, she pointed in the direction of the temple door, shook her head several times and abandoned herself to a torrential stream of talk.

She seemed to be amazingly polyglot, now speaking Italian, now English and French, or she resorted to a mysterious world language for none but the initiated. Most of what she said was lost on the wind, but I understood enough to realize that the temple was closed and would only be open to tourists later in the day.

I settled on the pillow and accepted a piece of chocolate that she held out to me with an incredibly dirty hand. She sat a while rattling her bags, arranging them in a special order the significance of which I was in no position to understand. Meanwhile she went on talking at random, as though to an absent or invisible listener.

At first I didn't grasp very much of what she was saying, nor was it likely that there was much coherence to her outpourings. I mostly listened to her voice, which was warm and alive and had an inflection that somehow didn't belong to any of the languages she tried to master. This peculiarity sharpened my attention more and more, making me listen with twice my usual sensitivity. From her rambling stream of talk I understood that something must have led her mind astray, that she couldn't be all there. Her account was hard to follow, but from the many repetitions I was gradually able to get hold of a story that both amused me and went straight to my heart. When she finally fell silent, she let out a deep, satisfied sigh and sat a long while looking at me with the gaze of a sibyl or a soothsayer.

The content of her prophecies in all their enormity was this: In one month, when Lent was over and Easter approaching, great events would take place in the Eternal City. For the first time in history the Pope would take a wife, thus making good his confession of faith in Santa Maria. And what's more, after the wedding he would retire and transfer his holy office to the Papessa. Ha-ha, what did I have to say to that? she laughed, looking at me with twinkling eyes. In five weeks she would no longer sit here freezing cold with her feet in a plastic bag, but would be picked up and brought in a gilded sedan chair to the Lateran Church in a solemn procession. And there the triple crown would be placed on her head, and she would be anointed and elevated to Papessa Giovanna the Second.

"Why the second and not the first?" she asked, apropos of nothing, when she had sat for a moment and read the scepticism in my face. Well, for the simple reason that there had already been a Papessa Giovanna the First. She would be glad to tell me about her tomorrow, if I came back to hear the rest. It was a long story, and now she was tired and wanted to sleep a bit, if I would be so kind as to excuse her. The Fortuna temple would open shortly, she said, at which time, out of deference to her future position, she would have to gather up her things and find another place to stay until evening came and the temple closed.

I thanked her for the invitation and promised to show up the next day at the same time. When I gave her my hand for goodbye, she seized it greedily and kissed it several times, before placing her finger to her lips and asking me to keep mum about what she had told me. No more must come out than had already transpired, she explained to me. The world was full of unbelief, and she had already suffered enough for her elevation. Tomorrow she would tell me more about that, if I decided to do myself the favour of paying her my respects.

I had become intensely interested in her life history, and as agreed I returned the following morning at the same time. Before climbing the stairs to the Fortuna temple, I stopped at the kiosk on Ponte Fabricio and bought a container of soft drink and a bag of cornetti that I wanted to offer her in return for the chocolate I had received from her the day before. I could see her from far away as she sat waiting for me, blowing me a long succession of papal kisses as I climbed the last few steps and entered the peristyle.

Our new meeting began somewhat awkwardly, because she refused to accept the treats I had brought her. I had to understand, she said almost sternly, that considering what was to happen to her, she could not break her fast. The only food she was allowed under these happy circumstances was a little birdseed and a few mouthfuls of water from special initiated water faucets. She had nothing but derision for the soft drink, telling me it was the devil himself who had planted the straw in the carton, in order to tempt a holy woman to partake of his dark juices. But I could see that she was sending long glances toward the bag with the fragrant pastry, and when I picked up a cornetto and offered it to her, she hesitantly accepted it and dug her teeth ravenously into it, after first making the sign of the cross over it and mumbling forth a long string of prayers.

When she had swallowed it and brushed the crumbs off her chin, she looked anxiously about her, as if to assure herself that no one had witnessed her sacrilege. Then she leaned back against the wall and closed her eyes for a long while. When she opened them again, she seemed strangely confused and stared at me as if she had never seen me before. I had to remind her of our conversation the previous day before she woke up and became a little more obliging. But it was only when I had kneeled down and, at her command, kissed the foot she extended to me from the plastic bag, that contact was again established between us.

To help her get started, I asked cautiously about the troubles she had undergone for her elevation, and she wasted no time in picking up the thread. The Eternal City had become an evil and corrupt place, she told me, nobody wanted to have anything to do with her despite her proven holiness and the honour that awaited her. The last few weeks she had run all about town and put up posters announcing her wedding with the Pope and her ascent of the Holy See. But people just laughed at her, and the paste on the posters had barely time to dry before the cardinals sent out their spies to search them out and tear them down.

She had also been to the city's churches and convents to announce the sacred event, but to no use. The priests met her with the greatest suspicion and did all they could to prevent the truth from coming to light. But her sisters, the nuns, were the worst of all, she confided in a whisper. Santa Maria, they refused to receive her one and all, and wouldn't give her a roof over her head until the great day dawned. The French nuns at the top of the Spanish Stairs had simply asked her to get lost, and when she resisted, they had caught her by her arms and legs and thrown her out as a blasphemer. But she had taken it all as a trial and had not lost courage. "I don't give a fig for them," she cried, raising one arm in a conjuring gesture. "Do you hear what I'm saying, I forgive them and don't give a fig for any of them!"

I gave a start as she flung out these last words, staring at her in the greatest amazement. "But of all things, you're Swedish, aren't you?" I cried. "And I'm Norwegian. We speak practically the same language, and here we sit and try to communicate in one foreign language after another."

A long silence followed, during which she gave me some rather hostile glances, as if annoyed to be exposed as simply a Scandinavian. But gradually she became gentler and gave me her hand in reconciliation. Her stream of talk had abated, but during the brief period we still were left undisturbed she produced an occasional outburst that gave me some insight into the story of her life. She now spoke mostly Swedish, but once in a while when she grew particularly beside herself she switched over to Italian or mummified herself behind her self-created sacred language.

Eleven years ago she had come to Rome as a young student on a fellowship, she told me. At home, in Uppsala, she was considered to be extremely promising, and she went abroad equally possessed by a thirst for knowledge and by ambition. Her subject was the history of religion, and she had intended to write her dissertation on Saint Birgitta of Vadstena. But everything had gone wrong for her, and she who had such great expectations for her stay abroad met nothing but one disappointment after another.

After a few years of exile she had become a shadow of her former self. She fell victim to melancholy, and a whopping headache sat like an iron ring around her forehead and made it impossible for her to concentrate. Having run out of money, she shut herself off from people more and more. When finally she had an unhappy love affair with an Italian, she was completely knocked out. At one time she had been committed to a psychiatric hospital for people without means of their own, a sheer loony bin where the insane raved and screamed around the clock like the souls of the damned inDante's *Inferno*. They had just decided she would be sent home for further treatment when she managed to escape and make herself invisible in the Eternal City.

And so, being homeless, she had roamed here for many years, she couldn't say how many, because a strange thing had happened to time: it had both become infinitely long and incredibly short. She had abandoned all hope and had sunk as low as could be, when her prayers were heard and everything was brought to a good issue. The message concerning her elevation at first sounded just like the cooing of pigeons, and she didn't dare put any trust in it. For a long time it was more of a nuisance than a message, just as one may feel the everlasting cooing of the pigeons as an irritating nuisance. But suddenly one day she understood that it was the Holy Ghost itself that had descended to earth and was speaking to her. Ha-ha, everybody else thought that the call was simply coming from an ordinary pigeon, she was the only one in the Eternal City who knew better. And now she sat here waiting for her elevation, taking a silent delight in her precious secret.

I was just about to ask about Papessa Giovanna the First, when I caught sight of a policeman coming up the stairs. He entered the portico with firm steps and approached our meeting place gesticulating so wildly it wasn't difficult to guess his errand. The Papessa made herself small and crept closer to the wall, as if she wanted to disappear into it. When shortly the policeman got there, he struck her a blow with his club and showered her with words of abuse that I wasn't able to make out. But I understood that the woman must be an old acquaintance of his and that it probably wasn't the first time he'd come upon her and ordered her to be gone.

I went up to him and placed my hand on his arm, asking him to be a little more gentle. But that I shouldn't have done, it seems. He turned brusquely toward me and spoke to me in the same coarse tone; he obviously took me to be a bird of the same feather as my papal friend. I was afraid he might ask for my papers, or take me to the police precinct without more ado, so I was quite relieved when he simply gave me a nudge and told me to get lost. Turning around before descending the stairs, I saw that the Papessa had risen to her feet and was collecting her things. I waved at her, called *arrive erci* several times and tried in the last moment to give her a sign to the effect that I would be back the next day. But she didn't take any notice of me. The policeman was on top of her, watching over her tidying-up, and the last thing I saw was that he gave one of her bags a kick to speed things along.

The next day she was not there when I came back, nor any of the following days. When I had shown up for an entire week and looked in vain for her in the streets around Bocca della Verità, I had to resign myself to not seeing her again. But the story of Papessa Giovanna the First had awakened my curiosity, and I wanted to find out whether there was anything to it or whether it was nothing but a fantasy.

In the Vatican Library there was nobody, naturally, willing to hear any talk about a female Pope. When I finally managed to make myself understood, I was surveyed from top to toe and turned away with strict admonitions to have respect for the sacred. Nor did my visits to other libraries lead to anything, and I was on the point of giving up my research when an archivist at a small library nodded with understanding as he listened to me.

Papessa Giovanna the First was certainly just a myth, he said. She had scarcely ever existed in the material space we call reality. But it was equally certain that she had won herself a place in history and lived on in the best of health in popular tradition.

He asked me to wait while he took a trip to the archives, and shortly afterwards he came back with an old folio and handed it across the counter. It couldn't be taken away, he said, but I could study it for as long as I pleased in the reading room. It was an old mediaeval chronicle called *Gesta Romanorum* which dealt with the tribulations of the Holy See in a burlesque and uninhibited style. On the whole it stuck to the chronology, but it embroidered the old myths and mysteries in such an exuberant fashion that it was repudiated by official tradition.

The old book was a wellspring of popular fantasy, and it was with repressed laughter that I read the first chapter about Pope Gregory the Great. As a reverend cardinal he had one day learned the horrible truth that he was the fruit of an immoral relationship between brother and sister, and that the woman he had married in his first youth was his own mother. To expiate the family sins he interrupts his career and sentences himself to exile on a desolate islet far out in the ocean. He remains there for seventeen years and has shrunk to a shellfish-like creature by the time he is proclaimed Pope and the cardinals come to fetch him. The envoys are in for a severe fright when they find him out on the islet, but before their mission has been concluded everything has turned out for the best. When the hermit steps into the boat he is no bigger than a sea urchin, but on the voyage across the sea he keeps growing steadily, until the man who steps ashore at Ostia is a great and awe-inspiring prince of the church who lets himself be hailed as Pope Gregory the First.

As far as Papessa Giovanna (also called Johanna) was concerned, her story wasn't quite that grotesque. She was a young lady of the nobility from Ingelheim, who had fallen in love with a prelate and took to wearing men's clothes to be able to live with him in the monastery at Fulda. Later they went to Athens together, where they studied theology and philosophy and distinguished themselves by their great learning as well as by their piety. When her sweetheart died, Johanna took the name Johannes Angelicus and was soon so famous for her wisdom that she was called to Rome as a cardinal. When Pope Leo the Fourth died in 855, she was elected Pope by a unanimous college of cardinals and elevated to the Holy See under the name John the Eighth. But her pontificate turned out to be sadly brief; after a lapse of three years her female sex was exposed under dramatic circumstances. She had become pregnant after a love affair with one of the servants at the Vatican, but had for a long time managed to conceal her condition behind the flowing papal draperies. Then one day, in the middle of the Corpus Domini procession, the time came for her to give birth. She began having birth pangs on the way from St Peter's to the Lateran, and by the time the procession had reached its destination she had given birth to a boy before the eyes of a gaping multitude. When the spectators had recovered slightly from the shock, they fell upon her in furious indignation and killed both her and the child on the spot. After that day a special ceremony was required before a cardinal could ascend the Holy See. He had to sit bare-bottomed on a night-stool that was so ingeniously designed that an inspector could stick his head in and reassure himself that the Pope was of the right gender.

The legend about Papessa Giovanna would hardly have come down to posterity if someone hadn't had the idea of putting up a relief sculpture of the event at some point on the route of the papal procession. The richly ornamented monument showing a female pope with a child on her arm was so beloved by the people that it lasted for seven hundred years, until Pope Sixtus the Fifth had the building torn down in 1585. The papal procession had during all those years avoided the critical point of the route and solved the problem by making a detour to the Lateran. But the place lived on in tradition and can even now be pointed out on Via San Giovanni in Laterano, not far from the abbey church San Clemente. Up through the ages the Holy See did whatever it could to suppress the legend, but it proved to be too tenacious for the Vatican to cope with. As late as the year 1400, a picture of the false Papessa was displayed in the cathedral at Siena, where it was worshipped and adored for more than two hundred years. The picture had the androgynous inscription *Giovanni VIII donna d'Inghilterra* and showed a woman dressed in the papal vestments, with all the insignia and the triple crown on her head. When it was removed by Pope Clement the Eighth, the fairy tale was not yet quite over. The Papessa appeared as the fifth card in the great arcana of the Tarot pack, where she finally found an enduring place for herself. Here she quietly occupies the Papal See, the crown on her head, the sceptre in her hand and the keys on the footstool, while being adored by two kneeling monks turning the shiny crowns of their heads towards the card player. Her expression is inscrutable – maybe she's secretly waiting for a successor to appear, a red-cheeked Swedish woman in heavy clothes who for the time being has lost favour and roams restlessly from one refuge to another in the Eternal City.

I didn't stay in Rome for long after my meeting with the Papessa. One day as I was on my way to the library to take some notes for my novel, I was so lost in thought that I stepped in front of a car and incurred a concussion. When I eventually recovered, I was so exhausted and penniless that I had to ask the Embassy for free transportation home. A long and humiliating negotiation ensued, during which it was discovered that I had no permanent address and had been roaming around Italy for eighteen months without a residence permit. From first to last I cut a wretched figure and wasn't always able to separate my own identity from that of the Papessa.

Every time I got to an obscure point in my life history, I did as she did and changed from one language to another. Finally I suffered a complete breakdown in front of the embassy secretary, launching into a torrent of words that ended in sheer madness. Like my papal friend I had to go through a stay in an asylum, before being sent home with a tag to the effect that I needed psychological treatment.

Thus began my long trek in and out of loony bins, just as hopeless and confused as my wandering back and forth across national boundaries.

All this I was recalling lying on Fisheye's abandoned sofa, now sleeping or napping, now raising my head and listening to the nocturnal stillness. Sleep and wakefulness became increasingly indistinguishable, and I no longer knew whether I was here or there when I suddenly jumped up at the sound of footsteps in the hallway. I hurriedly tidied myself up a bit and had already taken my seat before the PC when a young man with a vacuum cleaner appeared in the doorway. I stood up and indicated he could come in, and had an explanation ready when he wondered about my morning prowess. An urgent matter had forced me to have recourse to the night, I said, but now I was through and would briefly drop by the upper floors.

"I'm leaving the keys in the door," I called to him as I let myself out, "just let them stay there till I get back about half an hour from now."

In the corridor there wasn't a soul to be seen, but I could hear how the whole house was echoing with footsteps and commotion as I hurried toward the exit. A sense of unreality had come over me, and while hastening off to my next hiding place I couldn't get rid of a feeling that I was split into two persons. One hopeful and successful person who was to have a book reprinted and had visited the publisher on perfectly legal business, and another suspect and ghostlike person who wasn't much more than a shadow. I shivered in the chill morning air, noticing how the first person was becoming more and more erased, while the second was growing and making herself at home.

"Idun, my dear, don't lose courage," I said to myself. "You're going to have a book reissued and have nothing to be ashamed of. What's the harm? After all, the key is in the door, you just stayed there a little longer than was strictly necessary."

I tried to get over to the right side by breaking into a little laugh, but I didn't manage; it became distorted in the process and stuck in my throat as an unpleasant husky sound. I crossed squares and rounded street corners, still in the same faraway and somnambulistic state. The two persons continued rushing off side by side, one crescent, the other waning. Soon I was changed into my own shadow and could only glimpse my fleeing self by casting a quick glance across the bridge of my nose.

2

During the years before World War Two Vemund Hov stood in the pulpit and preached to a nearly empty church. As the novelty faded away and the rituals were reduced to a minimum, all the Lutheran Church could tolerate, church attendance shrank drastically and didn't pick up again until the war came and filled the pews with an entirely new congregation. High church members found him too learned, low-church ones insufficiently edifying, and most people felt, as they always had, that it wasn't seemly to make churchgoing into a habit. Only the Thursday musical services were well attended throughout, with the turnover that the course of events entailed.

Vemund Hov appeared quite unconcerned and took the ups and downs of life with great composure. He tended to his pastoral duties in an irreproachable manner, renounced the more colourful elements of the service and took care to insert a few more commentaries into his short, clear sermons. He was even magnanimous enough to shake hands with the spy of the parish council and to exchange a few words with him on the church square before they went their separate ways.

But he was certainly not altogether untouched by his waning esteem. As soon as he was back in the parsonage, his temper gave off sparks, and his irascibility, which had until then always had a demonstrable cause, would now come over him like lightning from a clear sky.

Nor, perhaps, was it his pastoral duties that wore him down or upset him the most. After Vemund and Mary had had the time of their visitation during that ardent summer and autumn of 1934, they drifted more and more apart from each other. Six years of matrimonial life had deprived their marriage of its glow and opened the door to a different and moreconsuming fire. The incompatibility that caused one of them to erupt in anger and violence, caused the other to respond with coldness and indifference.

Mary had been a young, childish woman when she threw herself into her life's adventure, forcing herself upon a man nearly twice her age whom she barely knew. Now she was left with a melancholy crank whom she simply couldn't understand. When he wasn't saying mass or singing like a cherub, he was lost in thought or given over to capricious merriment. He would change his mind from one moment to the next, making her a slave to his moods. He would laugh, sing, brood, joke, jeer and perform miraculous deeds without her being able to follow him or even having an inkling of what it was all about.

But worst of all were his fits of rage, his senseless berserk fury that chased him around the room and drove him to slam his fists into perfectly innocent walls and pieces of furniture. Mary would stand trembling in a corner until the fit had passed, petrified she might provide a target for the next blow. So far he had never laid a hand on her, but the blows fell so frequently and so near that one could never be sure. And even when it was all over and the turn-around came, things weren't as they should be. Then came the sudden, ardent embraces which she was unable to resist, and she was carried off to a delight and bliss she would have to pay for with a new, unwanted pregnancy.

The birth, in February 1935, of Mary's first child had instilled a deep and enduring fear in her. The child had Down's syndrome and lived just a few days. When she realized she had given birth to a deformed foetus she burst into tears and refused to have anything to do with it.

"It isn't my child! I don't want it!" she screamed, wildly flailing her arms when the midwife handed it to her. "It's a changeling and a monster which those disgusting gossips made me big with! Away with it! I don't want it!"

Gradually the tears turned into such violent convulsions that her milk dried up, and before a wet nurse could be found the child withered and died. The third day after the birth the little one was baptized at home and was named Josefine Charlotte, a name subsequently passed on to me, casting a life-long shadow over my identity.

Though Mary quickly regained her health and got over it, she was never the same again. Behind her mischievous face and light footsteps lay a burden of grief and self-reproach, and she never had the strength to love the three healthy, well-formed children to which she later gave birth. At times she would gather them around her the way a child snatches up her dolls, endowing them with a brief life. But before it became serious, she pushed them away again, shooing them off to the nursemaid, and then forgot about them for days on end. She couldn't bear hearing any mention of the dead child, as though it had disappeared without a trace. She went rigid and cold as ice when Vemund, in a mood of inexplicable tenderness, recalled the firstborn with bittersweet pet names like the "Half-wit", the "Fool", the "Dangle-head", the "Wood louse", or the "Moluccan Princess". It was he who tended the small grave in the cemetery, planted flowers there and raised a gravestone with the enigmatic inscription: *Emigravit.*

Shortly after Mary had risen from childbed she had a visit from her father, who offered his hand in a spirit of reconciliation and promised to forget the past. He wasn't the sort to set himself up as a judge when the Almighty himself had already intervened and punished her for her frivolous ways. The ban was lifted, accompanied by tears and embraces, and Mary once again gained access to her childhood home and her father's blessing. At least a couple of times a week she found a pretext to visit the shipping company's office, where she placed herself at the counter, casting long looks at the sunny spot by the window where she had sat in all innocence and struck up conversations with hearty young sailors and elegant officers. As a married woman she had lost all rights and had to put up with the fact that a bespectacled middle-aged person now sat puffing herself up in her old seat. But she was still sitting there in spirit, and she didn't miss a thing. As in her heyday she could keep a lookout from under her eyelashes, extend a well-formed silken leg, and turn her head at just the right angle when a sailor stepped through the door.

Unfortunately, with the reconciliation came the necessity to make peace with the Ark, where her conversion was celebrated with a long and distressing prayer meeting. She sat there listening, flushed and embarrassed, as the brothers and sisters sighed over her defection and praised the affliction that had brought her back to the fold. But Mary never became a whole-hearted member of the Ark, and after another argument with her father they agreed to a compromise in which the reconciliation remained in force, even though she turned up at the prayer meetings only once a week.

As the children grew older, it became established custom for them to dine at their grandfather's every Sunday. When they arrived at twelve o'clock sharp, mother and children found a richly laid table, and it was a tacit agreement that Vemund Hov stayed away. Since the dinner was set at such an early hour, the pastor's absence could be explained by the fact that the service was not yet over. At the very moment they sat down at the ship owner's table and Andreas Sand bowed his head over his soup plate to ask God's blessing on the meal, Vemund Hov was still in church, wearing his vestments, baptizing children or singing the praise of the Eucharist before distributing the bread and the wine. Afterwards he would sit alone at the large dining table in the parsonage eating porridge or a warmed-over dish that the housekeeper saw fit to put on the table. After all, to prepare an entire Sunday dinner for a single person was out of the question, or perhaps the pastor was of a different opinion? No, Vemund Hov had no objection, being so lost in his own thoughts that he scarcely noticed what he was eating.

By contrast, the dinner at the ship owner's house was a real feast, with soup, fish and meat, and a dessert that would make sweet tooths of all ages smack their lips. The cook, Maren, was a generous and big-hearted woman, positively swelling with culinary art; she was not at all of the same kidney as the housekeeper over in the parsonage. She had been so long in service that Andreas Sand had inherited her from his father-in-law, the fish skipper, when he took over the business years ago. At one time Maren had had to make do with gruel and salt herring, for the dear, departed Torjussen was a strict ascetic who regarded the belly as the seat of all evil. Andreas Sand didn't agree, for he was a man who lived at peace with his desires and whose gourmandise matched his enjoyment of all God's gifts. Once he had chewed his way through the daily fare for a few weeks, he left the table, aimed a jet at the spittoon and walked resolutely to the kitchen to dictate a new menu.

And Maren, in those days a young lady of twenty-seven eager to learn, steeled herself and rose to the challenge. She mended her ways almost immediately, dug her knuckles into the ingredients and changed from an unimaginative soup maker to an exceptional mistress of the kitchen.

Service under Andreas Sand also enabled her to develop her stock of innate qualities in other areas. If she had been loyal and reliable during the fish skipper's time, she now became loyalty and reliability personified, a vigilant defender of her master's interests and privy to his most daring enterprises.

After the war, it turned out that she had shared a great and dangerous secret with him and made certain that it didn't penetrate beyond the four walls of the house. For two and a half years the residence had been the hiding place of two fugitives, who wandered freely on the second and third floors without anyone outside the house knowing. If the authorities had tracked them down, it would have been a serious matter both for the ship owner and for her who was in on the secret. But, however incredible it may sound, nothing came out until the very last months of the war.

During office hours the employees must occasionally have heard footsteps upstairs, too many and too bouncing to be the housekeeper's alone. But when it became too crowded up there, they must have thought it was just the ship owner's daughter paying a call, with her little ones noisily running about. As a matter of fact, Mary never happened to surprise the two stowaways who lived their clandestine lives in the little cubbyhole in the attic. For months and years the watchful Maren saw to it they were out of the way when the family assembled for Sunday dinner. If she learned at other times during the week that the master's daughter was approaching, she made a sign to the secret guests and watched them till they had disappeared up the stairs to the attic. Andreas Sand was at this time busy with big construction projects for the occupying power, so who could suspect this co-operative man of hiding Jewish refugees in his house?

Anyway, the two lodgers hadn't come from far away, but had been the ship owner's next-door neighbours for several years. The long building of the shipping company sat on the town square, but one gable and a tall privet hedge looked out on a quiet back street. Diagonally across this alley there was a small tobacco store, where the ship owner dropped by almost daily to buy a cigar, a batch of writing paper or the daily paper. The owner was a young Jew with a very attractive wife, who frequently served customers in the shop, and a little son about the same age as the ship owner's grandchildren. On Sundays when dinner was over and the children had been dispatched to the back garden, it often happened that little Aaron slipped across the street and crawled through an opening in the hedge to join his playmates. When he failed to appear one Sunday in November 1942, the grandfather made light of it, but when the boy didn't show up the following Sundays either, Andreas Sand explained to his grandchildren that the shop across the street was closed and that the family had moved far away to another country.

While what escaped his lips was not an outright lie, it was no more than a third of the truth. True enough, the head of the family had been caught during the German raid and deported to an unknown place. But pure chance, or providence as the ship owner preferred to call it, had allowed the mother and child to escape. Visiting some acquaintances upcountry, they had got a ride home on the milk van. At the crack of dawn when the raid took place, they were sitting safely in the cab of the dairy van with no inkling of any danger.

But at home in Skipper Alley a ghastly sight awaited them. The front door was wide open, the shop had been turned upside down, and the street window broken. As they stood there, bewitched, staring at the destruction, they heard somebody calling them nearby in a low voice, almost a whisper. It was the neighbour, Andreas Sand, who had opened a window in the gable of his house and made signs to them to hurry up and get away. He said nothing about where they should take refuge, but the little boy understood the warning in his own way and pulled his stupefied mother across the street and in through the opening in the hedge.

It was just after six o'clock, the street was completely empty, and quite probably no one except the ship owner had witnessed what had occurred. But in the time that followed the air became thick with rumours, and after some delay the townspeople acquired eyes on every finger. One after another reported having been eyewitnesses and claimed, in the teeth of all known facts, that they had seen the small family being taken away – not only the husband, but also the wife and child. Some could recount how the boy had cried and resisted, but was comforted when given sweets by the enemy. Others had seen the NS troopers make shameless advances to the attractive Jewess, till her husband lost control of himself and rushed at them despite the odds. Others again had seen the shop being searched from one end to the other, until the Jews were discovered and driven out of hiding. In fact, there were even those who maintained that they had been present at the railway station as the Jewish convoy was leaving and had seen little Aaron stick his head out the door of the carriage just before it was closed and bolted. Nobody could say how all of these rumours, most of which bore little resemblance to reality, had arisen. Maybe the ship owner himself put them into circulation, to cast a smokescreen over events and thereby protect his secret lodgers.

But one thing is for sure: late that autumn in 1942 something radical happened to the lonely man in the ship owner's house, better known as a doomsday prophet, confidence man, jester, barracks baron, tax evader, and as the greatest philanthropist of the region. He grew warm and alive again after a long period of frost, and in the coming years he was to develop strangely tender and close links with the two strangers. He showered the young woman with gifts and attention, instructed her in the Christian faith, and was said to have baptized her single-handedly, once she was converted, in the name of the Father, the Son, and the Holy Ghost. The little boy became the apple of his eye and his declared favourite, at first perhaps in order to win the mother, but later wholeheartedly and with a playfulness he hadn't experienced since his courting days almost a generation ago.

At dusk, having had his afternoon nap, he took the boy on his lap and told him hair-raising tales of the sea, or knelt on the floor and helped the little one explore a new toy. That was something he never did with his own grandchildren, even though he loved them with a kind heart and took care of them in the best possible way. He might occasionally pat them on the head and ask how old they had become since their last visit. But nothing more came of it, and as soon as they had bowed and curtsied and dropped their thank-yous for dinner, he took himself off and left them to their own devices.

So there was a great commotion when, on Easter Sunday 1943, the children were playing hide-and-seek in the rooms and one of the twins came across an exciting toy in the grandfather's office.

"A doll's house!" she cried, completely forgetting that she had sneaked in there to hide. "Mama, Grandpa, come and look, a little three-storey house, with furniture in every room and tiny little people living there!"

The office was a place where the children were not allowed, so the grandfather, startled out of his chair where he sat dozing, was about to give them a severe scolding. But before things got that far, he realized the battle was lost and that he had to come clean. He entered the office, shushed his grandchildren, lifted the marvellous toy and held it at arm's length, pretending it was a surprise he'd been planning for a long time. Then he carried the house into the living room, slipped off his jacket and gathered the ecstatic children around him.

"Now, little brats, we'll have some fun!" he cried, at the same time whispering an admonition to himself: Hush, hush, you old blusterer, be sure not to let it leak out that you made the house for someone else. Do you hear? Not a sound about the little cave dweller confined in the attic, who was given a playhouse so he could get to know his prison.

To escape his dilemma, the ship owner went down on hands and knees and showed the wide-eyed children that the house was a reduced but accurate model of the one they all found themselves in at that very moment. When it also dawned on them that the small wooden figures exactly matched the occupants of the house, they were overjoyed, and Grandfather didn't have a moment's peace until he had picked up each and every figure and said who they were. There was the ship owner himself in his big office downstairs – oh, down there he was an altogether different sort of man and nobody's grandfather. There was the clerk and the shipper and the delivery boy, here the cashier in his glass cage, the accountant at his desk and the secretary behind the counter. Here was a fat client with a big cigar in his mouth, there an officer with gold braids on his jacket, and two young sailors who'd dropped by to pick up their pay.

In the same way he tackles the occupants upstairs, moving the ship owner up one floor and putting him where he belongs, in the grandfather's chair. Suddenly Maren jumps up and trips over to the stove, where the pots are already on the boil.

"But who is coming there? By golly, if it isn't the minister's wife with her three children in their fine Sunday outfits! Now, listen carefully as I pull this string, ting-a-ling, there was the doorbell, and Maren hurries out to open the door. Welcome, welcome, just go into the living room and wait a little while, then we'll be asked to the table."

"But who is living up in the attic?" asks one of the twins. She notices how Grandpa stiffens as soon as she has said it; for a moment he is quite unrecognizable. What's wrong with him, why does he look so dark and threatening, why does he shudder and look in another direction? But in seconds he is himself again. He straightens up and gives a little laugh, then snatches up the two mysterious figures and puts them in his waist-coat pocket.

"They don't live in the attic, you mustn't think that," he chuckles, emphatically patting his pocket. "They are two thieves who have sneaked up the back stairs to poke about in our drawers and steal our charts and all the other precious articles we have up there. Those blockheads haven't seen that it says KEEP OUT on the door. Or perhaps they've seen it, but think that the warning doesn't mean anything. But now they've been caught and thrown into gaol, and God help anyone who tries to break in a second time!"

The children sit there on the floor, their eyes in a wide-eyed stare as Grandfather spins his yarn. With his usual quick-wittedness he finds a new thread, interweaves it with other questionable material and creates a regular cock-and-bull story out of it. Afterwards the children are allowed to pat his chest and make sure that the two thieves are locked up and cannot get out of prison. They look more closely at the attic room in the little house and see that, indeed, it does say KEEP OUT on the door, and a little higher up there is another word that isn't so easy to spell either.

"Grandpa, why does it say CUDDY?" asks the boy, the eldest of the three and soon to begin school.

And the old man has his answer ready, explaining that the attic room was his first hole-in-the-wall on dry land when he quit going to sea. "You see, I was so used to sleeping in cuddies on the high seas that I felt almost unsafe living in a room on shore. So I borrowed paint and brush from the fish skipper and wrote CUDDY on the door with big letters. I can tell you it helped, the floor began to roll under me at once, and the berth lulled me to sleep. To be on the safe side I wrote KEEP OUT underneath, so that nobody would think it was a place where anyone could enter."

"Does that mean that we won't be allowed up there either?" asks the grandson.

"Of course, what else do you think? Keep out means keep out, and if anybody should try, he'll end up in prison."

For the remainder of that Sunday the three children sat spellbound, moving the little figures up and down the stairs, along corridors and in and out of doors, as their game required. But one of them fell into a reverie now and then and didn't join in fully. She couldn't forget the shadow that flitted across her grandfather's face, the wrinkle that appeared on his forehead, and the odd laugh he gave before snatching up the two thieves and hiding them behind the button on his waistcoat pocket. Was it really so certain that the two figures were thieves? Why didn't they look more sinister, and why was one so much smaller than the other? And since nobody must go up there, what sort of precious articles lay hidden in that little room in the attic?

They were thoughts she never managed to think through to their conclusion. They brushed her fleetingly once or twice and disturbed her, until she pushed them aside and found something else to think about. The whole summer went by, and it was already well into the autumn when one day she suddenly decided that she had to get up to the attic and find out whether somebody really lived up there. Her brother and sister had long ago lost interest in the little house in favour of a pinball game their grandfather had provided. The adventure with the thieves had been forgotten, and nothing suggested it had made an impression on them or awakened their curiosity.

One Sunday in mid-October she has a feeling that the time has come.

Grandpa sleeps in his chair, her mother is in the kitchen with Maren, and her siblings are quarrelling over the pinball game as usual. She quietly steals out through the sitting room door, down the long hallway that runs from one end of the house to the other, and begins to climb all those stairs. First, along the white-painted banister with the gold scrollwork, past a landing with a compass on the wall, and up yet more flights until she reaches the bedroom level. Then down another hallway to the back staircase without a banister, which leads in sharp turns from the courtyard up to the attic. She knows the way very well, because once the previous autumn, before the thieves began to play havoc in the attic, she had been allowed to follow Grandpa up there with an old trunk he wished to put away. She had seen no chests containing silver or gold, the attic was grey with dust and messy and full of all sorts of useless things. Before they went down again, her grandfather had lifted her up so that she could look out of the skylight, and for a dizzying moment she had seen, far below, the town lying there, strangely remote and Lilliputian, as only God and the angels saw it.

Standing still on the top landing, she is filled with dread. God who loves us little children, what if the thieves were lying in ambush up there, ready to throw themselves upon her! No, always go boldly where you walk, the thieves were only a couple of wooden dolls after all, so small that they fit in a waistcoat pocket. Pooh, they were no more dangerous than the sea goblin and the sea serpent and all the other monsters Grandpa liked to tell them about. Childhood faith, a golden bridge leads to heaven's gate, just hurry up, Idun, and do what the song says. There is the door to the attic, can't you see it's already ajar? Gentle Jesus, you who – didn't something move in there, and didn't she hear a voice mumbling softly? Keep and protect me, from sin, from sorrow, from danger. Stuff and nonsense! What sort of danger should there be? Ha, those thieves must have been really stupid, poking about in the attic when there were so many nicer things to steal downstairs.

She takes a few hesitant steps. Your angel me keep, who this day has guided my feet. Then she plucks up courage and cautiously opens the blue-painted door to the attic. First just a tiny crack, followed by a streak of light that slowly spreads, allowing the steps to come into view. But what is it? Isn't that a little boy sitting in the middle of the staircase, mumbling something to himself, no, not mumbling but humming a sort of strange bird call? He's so engrossed by what he is doing that he neither hears nor sees, he just quietly hums while holding out his hand.

"Come, Methuselah, come and take what I've got for you, hurry before something bad happens. Feel free to come out, little Mousedaddy, it's just me sitting here quite alone. Don't be afraid, no Germans can get you here."

When he catches sight of her he is startled, lets go of what he holds in his hand and darts quick as lightning up the stairs on all fours. But he changes his mind before he gets all the way to the top and settles down on the topmost step with his hands on his knees.

"But Aaron, what are you doing up here?" Idun asks when she finally dares to believe her own eyes. "You moved to another country, didn't you?"

"Ssssh," the boy whispers, placing a finger to his lips. "Mother is running a temperature and is asleep. We musn't talk very loud or we'll wake her."

He slides noiselessly a few steps down until he gets to the middle of the staircase, where he settles, making signs to her to come and sit beside him.

"But you moved, didn't you?" she repeats. She is not content until she has touched his chest and shoulders and made certain that he isn't a ghost.

"Dad moved," he says after a long silence between them. "Mama and I came home too late the day he left, so now we'll have to live up here till the war is over."

"What were you holding in your hand just then, the white thing lying over there?" she asks, though she can see very well what it is.

"Oh, only a bit of cheese for Mousedaddy. His name is Methuselah, and he watches out that no harm comes to Dad where he is now."

"Watches out, you say. How can a little mouse do that?"

"Let me tell you, he's no ordinary mouse. Maybe it's Dad who has taken the form of a mouse so he can safely come and visit us. I dreamed about that the first night I slept up here. Suddenly Dad stood in the middle of the room, and when I blinked my eyes he changed himself into a mouse. He stood there only for a brief moment, then he was gone. But before he disappeared he said that he would come back from Germany safe and sound, if only I remembered to give him a bit of cheese every day."

"But where do you get all those pieces of cheese from, up here in the attic?"

"Maren brings them, it's a secret we have together. And now you know it too, so now we are three."

"Do you really think it's true what happens in fairy tales, that people can change into animals?"

"Not always, only once in a while, when there's danger. You know, the Germans don't go after mice, only Jews. That's why Dad is able to change into a mouse and be in two places at once."

"Two places at once?"

"Yes, in a German prison and here on the stairs to the attic. You just have to snap your fingers to make the change happen."

He makes himself more comfortable and shows her how to snap people into mice. "The right hand up, like this, the thumb against the middle finger, see, and snap, it's done. But it works only when I'm alone. Mousedaddy sits in his hole and keeps guard, and he doesn't come out if others are around."

She sits motionless, staring dreamily at his thin hand, which again and again shoots up in the air and makes a small click. She squeezes her eyes half shut, and through the cracks she sees a little mouse sitting behind the wall, waiting for the all-clear. The mousehole is Germany, and the stairs to the attic is Norway, but only when the real click comes can he venture forth and throw off his mouse likeness.

"You know, it's my birthday today," he says suddenly, letting his hand drop. "Tonight after you've all gone home, Maren will come and pick me up, and there'll be a big cake with eight candles in the living room."

"Then your mummy will have to be there, too, won't she, if it's going to be a real birthday party?"

"That would've been great," he answers with a deep sigh. "But it won't work. Mama can't keep food down, she's been throwing up for weeks. Do you want me to tell you something creepy? I almost believe that someone tried to kill her yesterday afternoon, while I was downstairs for a moment. You should've seen all the blood in her bed, when Maren was here and changed the sheets."

"Since you're eight years old, shouldn't you go to school?" Idun says. She is afraid of blood and would rather talk about something else.

"But I do go to school. Grandpa gives me lessons every evening, and I've learned to read already."

"He's *my* grandpa, and the grandpa of Vidar and Urd. And I really don't think he's the grandpa of anyone else."

"That's what he says I should call him," the boy answers, more meekly. "I know I only have him on loan, until the war is over. But a grandpa on loan is a good thing to have when you don't have any other."

"Don't you ever get out any more, to get a breath of fresh air?"

"Not out on the street or down into the garden, if that's what you mean. But I'm allowed to crawl out onto the balcony and sit there, as long as I remember that I mustn't stand up."

"The balcony? Can it be any fun to sit there, behind the high wall?"

"I have a rabbit out there, I can feed him cabbage and carrots. And I can sit there and look at the sky, with all the clouds that travel by. They change all the time, and sometimes they have faces and turn into giant people who fly."

"You could take a walk in the garden once in a while, couldn't you, in the evening when it's dark?"

"Don't be stupid. There are plenty of holes in the hedge, though Grandpa has filled in the biggest one. What if a German came by and took it into his head to peek in!"

"Do you remember how much fun we had playing down there last autumn, when you came crawling through the hedge and joined us. Vidar and Urd wanted to capture us and make us their slaves, but we had them fooled. They hadn't counted with the four-footer "Idunaaron", who came storming out of the jungle and routed the enemy."

They laugh and move closer together, and everything is almost the way it used to be between them. But then he suddenly clenches his fist in the air and says, "I'll be jiggered."

"You shouldn't say that word," she says sternly. "It's almost like a swear word."

"Swear word, yeah? Grandpa says it himself when he is in a fix, so it must be something from the Bible, I think."

"I don't care," she says, shrugging her shoulders. "If you like to swear, just say it as much as you want, even on Sunday."

"I said it because I just happened to think of something. Your dad's a Nazi, right, and if he finds out that we're living up here, he'll go to the Germans and report us."

"My dad is not a Nazi!" she answers, her eyes flashing. He doesn't use the Nazi greeting, *Heil & sæl*, and he doesn't wear that shiny badge on his jacket. And besides he isn't the sort to report anyone."

"But you have to keep mum, just in case. God help you if you tell anyone where you've been today, and who you've been talking to."

"Cross my heart, I won't tell anyone. But now I'll have to hurry down to the others, before they start looking for me."

She holds out her hand for goodbye, and he takes it in both of his, reluctant to let it go. She frees herself with a tug, but when she notices his loneliness and his imploring look she promises to come back the next Sunday, to see whether Mousedaddy has fetched his piece of cheese.

He nods mutely, and his face lights up in a big smile for a moment. But when she turns around at the bottom of the stairs, she understands that he has changed his mind. He is perched precariously on the very edge of the step, his thin hand beating the air and his lips moving incessantly, until he finally manages to form a sound.

"Just you try to come up here a second time!" he threatens. "Mousedaddy knows you have a dad who is a Nazi, and if you blab he'll take a cruel revenge on you!"

She ducks her head between her shoulders and gives a little gasp. Then she opens the blue door and slips away without looking back.

She waits until she is near the bottom of the next flight of stairs before she stops to straighten her back. "Dad is *not* a Nazi," she whispers one last time. "And he's not the sort to report anyone."

3

When Idun maintained all her life that her father was not a traitor to his country, she was at once both right and wrong.

Vemund Hov never acknowledged membership of the National Union party, never used the ancient Norwegian salute, and did not wear that shiny badge on his jacket, to quote his six-year-old daughter. But in the course of those five years of war he did a number of unforgivable things that aroused general indignation and led to the sentence for treason in 1946.

During the trial the accused remained strangely silent, imperturbable, sitting on his bench like a spectator and letting everything happen as it might. Only when the prosecutor directly addressed him did he raise his head and give a brief, precise answer. The incredible thing is that he possessed proof of his innocence, but for some inscrutable reason neglected to make use of it.

When Vemund Hov was imprisoned in the late summer of 1945 and brought to trial a few months later, the indictment against him was contained in five points:

(1) He had been a member of the National Union since 1934 and paid his membership fee every year.

(2) He had been on friendly terms with the occupying power, and as early as the spring of 1940 he had given a sermon that urged reflection and reconciliation.

(3) He had allegedly denounced, in writing, a Jewish woman and her little son, who were in hiding someplace in town, to the local chief of police.

(4) He received visits from Vidkun Quisling and held services during a rally of NS troopers in town.

(5) For some unknown reason, he had locked up his youngest brother in the sacristy after an act of sabotage, causing the latter to fall into the hands of the Gestapo.

Of these five counts he admitted points (2), (4) and (5), but only on the understanding that he was being court-martialled. If the proceedings were civil, he didn't plead guilty to any of them.

He flatly denied the denunciation, pointing out that, even if the communication was written on the stationery of the pastoral office, it did not follow that it was written by him. The paper could have been stolen by one of many visitors to the office, and his handwriting imitated by someone with a talent for forgeries of that kind. The letter was never examined by a handwriting expert, something that might have led to an explanation.

In what follows we shall try to isolate the five points of the indictment, as far as it may be possible for a chronicler who hadn't yet turned nine when the trial took place. Needless to say, she cannot go about it too systematically, or simply trust her memory. As is her custom, she will take a broad look at the chronology and relate the events as they come up. She has ascertained the principal details by leafing through old newspapers, examining transcripts of court proceedings, and seeing what Vemund Hov himself had to say in his diary during the autumn and winter of 1944.

At the outbreak of war in April 1940 he kept altogether quiet and took care of his pastoral duties as usual; he even remembered to pray for the King and his house, once he had prayed for the Fatherland, the Government, and peace on earth and in men's hearts. No secret spy would have found anything to report, except for the fact that perhaps he reeled off the Common Prayer rather too quickly, without the fervour and empathy he displayed while saying mass. His sermons were brief and unbiased as usual, and when the war came the only liberty he allowed himself was to expand High Mass with a song or a recitation from the liturgy of the primitive Church. The parish council now had something else to think about than pursuing their pet ideas, so the pastor received no new requests to tame his fondness for singing and to strictly adhere to the evangelical Lutheran tradition.

It had long been rumoured that the parish pastor was pro-German, though no grumbler had been able to catch him out in so many words. Pastor Hov did not come out in the open, and the situation was still uncertain when the Norwegian forces capitulated and laid down their arms. But not long after, on Trinity Sunday itself, he mounted the pulpit and gave a sermon that caused his opponents to rub their hands with glee. Just what we thought, the parish pastor is a German sympathizer, or at any rate lacking in patriotic sentiment. Who knows whether he may not be a secret Nazi, who now sniffs the morning air and ascends from his crypt.

While, unfortunately, very few heard the sermon, it acquired wings all the more and spread far and wide. And since Vemund Hov never wrote down his sermons, there was no one who could remember them six years later and place on record what he had, or had not, said.

But the organist, who was summoned as a witness and was known for his rectitude, couldn't remember that the sermon was particularly sensational. The text was from Matthew, chapter five, and was read aloud by the witness in its entirety: "But I say unto you, That ye resist not evil: but whosoever shall smite thee on thy right cheek, turn to him the other also. And if any man will sue thee at the law, and take away thy coat, let him have thy cloak also. And whosoever shall compel thee to go a mile, go with him twain."

After the organist had given a report on the sermon as he remembered it, he added that, in his opinion, the very choice of text was an argument in his defence. If the pastor was referring to an actual situation, then he declared loud and clear that the Occupation was an evil. And he stood firmly on evangelical ground when he called for calm and cool-headedness. With his view of life as something priceless, there was nothing remarkable in the fact that he asked his countrymen to go two miles with the conqueror, when they were forced to go only one. Vemund Hov was, after all, a clergyman, a fact not to be forgotten, and he acted entirely in the spirit of the Sermon on the Mount when he ended his sermon by changing to direct speech: "Dear congregation, so let us love our enemies, bless them that curse us, do good to them that hate us, and pray for them which persecute us; that we may be the children of our Father which is in heaven: for he maketh his sun to rise on the evil and on the good, and sendeth rain on the just and on the unjust."

The organist concluded his testimony by maintaining that Pastor Hov's conception of life was on every point in keeping with the gospel he was assigned to preach. It was no coincidence that the appeal came from a man who had written a dissertation called *The Tree of Life* and who looked on existence as a gift from God. If existence was the sustainer of all things, it was vitally important to preserve it, even under the most threatening circumstances. Consequently, the Trinity Sunday sermon offered no evidence against the pastor, but proof of his will to peace and his Christian temper.

I cannot say how much weight was given to the organist's plea, but the newspaper reports indicate that the last part of count (2) was dropped before sentence was passed, and that the prosecutor concentrated all the more on the first part.

But before we tackle that, we have to embark upon a rather long previous history, which will also be of importance for the interpretation of counts (1) and (4). It deals with Vemund Hov's tangled family circumstances, and with the powerlessness and complaisance that took hold of him in his relations with those closest to him.

At the end of the holidays in the autumn of 1939, the town's secondary school had acquired a new teacher. His name was Balder Hov, brother to the parish pastor, but so totally unlike him that it was difficult to believe they were related. While the pastor was an inscrutable loner whom his townsmen had long ago given up associating with, his younger brother was a jovial yet aggressive person whom nobody could escape in the long run. In the course of a few weeks he managed to win the upper crust over to his side and to be admitted to the leading circles. He was regarded as something of a find and was received with open arms by those families that had tried in vain to capture his brother.

Balder Hov was a tall hulk of a man on the verge of obesity, with a few stray whisps of hair around a shiny crown and bright, sparkling eyes in a round moonface. His movements were amazingly light for his heavy, slightly peasantlike figure, and his attire was slovenly – unless he saw fit to irritate the town's philistines by wearing a gaudy waistcoat, a garish necktie, or odd socks. Endowed with a sweet tooth, he would clear a cake dish in a few minutes and then look hungrily about him for more. No sooner had he said hello to the lady of the house and handed her a box of candy than he seized it out of her hands, tore off the lid and consumed it all by himself. When he went visiting, he wasn't content with simply ringing the doorbell, but walked around the house and peeped through the windows if there was no answer. This became tiresome some months later, when his popularity waned and his hosts preferred not to be at home to him. When the visitor's massive figure appeared in the entranceway, it was too late to draw the curtains, so the family had to leave the room in a hurry or withdraw to a corner hidden from the window peeper. Once the door was opened, all hope was gone, and it availed little to explain to the visitor that his call was inconvenient. "Oh, you have company? Aha! I knew I was coming to a well-laden table! What? You're sitting at home completely alone? Lucky it occurred to me to come over."

Half a year after his arrival, the new teacher had become a byword in town, a walking illustration of pushiness and bad manners. His name became synonymous with "freeloader" and "having-one's-foot-in-the-door", and people threatened each other in jest with "doing a Balder Hov", being *bald*-faced or talking *balder*dash and stowing away an excellent dinner.

But all through the autumn of 1939, Balder Hov was the town's pride and joy, its main attraction. The men slapped him chummily on the shoulder, and their wives were eager to catch him and cozy up to him. Though he didn't have quite as fine a singing voice as his brother, it was adequate – and more than willing to launch into the oratorios that his hosts wished to hear. Soon he had formed a small male choir, a quartet playing light music, which was a great hit at the town bazaars and benefit performances. In addition, he acted in the amateur theatre and had the priceless ability to mimic every public figure and imitate every speaking voice. He overflowed with jokes and tricks, and in merry company he enlivened the party with an exceptionally deep and booming guffaw that nobody could ignore. He seemed oblivious to the fact that he was mostly unintentionally funny and went recklessly ahead, letting the others have a laugh at his expense. To be on the safe side, he made certain he was the first one to laugh, leaving the stragglers to keep up as best they could.

To keep his weight down, he obtained a racing bicycle and soon became a familiar sight puffing his way along the local roads. He wrote down precisely how many kilometres he had put behind him every day in a notebook, which rarely remained in his pocket for long when he inflicted himself on his regular hosts. As the evening wore on and the jokes and puns gave out, the notebook appeared at the table, and a thick schoolmasterly finger with a chewed nail pointed to the scores: Monday 11 September, 42km; Tuesday 12 September, 48km; Wednesday – unfortunately a flat tire and just 7km.

"But look here, folks, the next day 50km and the day after that 55km! What do you say to that, you layabouts? Tomorrow I'm going for 60km, and just you wait, on Sunday I'll celebrate the day of rest with a 100km lap."

He didn't notice that his lectures evoked merely smiles; he never knew how to stop before becoming a caricature of himself. Even his pupils made fun of his bicycle rides and joked about having a teacher with more than just algebra on the brain. When his back was turned as he solved an equation on the blackboard, they bent over to tread invisible pedals at their desks. He had a brilliant mathematical mind, able to catch every proof on the wing and to crack every nut on the spur of the moment. But his mania for *tours de force*, which made him a much-feared teacher, left him an absurd figure outside the classroom. The solar cross he wore on his lapel was like an omniscient eye that saw through all cheating and apathy along the rows of desks. But out on the highways it became a frantically flashing sign that counted the kilometers, forcing the pedal-pusher to assume a role in which he constantly had to surpass himself.

Balder Hov had been a member of the National Union since the party was formed in 1933. It was he who signed up Vemund when his brother returned from Germany in 1934, and who paid the membership fee for him during the coming years. When Vemund Hov sat in the dock after the war and denied that he had ever been a member of NS, nobody quite believed him. Didn't he know that he was on the party's membership list? the prosecutor asked at one point. Oh yes, he had had his suspicions, all right. But why hadn't he resigned his membership, since he didn't want to be a member?

"Because I never joined," the parish pastor replied, briefly and concisely. Afterwards he maintained a long silence, and when he was asked to be more specific, he looked in surprise at the judge and gave a weary chuckle. "Gladly, Your Honour, gladly. If it shouldn't already be obvious that someone who didn't join has no reason to resign!" Balder, his brother, was no longer alive at that point to offer a solution to the riddle. And because the pastor foolishly withheld his diary notes, the documents that might have thrown light on the true facts of the case were lacking.

How the old man at Hov, the almost hundred-year-old Thormod Hov, would have couched his answer if he had survived long enough to sit in the courtroom, is hard to say. His registration had also taken place behind his back, but in contrast to his son Vemund he was overjoyed to receive his NS membership number. Finally there was going to be a new order in the country, everything shipshape, so that farmers wouldn't have to wait around to no avail to have a lake sunk. Supported by two sticks and totally befuddled by age, he stumped his way around the village holding forth about the redress that would soon be granted Nether Hov. As the name of the homestead indicated, the small, waterlogged farm was once a Norse place of worship, where great sacrifices to Odin and Thor were made long ago. But treacherous Loki must have had a hand in the game, for the temple was moved elsewhere, causing the memorable sites to sink down into poverty and stagnation. His National Union membership was Thormod's final *idée fixe* and a compensation for the insult and injury he had suffered in his correspondence with the Government. After letting the whole community in on what was at hand, he hitched Sorrel to the manure cart and set out into the world, to spread the glad tidings to heathens and infidels. What happened to him on that final journey doesn't belong here, but it will be made clear when the time has come to open the last of Vemund's diaries.

But to go back to the phenomenon of Balder Hov and his rapid downfall from being the town buffoon and life-and-soul of the party to becoming a headache.

Although the teacher could scarcely be more solidly present, his behaviour betrayed a disguise that aroused curiosity and suspicion. The townspeople began to wonder, especially after Svallaug, his sister, moved in with him. She arrived in town in the spring of 1943, supposedly to keep house. They attracted attention from the moment they were seen together in town, because they walked on opposite sides of the street, occasionally crossing to the middle when they had something to say to each other. The brother walked as free as the breeze, gathering welcoming nods for them both, while the sister stared into space, her body all crooked from dragging a heavy suitcase.

And no sooner had they crossed the threshold than the door lock jammed, and afterwards nobody saw a glimpse of the sister again. When it was whispered that she had left, her brother could report that she was a bit shy and preferred to stay indoors. He did the shopping himself on his way home from school, was always the one who opened the door when someone rang the bell, and never took his sister with him when he went out in the evening, making the town feel uneasy. If at that time someone went to his house and tried to ring the bell, there would be no answer, but fleeing footsteps or a creaking door betrayed the presence of someone who refused to reveal herself.

Soon there were rumours to the effect that the brother was keeping her locked up, and this was followed by a suspicion that some unspeakable things were happening in the yellow house behind the secondary school. Some people claimed they had heard a woman scream, others had looked through the window to see brother and sister locked in an embrace, while still others could relate that they had seen the sister's deathly pale face peep out from behind the curtain up in the dormer window and then withdraw in a flash. Gossips hinted that she had been pregnant when she came to town and had good reason to keep herself indoors. Later in the summer some claimed to have seen the midwife enter the house in the middle of the night, and the teacher steal into the garden a couple of hours later to bury something in the ground. The midwife couldn't be made to utter a single word afterwards, nor was it necessary, because anyone could tell what sort of business she had had in the yellow house. Later the matter was cloaked in silence, and after a year and a half, when the pair of siblings met their deaths together, it had been almost forgotten. During the investigation of the two deaths, the ground was dug up at the place indicated by the witness, and true enough, a shapeless lump of organic matter came to light. But the find was in such an advanced state of decomposition that it was impossible to decide whether it was the entrails of a butchered animal or the last remains of a foetus. The midwife was no longer alive, and, after pressure from the local Nazis, the investigators let the matter drop.

Nor was it easy to fathom the relationship between the brothers, Balder and Vemund. The teacher was anything but a regular churchgoer, but if the weather was so poor one Sunday that it hindered him from the observance of his sacred fitness routine, he went to church and accompanied his brother back to the parsonage after the service. But anyone seeing them together didn't get the impression that they were particularly close. Balder always led the way, while Vemund shuffled silently beside him, tagging along in the name of sibling unlove. The visit to the parsonage rarely lasted long, and Sunday dinner was something of an ordeal, because Balder was used to living well and showered abuse on the food that was placed before him.

What the brothers had to say to each other during the scant hour when they sat together at dinner, became known only during the trial of one of them. The housekeeper, who was called as a witness, could relate that the teacher would sound off, while the pastor listened and hardly uttered a word. Did it look as though the brothers were enemies? No, not exactly enemies, because there never fell a malicious word between them. But it looked as if the pastor was silent on purpose, and for some mysterious reason gave in to his domineering brother. Now and then he responded to the other's torrent of words with a nod or a shrug, but somehow he didn't seem to be really there, and when he looked up his eyes were very strange. But the teacher was in his element and didn't pay attention to the mood at the table. The more silent the other became, the more he grew highly charged, until he sat there crackling and giving off sparks like a power generator.

Did she know anything about the sort of relationship there was between Pastor Hov and his departed sister?

Well, she was sorry to say, not much of one. Only once had the poor woman been a subject of conversation between the two brothers, and afterwards there was never any mention of her, not a word. Once in the autumn of 1943, the pastor had said that he would invite his sister for coffee one Sunday afternoon when the family was gathered.

"You shouldn't do that, you might come to regret it," the teacher said in a firm voice, clearly a voice used to having its way. The pastor gave a momentary start, and it looked as though he would lose his temper. But he seemed to understand who had the upper hand, because he soon calmed down and changed the subject.

Had she heard anything else that might be of importance for the proceedings?

Well, she didn't quite know – what might that be? Oh, by the way, wait a minute, one Sunday she had heard the teacher mention a rally of NS troopers that would shortly take place in town. The pastor was to officiate for the occasion, but looked like he would rather not as he squirmed in his chair. The housekeeper herself had been walking in and out, so she couldn't say for certain how the matter developed. But she could clearly remember what the pastor said when she entered the dining room to gather the plates.

"All right, brother, you're probably right," he replied, heaving a deep sigh. "It's my duty to hold a service every Sunday, regardless who sits in the pews."

But as soon as the brother had left, there was an end to the pastor's mildness. He rushed from one room to another like a madman, pitched into the furniture, swept the family portraits from the wall and snatched books out of the bookcase and flung them to the floor.

"'Rubbish!' he cried again and again; it sounded as if he was speaking to the things, but I believe that what he meant was the service. He even repeatedly kicked the piano, which he used to be so careful of. Someone had to come and repair it the next day."

But he did hold the service, as he was duty-bound to do, during the rally, and afterwards Vidkun Quisling and a few other VIP's dined at the parsonage. She had had to serve four courses. There was much eating and drinking, and nobody could complain about the spirit of the occasion. The pastor and Quisling supposedly knew each other since their youth, and it was quite evident that the pastor was glad to see him again. She had never seen him so elated, and when the rally was over Quisling came back; there was music and song, which made people stop in the street to listen. Balder, his brother, was sick in bed with influenza that Sunday, which may have been why the pastor had the courage to let himself go and throw off his depression.

How about the other brother, Steingrim, did he ever visit the parsonage?

Not very often, as far as she could recall. Three times altogether. The first time was as far back as 1937 or 1938, she couldn't remember exactly. The young man seemed strangely restless, couldn't sit still for five minutes, and stayed only one night at the parsonage. From the conversation between the brothers she understood that he had run away from home and was on his way to a city called Marsay or something, to go to sea. But he didn't seem cut out for a sailor's life, for a few months later he was back, shamefaced and crestfallen. The third and last time he showed up was in December 1944, at which time the pastor locked him in the sacristy and delivered him to the Gestapo. His brother had come straight from a piece of sabotage that had gone wrong and cost him his hand. It was the pastor who opened the door when he knocked, but she had a glimpse of him through the opening before the brothers went to the church together. Steingrim bled profusely, and to stop the flow of blood he had removed his cap and wrapped it around the stump of his arm. The cap was completely soaked with blood, and the man was so shaky on his feet that the pastor had to support him on the way across the churchyard.

What was the relationship between the brothers like, could she say anything about that?

It seemed good, strangely enough, far warmer and heartier than his relationship with the teacher. But the pastor was furious when he realized what his brother had got himself mixed up in and told him that it served him right if someone reported him to the authorities. After locking him up in the sacristy he quickly dropped in at home, but then went out again for a long time. It must have been then that he went to see his German friend, asking him to come and take care of the saboteur . . .

When Vemund Hov sat in the courtroom one year later he stubbornly denied having delivered his brother to the Gestapo. But during the subsequent cross-examination he cut a poor figure, unable to explain why he had shut up Steingrim in the sacristy. It was a whim that occurred to him, he said, a sudden impulse that he didn't have the time to consider more closely. He may have been trying to give his brother a hiding place, but it was also possible he had done it without any particular purpose in mind. He had to get the man out of the way, and the church had at all times been a sacred place where even evildoers could seek refuge.

"So you didn't support your brother's action when you helped him seek cover?"

"No, not at all. I'm opposed to subversive activity and cannot see it as a solution. When my brother showed up at my door, I felt most of all like telling him to get lost, and would no doubt have done so if he hadn't been so severely wounded. But to deliver him to the Gestapo – never, never!"

After this the prosecutor was silent for a while, leafing through his papers. He shook his head meaningfully and shifted his eyes from the documents to the accused.

"Well and good," he said at last. "So it was not you who first locked up the saboteur and then dropped a hint to the Gestapo. We are willing to believe you, even though we know that you were on an excellent footing with the occupying power at the time."

With that the interrogation took a new turn, and the prosecutor could play his trump card: the pastor's obvious friendship with a German officer, more explicitly SS-*Sturmbannführer* Otto Todleben, an extension of Terboven's arm and the region's highest military authority.

But before we go on to this last and damning part of the interrogation, we shall let the trial rest and see what is written in Vemund's diary for the autumn and winter of 1944.

4

Wednesday, 23 August. The dog days ended as bleakly as they began. Constantly pouring rain, with showers like real cloudbursts. Sun up at 4.52 and down 7.46 – if one can believe that the old fireball is still there behind the cloud banks. Temperature at six in the morning, 9.5° Celsius.

Returned home late Saturday night after a fortnight's summer holiday at Nether Hov. Don't you believe it! I had to grind away at farm chores from early morning till late at night.

When we arrived on 5 August, the farm couldn't have been in a worse shape. Steingrim, my brother, had run away from home in the middle of the haying season and disappeared without a trace. The haycocks were rotting in the fields in the pouring rain, and it was with great difficulty that Kjellfrid and I managed to bring them in.

Father is now so far gone because of hardening of the arteries that his head is all in a whirl. He thought I was a government envoy, sent to lower the Hov Lake according to the instructions he had given almost a generation ago. He became quite impossible when he realized who I was, and sent me to the back of beyond. But shortly afterwards he gave me a fatherly pat on the shoulder and said it would be terrific when the swamp had been drained and we could begin to sow wheat. It went back and forth like that during my entire stay. Now he would recognize me as the prodigal son and begin to scold, now we were great pals who would show the whole world and environs how a farm ought to look.

Poor Kjellfrid – she slaves her life away looking after the old man, in addition to having all of the farming dumped on her back. Father is now in his ninety-first year and cannot keep himself clean anymore. He's a filthy mess, urinates and defecates like a baby, and Kjellfrid has to be after him late and early, lest the whole house be coated with the stuff.

Besides, the old man wants to go out and meet people, he disappears as soon as her back is turned. Of course, the poor old fellow doesn't get very far with his two sticks. But sometimes he manages to stop a carriage on the road and get a ride, at other times he hitches the horse himself while Kjellfrid is in the woods to fetch the cows home. Then she has to get the milking done in a hurry and tramp from farm to farm to track him down.

Kjellfrid doesn't say much, but I can see it troubles her that the family is in such disfavour in the village. It was bad enough before, but after the war came the people at Nether Hov have become completely isolated. The old man isn't taken seriously by anyone, they realize what is happening to him. They may even find it directly satisfying that the best and brightest head in the community has ended up in total confusion. That in the end nature puts things straight and levels all differences.

It's a different matter with Balder. Before I arrived with Mary and the kids he was home for a few days and certainly didn't waste his time. Kjellfrid says that the people on the farms in the area are scared of him; they believe he may denounce them to the Germans and don't dare turn him away. He has an infallible nose for sniffing out a coffee party, and once he feels comfortable indoors he pretends not to notice the oppressive mood. Or who knows, perhaps he is so devoid of ordinary sensitivity that he really doesn't notice anything.

By the time he left he hadn't lifted a finger to help with the farm work, he had just wandered from one neighbourhood to the next expatiating on the world situation. One and all got to hear that Germany had almost won the war and that the situation was far from being as bad as the voice from London claimed. The Normandy invasion he dismisses as allied propaganda, he himself being better informed, knowing from a reliable source that a great German offensive is coming.

For my own part, it didn't take me long to sense the mood in the neighbourhood. I only had to take a walk down the road to get the message. People looked away, sneaking past me as though I were carrying an infection. And I certainly wasn't going to take the initiative. I strode briskly on, aware of a familiar feeling emerging in me: a kind of reverse pride, an antithesis to all theses, a quiet gloating over having to play the old game of one against all.

What is the matter with me, that at the age of forty-four I continue to go ahead recklessly, refusing to learn my lesson? One thing is that I don't try to make myself understood by other people; worse yet, I don't even try to become wise to myself. Wouldn't it be about time to find out what my attitude really is to the occupation of Norway? After all, I know that a German defeat is coming and that I find myself on the wrong side in the eyes of everybody. Why do I do nothing to save myself, why don't I see the writing on the wall and detach myself from the losing party? Can it be that defeat has a secret attraction for me? That I am a Nay-sayer and an incorrigible misanthrope who doesn't want to be where people are waving palms of victory?

For Mary the stay at Nether Hov proved an ordeal from beginning to end. She positively gasped for air when we entered the kitchen and rushed off to open a window that wouldn't come unstuck. The children got fleas on the first night, and Mary's extermination campaign was anything but low-key. Poor Kjellfrid, who doesn't know what cleanliness is, was lectured about it till she burst into tears and rushed out the door. But Mary kept at it, refusing to let her get away with it: the cracks in the floor were packed with filth, father stank, the flypaper was full of dead flies, the dishes were a mess, and the pots and pans were so ingrained with old dirt they must be scrubbed with scouring powder.

I was careful not to meddle; only once did I ask her to be a little more tactful. She snorted and turned aside, as though I were personally responsible for the world's filth.

Saturday, 26 August. The weather a bit lighter, but no sun to be seen. Not a puff of air, as if nature too had difficulty breathing. Temperature at six in the morning risen to 11° Celsius.

Tomorrow I'll deliver my sermon on the text for the fourteenth Sunday after Trinity, but my head feels completely empty. Difficult to get going with my pastoral duties after our stay at Nether Hov. Almost exclusively German soldiers in church when I gave the service last Sunday. I could see only six of my countrymen: three Nazis, one unknown person, and two of the faithful who come just to hear the word of God.

Worried thinking about Kjellfrid after our leave-taking five days ago. Immediately after breakfast, while the children were playing in the yard and Mary was upstairs packing, I asked my youngest sister to come into the living room and closed the door behind us. The old man was sitting on the bench in the kitchen, struggling with his morning porridge and shaking his spoon at the flies that were cleaning their feet on the edge of his plate.

I took out a few hundred-krone notes and told Kjellfrid that she should hire a boy to help her with the potato digging, if Steingrim hadn't come home by then.

She started when I mentioned Steingrim; then she bowed her head over the tablecloth and hid her face between her hands. I put a hand on her shoulders and asked what was the matter, but she just winced, and I had to wait a long time for an answer.

"Keep your money," she said at last, on the brink of tears. "We have disgraced ourselves all over Siljan, don't you see? We are shunned by everyone, and no decent man will dig potatoes at Nether Hov."

"I see," I said, but didn't take back the money. "Then let the potatoes stay in the ground until Steingrim shows up some day."

She turned to me, her eyes full of fear, and burst into tears, violent sobs. "Steingrim won't be home till the war's over," she lamented. "He has joined the Resistance and is far deeper underground than any potato."

"What are you saying?" I cried, shaking her arm. "Who is spreading such slanders about our brother?"

"He told me himself," she whispered. "He has always told me what he does, starting with his leaving home in 1938. I'm the only person who understands him and knows who he is."

"Now, just try to calm down and explain yourself properly," I said. "What did he tell you that time he left home and was going to sea?"

"He wasn't going to sea," she cried, convulsively closing her hands around the tablecloth. "He wanted to volunteer for the Spanish Civil War, but ran into so many obstacles on the way that it became too late."

"What?" I said, aware I was getting mad. "Are you telling me he was faking it, that he deceived me? When he came to the parsonage he said he had fallen out with Father and had decided to become a sailor!"

"I shouldn't have told you!" she cried, wiping her tears with her apron. "I promised him to keep quiet and not tell a living soul. Not the thing about the Home Front either."

I was so surprised I didn't know what to say. For quite a while I sat stroking her back, begging her to calm down. She shouldn't regret having confided in me, no, she shouldn't. I would keep the secret with her, and she could be reassured, my lips were sealed. The day might come when Steingrim required help, at which time he would need greater support than a frightened little sister could provide.

"But aren't you . . . ," she asked, sending me a long, scrutinizing look. "Hereabouts they say that not a single one of the sons at Hov is to be trusted, and that you are the most dangerous and cunning of them all."

"Do they now?" I replied, unable to suppress a chuckle at the bit about cunning. I was just about to say some soothing words to her when Mary stuck her head through the door and asked if I wouldn't come soon. Everything was ready for our departure, I just had to drive the car up and put the suitcases into the boot.

Tuesday, 29 August. Finally it's clearing up, as is my beclouded head. On Thursday, 28 September, I'll once more begin my musical devotions, the only part of my ministry that gives me a little comfort and uplift. I met with the organist yesterday evening to plan the programme for the whole autumn season. Handel's *Messiah* and the oratorio *St Paul* by Mendelssohn will be the most demanding tasks, but we begin a little more modestly with the song numbers *Ave Verum* and *Mors et Vita* by Gounod.

I'm certainly in need of a few bright spots right now, even my domestic life has unravelled and can't be repaired. Mary and I have lived apart since that terrible thing occurred between us Easter Sunday. Good God, what kind of person am I? I have managed to scare her so thoroughly that she shields her face with her arm as soon as I make a sudden movement. It's all over between us and I make no attempt to get close to her.

I have no idea what was the matter with me on Easter Sunday, everything was taking its accustomed course and I didn't intend to make a row. It was just before high mass; I was about to climb the stairs and get into my cassock, and Mary was standing before the big mirror in the hall fixing herself up for Sunday dinner over at the ship owner's house. Maybe there was something about her reflection in the mirror that annoyed me, the way she stood there tilting her head and preening herself. Suddenly I was overcome by a destructive urge, I stamped my feet and felt a wild desire to smash the mirror and her vanity with it. And before I managed to check myself, I had succumbed to a blind rage. My whole miserable life closed in on me, all the Sundays I'd gone to church alone, all those solitary meals at the dining table, the bachelor's existence I was condemned to every single holy day, while she was decking herself out preparing to leave.

Before I realized it I had rushed across the floor and pushed her against the wall, and while she stood there cowering I let fly at her in such a rough and violent manner that I won't ever be able to forgive myself for it.

When it was over I sat down on the stairs with my head between my hands, and I remained there for so long that at last the verger came over and asked what had happened. I jumped up, got into my cassock as I was supposed to, and reached the church a few minutes late; but I was able to go through with the Easter service, calmly and in the proper order.

Since then I have asked myself how it can be that time and again I forget myself in my domestic life, when I'm capable of such self-restraint in the discharge of my official duties. If I have control of myself in one place, with a little good will I ought to have it in the other place too, right? After all, Mary has not changed since I fell in love with her ten years ago. It's I who have become someone else, my vision hexed by a splinter in my eye. Her frivolity vexes me, and all the qualities I used to regard as merits have now become shortcomings.

So if someone is to blame in our relationship, it must be myself. I was a full-grown, thoughtful man who in a moment of weakness let myself be tempted by a young girl eager for adventure. I ought to have foreseen what the outcome would be when a melancholy savage got hitched to a playful innocent.

Now it's all too late, and I hope I have sufficient strength of will to leave her alone. Her coldness is unmistakable, she doesn't care for me in the least and has forgotten all the dodges she once used to catch me.

Sunday, 10 September. Sunrise at 5.33, sunset at 6.55. Temperature at six in the morning, 4° Celsius. Sparkling weather, but with a peculiar clarity in the atmosphere that portends darker and harsher times.

I sit down to write a few words about this, that and the other, before Mary returns with Vidar and Urd.

Once, last autumn, Idun suddenly refused to come along to the ship owner's house; she would rather come with me to church and afterwards to the cemetery plot. And this is the way it has been for nearly a year. She refuses to join the others, and her face takes on a sort of fearful look when someone mentions her grandfather's house. I cannot bring myself to question her, but something must have happened over there to frighten her, and burden her with something.

Right now she is sitting in the kitchen with Anna, who is helping with her knitting, which is full of holes and dropped stitches. The little girl is clumsy with her hands; in that respect also, she is different from the other two, who are extremely deft for their age. She doesn't have an easy time of it with pen and ink either. She splatters and makes splotches, so that the schoolmistress feels called upon to walk around the classroom and display her copy book as an example of how it should not be done.

Perhaps it was wrong of me to let the children skip the first standard and start right away in the second? The school board was against it, but I forced it through with the help of an old fellow student employed in the Church and Education Department.

Poor dear, she's a bit of a rum one, and I'm afraid she won't have an easy life. She's smart and thoughtful enough – as a matter of fact, I wonder if she isn't the one of the three who is most gifted. But somehow she is at once too slow and too advanced and doesn't develop in a regular and orderly way.

Mary never learns to watch out when someone praises our children. She has a weakness for praise, but always takes care to diminish it where Idun is concerned. It doesn't occur to her that the children stand beside her listening, she just gives her opinion loud and clear as if they weren't present. She has chosen one of the little girls for herself, and that means the other has been rejected and pushed aside.

In all fairness, Urd is good enough, quick-witted, unabashed, and already well on the way to becoming a beauty. Big blue eyes, a perfectly oval face, and a rosebud of a mouth that looks sweet, even when she pouts. But if old Francis Bacon, Lord Verulam, was right in saying that only the irregular is truly beautiful, Idun nevertheless takes the prize.

"Dad, do you think I'm ugly too?" she asked me one day in the graveyard; she had obviously picked up something. "Why haven't I got a face just like Urd's, since we are twins and born the same day?"

At first I grew angry and uneasy, but fortunately I managed to laugh it off and cheer her up with a little creation myth:

"It's a day in the spring of 1937," I say. "God has got an order for twins and has to start creating them. It ought to be a simple matter for someone who has created a whole world, but still a bit more difficult than when he creates one human being at a time. He gets out the best material he has: fine, soft, silky skin, golden threads of hair, clear eyes, muscles and bones that have never been used before. 'Let's see,' he mumbles in his beard as he sits there feeling his way. 'They are going to be twins, sure enough, but watch out nonetheless that they won't be just like two drops of water. Not bad at all,' he says to himself when Urd is all ready and the rough work on Idun is finished. 'The recipe is good, but I'll have to think up something new before I let go of the other one. After all, that's what being divine means, being able to make things almost alike without producing look-alikes.'

"He sits there pondering a little while before he knows what is required. Then he goes ahead and kneads the Idun-face one last time, makes a pimple in one cheek, raises one eyebrow an iota, and pulls the lower lip slightly forward. 'Do I dare risk it?' he asks himself when he gets as far as the eyes. 'Of course I do, I'm God after all!' he answers, and picks out the most radiant eyeballs he has, one blue and the other brown. When he has put them in place, he nods with satisfaction and chuckles behind his big hand before he nudges her off the cloud. 'There you are,' he calls down to the parents who sit waiting. 'The second twin took a bit of time, but I hope you will be satisfied and can see the difference.'

"Do you understand, my friend?" I say as I kneel down and plant flowers on the grave of my first-born. "God wanted to show that he could create Idun and not just a new version of Urd. That's why you've got one blue and one brown eye and a face that is all your own."

"But isn't it ugly to have two mismatched eyes?"

"No, it's exciting and interesting; you realize it's a face that God has taken special pains with. When we get home I'll show you a picture of a German poet called Goethe. You can't ever figure out his face, you have to go back to the picture and look at it again and again. It was said about him that an angel peeped out of one eye and a devil out of the other."

"You mustn't say that!" she cries, waving her arm to chase the words away. "I don't want to have a devil looking out of my eyes!"

"Calm down," I say. "With you it is two angels: one dark and one light, one smart and one clumsy, one merry, the other serious."

This is how we chat on Sundays when we go to look after the grave of the Moluccan Princess. Mostly we talk about what is nearest to us, about the flowers we're going to plant, the holes we dig in the ground, the earthworms crawling out and the birds sitting ready to devour them. But despite the difference in age and other natural obstacles, it happens occasionally that we transcend ourselves and go deeper than that.

"Emi-gra-vit," she spells, her index finger nearly touching the headstone. "Dad, why does it say 'emigravit'?"

"It means emigrated," I say. "It's written in a language called Latin."

"To emigrate, what is that?" she asks; for my latest-born is thoughtful and has the good habit of never letting go of a problem before it's cleared up.

"It means to move to another country."

"What kind of a country is it?"

"That I cannot tell you, because I've never been there. Some call it heaven or eternity, others are content to call it annihilation or the great nothingness."

"Won't we come back anymore after we have *emigravit*?" she asks, knitting her brows.

"No, then we won't come back anymore, unless someone remembers us and takes care of our grave. When you and I talk about the Moluccan Princess as we are doing now, then she comes to life again for a short while, until she fades away and disappears where she came from."

While we are cleaning the headstone and making it shine, I explain to her where I have the inscription from. That when I was living in Germany I once saw it on a monument to the painter Albrecht Dürer.

"At first I thought it would some day be on my own tombstone," I say. "But then the Moluccan Princess came and decided to emigrate, and I realized that she must have it."

"Her name is Josefine Charlotte," she says almost doubtfully, after staring at the inscription a while. "But Dad, then it's my name, isn't it, that's written on the headstone?"

I'm startled, but manage to compose myself and make light of it.

"You're also called Idun and she was not," I reply, stooping to gather my tools. "You see, your mother and I could never agree on what you should all be called. The first time I let her have her own way. But later I always added an extra name when I entered the baptismal names in the church register."

"Dad, can you tell me, was the Moluccan Princess a real princess, or are you just joking when you call her that?"

"No, believe me, I'm not joking. She came one day from the country east of the sun and west of the moon and stayed with us for a short while, until she became homesick and went away."

"It seems so strange when you think about it," she says long afterwards, when we're finished on the cemetery plot and stroll home across the churchyard. "I'm the twin who God kneaded one time too many. And I'm the baby sister who has stolen the name of the Moluccan Princess."

*   *

Monday, 18 September. The Lord be praised, the rally of the NS troopers is over. High mass took its course, nothing unusual happened, except that the attendance was overwhelming and the church occupied to the last pew.

By a kind of irony of fate the text for the day was "Render unto Caesar the things that are Caesar's, and unto God the things that are God's." I interpreted the text as best I could without an eye to the actual situation. My sermon was short, even shorter than the one that the chairman of the parish board choked on at my induction more than ten years ago. But on the other hand, I sang my two favourite hymns before the altar: "In heaven, in heaven" immediately after the creed, and "No man will win eternal peace" as I descended from the pulpit just before I proclaimed the benediction. The organist followed me with understanding on the organ, and I believe those old folk melodies gave back to the High Mass what might have been lost in my sermon.

At first I thought that Vidkun Quisling had not shown up, though I had received a hint that he would be present. But as I stood in the pulpit and read the text, I suddenly caught sight of him in the uppermost gallery. He looked extremely buttoned-up and forbidding as he sat between his two bodyguards; a shiver passed through me, and I thought the prospect for Sunday dinner at the parsonage looked extremely bleak. But in the midst of the sermon our eyes met and a faint smile lit up his face.

Fortunately Balder was sick in bed at home, so I was spared being browbeaten by his presence. My zealous brother had as usual acted behind my back, convened a troopers' rally, invited Quisling for dinner at the parsonage, and shut my mouth when I attempted a weak protest.

I hadn't seen Quisling since 1919 and cannot exactly say that I looked forward to our meeting. And indeed, it turned out to be rather stiff, with two reserved men shaking hands and trying to get back on speaking terms across a distance of a quarter century. Scarcely a word was exchanged between us on our stroll across the churchyard; my guest was so far away that he nearly stumbled several times, and I was annoyed with myself that I hadn't been able to oppose the arrangement.

But during dinner the tension dissolved, and when we began brushing up old memories the mood became quite animated. While coffee was being served, I sat down at the piano and sang two songs that I had chosen with care. First, Per Sivle's "They stood at Stiklestad in battle array" and then Welhaven's "Saint Olav stood at the fjord with his army" – both poetry in the high style that I thought must be in keeping with the Minister President's national temper and his religiously tinged idealism. I was not mistaken. At one moment I perceived a soft drone behind my back, and when I got to the last verses he joined in with a voice that sounded far from bad.

When he was about to leave shortly afterwards, he looked so lonely and forlorn that it wrung my heart. All at once I remembered a bitterly cold New Year's Eve in the Gjerpen parish, when an exhausted peasant boy knocked on the door of the parsonage and asked for shelter, and a young, rather gruff officer strode up and took him into a warm room. After the vicissitudes of twenty-seven years the situation was roughly the same, with the sole difference that the roles were now reversed. When I gave him my hand for goodbye, he seized it almost in panic, and when he finally released it he let his hands drop in a peculiarly despairing manner, as though he were tearing himself away from his last refuge in life. I noticed that his face was drawn and ravaged, and that the expression in his eyes was one of near-perplexity. But at the same time his bearing was straight, indeed, almost military in its erectness, with a will to hold out that bordered on the superhuman.

On second thoughts, lightning-quick, I asked him to give me the pleasure of coming back when the rally was over and stay the night with me at the parsonage. I didn't have to force myself to offer this invitation, for a profound gratitude had sprung up within me, and it was a real pleasure to reciprocate and keep the door to the parsonage open one more time. What would have become of me, it flashed through my mind, if the Quisling family hadn't seen my distress that New Year's Eve long ago, and had a big enough heart to look after me?

At first he turned away, looking almost shamefaced, and a sudden blush spread across his sallow features. Perhaps he, too, recalled something deeply felt that embarrassed him. But a moment later he nodded slowly, clicked his heels together as if he had received a military order and hurried off.

Midnight was approaching when he again knocked on my door, and it was almost half-past four by the time we finally went to bed. Anna had made up beds on the floor in the hall for his two bodyguards, and they lay down in all their gear, their pistols under the pillow and a watchful eye on every finger.

Quisling and I went into my study and sat down. To my surprise my guest produced a bottle of brandy and placed it on the table between us. That was a fortifying drink that had been banned at the Gjerpen parsonage, and I understood that the Dean's son had reached a point where he could keep going only with the help of such stimulants.

I can only recall in broad outline what he and I talked about during the four hours we stayed up together. But I do remember that we became remarkably close, as can only happen to two people when they have their backs to the wall and sense a common fate.

It was quite evident from my guest's manner that he considered everything to be lost, that doomsday was imminent and nemesis swiftly approaching. A less resolute and honourable man would have begun his retreat long ago, trying to salvage whatever he could. But in his tormented brain there was no thought of rescue, he kept swimming steadily and deliberately against the current and was prepared to go under. Indeed, it almost seemed as if his undoing increased his vitality and steeled his will to the point of inflexibility. National Union was his vocation and destiny in life, and he was firmly resolved to live or die with the movement; preferably live, but if necessary go under and disappear. It was with a kind of masochistic pride that he observed how Germany's allies deserted the cause one after another, until he himself was the only one who stood his ground, faithful to the last.

As the night drew on, he became more and more restless and uneasy, downed one cup of black coffee after another, tramped about the floor like a caged animal, and emptied the brandy bottle almost by himself. His speech became more and more incoherent, but I found it difficult to decide whether it was due to intoxication or to a more permanent impairment of his intellectual powers. At the crack of dawn his ardour flared up, and he spoke passionately about the ancient Norse chieftains, who had been both priests and kings. Almost in the same breath he told me that he was considering applying for the parish pastorship in Fyresdal. He was swollen with pride; obviously he would be glad to see himself in the role of a priest-king. At one point he bent forward and told me in a near whisper that he was of royal descent. He could trace his family tree as far back as Harald Fairhair and Ragnar Lodbrok, even further in fact; it stretched all the way up to prehistoric times, to the Volsungs and the principal West Germanic god, Odin.

As I sat listening with half an ear, I couldn't shake off the suspicion that something had gone wrong with him. He was speaking like a lunatic or like a voice in the wilderness, and had gone far beyond the point where he could balance his self-importance with sound criticism. The crusading spirit had always been alive in him, he told me, and if the times had been different he could very well have envisaged a career as a preacher and spiritual guide. But the Fatherland was in distress and had summoned him, and he had answered like young Samuel in Scripture: "Speak, Lord; for thy servant heareth."

His position as Minister President was nothing less than an offering, he went on, and if there ever was a resistance fighter in Norway, it was him! His lot was the hard one of the scapegoat, onto whom all parties loaded their iniquities, so that they could be expiated and driven away. Just imagine how the occupying power would have treated this country, he almost screamed, if he hadn't mediated and intervened time after time! But what was his reward? Sure, nothing but the old familiar formula: crucify him, crucify him!

Shortly after this outburst we went to bed, and he thanked me in almost biblical terms for my willingness to watch with him for one night. When I got up, rather late in the morning, he was gone, having left a note in which he thanked me for lodging and good company in more sober words.

I quietly dropped the note into the wastepaper basket and was about to cross the hall and open the office when I stopped short and clapped my hand to my forehead. In heaven's name, I had forgotten to tell Quisling the truth about my membership in the National Union. That I had not myself joined the party, so I was in a fix and barred from resigning.

Wednesday, 20 September. Another sleepless night, the third in a row. I lie tossing in bed for hours on end, drop off for a little while perhaps, then get up and take a walk through the house to the office and back. Flop down again, stare out into the darkness, doze a little, and then start all over again from the beginning. Won't I ever find rest after that long night of watching with Vidkun Quisling?

Fortunately I don't share my room with Mary any longer, but sleep on the couch here in my study. I have the entire lower floor to myself and don't need to worry about disturbing anyone with my nocturnal rambles.

What kind of man is Vidkun Quisling? I ask myself, and the answer proves to be uncertain and ambiguous. Highly gifted and full of good will. Hotheaded, but not vengeful. Rather deluded and stubborn, as happens to people when they shut themselves up in their own world, but honourable and deeply in earnest.

Perhaps, when all is said and done, it is this earnestness that is leading him astray. Without a grain of frivolity and natural cheer, even the best nature degenerates and falls prey to bullheadedness and messianic ideas.

The meeting with my old benefactor has certainly given me something to think about. I have once more begun to ponder my homelessness in the world, where it will take me and where it emanates from. Was it perhaps wrong of me to free myself, to break away from my family and the place of my birth? Would it have been better if I had instead become resigned to my condition and remained in the muck and fraudulence of Nether Hov?

The answer is no and again no, and when I roam at night in the quiet house it happens that I shout this "No!" so loudly that I give a start and stop my mouth with my hand. Resignation is not something that occurs through an act of will, I say to myself. It's something mild and clear that grows out of a patience I do not possess.

I know that, considering how I'm made, breaking away was my only salvation, and not a living soul can make me turn back. All the same, homelessness sits like a thorn in my flesh and is almost unbearable. It's probably this that the Bible calls to be damned, to know that you are travelling down trackless paths and yet feel certain that no other paths are open to you.

Last night the devil took me up to a high mountain, not to tempt me with the glory of this world, but to awaken my recollection and give me a view of a part of my life I had nearly forgotten.

I saw myself trudging through the streets of Kristiania on a raw autumn day in 1921, shivering in much too thin clothes and with feet so sore inside my leaky boots that the ground was burning under me. I regarded the down-and-out figure in a sort of slumbering clairvoyance, in which I was at once the observer and the observed; I dreamed, but was above the dream.

What could be driving the hopeful young man to roam about the capital in such foul weather, I wondered, though I knew full well. Was it the pursuit of happiness, the thirst for knowledge, or just a fleeting rendezvous in an entranceway? Neither. It was necessity that drove him, and naked self-preservation that steered his steps. For the miserable payment of forty øre an hour he went up and down stairs to tutor difficult huckster's sons in German and mathematics. If he could fit in five a day, he was just barely able to keep body and soul together and pay the rent for the miserable attic room he shared with another peasant student. While the sons of the gentry were sitting in the reading rooms, puffed up with theological conceit, he was constantly on the go, wearing out his shoe leather merely to survive. And while they let exegesis be exegesis and went on a spree, he slumped exhausted onto his stool to take a critical look at the notes he had managed to scrawl down at the morning's lecture. Too poor to supply himself with textbooks, he had to imprint everything in his memory and keep it in his untiring brain.

Several years were to go by before he improved his lot as a private tutor and could exchange the slow schoolboys for his own fellow students. By that time his roommate had expired from galloping consumption, and he could abandon his curled-up position on the settee bed and stretch out under the departed's pestiferous blankets. For a long time he wasn't able to go to sleep because he missed his friend's cough – that hacking, barking desire for life, that remainder of human breath and endurance that gurgled in the dying man's used-up lungs.

But little by little he won a name for himself in the theology department, although it was a recognition with many reservations and shrugs. He could afford to buy books and a winter coat, could keep hunger at bay and yet send a monthly shilling home to Nether Hov to start paying for his perfidy.

But he was never admitted to the Pleiades, the exegetical society that supposedly included the most brilliant minds in the department, but which in reality was an unbreakable ring of theologians from the right social circles who saw to it that the unworthy were excluded. A self-taught man with many oddities, unfamiliar with the accepted rules of academic debate, Vemund Hov was an all too unpredictable quantity for anyone to feel quite at ease in his company.

Where did he find the strength to hold out, how did he manage to preserve his gifts and his self-respect throughout such a long ordeal? Was he not already stigmatized as a divinity graduate, homeless, friendless and banished from good society? Condemned to be a Vemund Contrary who prided himself on defying circumstances and conquering life one against all?

Saturday, 23 September. My intellectual life is barren after six nights of insomnia, I can barely think a clear thought. Walk calmly about the parish, pretending not to notice the eyes looking askance at me from every side. The service last Sunday has left its mark, all right – not to mention the visitor I had at the parsonage afterwards.

Only my visits to the sick remain the same, and I meet no animosity where I show up. Notice to my surprise that I find it easy to make contact with ill and sorrowful people. My own wretched situation disappears, and a strange power flows into me from an unknown source. As a pastor I probably ought to call this source God, but in my doubt and unworthiness I choose to leave that question open.

I probably do not have the aptitude to be a spiritual person through and through. There are too many things that weigh on me and drag me down. My aspiring spirit has heavy lumps of earth under its feet; despite all attempts at escape it is still trudging in the swamp and wilderness of Nether Hov.

I often think of resigning as pastor, but cannot quite come to a decision. What is a pastor's mission? I ask myself. Is it not to be a mediator between the earthly and something that is so incomprehensible that no one can grasp it and make himself into a spokesman for it?

Enough. Maybe it won't be long before everything will straighten out by itself.

To get some breathing space I have transformed my study into a work-shop and use every free hour for practical tasks. Have just finished soling all of the family's shoes and lengthening the children's winter boots by adding new toes. Mary wrinkled her nose when she saw the result, called it patch-work and said that children of good family couldn't appear in public with feet looking like that. Her father had good connections with the merchants in town, she said, and could easily procure three pairs of new boots.

I felt I was losing my temper, but managed to control it and tell her calmly that in this house there was no space for any black market merchandise.

Unfortunately the children begin to take after her and to see things through her eyes. During the summer they were enthusiastic about the satchels I made for them and would carry them proudly over their shoulders, while the others held theirs in their hands. Now they make faces, finding the satchels tacky all of a sudden. "There they are, with their postboxes!" the children shout after them. Poor kids, they probably haven't seen a shoulder bag before. But no matter, the children must learn to be independent and to bear the brunt. Children will tease, and it's better that they get an earful for the postboxes than for something else.

However, they probably get to hear about other things too. Yesterday morning, as Idun and I were sitting down to eat together, she told me something that I'll have to think about more carefully. She gets pushed around on her way to school, and they call her a Nazi fatty, because she's a bit chubby and has a father who receives visits from Vidkun Quisling. She was on the verge of tears when she told me this, and I didn't know what to say to comfort her.

What about the other two? I asked. Weren't they also teased? She shook her head and said nobody dared do that. Urd was the girl in class who decided everything; she would have everyone on her side with a mere wave of her hand.

And what about Vidar? I wanted to know. Why, he was the leader among the boys. But how could he be, since he too had a father who was visited by Vidkun Quisling? Oh, he threatened them, so that no one dared call after him. If they didn't keep their mouths shut, he told them, it would be their tough luck. Then his father would go to the Germans and get their parents thrown in prison.

Friday, 29 September. The musical devotion yesterday turned out to be an exceptional celebration; it was as though we raised the roof. I almost feel like shouting *Selah*! – as the psalmist does when something pans out and succeeds beyond all expectation.

I had feared that only Nazis and German soldiers would show up, but that did not happen. Music lovers from the entire district filled the pews, also patriots and so-called good Norwegians.

It's the organist we have to thank for the fact that the choir hasn't broken up and been scattered to the four winds. During the early years of the war there were losses, especially of male voices. But our mastersingers evidently couldn't live without Lady Musica. Gradually they came back, one by one and in great numbers, until the choir was complete.

Our *Scola Cantora* scarcely has its equal any other place in the country – considering the size of the town, it is nothing less than a miracle. Perhaps it's not so remarkable that people come flocking, even though the pastor in charge of the program is somewhat dubious and rumoured to be a German sympathizer.

Mary had agreed to sing the soprano part and carried it off with such sparkle and sweetness it almost took my breath away. Again it was the organist who persuaded her to do it; when I mentioned the matter to her around Pentecost she just looked out the window, pretending not to hear what I was saying. In the middle of the oratorio I noticed to my great delight and pleasure that our voices found one another, and we came together in song with the same ardour and intensity as ten years ago. What if . . . No, no, old Adam, bethink yourself; you know, don't you, how long a happy man is allowed to remain in paradise.

When the musical devotion (the concert) was over, something happened that was so unexpected that I need some time to think it through. I'm still completely dazed and bewildered in my own mind, even after the lapse of twenty-four hours. Am I caught in a trap, or do I dare believe that something joyful has happened to me? God in heaven, can it be true that my isolation is broken, and that I have reached an oasis in the desert?

The choir was going to town the celebrate the event, and I promised to come along. But since I needed to collect myself a little, I asked the singers to go ahead, while I remained in church alone. A great weight had been lifted from me, and I hummed some stanzas of the oratorio as I walked up to the altar and kneeled down in silent prayer.

I do not know how long my meditation lasted, for at such moments I'm unaffected by time and space. Most likely only a few minutes had gone by when I suddenly became aware of a slight noise down by the entrance. As I got to my feet and turned around, I saw a German officer coming up the aisle, followed by his adjutant at a few steps' distance. He must have been waiting in the vestibule, for he came towards me with a resoluteness that showed he wanted to see me for a special reason.

My initial reaction was a blind dread and heart palpitations. It looked to me as though the hour of reckoning had arrived, that I would be forced to stop shuffling and to take a definitive position towards what was taking place in my country. The mere sight of that black uniform was enough to make me shudder and expect the worst. Throughout the years of war I have entrenched myself behind my ministry and kept away from the occupying power in order not to give offence and provoke indignation.

But it all came off quite differently from what I had feared. The officer's gait as he walked up through the church looked anything but military; I would be inclined to call it theatrical if it hadn't at the same time been so solemn. About midway he stopped to draw a deep breath, before raising his voice and greeting me with a succession of notes which I immediately recognized as the prelude to *Ave Verum*.

For a moment I stood as if thunderstruck, staring at the man in the black uniform. Then the musical spirit came over me and made me forget my intention to keep the occupying power at a distance. I walked toward him in the same solemn way, responding with the next stanza of the oratorio. And thus we continued the procession, moving forward step-by step and greeting one another with an antiphonal singing that rose and fell, until we stood face to face and the last remnant of irreconcilability between us had died away.

We sat down in the front row, and it didn't take long to make contact. Simply hearing the German language again sent long stabs of joy through me. It was in that beloved language that I was welcomed abroad, a form of compensation for all the hardship I had encountered at educational institutions in my own country.

His name is Otto Todleben – quite some name for a soldier, as if from the very first moment he was condemned to hover between life and death. Seven years older than I, born on 25 December 1892 in the old fort-city of Ulm, Württemberg. His military rank is *Sturmbannführer*, whatever that may mean. I made it clear to him on the spot that I am a born civilian, and that militarism is for me a sheer absurdity. I would have to disregard his black uniform with its death symbols, I said, if I were to look upon him as a human being and not a marionette.

He took it nicely and told me that for him, too, the military was somewhat of a makeshift solution. Originally he wanted to be a violinist and was well on the way towards his goal when World War One broke out, and he was called up as a lieutenant with the royal Bavarian infantry. It had been his intention to resign his commission as soon as the war was over, but during the offensive on the western front in 1918 he was hit by a projectile and lost three fingers on his left hand. For the officer this loss was not irreparable; he was transferred to the general staff, where he made his way quickly until he enrolled in the SS. But for the violinist the destruction of the sensitive left hand was fatal. He was through as a performing musician and had to abandon his dream of sometime creating a furore in the concert hall.

He is a man of exceptional intellectual culture, more widely read than most and well versed in the whole world of music. We have the same ideas and inclinations, but to all appearances he is more of a pure aesthete than I shall ever become. In the scant hour we sat and talked we only had time to give each other a number of catchwords, but they struck a sympathetic chord and opened up undreamed-of possibilities. We agreed to meet after the church concert (the devotions) in a fortnight, and since he couldn't think of a suitable meeting place, the upshot of it was that he would come to me at the parsonage.

I'm afraid it will mean that I make another blunder and let myself in for criticism. But let that go. I'm a pastor and not a *condottiere*, and I refuse to divide humankind into the categories friend and enemy.

Monday, 2 October. From time to time I occupy myself with a little piece of writing, which for want of a better title I've called the *Apology*.

It's not a defence on the Socratic model, but an attempt to look into our actions as human beings and see whether there exist any explanations for them.

Naturally, when all is said and done the inquiry is about my own actions, but my object is what is human in the widest possible sense. The question is whether our actions can be said to be strictly individual – and therefore unique – or whether we can justifiably infer from one person to another, and from one case to another.

If every human action is unique, it becomes doubtful whether the judicial system can be used as a standard. Doesn't the entire code of law become an illusion if it is impossible to establish a rule for how human beings ought to behave in a given situation? True enough, that paragon among thinkers, Immanuel Kant, asserts that our actions ought to be representative, that they must have a validity which makes them into a general law and a rule of conduct for others.

As an abstract thinker he is undoubtedly correct. That's the way it must be in the ideal world, where his categorical imperative and his *Ding an sich* are to be found. It's just that he ignores the fact that we are human beings of flesh and blood, that we are compelled to live our lives in a place incomparably more chaotic and imperfect than that in which the philosophers erect their abstract systems.

Seeing Vidkun Quisling again has made these speculations highly relevant. What will happen to him when the war is over? I ask myself. Will his idealism and his honourable intentions be permitted to speak for him, or will he be court-martialled and end his life before the firing squad? Will it stand him in good stead that the National Union was a perfectly legal party when it was formed in 1933? Or will new laws be passed, laws with retroactive force that make it a crime for a man to stick to his original point of view? Will a new kind of legal procedure be used, where questions are no longer asked concerning intentions and motives, but where only the outcome counts?

In that case the victors might just as well save themselves the trouble of taking legal action against Vidkun Quisling and kill him without any judicial fuss.

Saturday, 14 October. Another letter from Kjellfrid – the fourth since we left Nether Hov on 19 August. Mostly it is a repetition of the same complaints, but this time there's something in the tone that makes me uneasy.

She says that she's dead tired and can't go on alone any longer with the drudgery at Nether Hov. Father has become quite unmanageable, and if she doesn't keep an eye on him round the clock, he disappears or dreams up all sorts of shenanigans.

For the first time she voices something like a reproach against me. I am the eldest son, she says, I never signed away my right to the farm, so in the end it is I who am responsible for Nether Hov. The letter closes with a cry for help and makes me suspect that something terrible will happen if I don't intervene.

I sat down and wrote back that I couldn't possibly make myself free right now. She must be patient, I would come up after Christmas and straighten things out. I promised to find a solution before the end of the year, we would probably have to get father to the Old People's Home. Now be brave, sister, and hold out another few months, I wrote to her. When Father is out of the way, you will be free and can do with your life what you please. You're only thirty-seven years old and have the future ahead of you. As far as I'm concerned, we could very well sell Nether Hov, the sooner the better, I said. The farm was a swamp of memories, a place of strife and dissension that I would prefer to forget. The buildings were only fit to be torn down, the farmland was worth nothing, and our all-devouring landowner would no doubt know how to deal with the woodland.

I felt relieved after taking the letter to the post office, but tonight I feel uneasy again. What if Kjellfrid won't be able to keep it going until December? Suppose she's completely worn-out and her letter is a plea for immediate help?

I try to be reasonable, telling myself there is no imminent danger. Kjellfrid is young and strong, and she has managed to take care of the farm and Father for many years. Nothing has changed in a long time, so why shouldn't she hold out another couple of months?

But the devil take Steingrim, who simply skips out and leaves her in the soup! If I knew where he was I would haul him over the coals and tell him to take himself home as fast as he knew how.

Sunday, 15 October. When one speaks about the sun it shines! Or as the French express it more strikingly: When one speaks about the wolf, one can see its tail!

This morning when the service was over and I came out of the sacristy, a man stood waiting for me in the churchyard. At first I didn't take any notice of him, for he was standing at one of the cemetery plots, as though he had an errand there. He was ordinarily dressed, in a windbreaker and cloth cap; the peak of his cap was pulled down over his eyes. The most conspicuous thing about him was his full red beard, which made the face look outlandish, while it also reminded me of something. I had almost passed him when he turned around, and to my surprise I recognized my youngest brother, Steingrim.

Fortunately the weather was nice, so I could be certain that my other brother was on the road somewhere far away. After what took place between Steingrim and me, it would have been a great misfortune if a third party had been present and stuck his nose into our affairs.

I understood that he had been on the lookout for me to tell me something, and proposed that we step into the church and sit in the sacristy. The parish clerk, the sexton and the organist had gone home, so he needn't fear we would be disturbed.

I had not seen Steingrim in over a year and was shocked to discover how he had changed. It was not simply the unkempt beard he had grown, making him look like a tramp or some other shady character. His face was severely emaciated, his eyes hollow, and the strong, well-proportioned figure had developed a sort of stoop, as if overtaken by premature age.

After we had sat in silence for a while, I unsealed my lips and reproached him for having slipped away from home, leaving Kjellfrid in a fix. So as not to frighten him, I began by discreetly telling him about the letters I had received from our sister. But I soon flared up in anger, scolded him for his desertion, and asked him what he'd been thinking of, whether he had lost the last remnant of his sense of responsibility.

He listened to me in his usual good-humoured way, nodding gently and letting himself be taken to task. When I paused and looked expectantly at him, he stroked his beard bashfully, and I could see his mouth widen in a wry smile.

"Take it easy, brother, I'm in good company," he said with a little laugh. "If I'm not altogether mistaken I was not the first to turn my back on Nether Hov. First, the heir to the farm disappeared; one fine day he was over the hills and far away, without a word of farewell. Then the next in line – presto, he too was gone without explanation. Left behind was a boy of fourteen who had to do the work of three grown men."

I felt an old resentment tug at me but was able to restrain myself, realizing that he was right. I kept staring out of the window without saying a word for a long time, until I woke up with a start and fixed my eyes on him.

"Where do you plan to go now?" I asked.

"I've taken a job in the machine shop," came his matter-of-fact answer. "An easy job, brother, child's play by comparison with the slavery at Nether Hov."

"All right, it's probably best like that," I said after thinking for a moment. "I've just written to Kjellfrid that we'll have to rid ourselves of the farm."

I sat leaning sideways against the carved table, where the chalice and the tray with the wafers were still waiting to be put back in the cabinet. He sat directly opposite, straddling a tall chair which he had turned round so that he could rest his arms on the back.

"The liberation is rapidly approaching," he said all of a sudden, with a firm look in his eyes. "In a few months there won't be any Germans in this country any longer. But before it gets that far, you and I ought to consider what we can do to liberate Svallaug, our sister."

Taken by surprise, I raised my hand, but gave up and let it fall limply back on the table.

"What do you mean?" I asked. "Have you come to town to sit in judgement and be your brother's keeper?"

"Don't put on a saintly air, and spare us the clerical tone," he said almost gaily. "For a year and a half you've lived in the same town as our poor sister, who's locked up and imprisoned. Has it never occurred to you that it's monstrous, and that you ought to do something to liberate her?"

I was startled and felt threatened. The accusation came so suddenly that I could think of nothing better to do than to ask a counter question: "And what have you done yourself to help Svallaug get out of Balder's clutches?"

"Not much, but I've tried." He waited a moment, all the while clenching his fists and opening them again, as if considering whether to be open with me or keep his secrets to himself.

Then his decision was made, and he told me a story that was so wildly improbable that even while writing this I'm uncertain whether I rightly understood him. I sat listening to him in a strangely dreamlike state, as though his report were happening far away in another world, where phantoms and ghosts play their tricks.

If there's anything at all to the story, it goes as follows:

At the beginning of July, when Balder came up to Siljan for the holidays, the younger brother had been able to pry out of the elder one that Svallaug, his sister, was back in town alone with strict orders not to leave the house. His sister was not in her right mind, Balder claimed, and might do the most unseemly things if she was let out of doors, such as running half-naked through the streets screaming. Having assumed responsibility for her, he had to make sure that she didn't traipse about town causing scandal. And so he had stocked up the food-cupboard, telling her that he would be away for a few days and that, if she broke the agreement and showed herself in town, there would be extremely serious consequences. She must keep the door locked and let no one in, and otherwise take care of the house as usual.

When Steingrim had gained an insight into the matter, he pretended to agree with his brother and praised him for his family feeling. But already the same evening he took his youngest sister aside, and together they laid a plan to rescue Svallaug from her captivity. If she really was sick, she had to be taken to hospital, where she could receive the necessary care. But if she was simply locked up and cowed into obedience, everything within human power had to be done to liberate her. The greatest difficulty consisted in the fact that Balder was one of the big shots in the National Union, county leader in the party and hand in glove with the police and the judicial system. If they were to remove the sister, it could only be done by means of a ruse and in complete secrecy. Steingrim had good connections inside the Home Front, and his plan was to abduct her and get her settled on a farm in lower Telemark until the war was over.

So, when he left Nether Hov in the middle of the haymaking season, it was not in order to shirk work on the farm, but to carry out an action that he assumed would only take a few days. His best friend and fellow conspirator from the unsuccessful trip to Marseille in 1938 had already been initiated, and together they set out to take care of the affair.

At the beginning everything went according to plan. Late one evening Steingrim removed a windowpane in the yellow house and crept inside, while his companion waited with a horse and cart a few hundred metres away. The escape was arranged very well, the driver was dressed in simple peasant clothes, the horse was a none-too-spirited nag, and the bottom of the cart was strewn with bark and chips. If he was stopped, he could tell the entirely credible story that he and his wife had been to town with a load of wood and were now on their way home.

The failure of the action was due to something that the liberators had forgotten to take into consideration. Svallaug was completely unprepared, and when her brother suddenly stood in her bedroom, she was scared out of her wits and defended herself. All persuasion was to no purpose, she begged and implored him to go away and refused to leave the house at any price. Steingrim himself had become doubtful when he set eyes on her again. He had remembered her as a healthy and courageous girl, who lighted up the gloom at Nether Hov. But in the fifteen months Balder had kept her shut up, he had managed to subdue her so thoroughly that he cast his shadow across her even when he was miles away.

"Tell me one thing," I said when I had heard him out. "Why didn't you go home again when you realized that you hadn't got anywhere with your plans?"

"I haven't abandoned them, don't ever think that," he said, looking me in the eye. "I'll stay in town and bide my time, until I find an occasion to carry her away by force."

"No you won't!" I cried, jumping up. "The only thing you'll get out of it is that both of you will endanger yourselves."

He got to his feet in a curiously heavy, cumbersome way and came over to my side of the table, where to my horror he fell on his knees before me. "Give me the bread and the wine," he said, holding out his hand towards the means of divine grace that were still on the table. "I'm going away now, but we cannot part till I've received the benediction."

"Stand up and come to your senses," I shouted angrily. "Holy Communion is no miracle cure, and offers no forgiveness for future crimes."

He crouched at my feet for a moment, then rose and walked toward the exit, his head bowed.

"Goodbye, brother," he said, in a tone of voice that suggested he didn't expect to see me again in this life. "And forgive me if I've talked irrationally and brought disturbance into your life."

"So, you will be working in the machine shop?" I called after him.

"Yes, brother, I'll be there for the time being, biding my time."

Then he was gone. The last impression I had of him was his characteristic way of bowing his head in the doorway, as if forever condemned to walk in and out through the low doors at Nether Hov.

Monday, 16 October, 11.45, evening. There is something I can't get to tally, hence this postscript to what I wrote yesterday.

Can it really be possible that Steingrim has joined the Resistance Movement, or is it just something I have from Kjellfrid and magnify by my own gullibility? I am dumbfounded, because I find it improbable that my nervous and easily frightened brother should take such a perilous path. His naive openness alone argues against it: he would surely take good care not to let it leak out if it was really true that he had any dealings with that camp.

After our conversation in the sacristy yesterday I ask myself: Is my younger brother all there, or is he just one of many other dreamers and lunatics who bear the name Hov? After all, my father's side of the family is full of cranks, emigrants and tramps, so why should it be any different with him? Already as a boy he was an arsonist, and who knows if he isn't plagued by the same proclivities even today? What he has in mind is most likely a one-man enterprise. The Resistance surely knows how to screen its men and won't rub elbows with tramps.

Nevertheless I'm uneasy about him. In one way or another he escapes my calculations. I have to find out where he lives, so that I can warn him and explain to him my own view of the matter: Either the Germans will win the war and, with or against our own will, we shall be incorporated into the promised great-Germanic Reich; or, and more probably, the Allies will be the victors and we shall become part of an equally mighty great-Atlantic empire. Or the grand mogul will rise in the east and let his wild hordes roll over us. In any case, subversive activity is wasted effort. Little Norway is just a pawn in a larger game, moved hither and thither depending on what the Great Powers decide.

It's this game that, in all modesty, I have seen through and refuse to take an active part in. Peace and free will are just blinds; comrade Marx is right:

history acts for us. More than four hundred years ago that old political fox Machiavelli came to the same conclusion. The course of world history is a power game; anonymous forces incarnate themselves and become flesh, as is written. Treaties are made and broken, intrigues are formed, and the body politic is weakened, until the contagion permeates everything and plague breaks out.

That's why I am resigned and give myself up to the condition which Nietzsche calls Russian fatalism. Which already in my faraway youth – long before I had read a word of Nietzsche – caused me to lie down on the threshing floor of that slave driver Gardatun, firmly determined to suffer all, endure all, reconcile myself to all.

Wednesday, 18 October, 6 morning. The meeting with Steingrim has fulfilled its mission nevertheless, lancing a boil I have long been carrying in secret. He's right: it is almost unbelievable that for eighteen months I've known about my sister's imprisonment without doing anything to help her.

It is cowardice and weakness pure and simple, I know it very well. How many times have I not decided to take it up with Balder, without anything coming of it. As soon as I sit opposite my power-hungry brother, I lose courage and sidestep the issue. His massive body alone is enough to make me feel weighed and found too light. I'm locked up within the domain of his power, just as unaccountably as Svallaug is a prisoner in his house.

What is Svallaug's secret, since she is putting up with her lot and doesn't flee? During the summer she was alone in the house for a whole week and could easily have escaped. Can it be true that they are bound together by an improper relationship, as the gossip says? I doubt it. Rather, Balder's compulsive hold on her is psychological, as I ought to know better than anyone else. He has probably caught her at a critical moment, when she was disappointed and broken and didn't know where to turn.

The last I heard from her was that cheerful and happy Christmas card nearly two years ago. She wrote that I shouldn't be surprised if, sometime during the winter, she arranged a wedding party. Her master had become a widower, and since they had had an eye for one another more than twenty years, it was none too early to tie the knot, was it? "You probably laugh at me now, an excited old maid," she wrote. "But whether you believe me or not, I'm full of zest and not at all ashamed to make my marriage bed at the ripe age of forty."

I didn't hear from her again, and did nothing to find out why the wedding didn't come off. Had her expectations been too bright perhaps, had she been let down at the eleventh hour by the man she at long last could regard as hers? Did she carry the child of her seducer when she sought shelter with her despotic brother? Was it conceivable that the rumour was true, that the midwife had paid a nocturnal visit to the yellow house?

I winced at all these hypotheses, and to tell the truth I'm very reluctant to have them cleared up.

But I have to do something. My sister's distress has been brought home to me, and I can no longer pretend it is none of my business.

I give myself a fortnight's grace period. By the end of the month at the latest, I must have decided how to tackle the matter.

Saturday, 21 October. Found a pretext for going down to the machine shop (a.k.a. the machine works) to have a few words with Steingrim. Went poking around in the maze of the old shipyard for a long time before I learned that he works the night shift all this week and the next. No one could tell me where he lived. When he came to town this summer, he had found lodgings at the mission hotel, but as soon as he got a permanent job he had moved into a furnished room somewhere in town.

Though obliged to go back without accomplishing my object, I did get something out of my expedition. I saw the inside of an industrial concern operating at full capacity, while all other industry is shut down. The obvious reason is that the war is taking its course and that the factory delivers arms and machine parts to the occupying power.

It's quite ironic, but evidently my enterprising father-in-law has just as much luck in matters of this world as in those of the beyond. At the same time as he stands on the platform before his flock proclaiming the apocalypse and the last days, he is the main shareholder in an enterprise that is very much of this world and has long-range goals. Today the factory delivers hardware to the Germans, tomorrow it will negotiate contracts with their adversaries, if the wind should turn and blow from another direction. The speculator Andreas Sand knows how to protect himself from every side, all right; he operates high and low and has just as good connections up there as down here.

Before leaving the factory, I left a note for Steingrim in which I asked him to think it over and not do anything rash. He could always be sure that

I wished him well, I wrote, and if he should ever find himself in a difficult situation he mustn't hesitate to ask for my help.

Friday, 27 October. Today had my fifth and perhaps last meeting with Otto Todleben. After the musical devotions we leave the church separately and watch out that no one sees us together. Once I get back to the parsonage, it's a good while before I hear his car breaking on the gravel outside. I stand behind the window and see his shadowy figure cross the square toward the pastor's office, where he steals through the unlocked door like a modern Nicodemus. He's dressed in civvies, and his chauffeur drives off at once and comes back to pick him up only at the agreed time. I take care of the refreshments myself, so unless Anna is prowling by the door, no one but Mary knows who my nocturnal visitor is.

Most of the time we sing and make music, he has a fine, high-pitched tenor that now and then accomplishes wonders together with my own baritone. We sing hymns, *Lieder*, oratorios and parts from the great operas – the last often humorously and on the verge of parody. As a rule I'm the accompanist, but occasionally he pushes me aside and takes control of the keyboard. His right hand is incomparable, racing up and down the keys as if it alone had ten fingers at its disposal. But his ruined left hand is not to be despised. He combines the thumb and index finger into a formidable claw, which is like a veritable sledgehammer for marking the rhythm and producing syncopation. Then I join in, and we play four-handed with three and a half hands, until there's nothing but heavenly harmony and the world situation drifts away, a dark cloud on the far horizon.

Afterwards we settle in the old leather chairs in my study and tentatively speak to one another. Speech is a far more uncertain and risky medium than music, and during our first evenings we didn't get much further than a polite exchange of *bon mots*. He is a refined intellectual, and I am myself deeply indebted to German culture; in fact, I could almost say that I've been formed by its literature and thought.

But suddenly last night something gave way and things opened up between us. We dropped all evasions, and an intimacy arose of a kind that is rare between one man and another. It happened because he began telling me about the German offensive on the western front in the spring of 1918, the last great campaign before the Allies definitively broke through and everything became transformed into an inferno of fire and blood.

It took some time before he got going, and he's not a very good narrator. Time and again he came to a dead stop, staring into vacancy for so long that I feared he wasn't feeling well. He spoke more softly than usual, and now and then his voice dropped to a faint mumbling. Since in addition his account was disconnected and full of lacunae, it was sometimes difficult to follow. But from all the isolated episodes that made up his report, there emerged at length a scenario of such enormous dimensions as to seem almost unreal.

I listened spellbound, letting him take his time and refraining from hurrying him. Soon I was captivated and disregarded his mystifications and strange flights of fancy. He appeared before me as larger than life, that young lieutenant of the Royal Bavarian Infantry, as he led his assault party through no man's land toward the British trenches. A thick fog covered the terrain, and the soldiers could scarcely see their own hands as they dragged themselves forward, heavily loaded with bombs and machine guns. They trudged through mud, stepped over ditches, got stuck in barbed wire, stumbled over tree roots and corrugated iron, while enemy bombers droned in the air above them, rockets whistled past, and the northwestern sky was ablaze with fire from the British artillery. The field was strewn with the fallen, friend and enemy pell-mell; the stench of death and putrefaction was so strong that the showers of mustard gas felt like perfume. From everywhere came the moaning laments of wounded men abandoned by their company, men who still had a long wait before a merciful death would come. Here and there deserters and corpse robbers roamed about, pulling the boots off the fallen, taking their rifles and uniforms, and stealing their watches and valuables. Over on the other side, behind the barbed wire mesh, lay the enemy's foremost trenches, abandoned in great haste, which to their surprise contained a treasure-trove of provisions and arms and, even more surprisingly, a whole case of whisky. In some of the corridors there were still enemy sentries, who raised their hands and let themselves be mowed down without resistance. Farther on, along the river's edge, lay burned villages without a sign of life; the ruin of a church stood out sombrely against the red sky, flocks of cattle drifted aimlessly about, and inside a copse lay a small troop of Scottish veterans, who opened fire and held their ground to the very end.

When the assault party set out on its raid, it numbered forty specially equipped infantrymen; when it returned to the German positions a few hours later, only twenty-seven exhausted men were left. Of those, several were severely wounded, and the lieutenant himself had been hit by a grenade just before he ordered his men to withdraw.

Some months later his bravery was rewarded by the Iron Cross of the first degree, which he accepted with all due respect for the military ceremonial. His hand had then been operated on and mended in the approved fashion, and a special glove designed. But out there in no man's land something had befallen him that could not be repaired. Not only had he lost three fingers of his sensitive musician's hand, he had also lost his soul and his human empathy somewhere out there in the fog and the mire. After that raid in April 1918 he was, in his own words, game for anything, for pushing forward unflinchingly, surmounting every obstacle, killing systematically and in cold blood. War had become the fountainhead of all things, and the horrors he witnessed in Poland and Czechoslovakia twenty years later were merely its repercussions, pale abstractions.

"Reverend Hov," he said all of a sudden, drawing himself up in his chair and speaking directly to me as he concluded his account. "After the bloodbath on the borders of the Somme there were only two possibilities for anyone who had escaped with his life: either abandon the military slaughterhouse and become an apostle of peace, or shut his eyes and come to terms with human barbarism."

"And so you chose to shut your eyes," I replied after a long silence between us.

"Yes, as you can see," he said with a short, tired laugh. "I've served faithfully, and have in every way deserved the Iron Cross in the first degree. Now it only remains to go the whole hog and complete my destiny."

"Complete your destiny?" I asked, but checked myself and suddenly fell silent.

"Yes, *lieber Freund*, the suffering is over. Finally, at long last, I've become one with the name you've so often teased me with. I've become Otto Todleben, a living death, an empty shell devoid of humanity."

Tuesday, 31 October, 3 o'clock. Have just made an unsuccessful attempt to come to the rescue of Svallaug and set her free from captivity.

Shortly after twelve, when Idun came home from school, I sent her over to the yellow house with a letter she should try to deliver. I wrote my sister that I would pick her up with the car the following day and drive her to a place where she could live safely.

I had beforehand made an agreement with the organist's aunt, a widow who lives alone in a little house not far from the edge of town. She was willing to give Svallaug a secret hiding place until the war was over. The old lady hardly ever goes out, and receives visits from none but those closest to her. The only question was whether my sister dared to take the chance and was prepared to stay in hiding until the end of the war.

I told Idun to hurry up, because at two o'clock Balder would finish at school and could be expected home. She shouldn't ring the bell, but must steal round to the other side of the house and knock gently on the door of the glass veranda. Her aunt would no doubt look out the window to see who it was, and then she must pull the letter from her pocket and wave it at her. Then Svallaug would either open the door and let her in, or she would shake her head and withdraw from the window. If the latter occurred there was nothing more to be done, she just had to leave and hurry home to give me the message.

I was anxiously awaiting the outcome, and since time dragged on and it was already past one, I figured that she had succeeded. The moment couldn't have been more favourable: Vidar and Urd had dropped by with their satchels and run out again, and Mary was in town on one of her many errands. I stood at the window in my study keeping a lookout, growing more and more uneasy as it approached half-past one. But suddenly I saw her; she came running, looking strangely disturbed, running for dear life and turning her head all the time, as if she wanted to know whether someone was following hard on her heels. When she fell headlong into the hallway, she was so exhausted that she gasped for air, and a considerable time passed before I could get a sensible word out of her.

She had done what she was told and gone to the back of the house, and when she knocked on the door to the glass veranda, sure enough, her aunt had looked out of the window. But when she took the letter out and waved it, the other seemed to harden, and for quite a while her aunt kept standing motionless behind the window.

"Then I smiled to her and waved the letter still more," Idun explained, "and to make doubly sure I pointed at her so she would understand that the letter was for her. When I had stood there waving and pointing all

I could, it was as if she suddenly woke up. She gave a start and, pop! – there she was at the veranda door and let me in."

Then everything became so strange that she didn't know how to explain it. Her aunt held her close and rocked her in her arms, and she kept on doing it for so long that Idun had to free herself and remind her to read the letter. But she didn't seem to be very much interested in what was written in it, for she let it fall on the floor and again began kissing and squeezing the child, and talking to her in a strangely wild and impassioned way. Finally she let go, and while Idun stood there shifting her feet and wanting to get away, her aunt wrote a few lines on a piece of paper, folded it and stuck it in her coat pocket. Then there were fresh kisses and hugs, and before she was let go she had to promise to come back again and to tell her dad that he mustn't send her any more letters.

I unfolded the sheet of paper and read the few words, written in a hurry and with a trembling hand: "Dear Vemund," it said, "thanks for your thoughtfulness. But I cannot accept your offer. I have disgraced myself before God and men, it's all over, and it serves me right to remain where I am. Just leave me alone, and don't try to go against Balder, because anyone who does gets hurt. He shrinks from nothing, now you know. Your lost sister, Svallaug."

When Idun had come back to her senses and her tears had subsided, I asked her what had frightened her so, since she came running home as though the devil himself were after her. She shook her head, bit her lips and sat squirming a long while, refusing to talk. But at last I fished the truth out of her. Balder had come home ahead of time and was letting himself in when she came stealing around the corner of the house. At first she thought he hadn't seen her, but when she had almost reached the entranceway she heard that he was calling her. She acted as if she hadn't heard and started running, but all the way home it was as if she felt his breath at the back of her head, and she could clearly sense how his long arm stretched out to knock her down . . .

I realize that my rescue has failed and can only hope that my revealing letter won't fall into the wrong hands. I have asked myself if she could be carried off by force, since she herself has given up and doesn't know her own good. Possibly, but in that case someone other than me will be in charge of the operation. All my convictions are based on free will, and if I have the choice between coercion and impotence, I choose the lesser evil.

* *

Wednesday, 1 November. After agonizing over a long period, I've finally made up my mind and dispatched my resignation to the bishop. Anticipate retiring as pastor on 1 February, but willingly before then if arrangements can be made for a substitute. As cause I indicated "personal reasons", not wishing to say too much. I intend to find lodgings at an Oslo pension as soon as I'm relieved of my position, so my father-in-law will have to take care of Mary and the children till the war is over (and perhaps even longer). I've saved a few thousand kroner in the course of the last ten years and shall manage for the present. Perhaps it won't take long before I'm well provided for and won't have to worry about food and shelter.

Evenings I'm occupied with my *Apology*, but constantly come up against unexpected problems. It is one thing to solve a problem philosophically, it can be done almost too easily if one has the right training. But philosophy is not life, and time and again I experience to my great amazement that the premises do not hold when a problem closes in on me.

What is it that links the good intention to the good action, I ask myself, and with the backing of moral philosophy I arrive at the answer that it must be the will. I may have every imaginable good and worthy intention, but they cannot be translated into action until something in my being answers yes and consents. This "something" seems to be the will, and it's my experience that if I really have the will to do something with all my heart, then the action follows as a matter of course.

How then to explain the inability to act that so often hits me when things come to a head and everything is at stake? Can it be that, deep down, I do not want to and therefore pull back? There is a passage in St Paul that has always provoked a most extreme protest in me. Already as a divinity student I wrote a big "No!" in the margin of the seventh chapter of the Epistle to the Romans, where it says that "the good that I would I do not: but the evil which I would not, that I do." It is, God help me, sheer nonsense, typical of Saul, the Pharisee, and his pious equivocations. I have always been of the opinion that if we human beings are so deeply divided and perverse in our actions, then we are inferior to the beast, which is always true to itself and its purpose.

But what am I to think of my vacillating walk through life, where I constantly go astray and act in the teeth of all common sense? What are those impulses that cause me to turn aside and go down paths that can only lead to shame and humiliation? Am I a lax and weak-willed being through and through? Or is my will a shackled force that takes the law into its own hands in a terrible way when it's set free?

One thing tells against me: my attacks of rage. Here it's plain sailing: the evil that I would, that I do, when the thin layer of civilization is peeled off and the beast rears its head in me.

Friday, 3 November. Telephone call from the sheriff in Siljan. Father has been found far away in a state of utter prostration and has probably been lost for a long time. Nobody home at Nether Hov. The neighbour, Elias Kroken, came by a week and a half ago and took pity on the cows, which stood in their stalls bellowing with hunger. Nobody answered his knock at the house, and when he tried the door it was unlocked. No sign of life, the fire gone out in the stove, an indescribable mess everywhere, the latest leaf of the calendar torn off on 17 October.

Will go to Siljan as soon as I can arrange for a replacement. Feel terribly uneasy and full of misgivings. There's something ominous in the air, and I would be greatly mistaken if there isn't some disaster in store for me.

Monday, 6 November. Am sitting here in the kitchen at Nether Hov trying to compose myself a little. My eyes glide along the worn, scarred tabletop, and I recognize some streaks I carved in it nearly forty years ago. I had just learned my letters and was carving my name in the wood when Father caught me in the act and gave me such an awful thrashing that it's still sitting there somewhere, like a deep ache in my body. Only two letters were done when the knife was torn out of my hand, and even today the broken-off inscription jumps up from the wood and passes judgement on me: Woe to you, Vemund, woe, woe, woe!

Father has been placed in the Old People's Home, but he's so sickly and decrepit that he probably won't last through the winter. I've put the farm up for sale – the buildings have to come down, but a couple of neighbours are interested in buying the land to add it to their own. The landowner has already inquired about the woodland, but he cannot have his final answer until we know what the Highway Authority has in mind. The small country road that winds through the hamlet will no doubt be straightened and turned into a major road.

But where has Kjellfrid gone? It's not like her to disappear and let the cows stand in their stalls without fodder. The horse had been taken by

Father on his last long outing, it was found in a copse not far from the Gjerpen parsonage. It was tied to a tree, completely worn out from pitching and getting hurt in the shafts. The old man had probably forgotten where he'd left it when he started roaming on his own.

The farm is in a deplorable condition; obviously Kjellfrid gave up and let everything slide. Dirty pots and pans are piled up on the kitchen counter, Father's chamber pot sits in the middle of the floor with its stinking contents, the flypaper from this summer hangs from the ceiling, completely packed with dead flies. The rats are playing havoc in the pantry, scurrying in and out and helping themselves to the winter provisions. The dates not torn off the calendar in nearly three weeks, a sure sign that something is wrong.

Can she have set out to look for Father? Perhaps. It has happened before, after all, and more than once, that she had to scour the countryside to track him down. But no, she can't possibly have been out looking for him since 17 October. She would eventually have understood that it was useless and gone home again.

What can have happened to my brave and clever sister, Father's keeper and good mistress to the cows? She may have been the most gifted of us all, with altogether different dreams than to wear herself out at Nether Hov. Suddenly it's clear to me what a burden we put on her shoulders, as one after the other of us went away and left her behind alone. I noticed this summer, of course, that she was near the breaking point. But I went away as usual and turned a deaf ear to the cry of distress in her letters. In short: the good that I would not, that I do not do.

Walked about in the yard last night by moonlight, looking around in all directions. Was filled with wonder and understood nothing at all. The landscape here at Nether Hov is a dream, so peaceful and strangely beautiful that it seems like a manifestation of God on earth. A light mist hovered over the marsh, and the moonbeams appeared like a mirage through the veil of fog. Everything suddenly became luminous – the buildings, the marsh, the cliffs, Hov Lake, the shimmering road that curved through the evening hour.

But suddenly a large nocturnal bird comes sailing through the air; it seems to come from nowhere and flies on soundless wings into the golden sky. I follow it with my eyes and shudder; it's bigger and blacker than any bird I know, with a pair of wings that spread and cast long shadows over the earth. Is it a soul from the realm of the dead that cannot find peace, a secret messenger from the night and the depths? It lets out a long, wailing cry, then is gone, and I hurry inside and close the door behind me.

Wednesday, 8 November. Came home last night shortly before half-past seven. A great to-do at the parsonage. Idun had been gone for two days and was at last found in the woodshed out at Sandane, all dissolved in tears and afraid of the dark. The search crew brought her just as I was getting out of my car. The child seemed completely disturbed, so I realized it was useless to question her. She was given a bite to eat and sent to bed, and we let the nursemaid sit with her until she fell asleep.

This morning when the other two had gone to school, I went upstairs and sat down on her bed. By then she had more or less calmed down and answered my questions quite readily. Yes, she had been to school on Monday as she was supposed to, but on the way home she had been overcome by fright, just like the day when she had visited the yellow house. Someone seemed to be after her, wanting to catch her, but when she turned round there was no one to be seen. She didn't know how it had happened, but all of a sudden she was no longer heading home, but well on her way to Sandane. She never stopped running, struggling on as though in a daze, and didn't come to her senses till she had arrived and crawled into the outhouse at her grandfather's place. There she lay the whole night with an old horse blanket over her; she slept a little occasionally but was constantly anxious, jumping at the slightest sound. Fortunately she hadn't eaten her lunch at school, so she didn't have to be hungry. She was just wondering whether she would have to stay in the shelter all winter, and spend Christmas there, when she heard the sound of footsteps and many voices. Here they come to catch me, she just managed to think before the door to the outhouse was opened and the search crew found her.

She answered clearly and straightforwardly every question having to do with her hiding place, but when I wanted to know what had put her to flight she pinched her lips together, and a stubborn look came into her eyes. I tried to be gentle with her as long as possible, but she held her tongue and I got nowhere. Finally I became angry and began to threaten her, but that I should not have done. She let out a scream and tried to hit me, and her little face was so stern and showed such will power that I became quite alarmed.

Monday, 13 November. Another telephone call from the sheriff at Siljan.

205

Kjellfrid discovered, drowned under the turf that runs like a floating bridge from the farm over to the fields on the other side of the lake.

It was the neighbour, Elias Kroken, who discovered her. He was taking a walk to have a closer look at the two plots, Snipa and Tangen, which he had in mind to buy and use as a summer pasture for his sheep. The turf is full of water holes and treacherous deep pools, so one has to watch out and walk warily not to fall through. I would often sit fishing out there as a boy, wondering how large trees could grow on a layer of turf that lay floating loosely on top of the water.

When the neighbour was about midway across, something attracted his attention. A black shoe stuck up from a water hole, and when he grabbed hold of it he noticed to his horror that it was stuck on a human foot. He realized right away what was hidden under the turf and kneeled down to pull the drowned person out of the water. But the body was stuck and resisted when he tried to work it loose, and finally he had to give up and go home to get some help.

When Elias Kroken and his two grown sons at last got Kjellfrid out of the hole, they had first had to fell an aspen tree and cut away a piece of the turf. The tree had a powerful network of roots, and the dead one clung to these roots so it was almost impossible to get her free.

"I suppose she was unlucky and fell through, then she grabbed hold of the roots to get out again," the sheriff said, and I wasn't slow to join him in his interpretation. We agreed that the funeral must take place soon and quietly, before gossip set in. The sheriff offered to make arrangements for a clergy-man and gravedigger, and I promised that I myself and my two brothers would arrive in Siljan Wednesday afternoon at the latest.

But it won't be easy to get my brothers to come. When I tried to find Steingrim at the address the machine shop gave me, it turned out that he wasn't living there. I've gone from place to place all morning trying to track him down, but to no avail. The hotel where he took lodgings during the summer couldn't tell me where he had moved, his fellow workers just shrugged their shoulders, and a visit to the Population Register didn't help clear up the matter. I had to go home without accomplishing my mission, and face up to the fact that my youngest brother had disappeared without a trace.

It didn't go much better over at the secondary school, when I went to see Balder to reach an understanding with him. He wasn't going to be part of any funeral, he said, behaving so strangely that I cut the discussion short. My brother Balder has never been in the habit of looking you straight in the face, but today he appeared so queer and shifty-eyed that I was taken aback. His will to power had shrunk to nothing, he looked like a dog that has got into mischief and expects to get a beating from his master. I had meant to ask him if I could pick up Svallaug and take her to the funeral, but thought better of it.

Sunday, 19 November. Yesterday morning I was summoned for a sick call to the chief of police, who had had a stroke and was near death. I sat with him for almost two hours, waiting for him to become lucid enough so that I could give him the sacrament.

He was far away most of the time, and spoke so obscurely and incoherently it was impossible to make any sense of what he was saying. But once in a while he opened a pair of strangely alert eyes and looked at me. He has been a member of the National Union since the beginning of the war, but supposedly tried to cancel his membership sometime during the autumn. The stroke may have been triggered by the problems that this brought in its wake. According to what his wife could tell me, Nazis and patriots had been attacking him from opposite sides, and it was more than he could take.

After I had sat with him for about an hour, he appeared to become more lucid for a while, but a little later he told me something that was completely senseless. He mentioned a letter I was supposed to have written to him, saying he had put it aside without doing anything about it.

I never wrote a letter to him and tried to tell him so, but he had already dropped back into his mental darkness, and I understood that it was useless. Afterwards he was in a protracted coma, and in the next lucid interval I gave him the sacrament. He thanked me in a feeble voice and again said a few words about the letter, which he had locked away in a drawer without showing it to his subordinates. Jews were people too, he whispered, but it didn't make me much the wiser. I came to the conclusion that he wasn't fully conscious and perhaps was confusing me with someone else.

I left him soon after, and this morning I received the message that he had died. It's still a riddle what he wanted to tell me, and most likely I will never know what letter he was talking about.

Wednesday, 22 November. This morning I was visited by the bishop, who informed me that a substitute had been found. I could count on being released from my duties as pastor by 1 February, he said, if it really was my intention to retire. In the meantime everything would take its course through the usual official channels. The department would consider my application and most probably grant it, without prejudice. It was uncertain whether I was entitled to a pension after only ten years of service, since I resigned the position at my own request. But if the "personal reasons" I indicated concerned illness, I would be wise to procure a doctor's certificate as soon as possible. However that might be, there was no need to worry, he said. I was a free man, and nobody could prevent a pastor from leaving the service when it was done after reasonable notification and a substitute could be found.

The bishop was extremely friendly, settled down for a cup of coffee and stayed considerably longer than was strictly necessary. Nevertheless it was apparent that he was relieved by my decision, and took a stern view of the sum of offences that were accumulating in my record. We parted most amicably and agreed that I would move from the parsonage on 20 January at the latest, so that my successor could settle in before taking over the position.

As soon as he was out of the door, I wrote a few words to my father-in-law and sent Mary over to the ship owner's house with them. I told him I would be leaving town sometime in late January and asked him to receive his daughter and the three grandchildren and give them shelter for the time being. Mary was back after a scant half hour, and I understood immediately that the outcome was not as I had hoped. She looked quite miserable, and told me with a lump in her throat that the old man had been furious. He had torn the letter in two and thrown it on the floor, and that was the only answer he had given her to bring back.

Thursday, 23 November. I was sitting in my office this morning brooding on our prospects for the future, when a messenger appeared with a brief note from my father-in-law. I had reckoned without my host, he wrote, if I thought I could turn myself into a bachelor and escape my matrimonial responsibilities. He had no shelter to offer a married woman and her children, they had to follow the head of the household when the latter saw fit to move. He, Andreas Sand, would be the last to deplore the turn that events were now taking. But since he was no brute, he could report that he had taken action and fixed something up. Come New Year, a three-room apartment would be vacant in one of his tenement buildings in Oslo, and when they left the parsonage in late January the homeless family could move in there.

The letter was furnished with the ship owner's stamp and a long, extravagant curlicue, no doubt intended to represent his signature. I couldn't help admiring the man's strength of character and the unwavering dislike he had managed to preserve *vis-à-vis* a son-in-law who was unwanted and had brought him little honour.

Tuesday, 28 November. I can't postpone it any longer, I must get it down on paper. Balder, my brother, has committed suicide and dragged Svallaug with him. The cause of death is the taking of Prussic acid; the autopsy shows a dose in each of them large enough to have killed an entire population.

I note down the following in completely impersonal words and turns of phrase, the only way I can give an account of something that otherwise would drive me insane. I'm so hollowed out and empty inside that I cannot even feel any grief, and the best thing would probably be to close this book and never open it again.

The two siblings were found yesterday, a week and a half after death must have occurred. Balder hadn't shown up at school for several days, but nobody suspected anything; he had previously absented himself on account of a rally of NS troopers or other political activities. Only when more than a week had gone by, and his post began piling up in his letterbox, did the suspicion arise that something was wrong. The school's caretaker had been at the door several times and rung the bell, and finally I was fetched at the parsonage and the police summoned, and together we forced an entry into the house.

Brother and sister were lying on the bed in the bedroom in a strangely grotesque embrace, which made it look as if the sister had protested and resisted to the very end. On the night table, beside the poisoned cup, lay a folded letter that I put in my pocket unseen by anyone. It had obviously been written by Balder several days in advance and signed by them both at the last moment. The sister's handwriting was trembling and almost illegible, and everything goes to show that she was under duress when her brother carried out his insane enterprise.

The letter is composed in a bombastic style and betrays obvious signs of megalomania. The handwriting is so like my own that it gives me the shivers, and if I didn't know who was holding the pen, I could have believed that it was I myself who had written the letter in a kind of vicarious absent-mindedness.

"APPEAL TO OUR COUNTRYMEN," it reads in large block letters, framed by a number of signs that look like rock carvings:

My good Norwegians, however ignominious it may be, we have to face the truth. The battle is lost, and the great-Germanic Reich is coming to an end. The months are going by, soon we shall be writing 1945, and we have been waiting in vain for the *Wehrmacht* to start using the secret weapon that could have become the war's *ultima ratio*. After the defeats on the western front and the Red Army's apocalyptic advance there is no longer any hope of survival for the Aryan race. World communism will come upon us like the eleventh plague, the heroic spirit will die out, Jews and inferior people will move ahead and live off the fat of the land. Our Norse heritage will be wasted, the honour of ancient lineage derided, the pure blood sullied, and our native soil trampled by inferior races.

As descendants of the old heroes, born and bred in one of the gods' holy places, we lay down a protest against a coming world order where all greatness will be flattened out and where second-raters will hold sway. It is with the most profound grief and humiliation that we take the matter into our own hands and annihilate ourselves, before democracy and social levelling will finish us.

We give our lives as an offering to the ancient Norse heroic world, and it is our hope that the best of our countrymen will follow our example.

17 November 1944
Heil & sæl,
County Leader Balder Hov
and his faithful Valkyrie
Svallaug Hov.

The same day, 11.30 p.m. I've read this odd product many times in the course of the day and can only shake my head. What kind of person was he, that twisted brother of mine, and what was the cause of his delusion?

It feels strange that I know so little about someone who is my near relation and with whom I shared both good and bad until my seventeenth year. As soon as I'm reminded of him, a sense of estrangement comes over me that makes it impossible to acknowledge him as a brother and a kindred soul. How is it possible that a man with such brilliant gifts could be so backward and build his life on ideas that belong to a much earlier stage of evolution? Had the burden of culture become too heavy to bear for him, I ask myself, since he lost his foothold in his own time and rushed backwards through the centuries?

I tried many times in the course of the years to tell him that the myth of blood and race is rooted in a primitive tribal culture, where it strengthens co-existence and becomes an irrational gain. But in modern civilization it becomes a rational loss and a fall into the primeval abyss. The sanguinary intoxication that caused the ancient berserkers to feel at one with the gods, is today an eclipse of God and an invitation to barbarism.

It is this loss of a sense of reality and humanity that has made it impossible for me ever to join a party like the National Union. However muddled I've been in many ways, reason has always been my guiding star, which has lighted up my path and helped me resist the irrational temptation. I look at Nazism as sheer magic and dimly perceive a death instinct in its backward-looking ecstasy. The sense of communion engendered by that kind of mass movement has always frightened me; it can only be maintained by having consciousness disconnected and great portions of reality denied.

Monday, 4 December. There can no longer be any doubts about it: little Idun is weighed down by something that she doesn't want to come out with. She has become so shy and strange lately; she scarcely says a word, starts up at the slightest noise, and looks searchingly about her all the time when we go for a walk.

Yesterday when we were in the churchyard to attend to the grave for the winter, she suddenly seized my arm and said, "Dad, there's something . . ." But when I wanted to know what it was, she let out a scream and ran all the way to the other end of the graveyard.

When she came creeping back again, I was busy with my own thing and didn't let on. Soon everything was as before, and we helped each other cover the flower bed with evergreens. A little later she reached for me again and was on the point of saying something, but it came only to a faint mumbling. I've decided to leave her alone as long as she refuses to open up.

I've tried to force her, with no success. It's better to be patient and wait until the time is ripe.

But I notice that her strangeness affects me and occupies my thoughts more than is good for me. Can her silence have something to do with the ship owner's house? I ask myself. She never wants to go there anymore, and she turns quite pale when Sunday dinner approaches. If the other two tease her or chat about something from over there, she goes completely stiff with fright and covers her ears with her hands till they keep quiet.

I've tried to make Mary aware of the child's torment, but she just sniffs and evades the issue.

"Idun?" she says. "Who's that? You mean Finelotte, don't you? She can't stand losing at pinball, that's the only reason she gets obstinate and refuses to go over there."

After all that has happened the last few weeks, Mary and I have drifted even further apart. Not even music can bring us together. The Thursday church concerts have been cancelled for the present and will hardly be resumed in my time.

Yes, moving to Oslo will probably be the best thing for all of us, alas. Then we'll be among strangers the day it's all over and the shame comes upon us. Wednesday, 6 December. Suddenly came to think of Elias Kroken, the only one of our neighbours who showed up at Kjellfrid's funeral. He had picked a large bouquet of cattails on the turf, which in the near future will become his own footbridge over the lake. When the pastor had finished his sermon, Elias went quietly up and spread the soft, downy marshland plants over the coffin lid. I thought he did it in such a nice way, and that his action had a special symbolism, as if there was something he wanted to cover up and beautify before it went down to oblivion.

Kroken is one of the smallest and poorest farms in the Siljan parish, and the one that remained a small holding under the estate for the longest time. It has ten acres of good woodland, but the patches of ground are so wretched that the farm can feed only a single cow. Elias Kroken has worked in the sawmill nearly all his life to be able to buy out the place and save some money, so that he can now purchase a little of the land at Nether Hov.

According to the prevailing pecking order, which even operates at the lowest rungs of the social ladder, the family at Nether Hov felt greatly elevated above those poor devils at Kroken. Elias became a widower with several small children early on, and taken up as he was with work from morning till night, he had neither the time nor energy to find himself another wife. A number of devout and sharp-nosed housekeepers found their way to the small farm in the course of the years, and it was whispered that Elias lived in sin with them all and promised marriage to avoid paying them a salary. But each time it ended in the same sad way: the housekeeper held out for a year or two, then she got tired of slaving away without knowing the score and left, taking the cow with her as compensation for the pay she had been cheated of.

Elias bore his lot with great humility, took on even more extra work at the sawmill and saved slowly and steadily enough to buy another Dagros. As soon as the cow was settled in its stall, he advertised for the next house-keeper in *For Poor and Rich*, straightened his bent back and sized up his dwindling powers as a seducer. I remember him from my early youth as a mild and meek man, looking already middle-aged, though he wasn't much past thirty at the time.

It was this harmless man that we chose for our scapegoat at Nether Hov, and once played a prank of the nastiest kind imaginable. It was the last summer I was home; I was in my seventeenth year, Balder ten months younger, and Father an old man of sixty-three. The other members of the family don't count, being excused by their tender years and female subservience.

We had seen Elias Kroken's advertisement for a new housekeeper in *For Poor and Rich* and together set about writing a reply to it. It was Balder and the old man who led the way; they were both in high spirits and dying with laughter as they leaned over the tabletop while concocting their malicious taunts and jabs. I didn't protest, as usual, but was probably the only one of us who was aware of committing a mean and dastardly act. Therefore the lot fell on me, and I became the only truly guilty party in this intrigue of heartless innocence.

If only we had stopped at the mirth around the long table, it might still have been all right. But Balder made a fair copy of the letter in his most beautiful calligraphy, concluded by giving the box number and expressing the hope of a speedy answer, and posted the letter the next time he took a trip to town. Many years later, on my Father's eightieth birthday, the family were still not through smacking their lips over this dirty trick; the old man was completely ecstatic with gloating and laughed so uncontrollably that he ended up choking on the banqueting fare.

"Heh-heh-heh-heh! He got himself a punch in the nose, that sly fox at Kroken, who had no sense of shame and bedded one woman after the other!"

Elias Kroken was not a stupid man, and he obviously knew the identity of this "housekeeper", who expressed herself so wittily and was so well informed about his squalor. But he didn't let it cast a shadow on his neighbourliness, and he greeted us the same as ever, cap in hand, when he met one of us on the road.

I do not know whether Elias Kroken is what one can call a good man. Nor do I know whether the motives that brought him to the funeral were particularly lofty. But it gives you a good feeling in these latter-day times to meet a person without a grudge, someone who strews cattails on old insults, lets revenge rest and acts as though there were no evil on earth.

Monday, 11 December. Lord, my God and maker, won't misfortunes ever end! I feel as if I were in a Greek tragedy, where the family demons are raging and nobody can have any hope of being alive in the last act.

Yesterday, Sunday, at dusk, while I was straightening out some accounts, I suddenly heard a dull boom from the harbour. I ran up to the window, and shortly I saw a sea of flames rise toward the sky from the place where the machine shop is situated. At first I thought it was one of the many bomb attacks that allied planes carry out along the coast these days. But there was no air raid warning, and gradually I understood that the explosion must be due to sabotage. An icy terror caught hold of me, and all the uncertainty that had been gnawing at me in the course of the autumn resolved itself into one single thought, clear and corrosive.

About half an hour later there was a loud ring at the door. I knew who it was and hurried into the hall to steal a march on Anna. I was so agitated that my whole body trembled, and when I saw my hapless brother standing on the steps, I went out of my mind and railed at him. He stood there with bowed head without answering, his face covered with burns and his cap pressed against his right arm in a strangely awkward manner. With just a streak of light falling through the door, it took a while before I realized how badly wounded he was. In the meantime Anna had appeared in the door to the kitchen, and from behind her wide skirts little Idun peeped forth with a terrified look on her face. I made a disapproving gesture with my hand, and the housekeeper grasped the warning and withdrew at once.

I stood there in a daze for a moment, until my agitation gave way to a great gentleness. Steingrim was already going away, and I hastily threw on a coat and picked up the church keys hanging on the wall. "Wait a little, brother," I said, stepping onto the stairs and giving a searching look all around. "I'll go with you to the sacristy, where you will be well hidden, while I get a doctor who can take care of your arm."

We crossed the churchyard without meeting anybody and reached the sacristy safe and sound. After turning on the light and asking him to take his cap away, I saw to my horror that his entire right hand had been blown off. I tended him as well as I could, folded a napkin and used it as a compress, wrung out his blood-stained cap in the sink and lashed it tightly around the stump of his arm.

Then I helped him stretch out on the floor and asked him to stay completely quiet until I came back with the doctor. Running across the churchyard, I went over the town's whole medical profession in my mind and chose three who I believed were dependable and would keep a secret. At the first place nobody opened the door when I rang, at the second place I was told that the doctor was out on a sick call, at the third place the doctor himself came to the door and asked to be excused when he heard what was the matter. I was forced to try a couple of the places I regarded as more doubtful, and finally I got hold of an old doctor who had ceased practising long ago. It had taken me a good hour to run from place to place, and when we finally arrived, to our horror the door to the sacristy was open and the patient was gone. There was nothing more to be done and I hurried home, after thanking the decent old man for his good will and moral courage.

At the parsonage Anna could relate that she had been visited by three unknown men with a big dog and that they had directed their steps across the churchyard when the pastor was not to be found. The dog rushed along, its snout on the ground, pulling so hard at the leash that it could barely be restrained. It was sure to be a bloodhound, she said, and it wouldn't surprise her if the threesome were police officers in civilian dress.

I shut myself up in my study, where I waited all evening, expecting them to return and ask me to follow them. But nothing happened, and it looks as if the case will take its course without my involvement.

The same day, 9 p.m. The sabotage against the machine works is given a big spread in today's papers, and if one can trust what they say, all the perpetrators have been apprehended. Three of them were caught shortly after they had left the place. The fourth, who seemed to be the ringleader, had managed to get away and was at large for a few hours, until he was tracked down by the police dog patrol. He had stayed behind in the factory till the very last moment to check the timing mechanism and was severely wounded when one of the incendiary bombs exploded before it was supposed to. When he was found he was so exhausted from loss of blood that he was taken to the hospital in a state of unconsciousness. But he was expected to survive, and as soon as he had regained his strength he would go to gaol and be called to account for his deeds.

When I had read what the papers said, I went out and looked up *Sturmführer* Todleben in his quarters. He received me amicably, but shook his head with regret when I asked him to do something to save the lives of the four saboteurs. I pressed him to the utmost, having the nerve to remind him of our musical evenings and to ask him for an act of friendship. All pretty useless. For the three adult culprits there was no hope at all, and he was sorry that one of them was my brother. But he would do what he could to apply for a pardon for the fourth man, who hadn't yet turned eighteen.

So why don't you wake up, Vemund, and face the truth? Steingrim, your brother, is doomed and won't live till the year is out. And here you, old philosophical straggler that you are, sit so engrossed in your own thoughts that even the most bloody occurrences are enveloped in a veil of unreality. While you are filling a piece of paper with strokes of your pen, quite leisurely and without any cost to yourself, your brother is being patched up in the hospital so that his body can be intact and stand upright when facing the firing squad.

Tuesday, 19 December. Steingrim and two of the other saboteurs were executed today, after a hastily arranged court-martial. The fourth man was reprieved and sentenced to twelve years in prison.

I feel a great bitterness toward Otto Todleben. With his high rank, he could easily have used his influence and had the death sentence annulled. He could at least have demanded a regular trial, which would probably have taken so much time that the accused would have come away with their lives.

Have no wish to see the man again, and hope that after this he understands of his own accord that he ought to stay away.

*　*

Monday, 31 December. This morning, only a couple of hours ago, I was again unable to contain myself. And I who had promised myself solemnly that it would never happen again! I was overwhelmed by a terrible rage, which didn't let go until I had laid waste to everything around me. And now, here I sit completely drained of strength, without any idea of how to get through midnight mass.

It came over me like a stroke of lightning and grew beyond all bounds, making it impossible for me to get back to myself. In the end I was no longer a human being, but a savage monster foaming at the mouth. Vidar and Urd ran off to hide, Mary was sobbing with her head against the wall, and only when I had calmed down a little did I catch sight of Idun, who was standing over by the Christmas tree, her eyes fixed on me in a wide stare.

Things had been accumulating for a long time. It had already begun the night before Christmas Eve, when a card arrived from the ship owner's house to say that Mary and the children were invited to Christmas dinner on the twenty-fourth, between four and seven o'clock. I was a bit surprised by the proposed time, for my father-in-law never used to limit the length of the visits to his house. I couldn't help wondering what was going to take place over there for the remainder of the evening, since those who were closest to him had to leave the house so early. That the invitation didn't include me, I didn't take any notice of. I have for many years celebrated Christmas alone and made the best of the arrangement.

Idun refused to go along as usual and stayed home when the others set out. We lighted the candles on the table and ate a plateful of rice pudding each when the church bells rang in Christmas at five. Anna had asked me beforehand if I wanted something else, but I said she had done the right thing and played along with her wishes. Rice pudding was just fine, I said, that's what we used to have at Christmas in my childhood home, and tradition had to be honoured and respected.

Shortly after six o'clock – Anna had just brought a cake dish – Otto Todleben called, bringing a big parcel for *die schöne Frau Pastorin*. I invited him inside, but he excused himself and said he couldn't stay long. He was to celebrate *Weihnachten* with some countrymen in the next town, so the chauffeur would come back to pick him up around half-past seven.

While we were having coffee my German visitor waved to Idun and took her on his lap. I could see she'd rather not, that she resisted, but the *Sturmführer* didn't let go until she was rocking on his knees. He had himself a daughter the same age at home in the Schwarzwald, he said, and it was *eine Seligkeit* for a man of war to begin *die heilige Nacht* with a little angel of light on his lap.

Dressed in full uniform, he was rocking her up and down in a rather funny way, speaking a babbling baby talk to her and seemingly unaware of her aversion. For the first time I sensed something artificial in his tone and some affectation in his overall behaviour. The atmosphere felt more and more oppressive, and while making an effort to keep the conversation going, I knew in my heart that it was the last time I would have him under my roof.

It was nearly half-past seven and he had already risen to say goodbye, when Mary came back with the children. She was clearly animated by the visitor's compliments, chattered and laughed without restraint and was perfectly ecstatic when she opened the parcel and unfolded an elegant fur coat. After putting it on at his request, she turned around before the large hall mirror to admire it from every side. The gloom dissolved, and before the *Sturmführer* finally disappeared through the door he had sung a languishing duet together with *die Pastorin* and given her hand a goodbye kiss.

Mary was in a wonderful mood throughout the Christmas holiday, and everything seemed to be turning out better for both of us. She wore the fur coat to church both the first and second day of Christmas, and took care to show it off to advantage among all the shabby wartime garments in the pews here and there. I could see nothing wrong with that, but noticed the stir it caused and the many sharp glances she received. Only when the organist took me aside and asked me to persuade her to leave the coat at home, did I begin to suspect mischief.

"It didn't make a good impression," he said, but suddenly fell silent and attempted no further explanation.

I couldn't bring myself to mention anything to Mary, being reluctant to take away her joy and to destroy the bright, pleasant atmosphere that prevailed in the house. Every day between Christmas and New Year, she slipped into the soft pelt and went to town, so that nobody would miss out on the sight. Even in the evening, when the family was gathered around the Christmas tree, she kept the coat nearby; she would withdraw a little way from the rest of us and sit there caressing the soft fur while gazing pensively before her, with a smile on her face. Was her delight in the coat altogether innocent, I asked myself, or had she been made aware on her trips to town that it was not her rightful property?

For six days I saw her come and go like a supple and light-footed animal; then something happened that put an end to my uncertainty.

I received an anonymous letter in the mail, informing me where the fur coat had come from and who had owned it previously. Shortly before the war, the wife of one of the town's wealthy men had returned from abroad with this rare piece of fur, of a kind never before seen in this town and impossible to mistake for any other. The woman's passport was later provided with a special stamp, and she herself was one of the many Jewesses transported to Germany on board the steamship *Donau* in the fall of 1942. The rest of the story was delicately suggested, but easy to figure out: the fur had not been obtained honestly, but was taken from the store of confiscated belongings left behind by the deportees.

From start to finish the letter was couched in a matter-of-fact tone, and was obviously written by someone who simply wanted to prevent trouble. The writer begged me to pardon his communication, but advised me urgently to return the coat while there was still time. It was already looked at askance in town, and brought shame and dishonour to the one who showed herself wearing it. Rumours were flying from mouth to mouth, and there was a very real danger of a lynching mood developing if this provocative fur didn't disappear from public view.

I sat for some time with my head between my hands, feeling completely daunted and crushed. Then I ran into the hall, tore the coat from the hook and dashed into the living room, where Mary and the children were decorating the table for the New Year's Eve dinner. First I flung the fur coat on the floor and started trampling it, then I tore the tablecloth off the table with a tug, bringing all the dinnerware along.

I rushed around the room like a lunatic, tearing things down, tramping among family pictures and broken dinnerware and screaming "Rubbish!" again and again. On the coffee table lay two devotional books by Hallesby and Wisløff that Mary had received as a Christmas present from her father. I swept them off the table and kicked them from one end of the room to the other, until they ended up in a corner with the pages turned inside out. And all the while I was screaming and yelling the only word that comes to mind when I lose control of myself: "Rubbish! Rubbish! Rubbish!"

Finally I was so exhausted that I could do no more, went into the office and locked the door behind me. And here I sit, without the slightest idea how it's all going to end. For the written word gives no solution, I know pretty much all on that score. It can give you a temporary peace of mind, but reality reasserts itself and will have its way.

Nor would it change anything if I went into the living room and asked forgiveness. Certain events are so damning that they speak for themselves and silence all attempts to explain them. I can merely state that the year 1944 ended in a violent and humiliating manner and that there is no longer any hope for me.

P.S. The fur coat will be returned, that's the first thing I'll have to do in the New Year. It will be a painful affair, but there's no way around it.

5

Here my father's diary notes end, and he never picked them up again. During the seven years that he still survived, he was spiritually burned out and sank increasingly into a profound silence.

One day as I was sitting by his sickbed he told me in a whispering voice where the diaries were hidden, saying they were to be my paternal inheritance and asking me to take good care of them. But already the next day he ordered me to burn them, and I had to fight a desperate battle with him to change his mind.

In his lucid moments he didn't let himself off lightly, often calling himself a straggler and a philosophical fool. Then he would raise his head from the pillow and mock to his heart's content the written word in general and his own writings in particular. But suddenly he would stop in the middle of a sentence, pass his hand gingerly over his forehead and take it all back again.

"In the beginning was the word," he whispered, sinking back on the pillow, exhausted. "Remember that, Idun, in the beginning was the word, and everything good and great in the world has grown out of that."

Young as I was, I couldn't always follow him, because he spoke with many voices, and his self-esteem swung from one extreme to the other. When he called himself a philosophical fool, it certainly was not to say about himself that he was a poor philosopher. It was philosophy as such that he rejected, because it was always lying in wait and missed the boat. Apropos of this he liked to quote Hegel, comparing philosophy to the owl of Minerva, which flew out at dusk when the day was on the wane and the disasters had already taken place. To philosophize was to give oneself up to a melancholy backward glance, which could be perspicacious and full of insight but was lacking in power and will to intervene in the course of events.

In the same vein, if I am to believe the newspaper reports from January 1946, he proved unable to marshal any whole-hearted self-defence at his trial. During the three days of proceedings, he was difficult to make out and appeared to be divided against himself. Time and again he was building up a chain of reasoning, presenting convincing arguments and pursuing them to a certain point. But midway he grew doubtful, made more and more concessions and ended by agreeing with his adversary.

The reporters were many times completely bewildered and didn't know what to think of this strange man, who placed himself in such an adverse light. Was he just an ordinary idiot, or was he a secret ironist who amused himself on the quiet by poking fun at the entire judicial purge? What was it that, in the midst of a plea in his own defence, suddenly made him do an about-face and turn against himself? Did he stand apart deliberately, or what kind of odd duality was it that drove him to change sides as soon as he noticed he was getting the upper hand?

The newspaper editorials interpreted his behaviour in various ways, attributing all sorts of hidden motives to him, from the most honourable to the most contemptible. But the majority agreed that when the punishment turned out as severe as eight years in prison, the accused chiefly had himself to blame. If he had shown himself more trustworthy and had followed a more direct course, the sentence would hardly have been more than four or five years.

When on the third day the interrogation got as far as the pastor's friendship with *Sturmführer* Todleben, something unexpected happened to Vemund Hov. Having shown himself quite accommodating during the two preceding days, he now suddenly became evasive. He shrank into his shell, acquired a faraway look in his eyes, and sat silent for so long that the prosecutor had to repeat the question: How could it be that such a learned and thoughtful man as the pastor allowed himself to forget every consideration and formed friendship with the enemy at a time that was so hard and fateful for his country?

Vemund Hov was silent, his eyes set in a remote stare, as if he had caught sight of something that absorbed his entire attention at the far end of the courtroom.

"Has the accused nothing to say in his defence?" asked the public prosecutor.

"Oh yes," the pastor replied at long last, "a good deal could be said, to be sure. But it's uncertain whether it would make sense if considered more strictly."

"So let's hear, and let the court decide if it makes sense."

"Well, first of all I'm not aware that I have an enemy. I never declared war and I could never bring myself to hate a person simply because he was of foreign nationality."

"And what else?"

"Oh, nothing special, it's basically the same thing. I've never been able to recognize collective obligations. Each human being is alone with his conscience and must act in accordance with it. After all, old Talleyrand himself asserted that in wartime there exists no hostile relation between people, but only between states."

"You amaze me, Pastor Hov. Haven't you ever had a fatherland ?"

Vemund Hov was silent, shaking his head uncertainly for a moment. Then he gave an abrupt jerk, straightened up and struck the table with the palm of his hand. "There you said it, Your Honour! There you really put your finger on a tender spot!"

The public prosecutor wrinkled his brow and made an impatient gesture with his hand, before collecting himself and asking the accused to explain himself in more detail.

A long pause, during which the pastor shuffled his papers, as if it were a matter of life and death to have them arranged in a definite order.

"We asked you a question, Mr Hov. We asked you to give an account of your relationship to your fatherland ."

"Certainly, I heard; but that is a question I don't find it easy to answer. I've pondered it for many years, and it has made my hair turn grey. But listen: if you had asked me about my nationality the matter would have been clear, and I wouldn't have hesitated to answer that I'm Norwegian. But this thing with the fatherland is a more complicated matter."

"Go on, Pastor Hov. We are curious and all ears."

"Well, if it's true that our childhood home is the first fatherland we have, then I'm empty-handed and almost penniless. Then I missed out on the fatherland from the very first moment."

"Quibbles, Pastor Hov! Do not try to make us believe that you belong to the homeless! You were born in Siljan in lower Telemark County, a peaceful and picturesque place in the heart of the Fatherland."

Vemund Hov sat motionless for a moment, without saying a word. Then he nodded meekly, and his lips twisted into a wry smile.

"You're right, Mr Prosecutor, Siljan is a very paradise on earth."

"And it's not a fact, is it, that you suffered any want in your childhood?"

"No, not at all. I had food in my mouth and a roof over my head, and it's no small thing to survive. But if by home we mean a place where we know ourselves safe and feel we belong, then I've been homeless from the very first years of my life."

"Then perhaps you deny having committed treason against your country?"

"By no means, Your Honour. I've always known that I was full of treason. That I didn't belong anywhere and had nothing that I could call my own."

"And you never felt any shame or regret on account of this peculiarity?"

Vemund Hov heaved a deep sigh, and when he looked up his face was hollow and had a forlorn expression.

"Let shame and regret wait a little," he said, "they're both faithful companions that seldom leave one for long. Let me rather – if it doesn't take up too much of the court's precious time — "

"The accused has the right to use all the time he needs," the judge remarked laconically.

"It may be a digression," the pastor went on, directing his glance at the bench. "But perhaps Your Honour knows the poet Pushkin and his division of humankind into three categories. We are either executioners, victims or traitors, he says. Of course it's pushed to an extreme, but still there's some truth in his observation. As a young man I always imagined that the traitor stood in the middle, as a reconciling figure between two extremes."

"Go on, Pastor Hov, but do us the favour of coming to the point."

"Good, I'll try to be brief. It has occurred to me that if what Pushkin says is true, then the traitor is the only true human being. Rather a no to both sides than a yes that commits injustice or that submits to the yoke."

"And it has never dawned on you that this way of posing the question could be wrong? That there doesn't exist any such sanctuary between power and oppression?"

"Oh yes, Your Honour, that may very well be. But that's something one has to include in one's calculations. A dilemma is a dangerous place to be, one risks slipping to both sides or ending in sheer nihilism."

"And still you insist on playing the role of the traitor?"

"Yes, worse luck, I can see no other way. The dilemma is the growing point of all things, and I cling to this intermediate position, incurring the danger of losing my foothold and falling into one or the other ditch."

"Does that mean that you also include treason in your calculations?"

"Yes, Your Honour, under the circumstances, that as well. And not only treason against the Fatherland, but against your home, family and all time-honoured values."

"We are astounded, Pastor Hov! Can a pastor of the Norwegian state church advocate such amoral views?"

Vemund Hov raised his head, and his glance suddenly became alert and firm. "Just a moment, Your Honour, let us keep things straight. The amoral person does not know what morality is, and is in a sense innocent. Children and animals haven't eaten of the forbidden fruit, and all will be forgiven them. But in a case like mine it can only be a question of immorality."

"And what then? Would it sound any better to call a pastor immoral?"

"That is debatable, but I think so. The gospel is not mainly about morality, but about transformation. A pastor is not a state-appointed paragon of virtue, even though most people prefer to see him as such. He is a harbinger of the kingdom of God, who proclaims what is required to inherit eternal life on earth."

"And what, then, is required? Let us hear."

The pastor hesitated, looking about him with a questioning air, before he stood up and gave a lingering look at those present.

"Hm, this is not really the place for a Sunday sermon, but all right. At a certain moment in history there were some fishermen who saw the light and assumed the transformation. But the road was a long one, twilight came on and darkness fell. One of them began to be interested in money, another in the question of who would sit at the head of the table in the heavenly halls, a third went so far as to draw his sword. And with that the heavenly kingdom was lost. It's all long ago, but nothing has changed. Even today there are no merciful souls on the earth, none who are pure of heart, none who hunger and thirst for righteousness. A pastor in the Norwegian state church is a completely superfluous person. He does not proclaim the kingdom of God, but is only a sort of conjurer, whose magic changes the bread and wine into salvation and comfort."

"Was that perhaps the reason why you resigned from the ministry?"

"Maybe so, I cannot say for sure. Perhaps, too, I suspected that a day like this would be coming. Maybe I thought I could better hold my own once I was released from the church and only had to speak for myself."

The interrogation continued in this way throughout the third day, without the parties getting closer to one another or coming to any understanding. The counsel for the prosecution seemed more and more irritated and bewildered, and the newspaper reports relate that time and again he produced a handkerchief from the folds of his robe and wiped the perspiration from his forehead. The tone grew sharper as the day wore on, the man in the dock was showered by one piece of evidence after another. All along Vemund Hov was equally remote, his eyes set in a vacant stare, and he came back to reality with a start each time his adversary demanded an answer from him.

When the verdict was pronounced he received it with great equanimity and didn't seem surprised by its severity. He kept his stoic attitude to the very end, and didn't even neglect shaking the judge's hand when it was all over and he was led out of the courtroom.

But before the door of the courthouse will be closed for good, two more episodes must be mentioned. For the sake of emphasis, they are taken out of context in my account and given in reverse order, the last incident first and the first one last.

Well into the third day, just before the lay judges were to withdraw to return a verdict, a man got up at the far end of the hall and requested leave to speak. He was a very young man, almost a boy, a mechanic by trade and so direct in the way he expressed himself that he evoked smiles from the gentlemen on the bench.

After identifying himself, he added that he was one of the saboteurs who blew up the Sandane Machine Works and were sentenced to death in December 1944.

"It's not that I have any special liking for Pastor Hov," he said, "I don't care for his type, no matter what he has or has not done. I've been listening to him now for several hours, and I can't exactly say I'm any the wiser. As far as I'm concerned, he's a nutcase, and I'd like to see the guy who can figure him out.

"But I owe him something, that's the point, something really big and precious. Yes, Your Honour, I owe him nothing less than my life. That's why I've taken this trip and stand up to put in a good word for him. Where would I have been today if it hadn't been for him? Why, I would've been rotting in the cemetery down in my home town just like the other three.

"Wait a bit, let me explain myself. When I was in prison waiting to be executed, I had a night visit from a senior German officer. He came into my cell in full uniform, with jackboots, death's head in his cap, Iron Cross on his chest, and all. Christ, I almost thought I was seeing things when he stepped in behind the bars. What sort of business, do you think, could he have so late at night with someone who was condemned to death? Well, first he bawled me out in a mixture of German and Norwegian; fortunately it was mostly German, so I didn't understand much of it. But when he was through, he suddenly placed his hand on my shoulder and said I'd been pardoned. And for that I could thank Pastor Hov, he said; otherwise it would have meant certain death for me as for the other three. I was to be shot the next morning, Your Honour, but because the Pastor asked for mercy for me, it was called off. He said a lot more, but he spoke so poorly that I didn't understand very much. It couldn't have been what he meant to say, but it almost sounded as if it was the singing voice of the Pastor that had saved my life. The German's eyes literally shone through tears when he spoke about it, as if that and nothing else had decided the matter and changed the death sentence to twelve years in prison.

"Yes, you're right, Your Honour, the minutes are ticking. Just one more thing and I'll be through. I heard earlier that you wanted the Pastor to admit that he had reported his brother to the Gestapo after he'd shut him up in the sacristy. At first he tried to deny it, but you pressed so hard that you wore him out, and so he finally gave up. And the same way with the Jews he was supposed to have informed on. At first he tried to protest, but gradually he grew more subdued, and in the end he wasn't far from granting you were right. What is one to think of such half and quarter admissions? Well, I'm just asking. Don't you see that it really makes no difference? An over-clever clown who always sees things from two sides and feels he might just as well answer yes as no. Whether he's a traitor to his country or not, I cannot say. But informer, no, that I find hard to believe. As I've said before,

I don't have much liking for the man. But fair is fair, not least in the courtroom. Well, Your Honour, that's all, I think. But remember what I've said, and think it over before passing judgment, so you don't commit an injustice and sentence a man for something he never did."

Thus far the saboteur's plea, which was heard till the end and entered in the records, but hardly taken seriously enough to have any effect on the sentence.

The second episode may seem even more unimportant, nor was it perceived as anything other than a disturbance. When I still include it and let it stand as the conclusion to the chapter on treason, it is, as we shall see, for good reasons.

On the first day, right after the court had been convened, the door to the courtroom opened and a little girl with a schoolbag on her back came rushing into the room. When she had come a few steps forward, she stopped short and kept staring in all directions with an utterly perplexed look in her eyes. The moment she caught sight of the man in the dock she made a leap with her whole body, making her school things rattle in the bag, and darted forward to the upper end of the room.

"Dad, there's something – !" she cried in a thin, shrill voice, but checked herself and hid her face in her hands. "Dad, there's something – !" she tried again, but burst into tears and sobbed so frantically that the rest of her words were lost. And before anything more came of it, there were feet hurrying over the floor, voices shushing her, and gentle hands that caught hold of her and led her out of the hall. This was a place for grownups only, one of the voices explained, no children were allowed here, and now she must be a good girl and hurry to school so as not to be late.

Nothing more happened, and the entire incident was so brief that it's barely worth mentioning. But since the nine-year-old little girl is someone not entirely unknown to me, I shall dwell on the matter for a few moments and not make a secret of her errand.

Fourteen months earlier, in November 1944, something had happened at the parsonage that she alone knew about. It was a Sunday at dinnertime; her father had gone to Siljan to track down his vanished relatives, her mother and siblings were visiting over at the ship owner's, Anna was off, and only the nursemaid was at home to look after the house and one of the twins.

At a certain moment the doorbell rings, and when Maja, the nanny, opens up, the pastor's brother, the bike-crazy teacher, stands on the doorstep and wants to come in.

"What, nobody at home?" he says mistrustfully, forcing his way past the confused nursemaid, who had promised her mistress that she would keep the door locked and not let anyone in. "Well, just as I thought," he laughs when he notices Idun, who is leaning on the banister upstairs. "Come down here," he says, with the sweetest smirk at his command. "Look, Uncle has brought you some candy. Now the two of us will go into Dad's study and have a little chat."

Idun hesitates and withdraws a little, but when the uncle holds up the bag of sweets and rattles it, she takes courage and steals down the stairs, step by step. She isn't quite sure that she likes her uncle when he makes himself so sweet, and since that day over in the yellow house she has constantly had the feeling that he's right behind her and is going to catch her. But she's used to doing grownups' bidding, and when she's all the way down she sends Nanny-Maja a last imploring look and follows him obediently.

Inside the study, the uncle takes the bag from his pocket and places it on the writing table as bait, while his round face assumes an expression between excessive good nature and near menace.

"They're camphor lozenges," he says, and she can take as many as she likes as soon as she's been good and answered a few questions. "It's nothing dangerous," he insists, still in the same tone of exaggerated friendliness, he just wants to know what she was doing over in the yellow house that day when he came home from school early and caught her by surprise. Had she, perhaps, been prowling around the house for a long time, or was she there on some errand?

"I was just going to deliver a letter to Aunt Svallaug," she replies at last, after her uncle has overcome her resistance with his tricks.

"Ah, you don't say, a letter to Aunt Svallaug. Now, what could there be in that, eh?"

"I don't know, I can't read Dad's handwriting," Idun replies evasively.

"We-e-ll, so there was a letter from my brother, the pastor. Hm, I can already smell some intrigue. He wanted to see if he could liberate her, I imagine. Isn't that so, he was going to play the saviour and rescue her from the claws of the big, bad wolf?"

"I don't know," Idun whispers, squirming. "I was just going to deliver the letter."

"Oh, don't act more innocent than you are. You're full of secrets, I can tell from just looking at you, and you won't get out of this room until you've told me all you know."

"Leave me alone, I don't know anything more," the child cries in an anxious voice.

"Watch out now," her uncle says, leaning over her. "You don't know, do you, that Uncle Balder has an extra eye which can see through a little scaredy-cat like you?"

Idun raises her head and peeps apprehensively at the shiny badge he has on his lapel. It's an NS trooper badge, as she knows very well, but suddenly it seems to change into a glowing eye that burns its way into her innermost heart and sees what it must not see.

"I won't say it, I won't say it," she shouts, but now her voice is so thin that it is on the point of breaking.

"Out with it," the uncle roars, shaking her arm. "I'll keep you prisoner here until you let out all your secrets."

"It's just something that bad people believe," Idun whimpers, no longer in control of herself. "But it's not true. There are no Jews living in the attic at Grandpa's."

"What are you saying?" the uncle shouts, suddenly alert. "Let me hear, say it once again!"

"I tell you there aren't any Jews hiding in the attic of Grandpa's house."

"Ha-ha, indeed?" the uncle laughs, after sitting a while to assimilate the information. "Thank you, Idun, my niece. There you surely gave me a hint."

Idun jumps and lets out a little scream. It dawns on her that she has let the cat out of the bag and answered a question she wasn't even asked.

"Nobody is living in the attic over there, nobody lives there," she persists, her voice breaking as the tears gush from her eyes.

"All right," he says with a broad smile, pushing the bag of lozenges over to her. "We all know, don't we, that there aren't any Jews left in this town. The poor vermin have been dispatched, and good old Norway is finally free of Jews again. But take some candy, won't you, take the whole bag, for now you've really been a good girl."

He gets up and makes ready to go, but still hesitates a little and takes a few turns around the room. He steps restlessly back and forth for several minutes, looking searchingly all around him. Then his eyes meet the table-top, where he examines, one by one, all the writing materials standing on the green pad ready for use. Pen and ink in a special centrepiece, writing paper with the name and address of the pastor's office, and the pastor's own stamp with accessories. As if in a fit of sheer distraction, he takes the stamp, moistens it carefully and makes an imprint on the paper. He gives a quick sideways glance, and with the same absent-minded air tears the sheet from the writing pad, folds it and puts it into an almanac he has in the pocket of his jacket.

Idun sits motionless staring at the pad and the stamp long after he has gone away, as if the familiar articles contained some hidden misfortune. Then she slowly gets up and walks stiffly through the corridor and over to the other end of the house. If only I could tell Dad when he comes home, she thinks. Then there would be two of us who knew something, not only one, and I wouldn't have to be so afraid.

She stops for a moment in the dim kitchen hallway, looking helplessly around her; then she crawls into the broom closet to hide. There she sits with her head between her knees, mumbling softly to herself, until all ways out are closed and all hope gone.

"Dear God, help me," she whispers, "or I won't know what to do with myself. I've done something terribly wrong, but I didn't realize it till it was too late. Some words flew out of my mouth, and now they're stuck inside Uncle Balder's big, furry ear. Dear God and Jesus and all the angels, send a little ray of light into the closet for me, then I'll know there won't be any trouble."

No, there didn't come any light, everything was just as dark as before. "Where are you, God and his angels, can't you hear I'm calling you, that I'm in a terrible fix? I've done something wrong, I've done something wrong, and if you don't send me a little light I can't remain here any longer. Quick! Quick! Hurry up! Or someone will come over from Grandpa's house and tell us that the NS troopers have been there!"

V

Far Wanderings

1

Returned to the hospital again Monday 22 August, after being away for almost three months. Or after being on the road, I should probably say. For my absence was not according to regulations, and most people would no doubt call it an escape. I had been reported missing and was on the wanted list for several weeks before it was discovered that I was abroad, travelling on a stolen passport.

When I was finally found, deep inside the concentric circles of Amsterdam, I had a long detour on the Continent behind me, had crossed borders, seen memorable places once again, and faithfully walked in my own footsteps from somewhere in the sixties, seventies, and eighties. I was dozing by a canal at the very bottom of inferno, so spent and worn out that it was a relief to be picked up, stripped of my borrowed feathers and taken charge of.

For three weeks I've been lying stretched out on my bed more dead than alive, so amnesiac that I barely knew who I was, or where I had been for so long. But yesterday morning things slowly began to brighten for me, and today, 12 September, my head is sufficiently clear to enable me to sit up in bed and take stock.

I'm still committed, and after my latest disappearance there is no prospect of ever being discharged (apart from any escape I may achieve through my scribblings). I'm reminded of the terror that seized me the first time somebody in this place mentioned that I might be discharged. I thought immediately about my unfinished work and was on the point of calling out that it would be a disaster if that happened. I wouldn't be able to go on living, I wanted to say; if I was no longer able to recreate my ruined life and transform my grief into beauty, they might just as well bury me.

As a consequence of my absence – or my "breach of confidence" as the head nurse calls it – I've lost my precious private room and have been given a vacant space in a ward with six beds. At this moment, as I write, I'm sitting behind a screen trying to gather my thoughts, while around me people are yelling and screaming, talking in their sleep or in delirium, singing litanies and dirges, mumbling gibberish, crying crocodile tears, and letting out trumpet fanfares as a special greeting to my oversensitive sense of smell.

Before continuing my story where I dropped it in late winter, I shall have to make another quantum leap and insert a section where I explain in more detail the circumstances of my going away (my breach of confidence, my disappearance, my defection, my absence, my vagabondage). This reckless adventure, which may look like a whim or a sudden impulse but was, in reality, a deliberate and carefully planned escape. For once I cannot excuse myself by saying that it was something that "came over me", but have to admit that I'm a cunning and conspiratorial person who weaves intrigues and deliberately opposes the system.

As has been mentioned, I had agreed with my publisher to drop by some day in late May to sign the contract and receive an advance of ten thousand kroner. The editor and I had put our heads together, and he had promised to have the money ready in cash, and preferably in not too large denominations. I cannot tell whether he saw through my intentions, but he showed himself a true friend and took my side without reservations. I could feel quite confident, he said, because the hospital wouldn't know anything about the payment until sometime in the New Year, and my other superiors weren't going to be informed.

The day before I was to show up at the publisher's something unexpected happened, one of those strange flukes that almost seem like an intention. Not only did it strengthen my decision to skip out, but it came to me like a secret hint, made freedom of movement possible, and expanded my travel plans to a virtually dizzying degree.

My twin sister, who over the years has hardly ever visited me, suddenly appeared in the ward and proposed that I should go home with her. A good idea had occurred to her, she said, and she would like to know my opinion of it. She had thought she would have me join her in one of her TV programmes, and she had come to discuss the matter with me confidentially. And since my headquarters in the loony bin weren't quite the right place, she had requested a few hours' time off for me, so that our conversation could occur in the quiet surroundings of her home.

Urd is the medical director's sister-in-law and a well-known media hand, so she had no difficulty procuring my leave. She simply signed a paper promising to take good care of me and to bring me back to the madhouse well before supper. Then she pushed me with a slight nudge over to her right side and put her arm under mine, so that we could stroll out into the open like a pair of real *Doppelgängers*. Practically the same height, both of us slim, I almost emaciated, in contrast to the way it was in our childhood, when I had the most meat on my bones. One dressed in expensive, exquisite clothes of the latest fashion, the other more dubiously attired in casually assembled garments. The same shape of face, with a high forehead and round cheeks, just slightly more irregular in one of us and with a dimple that in the course of the years had turned into a crack. Longish blond hair, in my case rather messy and with touches of grey, in hers well-groomed and touched up in the approved fashion. Large, deep-set blue eyes, with the sole difference that one of my eyes has a troll splinter in it, making it shade into brown, grey and green tints. But when we walked the way we always used to, I on her right-hand side and at the very edge of the sidewalk, the passersby saw a pair of twin sisters who were blue-eyed and looked very much alike.

When we got to the parking lot she pushed me into the back seat of the car and quickly locked the door, as though I were a convict. I cannot say whether she found it distracting to have me sitting beside her, or whether she was afraid that the crazy woman would have an attack and frighten her, making her lose control of the vehicle. On the trip to town we sat in our separate cubicles without exchanging a word, but Urd hummed demonstratively to show that the mood was by no means depressed.

The apartment, situated in a side street to Bygdøy Avenue, was one of those luxury ratholes that turn their backs on the city and have a panoramic view across the Frogner Bay toward Oscarshall Palace. I may have happened to think aloud and say something wrong, because Urd's face tensed up; she impressed upon me that the apartment was a real find. It had cost three and a half million, she said, they'd been on a waiting list for years, and everyone who came there envied them the location and the magnificent view of the sea.

To pacify her I followed her around the place, inspecting the paintings and antiquities, nodding at random and playing along, while giving a friendly thought to music and literature, which couldn't be the object of speculation and investment but was the sort of stuff that dreams are made of. We came past Father's carved bookcase, and I noticed that it was cleared of books and converted into a display case for all kinds of sham old silver. On the opposite wall the shelves were full of technical books, encyclopaedias, lamps, and knickknacks, with a lone bestseller or detective novel here and there – not a single work of literature of any worth as far as the eye could see. What would Father's vanished library be doing here, I thought; maybe it was a good thing that Goethe's *Faust*, Shakespeare's *King Lear*, Dostoyevsky's *Crime and Punishment* and Dante's *Divine Comedy* had ended their days in the garbage dump. When Father bought them, he was an impoverished student who could barely afford to eat his fill, so the books he left behind were not leather-bound but unbound coffee-stained copies he'd literally read to pieces.

Urd went to the kitchen to prepare tea, and I sat there wondering in what way she could be of any help to her patients. Father always used to say that there were three sources of insight into the human psyche: first of all, the courage to look into one's own mind, then literature, and finally observation of other people. It appeared that my intelligent sister had access only to the last resource and by and large depended on her theoretical knowledge. Who knows, I thought, perhaps it wasn't an advantage to be so quick-witted as to understand everything on the spot, without first having to meditate on it. Perhaps one disposed of the problems too fast and came too easily to one's conclusions. There was something in Urd's facile intelligence that had always made me sceptical; it somehow seemed to know everything beforehand and was so clever that I couldn't put any trust in it.

Shortly after Urd had gone to the kitchen I noticed that one of the drawers of the writing table was slightly open, and since I've never been able to restrain my curiosity I pulled it out and rummaged in it a little. At the very bottom, under her writing paper, photo album, almanacs and psychological journals, I caught sight of her passport. I gave a start, afraid to touch it before turning an ear toward the kitchen to make sure my sister was still out there clattering pots and pans. Then I opened the red booklet, with its lion, cross and crown, and inspected the names on the first page. "Sand, Kathrine Elisabeth," I read; the paternal name, Hov, was gone with the wind, as was the name of the Norn, Urd, "she who shall come into being". If I knew my sister correctly, she had tried to have her silly, scarecrow name, Thrinebeth, included in the passport, but had cut no ice with the Oslo police authorities. In my mind's eye I could see her standing at the counter arguing and insisting, just like Mother when she would stand before the window at the post office refusing to accept stamps with "Noreg" on them.

Suddenly I noticed that it had gone quiet in the kitchen. I turned around and gave a quick look at the door, and without quite knowing what I was doing I pushed the drawer back in, lifted my skirt and stuck the passport in between my knickers and my tights. I had violent palpitations, but my thief's fingers were lucky, and there was still time to straighten out my dress and wipe the agitation from my face before the door opened and Urd came in, balancing the tea tray in her hands.

While the tea was poured and we helped ourselves to the delicious sandwiches, we were both rather embarrassed, and the conversation skipped from one thing to another. I was on tenterhooks, but the depth psychologist Thrinebeth Sand didn't appear to have a particularly deep insight into her depraved sister; in any case, her x-ray eyes never managed to penetrate below my belt. In between some elegant nibbles, she told me the latest news about our brother, Vidar, alias Nicolai Sand, who lived everywhere and nowhere and enjoyed a varied existence as a "perpetual tourist". When he took over the shipping company in 1970, times were hard for Norwegian shipping, and one of the first things he did was to lower the Norwegian flag on his fleet and seek a tax shelter in Andorra. He had kept the country house at Brekkestø, which was his house and his real home, where he lived as long as he could without getting into conflict with the law.

What she did not relate, but I knew from another quarter, was that my brother, Vidar (Nicce), an inspired speculator, had risen in the world and become a billionaire by means of all kinds of ingenious tricks. Sometime in the late seventies he had performed a feat not dissimilar to the one his quick-witted grandfather had brought off in the mid-twenties. He had chartered an East European tanker fleet on extremely favourable terms and stood idly by as his stock steadily kept climbing on the stock exchange. While the freight prices just rose and rose, he had at his disposal eight tankers and earned $20,000 a day on each, in return for paying the owners a negligible fixed percentage. During the Iraq-Iran war he had a fleet of seventeen tankers as old as the hills, with Philippine crews that transported oil to Iran from Kharg Island in the Gulf. As time went on, his clients began to complain that they received fewer barrels than the papers indicated, the insurance companies raised an outcry, and the newspapers brought out their bold type, and soon the good Nicce was involved in a suit which questioned his very credibility. A suspicion had arisen that the ships had used part of the crude oil for fuel, a very hazardous procedure, since the mixture was highly explosive and could endanger the lives of the crew. But, as always, Nicce knew how to thread his way through difficulties. With the help of astute attorneys he managed to weaken the state of the evidence, and so it ended with a settlement in which he paid a penalty of a couple of million for "negligence". –

Time was passing at Urd's tea table, and when the old grandfather clock in the corner beat four feeble strokes, I began to wonder whether she had changed her mind. But then she suddenly put away her cup and came to the point.

"I suppose you've heard of my Friday programmes?" she began, making some limbering exercises with her right little finger, which she had held elegantly extended during the tea drinking. "They've become extremely popular, even if I say so myself. No other programme attracts so many viewers. I'm constantly stopped in the street, and every week I receive heaps of letters from grateful people."

I had seen most of the programmes in the parlour at the hospital, but restrained myself and pretended not to know anything about them.

She narrowed her mouth and cast a long, scrutinizing look in my direction. Then she quickly passed her hand through her hair and began explaining the point of the whole thing. The programme was intended as therapy for the entire population, she said, that's why it had received the best prime-time slot in the week, Friday at eight. She herself used to sit on one side of an ordinary coffee table, while the "victims" – as she jokingly called them – sat on the other side with their backs to the camera. In rare instances the clients came forward openly, if they had a position that gave them sufficient self-confidence. But the rule was complete anonymity, or as much protection as the individual client needed. She had considered an arrangement around the table where the participants were occasionally visible in half-profile, thus offering a thrilling alternation between openness and mystery without anyone running the risk of being recognized.

I nodded, and to obviate any possibility of mimicry I took a draught of the tea and munched hard and heartily on the cheese sandwiches. Urd is a person who demands approval, and it would have been a terrible disaster if I chuckled or allowed my face to betray what I really thought of her undertaking.

"In the course of the winter I've completed a series that I've called *Confession*," she continued. "It became a great success, much greater than

I had anticipated, although I know very well that the absence of confession in our Protestant countries is felt as a deprivation. It wasn't difficult to find 'victims'. People signed up voluntarily, and in such numbers that I could pick and choose."

"But now you intend to close the confessional and withdraw absolution, don't you?" I said, no longer able to restrain myself.

"Don't try to be funny," she said, more sharply than was necessary. "*Confession* was really a unique programme and deserved a longer life span. But the viewers want change, and when a programme has appeared on TV for a couple of years, renewal is necessary. I've been turning it over in my mind, trying to find something that could keep their interest alive, and have rejected one project after another. But suddenly I had a good idea. Please, listen carefully, and don't interrupt me till I've finished my explanation."

I didn't say a word, because I had that very moment something else to worry about. The passport had slipped down along my lean stomach and was now chafing my skin in the cleft of my thigh.

"To make a long story short," she said, "I've decided on a series that I'll call *The Unhappy Twin*. It's still at an early stage, so I'll no doubt be sitting in my think tank for most of the spring and summer. But I can tell you this much: it will be an exciting programme, with a rich assortment of different human destinies. All twins are first and foremost individuals, that's my thesis. Even with identical twins there will be great differences in endowments, intellectual bent and living conditions."

"I see," I said, without moving a muscle. "You want to put together a panel consisting purely of unhappy twins."

"Exactly, that's the plan. For therapeutic reasons I'll concentrate on the unsuccessful twin. I'm going to show that the characteristics of a pair of twins are distributed very unequally and that one of them will always be the loser."

I nodded piously, pretending to play along with her construction, while I cautiously jiggled the passport under my knicker elastic, until it rested against my bare flesh.

"Listen, why don't you instead call your programme *The Dubious Twin*?" I said after a considerable silence.

"Why?" she said, casting me a suspicious look.

"Oh, I just happened to think of one of the books of the American humorist Mark Twain, who once declared that he was born of poor but dishonest parents, and who on his deathbed forestalled the gossips by saying that the news of his death was greatly exaggerated."

"You disappoint me," Urd said, heaving a deep sigh. "This is not a joke. Oh yeah, a nice impression that would make, if people started thinking that my studies of twins were entertainment."

"No, no," I said, backing down. "I'm sorry, it was just something that occurred to me."

I held out my hand, and Urd was gracious and squeezed it between two fingers. But suddenly she jumped up and began to gather the dishes with every sign of being in a hurry.

"Good heavens," she cried, "it's nearly half-past five. Hurry up and get ready, so we can be back to the hospital in time."

"Think about my proposal," she said a little later, as we stood in the entrance hall putting on our wraps. "You don't have to give me a final answer until sometime in August. But no nonsense, remember!"

"I hope I've understood you correctly," I said when we stood in the street and Urd was unlocking the door of the car. "You will sit facing the viewers and be the successful twin, who has made something of herself, isn't that so? And I'll be on the panel, sit with the other losers and speak about my experiences as an unhappy twin."

"Now you aren't being very nice," she said, pushing me into the back seat. "But you've grasped the main point and that's the most important. Think it over and promise me you'll keep faith with the basic concept, then we'll talk again sometime in the autumn."

I returned to the ward bubbling over with high spirits, which lasted the whole evening and caused me to snicker unabashedly in front of my keepers. "The un-hap-py twin," I mimicked over and over again in Urd's drawling, microphone voice. Can it really be possible, I asked myself, is it my intelligent and well-trained sister who takes on projects of that kind? And in full seriousness, without any countervailing ideas or ironic mental reservation! What can one expect from a poor guinea pig like myself, I thought, when a Ph.D. in psychology loses her head to this extent and goes astray?

Suddenly a treacherous thought struck me, making me laugh out loud. What if I rejected her plan and took matters into my own hands? What if I gave a half turn to the stage and invited the audience to a programme far more shocking and authentic than *The Unhappy Twin*? In the midst of all

240

the psychological fumbling I could turn around to the viewers and introduce myself as the doubtful twin, the one who broke agreements, threw up the game and showed her true colours, having no need whatsoever of the anonymity that was conferred upon her. "Good evening, big and small snoops," I could cry out through the screen and into the thousand homes. "Move closer together on the sofa and take a look at that terrible twin sister of media queen Thrinebeth Sand. Get to know her *Doppelgänger*, her shadow, her evil genius, the subconscious in person. The regular programme has been cancelled, and we are beginning a new series that will show the other side of the coin. In a number of revealing happenings we shall see what takes place between human beings when plans are thwarted, masks fall, chaos threatens and the unpredictable itself pops up and gives the lie to all calculations."

When the light was turned off, I placed my head on the pillow in an animated mood that rushed to meet tomorrow and threw me into its lap. My only worry was, who would go with me to the publisher the following day and see to it that I didn't indulge in any capers? I hoped it wouldn't be Sister Sigrid, the only one in the ward who took me seriously and treated me as an equal. But I took comfort in the thought that it would no doubt be a more subordinate person, whom I could run circles around without scruples and deceive to my heart's content.

Before I went to sleep, I had the entire escape route clear in my head, from the moment of leaving the office of the editor, after a quick visit, until I stood on board the Danish boat a couple of hours later and with a sigh of relief saw the strip of water between Pier Two and *Queen of Scandinavia* expand and turn into the Oslo Fjord. I felt so carefree and light-hearted that it was as though I were already on board, and my race through a labyrinth of hurdles was happily over.

But it was a restless night, one nightmare followed another, and I couldn't say how many times I raised my head from the pillow and looked around the room in bewilderment. My escape had started, I was already going down trackless paths, anticipating all the terrors lying in wait for me on the way. Now I would run for dear life through the streets of an unknown city, just as terror-stricken as when I was small and thought that Uncle Balder was after me. Now I would be treading in a huge fishing net, which wound itself round my feet and turned every step into a trap. And the next moment, without having climbed up, I was balancing on a thin branch in a tree top, while a monster was snapping at me underneath, waiting for the branch to break and the fugitive to fall. But the branch did not break and I did not fall, for suddenly I was at the window of the passport control in a foreign country and had forgotten how to stand in order to match my description. Madame Kathrine Elisabeth Sand, you can't fool us, said a voice in a language I'd never heard before, but which, strange to say, I still understood. Your identity is false, and we'll be obliged to detain you. Your eyes are not blue as it says in the passport, but have an indeterminate colour that affords grounds for suspicion. Come here, follow us, and we shall examine the matter more carefully.

By morning I was so exhausted that I almost wished something untoward would happen and prevent me from going through with my purpose. For example, that it would be Sister Sigrid, the charge nurse, who followed me to the publisher's, my protector and thoughtful friend, whom I couldn't possibly deceive. As the morning hours went by, I grew more and more fidgety and perplexed. What was pushing me into this adventure, since I knew in advance that it would end in the most extreme misery? What obscure urge was getting the better of me, steering my steps towards homelessness, horror, shame and humiliation? Was it a blind will to live, the beginning and origin of all things? Or was it the emptiness and despair that knows all is lost and that there is nothing left to lose anymore?

I didn't know. I only noticed that the shadows were gathering around me, that everything uncertain and dreamlike in my life was closing in, craving a visible form. Dread and danger, I thought, would they ever leave me alone and stop chasing one another? Wasn't nearly any danger preferable to all this nonsense, these figments of the imagination, which threatened my sense of reality night and day? What was the most dreadful thing, I asked myself: to stand before the passport control in a foreign country insisting on one's false identity, or to writhe under this omnipresent eye that searches you to the bottom of your soul and wants to know who you are?

If only I were in my little apartment in the Homansbyen section writing a novel, I thought. Then freedom would be the same as necessity, all my steps would lead to the goal, and the question of who I am would find an answer.

It was approaching half-past two, and I was on the verge of abandoning my purpose, when my escort appeared in the doorway saying we were leaving. It was a ward sister that I didn't know and whom it wouldn't be difficult to fool. All the same I felt a bit sorry for her as we sat side by side in the car. My little friend, you imagine you are on solid ground, I thought, glancing over at her self-assured profile. But don't rejoice too soon. In a couple of hours your passenger will be gone without a trace, and you will be obliged to return to the loony bin, alone.

In any case, I had no reason to complain about the surveillance, every conceivable allowance had been made to prevent the visit at the publisher's from being humiliating to me. My escort was not in uniform, and it had been agreed that she was not to come with me up to the editor's office but to wait for me in the lobby. I told her that my business might drag on, maybe until closing time. Not only was I to sign the contract and look at the new dust jacket for *The Papessa*, but the editor and I were also to examine the two books that would reappear in the autumn and discuss whether any corrections had to be made before they went to the printer.

"Just take all the time you need," said Sister Agnes. "I've brought my knitting and *See and Hear*, and won't have any trouble passing the time."

I waited until she had installed herself by the bookstall, in a strategic spot where she could keep an eye on all who came and went. Then I raised my hand in a gesture of deliverance and walked with firm steps down the long corridor, past the production department and up the stairs to the second floor. In passing I cast a stealthy glance at one of the office doors, where some months ago there had been a bunch of keys in the lock. That was not the case now, nor would that kind of coincidence influence my plans on this occasion.

The first thing I said when I entered the office of the editor was that I was short of time and could only stay for a few minutes. He took it very nicely – in fact, his face brightened up – and said it suited him fine. He had just been called to an important meeting and found himself in a predicament, not knowing "which god he ought to serve". Now everything was straightened out and we could rest easy. We would make up for it the next time we met, he said. He would send me an invitation when the books for the autumn season were to be presented, and if possible we would go out for dinner afterwards.

When I had put my name to the contract and stuck the envelope with the money in my purse, we went together into the anteroom. The escape route was clear, and I asked with a little laugh if I could borrow "the literary lavatory" down the hall (not to be confused with the previously mentioned "production lavatory" downstairs). That I could, and after uttering a few concluding words and shaking hands, we went our separate ways. He to the important meeting which had nearly clashed with our appointment, I into the innermost part of the building, past the caves of the bosses, around the turn by the cloakroom, and over to the ladies' lavatory near the back staircase.

Inside I opened the envelope with the ten thousand kroner and divided the amount, leaving eight thousand in my shoulder bag and putting the remainder into a cosmetic pouch I had sewn during therapy and was wearing in a string on my chest in honour of the occasion. These two thousand kroner were to be my reserve capital, which could be touched only if I got into difficulties.

Once I was ready I went onto the back stairs, looked through the window to see if the path was clear, took the stairs in a few quick jumps and strolled calmly across the courtyard and out the gate, which was wide open, as though by request. Anyway, if someone had seen me, the sight wouldn't have been very sensational. An unknown woman with a shoulder bag who was leaving by the stockroom entrance and crossed the square with measured steps, without either dawdling or being too much in a hurry. It was exactly fourteen minutes past three o'clock, and less than a quarter of an hour had passed since I entered the publishing house from the other end of the building.

Some distance down the street I hailed a cab and dropped by my apartment in Homansbyen, where I changed my clothes and got out the gold chain with the rubies, which was to be my protection in extreme distress if everything went wrong. Then off to Den norske Bank on Railway Square, where as a matter of course I changed my Norwegian kroner into German marks and Danish kroner. All along I was filled with a pleasant equanimity, an unfaltering confidence that everything would go according to plan and turn out well.

Once my financial affairs were in order, I stepped out on the square, glanced at the clock on the old East Railway building and dropped in at the bakery to buy a Danish. And while munching on this innocent piece of pastry, I went unhurriedly over to Fred Olsen Street, crossed at the traffic lights on Rådhus Street and entered the harbour area. The clock on the tower showed a few minutes past four. Sister Agnes was sitting faithfully at her post, no doubt, counting stitches while steeping herself in the customs of the rich and famous. Still, it would probably be several minutes before she began to suspect something and, lifting her eyes from *See and Hear*, gradually awoke and regained her ability to see and hear.

When the ship glided away from the shore, nothing alarming had yet happened; the ticket had been stamped and handed back, nobody had stopped me on the gangway, no loudspeaker had blared out the feared police bulletin. But as I stood there, leaning against the railing on the upper deck, I knew that the alarm must already have been sounded at the hospital. In an eerily faraway manner, as though I weren't involved myself, I imagined the commotion over there: running feet, medical records being turned upside down, telephones ringing, and undercover agents setting out to comb the city from one end to the other.

I wonder how long it will take before Urd discovers her passport is gone? I thought long afterwards, as darkness came on and I noticed I was cold. Suddenly it dawned on me that I was a traveller without luggage and that someone might already have noticed.

2

When today, six weeks after my wretched return, I am to try and explain my escape, I come up against two decisive problems (which may, in the last analysis, be one and the same).

One has to do with the lapse of time and with the age-old question of how movement hardens and becomes stagnation. To sit behind a hospital screen and write about an escape is not the same thing at all as to be escaping; something else has come in between, a magic hand has been raised, changing time into eternity.

In real life the pursuer overtakes the pursued by dint of his greater speed and efficiency. The latter may have a greater or lesser head start, but time is on the side of the pursuer and allows him to catch up with his victim. In my eternal backward glance, such a conclusion never occurs. I walk, steal ahead, hurry up, running as though my life depended on it, but when I turn around to look back, the pursuer is always just as far away or just as near. The arrow that is launched stays still in the air, Achilles chases the tortoise without ever getting his hands on it.

The other difficulty is that I've been wandering so many times that one period of time shows through another and assumes the character of a repetition. I'm not always able to tell them apart and to say what happened when. As in a hall of mirrors I see one fleeing figure behind another in an infinite succession that cannot be isolated or dated. The years 1963, 1968, 1971, 1976, 1980, 1987 or 1994 are sort of loosely attached to them, the figures are interchangeable as they stand there, motionless in the field of vision, hurrying on towards the vanishing point.

Because of these memory displacements I have several times been on the verge of abandoning this part of my story. But it refuses to be turned away; it gnaws at my recollection day and night, torments me with anxiety and uneasiness, and pops up like a spectre in my dreams. I'm forced to take the plunge and make myself familiar with these scenarios, which may be confusing and complex, but still possess a density that makes them look like pictures.

First picture: Ghosts.

Idun Hov seems to appear from nowhere and finds herself, just like that, in a small Danish town, more specifically a village by the Sejerø Bay in North Zealand, not far from that spit of land which once had a regular passenger service to a town in southern Norway. Whether she's here for the second, third or fourth time can't be cleared up. The only thing that can be said for certain is that it's not the first time, when everything was up in the air and the misfortune hadn't yet taken place.

She walks about the streets of the town for a day or half a day, ostensibly without any definite errand. But there is a somnambulistic air about her, and something peculiar in the way she looks at the passersby. It's a look that is at once faraway and scrutinizing, and that may occasionally become so bold that she gives a start and hastens to withdraw her eyes.

It's not everyone who attracts her attention, most people are allowed to pass by without her taking any notice. If it is the second time she's here, she is looking for a child around eight years old that matches a vague model she has in her mind. It may be a boy with black hair and dark, shining eyes, a descendant of the little Jewish boy, Aaron, whom she once surprised in her grandfather's attic. But it may just as well be a little girl with blond hair and queer eyes, very much like herself as she was that Sunday long ago when she stole up the stairs. But the child she's looking for is no perfect copy, and all kinds of combinations are possible: a boy with blond hair and dark eyes, a girl with queer eyes and dark hair, a boy with blond hair and queer eyes, a girl with black hair and dark, shining eyes, and so on and so forth, in every conceivable variation.

If it is the third time she's visiting the town, she's looking for a grown-up man or woman, a person of the same light-dark appearance as the one she's trying to find. Sometimes she's taken aback and opens her eyes wide, or she turns around like a flash and rushes back to look more closely at someone or other. But always to no avail. Recognition never occurs; she never meets anyone who corresponds to the diffuse image she has in her mind's eye.

If it is only the second time she's here, she cautiously approaches a little red-brick house on the outskirts of town. She walks right up to the door several times and then again withdraws, before she finally takes courage and knocks. She stands on the stairs in a sort of daze for a moment, like the first time she was here when nothing had yet happened. Then she raises her eyes, looks into the face of a woman, a total stranger, and asks timidly whether Ida Andersen, the midwife, is still living there. What are you saying, is she dead, can it really be true, how long ago? Six years ago – imagine, already in 1957! Goodbye, thanks for your help, I'm sorry, no, that was all. She turns upon her heel and flees, while the strange woman goes in again, or remains standing in the doorway shaking her head in wonder.

If it is the fourth and last time she appears in town, it's without any kind of purpose; she's a shadow of her former self, and her visit is a sheer haunting. Nonetheless she roams about the streets for hours, startled and unnerved by the faces of men and women she scrutinizes, rounding one corner after another, until she gives up and sinks down on a doorstep in exhaustion.

Second picture: On the stage

After many futile attempts, Idun has finally managed to get an appointment with Mr X, actor and director at the Royal Theatre, and is to show up without delay for an audition.

The year can in this case be given with great certainty as 1967. She has lived in Copenhagen for nearly eight years, and, thanks to the musicality she has inherited from both her parents, she speaks Danish almost without an accent.

The audition means so much to her that its outcome has become a "to be or not to be." For seven and a half years she has kept body and soul together by taking night shifts at the city hospitals. She's near breaking point, dead tired of making beds and lifting patients heavy as lead, taking their pulse, measuring their temperature, changing bandages, counting pills, and running in and out through the corridors with bedpans and urinals. Capricious Lady Fortune, goddess of luck and chance, once took her by the hand and led her into nursing. Now she's calling upon the equally capricious Lady Thalia, trying out for better luck.

Actor X is a refined elderly gentleman, more than twice her age, with silver-grey hair, light, almost feminine movements, and a voice coloured by the dramatic intonations of a long life in the theatre. He sits beside her on the couch, takes her hand and, when he notices how nervous she is, pats it soothingly.

"I knew you were Norwegian as soon as I glanced at your letter," he says with a little teasing laugh. "No, no, there were no slips of the pen, not a single one, my sweet friend. But something in the tone tickled my ear, it was unmistakable. Cheer up, little Idun, you write and speak excellent Danish, and that touch of a mountain accent is simply charming."

She steps onto the podium and begins to recite her lines: first Medea's long speech of revenge upon her enemies, then Ariel's warning to Prospero in the third act of *The Tempest*, and finally Rebecca West's fateful exchange with Kroll and Rosmer in the final scenes of *Rosmersholm*. She gives the men's voices in a whisper, like a prompter, but when one of the women has the floor she takes a deep breath and raises her voice to something like a muffled scream.

When she has finished and looks down at her auditor, he sits remote and motionless without saying a word, and she quickly sets to work on her extra numbers: the monologue "Myself" by Henrik Wergeland, "Ode to a Grecian Urn" by John Keats, "I long for the country of nowhere" by Edith Södergran, and finally a sad little poem of unknown origin.

She drops her hands and throws an inquiring look at her judge, but he still doesn't say anything, just gets up slowly from his seat, takes a large white handkerchief from his breast pocket and brushes his face with it. Her heart sinks, and she's full of misgivings when he finally makes a sign to her and asks her to come to the dressing room where they were sitting before.

But inside the small semi-dark cabinet something quite unexpected happens. He leads her up to the sofa, pushes her gently down into the soft velvet and sits down on a stool nearby. He sits there for a long time, fixing her with a penetrating glance, a deep wrinkle on his brow.

Judging by his silence and his distressing mimicry, she can expect a crushing sentence. But suddenly he seizes her hand and holds it between both of his, while he explains to her, very calmly and with great authority, why she is not an actor. Her passion and her sympathetic insight into the texts have made a profound impression on him, he says, he falls down before her artistic temperament. But the theatre is not the place for her, and she will spare herself great disappointments if she dismisses the idea of becoming an actor once and for all. Her voice is much too small and frail and becomes shrill in the great scenes. And that's not all. She's too introverted and physically shy to be able to give body to a dramatic text and project it beyond the boards. And what's worse, her body language contradicts her speech; she resembles an aerial spirit when playing a goddess of revenge and a goddess of revenge when she should be an aerial spirit.

"But believe me, no harm has been done," he says with a special light in his eyes. "The art of acting is not the only art, there are other languages than body language, and other voices than those that are audible. Little friend, go back to your own house and don't be sorry that you cannot be a member of the troop. You see, we actors are only half men, drawing our existence from the auditorium and unable to live a single day without applause. We are greedy cannibals who never can get enough, we swallow our audiences whole. Tell me one thing, by the way, who had written the little poem about the lost child that you read at the very end? Lo and behold! Just as I thought. There you might have something that could unfold and grow into something bigger."

In the course of sharing a bottle of wine and discussing her future prospects, the atmosphere has changed; his voice is more intimate, and quite imperceptibly he has taken to calling her by her first name. He makes a movement as if trying to embrace her, but pulls back and tells her once more that he cannot help her become an actor. He won't even advise her to become a walk-on, for a walk-on is a disguised actor who is simply waiting for a part. The only thing he can do for her is to get her a job as a wardrobe mistress, if she's really in earnest about wanting to quit nursing. It's not exactly a brilliant offer, she deserved far better, but some good might come of it. The salary is modest, but enough to get by on, and the work is so easy that she will have time to concentrate on her own things. She will be close to dramatic art and, not least, be welcome to visit him in his den and keep him company after the theatre.

When he leans forward and opens the top button of her blouse, she offers no resistance, feeling her will go slack and her limbs heavy. His movements become bolder, and in mute rapture he strips her of her garments, one after another, stretches her out on the sofa and kisses her naked body time after time. She lets it happen in a state of dreamlike ecstasy, as if it were a last extra number and the only possible conclusion to her performance.

But when she holds out her arms to pull him down on her, he raises his hand and holds her back. Without saying a word, he gives her to understand that this is not a mutual act, but an initiation, a means of grace, a mystical communion. She closes her eyes and surrenders obediently to this strange ritual, where she herself lies naked and full of wonder-working powers, while he bends humbly over her and kisses her body from top to toe. He does so with near-religious devotion, as if he were bending over the sacred host and absorbing its life-giving juices. He is untiring in his adoration, not a single part of her body is left untouched, and when she opens her eyes and looks at him, his face is empty and dull, like that of a holy man when the exaltation is past and he sinks back into a lower sphere.

When she is dressed, he accompanies her out and mentions a day when she can begin in the wardrobe. And he would very much like to see her in his private apartment the same evening, he adds in a near whisper, if she can endure him and doesn't feel too much put off by his overtures.

Third Picture: Trip

Idun and her theatrical friend Hamlet are sitting in Boom Inn in Farver Street, smoking hash in a mixed company of actors, budding authors, would-be philosophers, musicians and other adventurers. The rooms belong to the theatre group Secret Service, to which she has been introduced by her friend and where she helps out with odd jobs: puts up sets, translates dramatic texts, substitutes as prompter and dresser, airs the premises after closing time, wakes up stragglers sleeping in the corners, and administers first aid if anybody has taken an overdose.

Spirits run high at the gathering, at times verging on the apocalyptic, but by and large there are no drug addicts among the members. Most are simply young people looking for a high, eager to expand the limits of perception and try out new adventures. Although the air is so thick with smoke that it can be cut into cubes, their brains are luminously clear. Drama, philosophy and psychology are discussed, poems recited and music played, accompanied by flying stunts on the trapeze of possibility and runs up and down the scales of laughter.

Hamlet's civil name is Torben Nielsen, neither more nor less. His nickname stems from the star turn he performs whenever he can gather an audience around him. He assumes a world-weary pose, with an authentic skull in the palm of his hand, and declaims in rapid succession these immortal lines from Shakespeare's famous play: "Words, words words, there is more between heaven and earth, oh my prophetic soul, there is something rotten in the state of Denmark – the rest is silence."

On the calling cards he strews about him it says "royal actor", a reference to the venerable drama school in London where he is supposed to have cultivated his talent for the stage. But the truth, I'm afraid, is somewhat more modest. That he drew attention to himself on the other side of the North Sea is beyond doubt, his scripts are packed with autographs and special greetings to "the promising young prince of Denmark" from none other than Laurence Olivier. But in his usual rush he backed out midway, when the lessons in voice, dance, fencing and declamation had caused him to feel fully trained. Since then he has fought his way through as a stagehand and walk-on, and is still looking forward to getting a part. His weakness is that he's at once a greedy eater and a poor one: he munches and chews and swallows like very few, but loses his appetite before the table is set. He has got a talent for beginnings, and is full of running starts and exuberant ideas. But since he has turned his life into theatre, he doesn't have very much to do on a stage.

She became acquainted with him six weeks ago, while he was a walk-on and she wardrobe mistress at The Royal Theatre. One evening as she stood by the counter handing him his large artist's hat, he looked her straight in the eye and began flirting tempestuously, pulling out all the stops, without any opening or introduction. And since Idun has never been able to resist eccentric men, the matter was decided on the spot. Goodbye Royal Theatre with appertaining privileges, goodbye my old, silver-haired friend with your quaint inclinations. This evening she will not be lying on a dark-red sofa distributing the holy sacrament, but sit on the back seat of a battered old Vespa and allow herself to be carried off to far less refined fun.

Officially he's her fiancé and he makes no secret of the fact that it says *Yours For Ever* inside the small worn gold ring that he's wearing on his left hand. But strangely enough, there's no name in the ring, and no date. Idun smiles shyly, holding out a hand with her own ring, which looks new and bright by comparison. She's still blissfully ignorant of his most recent past, and of the domestic drama that preceded the courting at The Royal Theatre.

That very day he had fallen out with his fiancée; after endless complications she had had enough of his play-acting and had shown him the door. And since he didn't have a place of his own but put up here and there with his changing female friends, he was suddenly without a roof over his head. The eviction occurred so suddenly that he didn't even have time to remove his engagement ring and chuck it after her. Only far down the stairs did he slip it pensively off his finger, hiding it in his breast pocket as so many times before. The following morning, on their "wedding day", he shows it to Idun, hints something to the effect that it is a family treasure and suggests she go to a goldsmith and order a ring with the same inscription. Then they would be an engaged couple, he explains to her, and nothing on this earth could part them.

And with that he has moved in with her, full of enthusiasm and the charm of novelty, but without putting as much as a krone into the kitty. Idun receives him with open arms, unconditionally, like a lily in the field. She has never been in the habit of worrying about the day tomorrow and shares her bed and board with him as a matter of course. But after a few weeks have gone by she begins again to take night shifts at various hospitals, not full-time as before, but as many times a week as necessary to put something in the pot.

But right now they are both sitting in Boom Inn smoking hash, after they have taken their turns in the evening's performance. He's already quite high, and at regular intervals he leans toward her and whispers extravagant sweet nothings into her ear. She herself smokes in moderation and mostly for the sake of appearances, and is regarded by everyone as a slightly absurd novice who has still far to go before she sees the light. They wave encouragingly at her through the clouds of smoke, showing by signs and gestures how to get through purgatory and into ultimate bliss. When the pressure becomes too strong, she raises the pipe to her lips and takes a drag, but the high doesn't tempt her and she does what she can to evade it.

But she's far from being a novice; on the contrary, she harbours in all secrecy an experience that makes her into someone who is more than usually initiated. Slightly more than a year ago she took part in a seance that she won't very soon forget and that makes her trips in the Boom Inn seem like child's play. She went around looking for her lost self several days afterwards, and when she finally managed to overtake herself she experienced such a sense of estrangement that she vowed to stay away from drugs for ever.

One evening when she had a night watch at the Bispebjerg Hospital, an intern took her aside and asked if she would be interested in being part of a psychophysical experiment. He, another medical student and a clinical psychologist had agreed to meet one evening and investigate what influence the vegetable poison hashish had on human consciousness. One of them would simply register the effect and take notes, while the three others took a precisely measured amount of hash in tablet form.

When they came to her, it was because they thought it might be interesting to see whether the female psyche reacted differently than the male in any way, and of what significance body weight was for the expansion of consciousness. But an experiment like this one was not generally recognized by medical science, he explained, so it was absolutely necessary that they could rely on her discretion. They had chosen her and no one else among all the nurses in the medical section because she was a foreigner and not bound by the Danish hospital ordinances. They had also noticed that she kept to herself and had no personal relationships with the other sisters. Therefore it would be easier for her not to let on, rendering the experiment safe from one's friends' chatter and slips of the tongue.

She hadn't thought it over for long but agreed at once, saying she was willing to participate. But in the following days she got cold feet, and as the time of the experiment drew near she became more and more anxious and uneasy. At the same time her curiosity increased, and she caught herself wishing she was the one who would observe and take notes, while the three others swallowed the pills and gave intoxication free rein. The upshot was that she steered a middle course, deciding to play a double role. While sticking by the agreement, she would wait and see, putting aside a portion of the pills that were to be taken. That way she could delay the high and postpone taking the remainder of the dose until she'd seen what was happening with the other two.

The four conspirators got down to business and met in the bachelor's apartment of one of them at the appointed time. The two male subjects on an empty stomach, as agreed – it would speed up the high and intensify its effect. Idun's stomach, on the other hand, played apostate; in the teeth of all regulations she had eaten constantly all day and taken in a particularly nutritious meal just before leaving home. And since her betrayal was already in full swing, it didn't cost her many scruples to let half of the eight tablets slip into her pocket, before she put her head back and swallowed the remaining four.

From the very beginning the atmosphere in the room was uncertain, all four being full of expectation but also rather anxious about what the night would bring. It was still only shortly past seven-thirty, and they figured that several hours would go by before the high was at its most intense and the subjects reached their final phase. To calm down and pass the time of waiting, they took to playing bridge, first in real earnest and with well-considered bids, later more and more carelessly as two of the players began showing signs of their thoughts running wild. For a while everything took its course, with rash leads and spasmodic fits of laughter; then the bids became more and more senseless, until the game dissolved and the subjects threw down their cards to the accompaniment of loud bursts of laughter. All along the observer had his writing pad beside him on the table and was diligently taking notes, while Idun found herself in a strange limbo between dwindling presence and incipient absence. Now something would go to her head and force her to burst into an idiotic laugh, now she would be overcome by uneasiness and fright, now she would sharpen her attention and glance to both sides to see how far gone the other two were in their intoxication.

At a certain point the subjects were given a book and were to read aloud from it in turn. At first there was nothing particularly remarkable about their reading ability, apart from the fits of laughter that also in this case turned up at the most inappropriate places. But gradually the reader began to stutter and stammer, invented completely new words, gathered them into long strings, shifted them around, distorted them and fumbled for them, until he sat as if in a trance, staring uncomprehendingly at the text. At last they both gave up, one excusing himself by saying he'd never learned how to read, the other getting angry and insisting that it wasn't his job to decipher secret cryptograms.

The next thing that happened was that they could no longer speak clearly and were unable to hold on to a thought. They would get stuck in the middle of a sentence, having forgotten what they wanted to say, or went on in a fashion that betrayed completely derailed associations. It was now a quarter past eleven, there was no more laughter, and an eerie gloom fell upon the room. Idun was still sufficiently alert to be able to help with taking the pulse of the two subjects, who now gave the impression of being completely frantic. Oddly enough it was altogether normal, but they both had violent palpitations, their eyes were bloodshot, and they were constantly trying to vomit without being able to.

Suddenly, as if by a common impulse, they jumped up from their chairs and began to tramp around the floor in a sort of clumsy dance, as if they were hearing a faraway music and were compelled to dance to it with heavy leaden weights on their feet. Laughing even more idiotically than before, they occasionally let out deep groans, peered anxiously about them and screened their eyes as if to protect them from a too strong, blinding light. For a moment, one of them stood listening into vacancy with his hand behind his ear, while the other made the most horrible faces, pointing to something in the ceiling that seemed to give him a fright. Then they collapsed on the floor at an interval of a few minutes and fell into a deep sleep.

Idun got to her feet and found some rugs to cover them with, but noticed that she was wobbly and had difficulty keeping upright. The experimenter was as unperturbed as ever, taking notes and sending her a glance now and then as if there was something he couldn't figure out. She felt she owed him an explanation and tried to tell him that she had taken only four tablets, but heard with half an ear that she said something altogether different.

"Doctor, I've only taken four cockroaches," she said, breaking into the same unspeakably idiotic laughter that she was familiar with from the other two. And no sooner had it escaped her lips than it turned around, lost its harmless tone and prolonged itself in a piercing scream.

For now the nightmare was upon her. It came crawling out of every corner and crevice in the form of ants, beetles, cockroaches and spiders, which grew on the way and turned into strange reptiles, which again changed before her terror-stricken eyes and became hybrid superhuman creatures, half animal, half human, like the old Egyptian gods. She let out a scream, but felt at the same time that it was someone else who screamed. She laughed her little affected laugh, but it wasn't her own laughter, it was full of alien malice and came pouring out of the demi-gods' wide-open mouths. Something monstrous was digging its teeth into her, and she was chewed and crushed between a pair of huge jaws, as on that terrible picture above the piano at home in the parsonage, where Saturn devours his own child.

She made a last effort to get back to herself, but wasn't able to; it was as if she'd been struck by lightning and split into two people who were incompatible. One of them sat as though dazzled, screening her eyes with her hand, while the other was luminously clear, a witness to her own disintegration. If only I had pencil and paper, she thought, I could write it all down with the greatest accuracy. But in her innermost self emptiness was spreading, and she barely had time to think a thought before it was gone, leaving her with a mysterious dread.

"There, there, there, easy, easy," she heard someone saying, as though from far away and in a language she only half understood. Just then she seemed to be caught by a gust of wind and carried into an endless gyration; it was as though she were flying through the ages and was flung around the world several times. When she opened her eyes she was no longer in an apartment in the inner city of Copenhagen, she was not twenty-nine years old and a night nurse at Bispebjerg Hospital. She was almost exactly twice as old and sat curled up against the wall of a house in Amsterdam, robbed, half-naked, without memory, her whole body shaking after an overdose of Ecstasy.

"There, there, there, easy, easy," the voice repeated, but this time it was not the outlandish voice of a Dutch social worker, but the distinct and familiar voice of a young Danish doctor who had carried out a rather dubious psychophysical experiment.

Fourth Picture: Beyond All Reason

Idun and Hamlet climb onto the Vespa, a. k. a. "The Rolling Seven-League Boot", and head south to enjoy their first and last holiday together. Although neither is in the flush of youth any longer, they have agreed to live from hand to mouth, to stay in shabby hotels and earn their keep as best they can.

For as long as they stick to the motorway, they continue to eat into their provisions and savings; they will only feel in their element when they have crossed the Alps and the plain spreads out before them. The crash helmet hasn't yet been invented, or it is discarded in favour of luck and chance. In different ways, they are fearless travellers, who do not mind taking Death along as a stowaway. Speed and the risk of bodily injury are simply extra challenges, an adjuration to the forces of fate to let life live, or to strike, if that's the way it has to be.

Idun's long, golden tresses trail like a luminous comet's tail behind them and provoke no end of catcalls when they drive through urban areas. She steals more than her fair share of the attention, and Hamlet passes a hand over his closely cropped head, beseeching the gods of fashion for a more eye-catching male coiffure. He forgets that they have already heard his prayer and are trying out a new hairstyle on four young men in faraway Liverpool. But, oh dear, his days and the hairs on his head are already numbered. When the time will have come for longish hair, he will be beyond all whims of fashion, earth will hide his delicately shaped cranium, and no one will see how his hair follows the latest fashion as it grows out.

Hamlet was born jealous and never tires of comparing himself to anyone who comes his way. Mostly the comparison turns out well, for he's a handsome, supple young man who knows how to appear to his best advantage. The world is his hall of mirrors, which glorifies him from all angles and reflects his physical splendour in countless duplicates. He cannot pass a shop window without turning his face to make certain that no mortal has a more perfect figure. He moves across the asphalt like a ballet dancer, with a light, springy gait whose flawless glides and leaps make him seem at times to float above the ground.

When he saw Idun for the first time, in the wardrobe at The Royal Theatre, it was easy to outshine her. She looked rather lost, bringing out his protective side and appealing to his better nature to take pity on her. But since then things have happened that couldn't be foreseen, she has risen in the world and is almost outshining him. Just before they left for the holidays she was informed by a venerable publishing house in Oslo that her collection of poems had been accepted and would appear in the autumn. Hamlet raises his eyebrows and cannot believe his ears. Idun a poet? Who would've believed it? Someone who used to walk around looking like her own shadow and maintained a precarious balance on the edge of nothingness! An entire poetry collection overnight, that was too much for anyone to swallow. The only explanation must be that Norway was an intellectually retarded, backward country, where anybody could get their doggerel published.

"Come to Norway!" he says cuttingly, pointing a teasing index finger in her face. "Ha-ha! Come to Norway and you'll see what real poetry is like, yes sirree! So, what the hell!" he mutters, a bright idea having occurred to him. What if they both moved to Oslo in the autumn and settled in that hip-hip-hurrah country where it was so easy to make one's fortune? In a couple of years he would no doubt be one of the leading men in the National Theatre, and Hjalmar Ekdal, Doctor Stockmann, Oswald and Solness the masterbuilder would all fall flat without him. "Haw-haw, come to Norway and you'll see some real acting, sure thing. If only they recognized their ignorance up there and came to old Denmark for their dramatic talent!"

Idun does not defend herself, simply smiles in embarrassment as she sits on the other side of the table in the roadside inn. She realizes an argument is brewing. But she senses a vulnerability behind his apparent self-assurance, some ancient, incurable hurt that has nothing to do with her. And so she holds back, smiles uncertainly, not wanting to be the one to rip the plaster from the wound.

Hamlet leans across the table and angrily examines her thirty-one-year-old young girl's face, where age hasn't yet left any visible traces. How does she manage to keep it so round and smooth, while anyone else would have already begun fighting the wrinkles? He's two years younger than her, but because he burns his candle at both ends he looks ten years older. His face, with its noble lines and deep-set eyes, seems to have been made for playing the juvenile lead, but as soon as he moves a muscle it betrays its fragility. The thin skin is stretched taut over the high cheekbones, and when he makes a face his features become hollowed, giving him an air of near-senility. She becomes all tenderness and would like to press this haggard boy's face against her breast and pat and stroke it into a deep self-confidence.

But their love games are rarely about tenderness. He is overwhelmed by brutality and turns into someone else as soon as desire awakens in him. Before he can do anything with her, he always must resort to violence, to punching and pushing her, chasing her across the room, pulling her by the hair and throwing her roughly on the mattress. While in the process of subduing her, he calls her a snake, a vampire, seizes her by the throat, bites her breasts, spits in her face, and growls like a rabid dog as he forces his way inside her like a victor in a vanquished and plundered city. If he's ever denied this foreplay, he lies on top of her like a dead weight, sweating and groaning, incapable of getting a hard-on.

Only when it's all over does the lover seem to awaken in him, released from his curse. He bursts into tears, clings to her, kisses and caresses, and extols her divine body, wrapping it in the most tender words of love. And while hiding in her tresses he promises to mend his ways – by God and all His angels, things will be different! The rapist will go to confession first thing in the morning, and afterwards he will turn over a new leaf and become her lover, before the face of the Lord.

While attending the drama academy in London he changed his faith and converted to the Anglican Church, he tells her. He is almost a Catholic and intends to go regularly to confession when they have arrived in the Eternal City. And it would give him great pleasure if she decided to accompany him on his tour of the churches, and also go to confession herself as often as possible. Who cares if she is a Protestant, he'll explain to her what confession is all about so that she won't betray herself. No father confessor has yet discovered that he's only a quarter Catholic, who gets by because of his knowledge of Latin and the sacred jargon. He has always loved ritual, the more the better, and God becomes far, far bigger and more glorious when invoked in Latin.

But Idun refuses to go to confession. At most she is willing to wait for him outside the church while he kneels in there, wallowing in his false contrition. However, she is not certain that he is a complete fake; there is a duality in his nature beyond her understanding that may well contain a profound piety.

When he comes out again he is transfigured, and the morning goes by without discord. They walk the streets hand in hand, embrace and kiss, beaming with love and making sure that no passerby misses their romance. Conquering her shyness, Idun lets it all happen, she knows how much it means to him to display his feelings. They buy a bottle of wine and a bag of cornetti, and shortly they're having breakfast on Palatine Hill, or they climb the Capitoline and share their bread with the hungry cats.

Then they lie stretched-out on the grass, drinking Chianti from the same bottle while letting one another in on the painful childhoods they each suffered. Idun tells about her beloved and feared father, about his singing and chanting, his kindness and his attacks of rage, about the sentence for treason and the five years' confinement in a prison she has only seen from the outside. He responds with brief, enigmatic hints about his own father, a Supreme Court attorney who defended the small and the weak in court and then went home to his villa in Gentofte to proceed against a cowed wife and a little frightened son. Sitting head to head, they fall into a common destiny that makes the stories of their lives merge into one and the same story of shame and humiliation, estrangement and dissimulation, and an uncontrollable urge to step forward and throw off the yoke.

But the idyll never lasts very long. On Corso Vittorio Emanuele he suddenly grabs her, holds her out over the railing of the bridge and threatens to throw her into the Tiber. Or the sight of the old arena in the Colosseum awakens the beast in him and makes him come at her. "On your knees!" he orders. "Abjure your faith and worship the true god, or you're finished! Grrr, the god craves human flesh! Just you wait, I'll sink my teeth in you, drink your sweet blood, skin you and swallow you whole!"

Occasionally he treats her so roughly that the natives flock round them, and a chivalrous Latin steps in to defend her. But it always ends the same way: the Beast laughs and presses the Beauty to his breast, the deliverer has misunderstood the situation and abjectly withdraws.

After the siesta, as soon as the streets begin to fill with people again, they place themselves in some market or at a street corner to earn a few thousand lire for their daily bread. Unfortunately, the star turn with the skull proves a fiasco. The spectators do not like such a frivolous treatment of death, they do not understand English, have no idea who Shakespeare is and feel they're being hoodwinked. The death's-head grins at them with long, yellow teeth and becomes a *memento mori*, sending a shudder of mortality through them. The few who applaud let it be clearly known that they assume the scene is a macabre jest. Hamlet drops his hand and mumbles the final "the rest is silence", realizing that if he and Idun don't want to go to bed hungry, he'll have to change the programme.

Having a fairly good tenor voice, he tries to mollify the public with dear, familiar operatic arias, songs that every Italian loves and knows by heart. But he has no success with that, either. The local opera singers won't allow their bewitching *Carmen* and celestial *Aida* to be profaned by a Scandinavian, and certainly not in a voice that breaks in the higher notes and shifts teasingly over to falsetto. They snort and jeer, causing the singer to lose courage and give up in the middle of one of the great scenes.

It goes somewhat better when he takes to whistling fragments from Corelli. He has a pure, tremulous tone, and though he is not able to bring off a *concerto grosso*, he does very well and obliges with little miracles of imitative art. The listeners applaud and play along with him, and when he has finished and counts his earnings, there are not just small coins in the hat but also some big notes.

But, by and large, the profit is too meagre to feed two hungry tourists. Fortunately Idun has shown some foresight and holds in readiness a number that never fails. She dresses up in a nurse's uniform, puts on her most gracious Samaritan smile and offers to take the blood pressure of the passers-by. "One thousand lire per patient", it says on a sign she has put up on the sidewalk. It's a hot day and the crush of people is staggering – so many per-spiring, overweight gentlemen push forward that they have to queue up and wait their turn. The thousand-lire notes drop like dead leaves into the hat, and Idun lifts her finger and admonishes her patients to tighten their belts.

Hamlet withdraws a few steps; from the corner of his eye he looks jealously at the lucrative business, which reduces his whistling to sheer birds' twitter. He endures it in silence, but cannot hide his malicious pleasure when one day a police officer turns up, not to have his blood pressure taken, but to ask whether the nurse has a license. "*Licènza! Licènza!*" the officer shouts, waving his arms, and when Idun is unable to produce a permit he gives her a warning and tells her to get lost before being fined for disturbance of the peace.

When evening comes and darkness falls, Hamlet gets even: he gets onto his Vespa and drives out on his own private adventures in the night. Idun looks questioningly at him, eager to come along, but he brushes her off and starts the engine.

"Go up to your room and write poetry," he says with a laugh. "Spit out a little more great poetry, then maybe you can publish two collections come autumn."

He stays away for several hours, sometimes until dawn, and she lies tossing in bed at the pension, thinking of all the misadventures he may run into. If he falls into bad company, he thinks up all sorts of crazy tricks, as she knows from his capers at home, in Denmark. He may already be dead drunk and try to balance himself on some roof, or running around a cemetery dancing his necrophiliac dances. She saw him once in the Assistens

Cemetery in Copenhagen, poised above the family plot while invoking the spirit of his powerful father. She recalls all those times he has called her up in the middle of the night, asking her to come to this or that restaurant and help him out of a quandary. When the bill was paid, she would walk him through the streets, supporting him to keep him upright, just like that time long ago when her father had suffered a stroke and been released from prison. She can still feel the heavy man's arm resting on her shoulder, and in some strange way it's one and the same arm that weighs her down to earth. Both her father's paralyzed arm and the arm of a dead-drunk young man who cannot keep on his feet by himself.

Time after time she jumps out of bed half asleep, thinking she hears the familiar hum of the Vespa. But what's that? Amid all the misadventures she has dreamed of, she has never had sufficient imagination to envisage this! The scooter radiates an almost spectral light as it stands against the grey wall, and nearby, under the street lamp, two human figures stand locked in an embrace. He's found himself a new sweetheart! it flashes through her mind, sharp and painful like the thrust of a dagger. She quickly withdraws, and when she again dares go up to the window they are saying goodbye. But – what in the world? Can it be possible? The couple down there kissing each other for the last time are – two young men! They are standing close together in the yellow light from the street lamp and have difficulty tearing themselves away from one another. Good God! He's found himself a male lover! He's . . .

She jumps back into bed and pulls the blanket on top of her, and when he comes up at long last she pretends to be asleep. Early next morning while he's still soundly asleep she collects her things, packs her rucksack and prepares to depart. Before leaving, she bends down one more time, the last, over his peaceful boyish face, on which sleep confers an expression of touching innocence. She knows that this grown-up child needs her, that he loves her in his own divided way and will desperately start looking for her when he awakes in the late morning. But he won't be able to find her, she will have yielded her place and is out of his life for ever.

Fifth Picture: On the Road

Idun hurries along the highways like a fleet-footed messenger, unable to spare a single moment if her message is to arrive in time. Her long, slim legs move like drumsticks against the hard road, as if beating the time to an inaudible music. Her back is hidden by a big rucksack, her arms lunge out, flying through the air like wings. One eye squints at the roadway, and her thumb waits in readiness to make the sign. Everything about her light, rhythmic footsteps summons adventure, and her blond, flowing hair is the very bait that will make motorists and truckers stop and pick her up.

The year is rather uncertain. It could be August 1968, shortly after she fled her friend Hamlet. But long wanderings are always her refuge when crack-up threatens, so the year could just as well be 1972, 1975, 1980, 1988, 1994. If it is 1994, her back is not quite as straight as before, her long legs are a touch stiffer, and her blond, fluttering hair slightly streaked with grey. But in passing she still looks like a young girl, and the drivers hit their brakes and wave to her to jump in and get a lift.

In 1994, to be sure, some of the men are taken aback when they see her face close up. But most of them don't let on, and only very rarely does someone slam the car door in her face.

With her many years of exile behind her, she can make herself understood by means of a modest vocabulary in German, English, French and Italian. She gets along best with the truckers – they chatter at their ease, apropos of nothing, gesture with the hand that isn't on the steering wheel, share their packed lunch with her, offer her a cigarette, and tower beside her like a reassuring counterweight to her emptiness.

Only once do things go wrong. It's the summer of 1975; she has turned thirty-eight, but despite the hardships she has suffered on the highways she looks twenty-eight. A motorist of indeterminate age with a hard face clears the seat and makes space for her. He lacks the natural hospitality of the others and has shifty eyes, it looks as though he is up to something. She's on the point of changing her mind, but her feet are aching and he pats the seat impatiently and asks her to be quick. During the ride he touches her repeatedly, and soon he puts his hand on her thigh and doesn't remove it when she asks him to. She gets frightened and wants to be let off, but he pretends not to hear and turns onto a side road at the next intersection. They drive into a forest, and on a deserted stretch he stops the vehicle, throws himself over her and locks her arms against the back of the seat. Mumbling unintelligible words and panting like an overworked cart horse, he tears her clothes to bits and penetrates her. A few minutes later he has taken what he was after and pushes her out the door. She stands as though paralyzed by the roadside, seeing him turn the truck, wave through the window and rev the engine, while shouting something to her that's supposed to mean: "Ha-ha, you roving whore! This time you had to turn a trick for free!"

A few weeks later she's settled in Rome, where she has found shelter in a basement on condition that she sweep the courtyard and run errands for the landlord. In the autumn she feels unwell, vomits in the morning and doesn't know what to think. Finally she goes to a physician for the poor, who gives her certainty and promises to interrupt her pregnancy without compensation. They agree on a time, but as the day approaches she becomes more and more uncertain and uneasy. She has always wanted a child, since that time more than twenty years ago when they took her newborn child away from her. But not a child like this! comes a protest from inside her, not the child of a coarse and revolting rapist. Why not? says another inner voice, a child is a child, and it's always innocent. Life isn't easy to understand, and who knows whether something good and beautiful might not come of an ugly act of violence.

When the day arrives she has made up her mind: she goes to the doctor and thanks him for his offer, but says that she wants to go through with the pregnancy. When her time draws near, she will go back to Norway and have the child there, accepting it as a gift from the unknown. She's an author, she explains to him, she has already published a poetry collection and three novels, so she knows what it means to let herself in for uncertainty. With a bit of luck she'll manage to keep the wolf from the door, so she can provide for herself and the child.

Four months go by and she's already getting ready to leave, when she overstrains herself by lifting a trash can and feels a sharp pain shoot through her body. She walks hunched up the whole day, holding her hands protectively against her abdomen, but the pain does not stop and she wakes up at night to find her bed full of blood. Providence, fate, chance has chosen for her, and as always she resigns herself and takes it as a sign. Necessity belongs to her; where that is concerned she herself makes the decision. But chance is an alien power that acts blindly and doesn't ask anyone's permission.

She manages to keep body and soul together in Rome through the winter and to meet her alter ego, the Papessa, before cracking up and being sent home at the expense of the consulate. She sees the prison-like asylum for the first time and lets herself be taken there, empty-handed, disturbed and without any clear identity.

Sixth Picture: Ideological Sweat, Exhaustion and Fall-Back on Woman's Oldest Profession

In 1972 Idun and her Danish friend Susanne roamed about the Rhône Valley all summer, keeping alive by digging root crops, harvesting grapes and working in the silk mills.

Susanne has a Master's Degree in literature, but as an orthodox Maoist she holds the view that every academic should familiarize herself with how the proletariat gains its daily bread. It is simply her duty as a human being, she says, to renounce inherited privilege and experience the struggle for existence at the very bottom of society.

They gather their experiences in sombre machine rooms and under a scorching sun, gasping with exhaustion as they walk side by side, while Susanne, the Dane, gives Idun, the Norwegian, increasingly angry lectures on the injustices of class society.

"Dear sister, being an author and all, you must surely understand that you'll never write an honest novel as long as your body hasn't experienced what exploitation is."

Idun nods and doesn't object. She too finds herself somewhere on solidarity's left, but hers is a somewhat more indeterminate position, which is close to a sort of anarchism. Susanne groans and lectures, and Idun groans and says amen to everything – sure, she completely agrees, of course she does.

But her sweat is due to more obscure reasons than that of her Danish friend, and she hardly knows what to think about this self-torture anymore. After all, she and Susanne are only sort of visiting proletarians who can quit any time, while the rest of the work crew are condemned to remain where they are for life. The only thing she learns by this gruelling toil is how it drains the organism of its strength, until her brain is empty and unable to think a clear thought. No wonder their fellow workers shrug their shoulders when someone tries to explain to them that they are oppressed. They don't give a hang about edifying talk, that's quite obvious. When the day is over they want to relax and enjoy themselves with fun and games and dancing, before the slave drivers summon them at the dawn of another day. What concern is it of theirs that two strapping nymphs from the extreme north pat them on the shoulder, wanting them to believe that they are in the same boat?

In this way, one week goes by after another with thesis and antithesis, without the discussion resulting in that famous higher entity. Susanne and Idun become more and more exhausted, and in the end they no longer have the strength for any ideological debate. All interpretations have become superfluous, they have turned into two living examples of the deadening effect of exploitation. They stand in the machine room spooling silk thread, empty-headed like two automatons, or stretch dizzily up along the grapevine to pick a cluster of grapes and drop it into the basket. Their backs ache from their bent-over grind in the sugar beet field, their faces glisten with perspiration, and their chapped hands are a mockery of all bookish occupations.

Late one September day, with a low sun on the roofs of the buildings, they arrive in Paris, where they intend to stay through the winter. They are trudging through one of the suburbs when, all of a sudden, Susanne stops short and claps her hand to her forehead.

"What the hell!" she shouts out of the blue, shaking her fist at the sunset. "Idun, wait a moment till I simmer down and I'll whisper something in your ear. You know something, darling? Enough is enough! We won't prostrate ourselves before a factory owner and beg him to give us a chance, not on your life! Instead, we'll lie down in a different way and fall back on woman's age-old profession."

It takes some time to persuade Idun – as usual, the M.A. is the more quick-witted of the two, while the writer needs time to weigh the pros and cons.

"Why, look here," Susanne snorts, in her eagerness to move things along, "what could be wrong in selling your own body? We live in a society where every conceivable piece of junk and trash is offered to the highest bidder. And you and I have two splendid bodies, a real feast for the eye; they are our very own, we haven't stolen them from anyone, which cannot be said for many other goods in this damn, rotten capitalistic society! Come, my friend, we'll brush and adorn ourselves from top to bottom and go to the Bois de Boulogne, then you'll see we'll screw up the value of our natural goods and get a fair price."

They rest in a cheap hotel to gather strength for the following night, examine carefully the rags they've brought and agree to invest in a spanking new hunting outfit. Dressed in mini-skirt and fish-nets above tall stiletto heels, they step onto the boulevard like two outsize temptresses. Idun's blond and Susanne's flaming-red hair flutter in the breeze, their slender bodies snake their way through the throng until they find themselves in the right hunting terrain. Here their movements become more sluggish and sauntering, while they're continually on the watch, keeping an eye on the big limousines that roll by, slowing their speed.

Shortly Susanne is picked up, but Idun, who is constantly on the point of changing her mind, turns down one offer after another. She has nearly given up and stands looking about her in bewilderment, when she catches sight of a large black car that has stopped nearby. A window is rolled down, and a middle-aged gentleman with a refined face and mild grey eyes accosts her. His language is so polite and his figure so unintimidating that the situation feels almost normal, and when he opens the door for her she plucks up courage and quickly climbs in.

As they head for Neuilly they sit side by side without a word being said. He clears his throat and fidgets, until he finally happens to remember something and asks, almost timidly, what her price is. Fortunately she has discussed the matter with Susanne in advance, and after a good deal of disagreement they arrived at two thousand francs. Idun had been of the opinion that it was far too much, but with her usual authority Susanne declared that it was an absurdly small amount.

"Two thousand francs for a whole female body, do you really think that's overcharging? And an adventure to boot, an encounter with a dream, seduction incarnate! Come to think, it's settling for a bargain price, that's what it is. But since the world is a mean and shameless place, we'll take what we can get."

The car stops before a large, yellow apartment house in a quiet street, and she understands that they've arrived. He takes her by the hand and leads her up the stairs and into an apartment that appears to be surprisingly small and modest by comparison with the large car.

"*Non, non, non,*" he doesn't live here, he explains in a stammer, this is just his studio, where he occasionally retires when he has to do important business.

Looking about her, Idun feels that the room is strangely shut up; the door is padded, the walls thick and covered with bookcases from floor to ceiling. This thing with the bookcases sets her at ease; she examines them closely, telling herself that a man with so many books couldn't possibly do her any harm.

He places the agreed-upon sum of money on the table, pours out two glasses of wine, and greets her in an almost solemn manner. But there's something in the air that makes her uneasy, as though this harmless ritual were the last orderly, normal move, before the scene changes and hands her over to enormity. The situation seems precarious, and the slight gentleman seems far too polite and yielding, as if his evil genius were lurking in the wings and might pop out of the padded walls at any moment.

Suddenly he opens the door to the next room, making a sign that she should follow him. They hesitate for a moment on the threshold to the pitch-dark room, which has a sunken ceiling and where the only window is blacked out. Then he turns on the light, and she stands spellbound staring at the odd fixtures, which make the room look like a torture-chamber more than anything else.

In the middle of the floor stands an oblong crate, reminiscent of the vaulting horse she never managed to jump in her gym classes. But those chains that hang down along the sides turn it into something altogether different, something outlandish and uncanny. Chains and handcuffs are also fastened to the wall-bars, and riding whips of all sizes and shapes are stuck between the crossbars. In the corner stands a life-size female figure, dressed in a military cap and a tightly buttoned uniform jacket, which forms an odd contrast with her bare thighs, her garter and the tall, polished boots.

Oh dear, it flashes through her, he's a sadist! He gets his pleasure from locking up strange women and keeping them prisoner until he has flogged them till the blood flows. She steps back, letting out a muffled scream, but he places a soothing hand on her arm and explains to her that she has nothing to fear. The one who must be chastised and punished in this room is none other than himself, he says in a voice that is so gentle that it's almost like a whisper.

When she gives him an uncomprehending look, he assures her that he is an evil and depraved person who deserves to be punished. He once saved his own life at the expense of seven other people, he says, and they were people who were close to him and whom he loved above everything in the world. He ransomed himself by sacrificing them, saw them being taken away without a moment's thought of joining them and being with them in their last hour.

"But now the hour of retribution has come," he says in a strangely flat voice. What he requires of her is that she put on the outfit she sees on that figure over there. While he himself strips and becomes penitent, she will put on the military cap and the uniform jacket, the garter and the military boots, and chain him to the place of execution in the middle of the room. Then she shall choose a whip and give him a good beating, not minding whether he whimpers and asks for mercy, and continue until he's got what he deserves and is completely done for. Only when he no longer lets out a sound has the punishment been meted out in full measure, and she can put the whip away and undo his chains. As she will see when he has undressed, it's not the first time he has imposed this punishment on himself; his body is covered with old scars and fresh marks from a retribution that will continue for the rest of his life.

"I can't do that," she answers when he has finished his instructions. "You'll have to excuse me, monsieur, but I'm against violence. Since I became an adult I've never hit another human being, and I never will."

"Ah, you haven't?" he says, with a hateful gleam in his eye. "We'll see about that, *nous verrons, ma chère dame*! I'll keep you locked up here till you do as I command, even if you'll have to stay here till you rot!"

"You may do with me what you want," she says in a firm voice. "I have no idea what may have happened to you, that you want to punish yourself in such a terrible way. But I tell you once more, I'll never do as you command."

Wincing at her words, he rushes frantically over to the wall-bars and takes down the biggest whip, which has a scourge set with sharp bits of metal.

"You or I?" he screams, stamping his feet. "If you refuse to use it, I will."

"Do as you please," she replies, feeling an almost peaceful indifference descend upon her. "I don't know you, but I understand that you must have had some ghastly experiences. But please, spare yourself and don't let the evil continue."

After looking about him in perplexity for a moment, he lowers the whip and lets it fall on the floor. His eyes change their expression, again taking on the gentle look they had when he asked her to get into the car.

"Come," he says, leading her back to the room with all the books where they were before. When she gets up to say goodbye much later, the whole night has gone by, and he has quietly and with long pauses initiated her into the story of his life.

In 1942, when he was only twelve years old, the occupying power struck at his home town, Clermont, and his entire Jewish family was sent to the Buchenwald camp in Germany. His grandfather, grandmother, parents and three small siblings, the people he held most dear in this world. They remained there just a few months, suffering privation in many ways; still, that was as nothing compared to what awaited them when they were moved on to another camp, one of the so-called *Vernichtungslager*. First the two old people were taken to the gas chamber, then the father, who was sickly and suffering from diabetes. Soon the mother was showing signs of poor health, and he began to understand what was going to happen to all of them.

"But I was stubborn and refused to succumb," the strange gentleman went on. "I was firmly resolved to survive, whatever the cost. I hadn't yet turned fourteen, but I went to it with a courage born of desperation and did a grown man's work when I was sent out for labour service. One evening when I returned to camp, my mother and my little sister were gone, and I went aside and swore to God that I would save my two younger brothers. If I didn't, all would be lost, and I didn't deserve to stay alive.

"It was then that I changed and became a yes-man, a timeserver; until then I had been an unruly little fellow, full of contempt for our guards and hangmen. I began to make up to them, was always on the lookout for praise, and did every conceivable favour for them without being asked. This made me disliked by my own people, but my popularity with the master race increased, and I became a sort of prize Jew, an example, showing that not all members of my despised race were equally inferior. When I would meet the Commandant or some other superman once in a while, I even had the gall to click my heels and give the Nazi greeting. At first I justified myself by the thought that it was something I imposed on myself to save my brothers, who were already so pinched with hunger that they looked like two little skeletons. But it was not solely for their sake, of course, for I continued my betrayal after they were gone and I had no one but myself to worry about.

"Due to my fraternization I was not as starved as the other children, there was always someone in the kitchen and the dining room who would give me an extra ration on the sly. I grew up to become a handsome young fellow in fine condition, someone who never neglected to bow and scrape. My stay in the children's section was nearly over, the day I turned fifteen I would be transferred to one of the men's barracks. As the time drew near I noticed that our top female guard, the she-devil Ursula as we used to call her, was more and more often sending me long looks and summoning me for no particular reason. I was still enough of a child not to understand her purpose; it only dawned on me one evening in the late winter of 1945, when she sent for me and answered my knock on her door in an extremely surprising outfit.

"My dear guest," he said after a long silence during which he cradled his head in his hands. "You remember the female figure I've got in there, the one I wanted to force you to imitate? That was exactly how she looked, Ursula, the she-devil, when she opened the door to her adolescent Joseph and pulled him inside. She even had the whip in her hand, but she promised not to use it on him if he was *gehorsam* and obeyed her orders.

"At that moment the Russians were already near Berlin and, in the panicky mood that prevailed, the extermination picked up speed; most of the children in my barracks had already been sent to the gas chamber. My own panic was no less pronounced than that of the hangmen, and for several dizzying weeks I was the young lover of this terrible woman, who never forgot to remind me that I did my amorous service with death hanging over my head. She trained me in the crudest kind of horseplay, forcing me to sing the first stanzas of the Marseillaise while she held me tight, as in a vice, diverting herself with me. I did everything she demanded of me, and to my horror I noticed that I too experienced pleasure during these forced embraces. And in this way I managed to keep alive, while the camp was disintegrating more and more and getting emptied of prisoners. When the evening's nightmare was over, I fell on my knees before my bunk, knocked my head against the bedpost and vowed that, should I survive, I would do penance and punish myself for the rest of my life.

"I see you're interested in my books," he said much later, when the day was already breaking and the milkman had started rattling his bottles on the stairway outside. "You're probably surprised that someone like me has so many books. What can I possibly get out of them in a place like this? But believe me, it's not as strange as it may seem. As you can see, they're mainly old classics, books that deal with situations that are not very different from my own. They are stories about fidelity and betrayal, crime and punishment, emptiness, callousness, repentance and expiation.

"Look, right here on the table lies the book that I like to lose myself in more than in any other. I don't know whether you're familiar with the first thirty-three cantos of Dante's *Divine Comedy*, the descent into the abyss of hell where every human soul has its special circle of damnation. You are?

271

Then you no doubt remember the icy region at the bottom of the inferno, the ninth circle, where the traitors, the betrayers and the cannibals are found. Do you remember Count Ugolino and his sons in the hunger dungeon, where they had been incarcerated by Ruggiero, the treacherous archbishop? The Count was no ogre on the first day of his captivity, he loved his sons with all his heart and could only think of how to liberate them. But time went by, his hope dwindling while hunger gnawed at him. On the fourth day, without food and water, his son Gadda throws himself at his feet and cries, 'Father, why don't you help me?' Soon after, all his sons have died from hunger. For a few days the Count gropes over their lifeless bodies – hunger has blinded him – calling their names as if in delirium. 'Then fasting had more power than grief' – the Count turned cannibal. He had crossed over into the realm of the monstrous.

"Goodbye, my unknown friend, and thanks for coming in time to rescue me from the hunger dungeon. No, wait, you're forgetting the two thousand francs I've put out for you. What, you don't want them? Oh please, do me the kindness to take them. Your friend is right in saying it's an absurdly small amount. True, you broke the agreement and refused to obey my orders, but you've done something else and much greater. You've released me from my nightmare and helped me make peace with myself."

Seventh Picture: The Last Circle

It's in mid-August 1994, fairly late in the evening, just before the street lamps are lit and face their reflections in the water.

Idun sits curled up by a wall in Amsterdam, more precisely the Old Town, near a canal that shuts her up in the last circle of aberration. The rain is pouring down from the sky, as it has done all day. She sits there half asleep, far more down-and-out than her papal friend by the Fortuna Virilis temple. The water trickles down her back, her hair hangs in wet wisps, and she doesn't have a plastic bag to put her feet into. Her money has been used up or stolen, including her last reserve capital hidden in a purse on her chest. The gold chain with the rubies is gone, everything is gone, her memory as well. The fairy tale has been told, the flight stopped, the footprints erased; a blind will has seized her and set her down beside a well of oblivion.

The last thing she can vaguely remember is her lodging in Berlin, which she left ten or twelve or fourteen days ago. She had entered a church to go to confession, possibly at the request of her departed friend Hamlet, only with a delay of twenty-five years. It didn't take the Father long to discover that she was a Protestant, but he listened sympathetically to her distress and gave her absolution when he had heard out her gibberish. When she was about to go, he detained her, saying that if she was homeless he could provide her with a roof over her head in one of the shelters run by the church. He understood from her confession that she was an educated person, he said, and would do whatever he could to stop her descent down the slippery slope. Even if she wasn't a Catholic, she was welcome to come to communion, he had begun to take an interest in her and would do his utmost to get her on her feet again.

But the good Father was no doubt more sympathetic in the closed room of the confessional than when listening to the reunited roar from the big city jungle. After the fall of the wall, other barriers had collapsed as well, and chaos was eating away at an increasingly fragile order. The nuns who managed the shelter were pious and gullible women who measured the world by their own standards. They assumed their good works would instil gratitude, and couldn't imagine that the occupants might bring their own tricks and vices into the house. True enough, men and women were lodged at opposite ends of the building, the bells rang for mass, the daily bread was blessed through prayer and the sign of the cross. But the dining room and the lounge were common territory, where depravity spread in secret. Dirty money was passed from hand to hand under the table, a dubious address was whispered into an ear, drugs were sold to the highest bidder, pimping and prostitution walked on padded paws over the newly scrubbed floors.

After a week's stay Idun's will was broken, and she was once more in thrall to intoxicating drugs. During the first two days she fought against it and pretended not to understand when someone showed her the card with the little yellow, smiling face, the so-called "Smiley," which she very well knew was an offer of drugs. But by the evening of the third day her emptiness had grown so huge that she took out a thousand-mark note and bought six tablets of the new elixir of happiness, Ecstasy. She had never tried it before, and the dealer explained to her that if she was a novice, she would only need one or two tablets to have a trip.

She went into the dormitory, lay down on the bed, swallowed two of the tablets and experienced the loveliest and most luminously clear night she had ever had. Her old recollections of hash and amphetamine paled to insignificance, a veritable eclipse of the sun by contrast with the powerful illumination she now partook of. Her eyes and ears were opened to their utmost, and the least perception emerged with a clarity and sharpness that made the universe seem transparent in every particular in an instant of time. A few days later she had to take out another thousand-mark note, the last one before she would be forced to tap her reserve capital. Going into town with her suppliers, she was introduced to a world so light and sparkling that she felt as though she were walking the gold-paved streets and soaring through the pearly gates she had sung about in vain as a child, when she followed her grandfather to revival meetings in the Ark.

When she searched through her things in the morning on the eighth day, she discovered that the gold chain with the rubies was gone. She remembered having worn it when she went out in the evening, but at a certain point she must have taken it off and exchanged it for a pack of yellow tablets. That last night had been filled with mental aberrations and unmentionable adventures, she hadn't managed to get back to the shelter before the gate closed and had to roam the streets until daybreak. As the small hours of the morning crept by, her ecstasy faded away and gloom stole upon her, making her suspect there was a different face on the reverse of the smiling yellow tablet.

The following day she was summoned to a conversation with the prioress, and, considering how things looked, it wasn't difficult to guess what awaited her. Instead of accepting the condemnation and being turned out, she packed her sparse possessions in a hurry and left, as so many times before. She had three hundred marks and ten yellow tablets in her possession when the train fare from Berlin to Hanover had been paid. In the train she was taken sick, with convulsions and anxiety attacks, which suddenly turned round and lifted her into a nirvana of felicity and peace of mind. As the day wore on, the transition from one state to another became more indefinable, and when she continued her journey on foot she had long since ceased to feel the difference between high and low. She forged ahead, her blond, greying hair looking like a halo round her head, made the sign with the thumb of her left hand, and climbed into strange vehicles without any idea where she was going.

The rest was a dark hole of oblivion, with a few brief gleams of light that now and then fell upon the fractured history of her life. She was swimming in the Aegean Sea, pursued by a young Adonis to whom she had promised a kiss if he was able to overtake her. Did he get the kiss or did he not? She didn't know, for in that moment darkness fell, and when she was struck by the next flash of recollection, she was in an altogether different place. She was a prisoner of the crazy monks in their monastery on Lago Maggiore, that false monastic order that was in reality a league of death, bringing drug addicts into the mountains with the intent of seducing them to a collective suicide. Was it something she had dreamed, was it the beginning of one of her unfinished novels, or could it really be that she had managed to outwit her gaolers and make a last-minute escape from their diabolic *Purgatorio*?

It was never to be cleared up, for the next moment, without any kind of logical connection, she found herself as a night watch in a private clinic in the Greek coastal town of Loutraki. It was the night before the big earthquake, which tore the roof off the building and peeled off one longitudinal wall, so that the sickbeds were suspended like trapezes along the open facade. She is busy bringing the patients to safety when one of them, who proves to be a famous ship owner, becomes interested in her. He has only dislocated his shoulder, and after recovering from the shock he hires her as his private nurse and carries her off to his coasting vessel, *Jocasta*, which sits waiting for him in Piraeus. The ship is packed with exclusive guests whom she is to tend and nurse for imagined ailments during a cruise in the eastern Mediterranean. Just before *Jocasta* is to put off, two unknown visitors come aboard, sent by the hand of fate to cast shadows on the sun deck and infect the frivolous passengers with a lethal virus.

Raising her head abruptly, she looks about her with wondering eyes. Dream or invention or vanished life, how to remember what was one thing or the other? Wasn't it a fact that she had once published a book about these events, a half unreal dream journey that began with the big earthquake and ended with shipwreck and the solution of ancient riddles? And wasn't there something to the effect that the book had been rediscovered and rescued from the pulping mill, just as miraculously as the fictional narrator had rescued injured patients from the collapsed hospital in Loutraki?

There is no time for reflection, for suddenly she plunges backward in time and space and doesn't know who she is until she opens her eyes in Ulleval Road, Oslo. She's a lanky little girl of thirteen taking a walk with her brain-damaged father, who has just been released from prison. Her father is paralyzed on one side and leans so heavily on her that she's nearly collapsing. Stopping from time to time, he uses his stick to poke at an old

275

comb or a rusty nail lying on the pavement. Then she has to hurry and pick it up, because her father was born in poverty, and his unfailing motto is: Pick up everything you find and keep it for one hundred years, some day there will be a use for it.

She quickly bends down to the pavement and picks up the precious objects, though she knows they will end up in the dustbin before the day is over. Her mother will make short work of them as soon as she gets home from the office, and her father will have long ago forgotten what was to be kept for a hundred years. After his latest stroke his memory is like a sieve, where all ideas and commands trickle through and get lost.

"Dad, there's something," she says tentatively after picking up a rusty hinge and putting it in her pocket, "there's something I would like to ask you about, but I'm not sure I dare to."

"Just speak up, don't be shy, your old dad is no longer a dangerous man. As you know, he cannot take ten steps without having someone to lean on."

"But you must promise me that you won't be angry, because that's no good for your head. I just want to ask, why do you beat us?"

"Hm, that's some question, all right. But I'll tell you. When I have time to think things over, I'm a peaceable man, who can tolerate practically anything. But there is a beast inside me that's hard to control. If I'm not careful it breaks free, and that's when I start raving and hit out in all directions. I don't know if you understand, but that's the way it is."

"Oh yes, I know," she says, looking down at her shoes. "I too have such a beast inside me. But I've promised myself that it won't ever be let out."

"What do I see, little Idun has learned by bitter experience. But look out that the beast won't jump at you and tear you apart inside."

"Sometimes I notice that it's getting ready to pounce. Then I'm thinking such nasty thoughts that I can't tell a soul about them."

"You can tell me, can't you, now that we're talking about it?"

"You mustn't get angry, because then a vein will burst in your head. Well, sometimes I wish you were dead, so I wouldn't have to go here every single day dragging you along. And then I become so scared that it might happen. Just because I've been so mean as to think it."

"Take it easy," he says with a little laugh. "Nobody dies because there's someone who wants to get rid of them."

"Yes, but I don't want to be rid of you, it's only the beast that wants that. You've no idea how scared I get when it comes over me. I have to run and hide, or flee far away to some place where no one can find me."

"There, there, my child," he says, stroking her hair with his healthy arm. "Your old dad will die when the time comes and not because his little daughter is tired of dragging him everywhere."

"Dad, there's also something else," she says, trying to straighten her back a little under that heavy arm of his. "I have, I have, I have – denied you."

The father stops and turns around with unexpected suddenness. "Denied me, what's that supposed to mean?"

"Well, they used to tease us so terribly in that school we went to. They must have found out about something, because almost every day they asked me how my dad was getting along in prison."

"And what did you answer?"

"I told them they were mistaken, that they must be talking about someone else. My dad was dead, I said, he died long before the war, and I didn't know anyone who was in prison."

"Don't take it so hard," the father says gently. "If you remember your Bible stories, you know that you are not the first one to deny a dear friend."

"You mean Peter, who said he didn't know Jesus? But Peter repented and went off and wept, I didn't. I only told them off every single time and said I didn't know who they were talking about."

"I see," he says remotely, poking at a hole in the asphalt with his stick. "It wasn't easy to be the children of Vemund Hov right after the war. There were so many mean things written in the papers, and it was mostly so distorted it was unrecognizable."

"I could've been courageous and defended you," she cries in a piercing voice. "But I didn't budge, I just said I didn't know you."

"There, there," he says, almost frightened. "Now it's the beast that has dug its claws into you."

"I tried once to get to the prison and tell you about it. But they wouldn't let me in because I didn't arrive with a grown-up."

She gropes for his dead arm and is about to adjust it on her shoulder when she discovers that he isn't there. She's seized by the wild anxiety of negligence, because it is her task to go for walks with her father and see to it that he gets home in good condition. She has to hurry home from school every day and help him get dressed, take the little pillow he usually sits on and accompany him down Sofie Street and along Johannes Brun Street to the Sten Park, where they rest before going the same way home again.

277

But suddenly she has lost him, and as she tries to keep a lookout for him the street scene spins around so that she has to support herself against a wall to keep on her legs. When earth and sky have settled down, she's no longer standing at Adamstuen in Oslo but on a small, triangular market place in a foreign city. Over on the other side there is a church, and she sees a clergyman in canonicals coming out of the door. There is something strangely familiar about the figure, and suddenly she realizes it is her father stepping solemnly across the square and disappearing into a side street.

She makes haste and runs after him, but the gowned figure also starts running, with long, springy steps, as if about to leave the ground any moment. She goes off in pursuit, and for a brief eternity the daughter chases her fleeing father, calling him in a thin, lamenting voice.

"Wait for me, Dad! Don't leave me! Take me with you wherever you're going!"

At length they come to a cemetery, a strangely mysterious place that seems at once familiar and strange. She loses sight of him for a moment when a funeral procession passes by, a miserably short procession that merely consists of a woman and three half-grown children. A single wreath rests on the coffin lid, so close to the edge that it may slip down any moment, and one of the children rushes forward, nudges it in place and, in tears, keeps running beside the coffin with her hand on the wreath.

When she catches sight of him again, the cassock is gone; he is running barefoot between the patches of snow, wearing the white shirt with red edgings that he lay in on his deathbed. In his hand he has a sheet of music, whipped and torn by the wind, and his big voice is singing an oratorium, loud enough to raise the dead. He moves forward in great theatrical leaps, just like Hamlet, her Danish friend, when he danced his sombre ballet on the family plot in Copenhagen. She tries to call him one last time, but to no avail. The figure hurries off, becoming more and more transparent, and to her horror she sees that he disappears under a tombstone at the furthest end of the cemetery.

She approaches apprehensively step by step, stands still before the grave with an old schoolbag in her hand and reads with a sense of surprise what is written on the stone. *Vemund Hov, one-time parish pastor*, it says, *born 1. 1. 1900; died 19. 4. 1951.* She stares at the inscription with a faraway look in her eyes and reads it to herself several times in a low voice, each time feeling that something is missing.

All of a sudden she knows what it is, opens her schoolbag, gropes around in it and takes out a brush and a small can of paint. Kneeling before the tombstone, she removes the cover of the can, dips the brush in the paint and writes, with neat large letters, *Emigravit* under the line giving the dates of birth and death.

When she's finished, she looks about her in fear; but the cemetery is deserted, not a soul to be seen anywhere. She gets up, brushes the dirt from her skirt, throws her paint paraphernalia in a rubbish bin and casts a last look at the inscription on the tombstone. For a moment she stands as if in a daze, looking helplessly in all directions. Then she lets out an animal-like scream, grabs her schoolbag and rushes headlong down the gravelled path toward the exit of Our Saviour's Cemetery.

Millions of years afterward, when all is lost, she's dozing by a wall in Amsterdam, without the strength to stand up and go on. The darkness is thickening around her, the moments of lucidity are becoming increasingly shorter and rarer. The local citizens pass by without noticing her – once in a while she receives a kick, as though she were a bagful of old rags or some other lifeless object.

When she lifts her head at long intervals, a fleeting thought brushes her: Who am I, why am I sitting here, what has happened to me, will this be my last place in this world? But before she finds an answer, darkness overtakes her, and her head sinks back against the wall.

She opens her eyes and stares down into the well of oblivion, where her reflection is becoming more and more blurred. Then she plunges down through the many ages of her life and hits the bottom.

VI

The Memory Book

1

Time, that glutton, has devoured another three months of the course of the world, and I write 12 December without my knowing where the days and weeks have gone.

Due to the noise in the room, the confusion in my head, my anxiety attacks and my swiftly changing thoughts, it has not been easy to hold together, and it is with a sense of wonder that I turn over the leaves of my manuscript and find that I've managed to write almost fifty pages. A good part of it is so rambling that I'll have to trash it, but enough remains to make my flight through the ages come vividly alive for me.

Here everything is so hopeless that I would perish from non-existence if I didn't have the ability to transport myself in imagination to other times and places. This is the closed section, which means that we are locked up and watched over round the clock. A sharp neon light falls upon us from the gas tubes in the ceiling, the corridors re-echo with noise like an indoor pool, and in the lounge the TV is on from morning till night, whether anyone sits in front of it or not. This is a place for the lost and the damned, where the whole technical apparatus will continue to take its course long after everyone is dead.

Sigrid, the charge nurse, has been my sole hope in all the hopelessness. She pays me a visit a couple of times a week, instils courage in me and takes care of the manuscript pages I have finished. Before handing over the pages to her, I copy some of them in a memory book that I have. Just to be on the safe side, when there is something I'm reluctant to lose sight of. I'm always afraid that the written word is going to disappear, it's the only thing I have; without it, life itself would crumble and be lost.

My fellow patients in Ward 6 are five middle-aged women who receive no treatment and are only preserved like a collection of living dead. At first they frightened me, and I got a real taste of what it means to be locked up in a madhouse. But as I have come to know their peculiarities, I feel more and more like one of them. They are the way I would be if my inner defence broke down, if I lost the ability to step back and look at my own life history with clear, attentive eyes.

A poor old thing, who may not be much older than me, walks about the ward looking for her silver, which she has hidden in such a safe place she can't find it. She looks high and low, mutters softly to herself, and shouts at the male nurses, believing they have robbed her. Then she settles down without any fuss, having forgotten the whole matter. But soon she starts up again, with renewed energy and increased suspicion; nobody is going to tell her it's not the first time she has missed her treasures. I'm sitting behind the screen, wishing for her sake that she will one day lose her memory altogether. That not only her silver spoons, but also their disappearance will have been blown out of her tormented brain. And suddenly I know what it means to be senile. It's not to be completely out of it as most people think, that would be a perfectly blissful state! No, it is to wander about in a border-land, to balance on the dividing line between memory and non-memory.

Another woman sits on the edge of her bed putting on one pair of knickers over another, because the young doctors think about nothing but sex, she says, and they're constantly after her. She has barely escaped being raped several times, she tells me. Oh sure, she has tried to complain to the head nurse, but it didn't help. But fortunately the doctors are busy when they come for inspection. So, hee-hee, if she just takes care to protect her virtue with many pairs of panties, they won't get anywhere with her.

A third woman believes she's the Virgin Mary and chosen to give birth to baby Jesus. She raises her head from the pillow in the middle of the night, looks about her watchfully and steals into the corridor to keep a lookout for the Holy Ghost. She comes back a little later, followed by the night nurse, who leads her over to the bed with a firm hand and waits till she has lain down. But soon she is on her feet again, or she sits up in bed and turns on the light. After she has been staring into vacancy for a while, a radiant smile spreads across her hollow-cheeked face, and she whispers so softly that only I, lying in the next bed, can hear her: "Behold the handmaid of the Lord; be it unto me according to thy word!"

Then there is the poor, disturbed woman over by the window who thinks that the radiator is her dog. Maybe she once had a dog that died or ran away and has never got over it. The light of reason died, a string broke in a mind that was too highly strung to begin with. Her memory of the peerless Fido has gone astray in the convolutions of her brain and has become a creative force which can even bring to life an object that is as dead as can be. Time has stopped, all processes have merged, yesterday, today and tomorrow are contained in one and the same moment. Sitting lost in her corner, she strokes and pats the lost one, wheedles and nags apropos of nothing, or sings a little tune, before suddenly jumping up to aim a blow at her best friend.

"Peep, peep, little curly one, can you guess what Mummy has got for you today?" she says, keeping her hands behind her back. "Sit nicely now and give your paw and you'll get your bone. No, no, don't growl, did you ever hear the like, such a wild fellow! Bow-wow, take good care of the house while Mummy is away, so that thieves won't break in and steal anything. Tra-la-la, now we'll soon take our morning walk, if only I could remember what has become of your leash. Oh, shame on you, to do your business on the floor again! You deserve a spanking, you filthy cur!"

And finally there is the completely uncontrollable woman in the middle of the room, who must be strapped to her bed if the rest of us are to have any rest at night. When she is at her worst, she sweeps water glasses and vases down from the night tables, or she smashes them against the wall, producing a shower of broken glass. In calmer periods she's spared the strap, but even then she's not at peace with herself. Suddenly she will wake up and not know where she is, thinking that someone has locked her up in a morgue. Then she pads about from bed to bed listening to our breaths, feeling our foreheads and shaking us, and doesn't quiet down until she has assured herself that we are all alive.

The bed I sit in was left vacant by the little terror-crazed woman who couldn't stand hearing the tower clock strike the hours. She died of fright while I was out wandering, and when I was brought back to be punished, the bed had been made for me. So now it's I who sit here keeping watch, listening into the night with her ears and waiting for the striking of the hours with her heart palpitating in my breast. I have tried to tell the male nurses how I feel, but they just smile and start talking about something else. Nobody understands any other afflictions than their own; in this respect all human beings are cold as ice and without sympathetic insight. When I was staying on the other hallway and heard about her fright, I felt sorry for her, but didn't let it get to me. Today I'm the one who is patted on the back by well-meaning nurses, who assure me that the strokes of the clock cannot do me any harm. I know that well enough, there's no need to tell me. But something inside me breaks every time the clock strikes, my spirit is crushed, and I just barely manage to recompose myself before the next striking of the hour. It's as though a sentence or an execution awaits me at dawn, and the countdown takes place with merciless precision, with me being unable to defend myself or ask for mercy.

Fortunately the terror releases its hold on me when the morning routine begins, and during the daytime hours the racket in the tower is so remote that I scarcely notice it. I'm split in two: one calm and composed day person who sits behind the screen keeping her records, and a night person who is scared to death and lies awake with all her senses in readiness for instant action. I drop off occasionally, no doubt, but the passage of time has become a kind of obsession with me. Anticipating all things, it grants me life from hour to hour as a postponement and an extended deadline.

What more is there to tell about these corridors of perdition, where everything vanishes the very moment it comes into being?

Oh yes, at the end of October I had a visit which I cannot pass over in silence, although it was so humiliating I would rather not mention it. When it was over I was so frightened that I saw danger everywhere and came back to my senses only after being given a sedative. Sister Sigrid was summoned to attend to me, and when it was all over she didn't let the doorman off lightly. She said outright that the visit should have been prevented, and that the personnel must be more careful about who was allowed into the wards.

About the same time something else happened that was almost equally nerve-racking, but which in a strange way has kindled a small flame in me. I had a letter from someone I haven't seen for ages, nor heard anything from since that day in the late summer of 1954 when we went our separate ways. The letter was mailed in Jerusalem of all places, and the content was no less fantastic. Before I had finished reading it, my eyes were swimming and I wasn't able to continue. I kept staring at the dancing letters in a daze, while a faint hope was kindled and extinguished behind my blinking eyes. Then I quickly folded the sheet and hid it inside the Bible everyone in this ward has in her night table drawer, regardless of whether they know how to read or not.

Several days passed before I dared take it out again and look more closely at what was written in the last few lines. But even then I was unable to see that it had anything to do with me and my near future. I went on like this until well into November. I took out the letter and put it away again, read it forwards and backwards, spelling myself through it without being able to grasp the message. I had read the letter to bits and still didn't know what to think of it, when the letter-writer suddenly showed up one day and stood before me in person.

Since then he has visited me every day, though he's unwelcome here and practically had to force his way in the first time he came. But he has managed to make himself respected, and no one dares deny him admittance anymore.

As a specialist in psychiatry he has done a thorough job, examining my case from every conceivable angle. He collected all my data, had a look at my medical record, called a meeting of the doctors and the nurses, and acted with an authority that has shaken the entire menagerie from top to bottom. The two assistant physicians look suitably crestfallen, the nurses whisper in the corners, and the medical director hasn't made his regular visits for more than a week. My visitor is letting things take their course, while being careful not to do anything rash. The result of his examination will soon be at hand, he says, and judging by the sly smile on his lips he knows already what the outcome will be.

I probably ought to confide to the blank page that he has made a proposal that will change my whole life if I accept it. I know he is in earnest about it and that he has the strength to carry it through; the question is whether I have sufficient confidence and courage to take the hand he holds out to me. He has given me time to think it over until 31 January, when he will go back to his faraway homeland and take me along, if I decide to join him.

To calm down a little and get a break from the agonies of making a choice, I once more concentrate on the history of my life, flipping the pages of my scribblings forwards and backwards to see if there is anything that can give me a clue. Fortunately I've had sufficient foresight to work up the material in several versions. First a draft that's full of insertions, deletions and additions. Then the clean copy which Sister Sigrid is keeping for me. And finally, as a last safety measure, I have copied several sections into the memory book I've already mentioned. It has followed me through every vicissitude for more than forty years and is filled nearly to the last page with diary notes, drafts of poems, copies of letters and other important information.

As I very well know, my urge to preserve things is getting out of hand. But as we shall see, it has made itself useful at least once by rescuing a precious document from oblivion.

2

In August 1951, four months after his son-in-law's death, Andreas Sand wrote a letter to his daughter and called her home.

He had let the summer go by on purpose to keep her on tenterhooks, just as he thought he was punishing her in 1945 when he provided her with an office job in Oslo and demanded that she support herself.

But the work in Fred Olsen's shipping firm had come to Mary as a gift from heaven and buoyed her up in the darkest moment of her life. She enjoyed leaving home in nice clothes, her hair newly washed, was popular in the workplace, joined a choir and acquired new friends. She visited her husband in prison as seldom as possible without offending against common decency, and never took her children with her.

As soon as Vemund Hov was imprisoned in the Oslo Penitentiary, she had removed the old nameplate on the door and put up an elegant brass plate, with *Mary Sand, Secretary* written in Gothic lettering. When her husband surprisingly returned from prison one day in September 1950, she told him she had replaced the old nameplate for the sake of the children. And Vemund nodded humbly and agreed it was no doubt for the best. The five years in prison had broken his will, making him almost too manageable. His fits of rage were less frequent and manifested themselves mostly as involuntary twitches in his paralyzed arm.

When he took to his bed, Mary made arrangements for a woman living on the same stairway to check on him a few times every morning, and at two o'clock Idun would hurry home from school and assume responsibility for him. The nursing felt like nothing new to the precocious but childish thirteen-year-old; it was a vote of confidence and a continuation of her care by other means. During the last lesson she was already preparing to leave, and she didn't understand much of what was going on in class. As soon as the bell rang, she grabbed her schoolbag and started running, while the others gathered in groups in front of the school gate. She remained at her post all afternoon, and the evenings when her mother was out she didn't leave the sickbed till well into the night.

She brought her father his dinner on a tray and fed him one bite after another, placed his documents and writings on the bedspread and read aloud from them. She fetched the bedpan and the urinal for him and wiped his behind; at the end she scarcely dared leave the room for five minutes for fear he would be dead when she returned. She watched over him with a peculiarly intense alertness, interpreted his slightest hint and put herself in his place with all the empathy at her command. She almost forgot she had a life of her own, walked round as if in a dream, had no friends, and was the object of amusement in class with her absent-mindedness and her way of expressing herself, well beyond her years. She often forgot to do her home-work, or she did it at intervals, when her father slept or dozed.

During his lucid moments she took down from dictation the last sections of the so-called Apology, scratching the sentences in an ordinary notebook, and bit by bit made a clean copy in a book that was already crammed with her father's semi-illegible characters. When he began to brood, he was always ready to repudiate it, and he flew into a rage when Idun refused to do his bidding and burn it. But when the spirit was upon him he called it a work for the future, which had to be protected against the intellectual rats and bats until its time had come. Perhaps the dying man could foresee that he had created a monumental work, which would live on after he was gone and make a lasting impression. Or maybe he dimly perceived with what remained to him of sound judgement that the Apology was doomed, that it was an abortion, a gigantic swelling, a discharge without order and moderation, the last sparks from an overtaxed and burned-out brain.

After it had ended up in the rubbish tip, Idun got out her worn and smudged notebook and read it over and over again until she knew the sentences by heart. These notes with their childish handwriting and profound content remained a sacred treasure all her life, and wherever she moved she always found a place where they could be kept in safety. The last hiding place was a hole behind a wall in Homansbyen, where what remains of Vemund Hov's lifework is bestowed, perhaps to see the light of day only sometime in the next millennium, when the building is demolished.

But so far the calendar showed only August 1951, and break-ups and upheavals were in the air. When Mary received the letter from her father, she became so furious that she locked herself up in the living room for a whole Sunday, refusing to come out when the children called her and pounded on the door. They could hear her stamping her feet and talking to herself, and now and then it sounded as though she was crying.

But on Monday morning she stuck a dishevelled head round the door and announced coldly and calmly that they were going to move. A doomsday atmosphere settled on the house, and the clearing out that has already been referred to in these pages was perpetrated. As soon as the rubbish truck had parked down the street, everything moved very fast; the apartment was cleared and stripped of every reminder of a person who had been known by the name Vemund Hov. The bedclothes, mattresses, shoes, his two worn suits, his overcoat and hat, his walking stick, briefcase and books were carried out, in addition to all the trifles and curios that were to have been kept for a hundred years. The mother presided over doomsday with the relentlessness of an angel of vengeance, with the ready help of her two minor angels, who were racing down the stairs with anything that had been condemned to instant oblivion, coming up empty-handed again to fetch a fresh load. By sheer coincidence three diaries were saved, besides the above-mentioned notebook that was lying in Idun's schoolbag and looked confusingly like an ordinary exercise book.

The tale of the three diaries is easy to explain and becomes uncertain only because of the use that is made of them in this narrative.

The day before the van full of furniture was to leave, Idun was assigned to clean out the closet in the back entry and to wash the shelves. She had moved out almost all the suitcases and boxes, when she caught sight of a small brown cardboard box in the corner. It attracted her attention because of the string that was wound about it several times and sealed with a ball of intricate knots. She sat on the floor and began to untie them, opening the two flaps of the cover filled with expectation. When she saw the contents, she forgot everything else, and a full hour or more went by before she was torn away from her absorption. In the box were twenty-nine small green, brown and burgundy almanacs that her father had used as diaries. There was not much writing in most of them, apart from accounts, household remedies, addresses, and a few notes about wind and weather. But some had been expanded by the addition of extra leaves, and these inserted leaves had been made the most of in his rather crabbed handwriting, which didn't change greatly in the course of the years.

She leafed quickly through the books with not very much written in them and selected three, which she put aside behind her back after hurriedly looking through them. One was from her father's very first youth, and once she had started reading what was written under New Year's Day 1917, she couldn't tear herself away. She sat there turning the leaves as if in a daze, and had read as far as Palm Sunday when she heard footsteps in the hallway. She started up and just barely managed to push the three diaries out of sight before the door to the closet was opened wide.

"Idun, what are you up to?" her mother asked with reproach in her voice. "We have a lot to do, don't you know, and here you're forgetting yourself as usual."

Idun looked up, but was still so rapt and far away that she wasn't even able to look guilty.

"Ah, you've found that box, well, I thought so," her mother said, stepping into the closet and starting to gather up the almanacs. "This is not for you, my friend. Why don't you just let me take care of these old things, they're not worth keeping anyway. Get up, will you, and finish your washing. I can't tell you how sad I feel, having a strapping daughter who shirks work and can't be trusted."

Idun moved aside a little, but no further than that her dress still covered the three precious books, where the years 1917, 1934 and 1944 were printed on the covers in worn gold lettering. When the mother had made off with her booty, she got up on her knees, lifted her skirts and stuck the books inside her knicker elastic. Then she stood up and began to wash the shelves in the closet with uncharacteristic energy.

Before she undressed that evening she found a temporary hiding place for the books in the checked cloth bag where she kept her knitting from school, the tape measure, the needlework manual, and some clumsy attempts at hemstitch. She didn't take her eyes off the bag during the four hours she sat in the train, and had barely gone through the door in Grandfather's house before she started looking for a safer place.

3

The ship owner's house in Strand Street was unchanged from the outside, with its grey slate mansard roof, its front steps with the wrought-iron railing, and its long rows of windows in three storeys.

But inside there were great changes. Andreas Sand no longer inhabited the house as a solitary magnate with secret lodgers in the attic, but was surrounded by a numerous family. In 1948 his two sisters had returned to Norway from Georgia, U.S.A., one unmarried, the other a widow with two teenage children. He had let them have one large and two smaller rooms upstairs, and when Mary arrived with her three children, the bedrooms were overcrowded.

For unknown reasons Andreas Sand had moved out of the big bedroom looking east, which had been his throughout the years, and settled in a much smaller room over by the staircase that led down to the kitchen area. He had always delighted in rising with the morning sun, but now it seemed that the evening sun gave him greater joy. In the adjacent room he had installed his private office, which had previously been on the second floor below. Beyond the office was a bathroom and a clothes closet, and one had to go through a locked door to get to that part of the third floor where all his relatives were staying.

With such a division into spheres of influence, it was scarcely possible to hear whether anybody was stealing up or down the kitchen stairs at night. Andreas Sand had slept poorly ever since the war, and if a particularly keen ear happened to pick up a creaking noise on the stairs during the night, it could only mean that the insomniac was taking a trip down to the kitchen to cut himself a slice of bread and put on the coffeepot. Previously, when the ship owner rang, it was the tireless Maren who got out of bed to bring him his midnight snack on a tray. But Maren was no longer there to be roused; surprisingly, the old maid had married and moved to another part of the country when the war was over. At about the same time the Jewess in the attic learned that she was a widow, and as soon as she dared to show herself in the light of day she was promoted to housekeeper and moved into the room behind the kitchen that had previously been Maren's.

Her son, who had turned sixteen in 1951, still lived in the attic, and as the house became invaded by relatives he was the only one of the lodgers with his own room. The ship owner's former bedroom was occupied by his two sisters, and when Mary returned to the fold the end result was that she moved in with them. Mary's cousin, Signe, who was fifteen in 1948 when she crossed the Atlantic, was staying in the guest room. She was now eighteen and made a wry face when she had to make space in the big double bed for the twins, Idun and Urd, who were just two little girls around fourteen. "Why crowd each other like that?" she complained. Wasn't the house one of the largest in town, and weren't there two empty rooms downstairs?

But Andreas Sand was inflexible and had his will. It was only wholesome for near relatives to live close together, he said, that way they learned to have consideration for each other and to restrain their selfishness. He turned a deaf ear to their youthful protests and gave long speeches about the blessings of family life. The dressing room furthest down the hall was only eight square metres, and yet he didn't consider it too cramped to house two young boys of fifteen and seventeen. The couch of Gore, the Norwegian-American, was replaced by a set of bunk beds, while the young man clenched his fists in his trouser pockets and indulged in language that his uncle was fortunately unable to make out.

As time went on he learned to swallow his pride, contenting himself with casting envious glances up the stairs to the attic, where the intruder Aaron had a room all to himself. The frictions between the two cousins ceased, but the elder showed his contempt for the younger by freezing him out and never speaking an unnecessary word to him. Who could have thought that one day they would hold out their hands to one another and become so inseparable that the old man had to intervene and drive them apart by force? But that is an altogether different story that will be brought to light in due time.

Nor was it easy for Mary to put up with an existence where she had two strict and bigoted aunts right next to her. For six years she'd been free as the breeze, and all of a sudden she found herself idle in a family ghetto where she could barely move without being watched over by penetrating eyes. The two American ladies were all over the place, and wherever they set foot on uncultivated soil they discerned a mission field. It wasn't for nothing that they had spent a near-generation in a small town in the state of Georgia, where competing sects and religious communities were to be found on every street corner.

The two busybodies invaded the kitchen with their embroidered table-cloths and ornamental towels, which were to teach the Jewess Christian customs. "Pray and Work," it said on the oblong tablecloth they placed on the kitchen counter, and a church in blue cross-stitch with an extra tall cross on the roof showed where the place was for true prayer. On the tabletop they spread a somewhat larger cloth that announced that "The Early Bird Catches the Worm" – an allusion to the fact that the housekeeper overslept now and then, so that the ship owner's sisters had to come to the rescue and take care of breakfast. And if none of these admonitions should penetrate, the ornamental towel hanging beside the sink declared that the fear of God, along with frugality, was a great gain.

Ruth, the Jewess, was an unassuming woman who adjusted to the new domestic discipline and washed and ironed the admonitory tablecloths with the greatest care. She realized that her position in the house was uncertain, and that she had to watch her step even more closely than she had done during the war. She lowered her eyes when the omniscient ladies complained about the decline of morals in the old country, and didn't raise them again until their torrent of words petered out. Once in a while a fleeting smile flitted across her face, but it was impossible to tell whether it was a smile of admission and subservience, or a secret amusement at the way the sisters pronounced Norwegian words. Andreas Sand's two sisters had been in their first youth when they left Norway in the 1920s, and while abroad they had completely forgotten how to shape the vowels of their homeland with their lips. But most comical of all was the consonant r, which had lost its clear, sharp lingual sound and flowed around their oral cavities like an incipient toothache.

The two sisters, Severina and Theodora, had been members of a Baptist congregation in Georgia and put pressure on their brother to procure a submersion tub for his house of worship. But though Andreas Sand had once had the audacity to baptize the Jewess Ruth, he stubbornly insisted that the Ark was not a sect and that adult baptism must never take place there. But gradually he gave in to other persuasions, made more space for the confession of sins and praise of the Lord, and soon became a warm adherent of faith cures.

When he placed his hand on the sick person's head, he closed his eyes and began, in a soft, mumbling voice, to place the cure into the hands of the higher powers. But at a certain moment he raised his voice, and shortly it sounded as though he was ordering the deity to step down and prove His omnipotence. While the congregation sat as if paralyzed, their vociferous leader stood on the podium, hurling his demands at heaven and reeling off long passages of Scripture, only lowering his voice when he was certain his prayer would be answered.

He made it a condition that the sick did not go to the doctor, but gave themselves over completely to the healing power of the laying-on of hands. Sensual by nature, he enjoyed every form of touch, and if the patient was young and attractive enough, he concluded his treatment with a series of slow strokes. A couple of miracle cures gained support for his method, and, in the years immediately after the war, the Ark experienced an upswing that rivalled the following it had during its very first years.

But the backlash came, casting long shadows over his whole family. Sometime in the mid-1950s Mary complained of pain in the abdomen and asked her father's permission to consult a doctor. But he had already begun his miracle cure on her and wouldn't hear of any interference. For eight months his daughter submitted to his laying-on of hands, and from time to time she thought that the pain eased off when the stroking was over and he concluded by raising his arm and crying, "Out you go, you evil spirit!" But the outcome was that she ended up on the operating table, and when she came back from the hospital, pale and debilitated, her rebellion was crushed, and she became the pious and obedient daughter he had so long missed.

After this, Andreas Sand no longer had any problems with her; she became a faithful member of the congregation, needed no instructions, and was in every respect her own taskmaster. Together with her aunts, she went in for missions and charity, knocked on the doors of well-known sinners and picked up down-and-outs in the street, so that they could sit at the end of the ship owner's table and benefit from his soup pot and devotional books.

Andreas Sand had greatly deteriorated in the course of the war, and already in the early 1950s he looked like an old man. His hair was completely white, his face hollow, and there wasn't very much left of the suppleness that at one time had enabled him to walk on his hands on the roof of the Ark. The only youthful thing about him were his eyes, those sly, wide-awake blue openings that were always on the lookout for heavenly grace as well as earthly profit.

Immediately after the war he had been summoned to an interrogation at the police station. The atmosphere in the town was agitated, and so many voices were heard accusing him of collaboration with the Germans that a showdown was inevitable. But it ended short of a trial. The ship owner had powerful connections and defended himself so well and so credibly that the matter didn't go beyond this summons. He washed his hands according to the best models, and persevered until he was without blemish. True, he was the principal shareholder in the machine shop, and had made a good profit from it throughout the five years of the war. But after all, once the Germans requisitioned it for their own purposes, it was not within his power to close it down. Such freedom of action didn't exist in wartime, and if he had withdrawn, someone else would immediately have used the opportunity to jump in. And besides, the enterprise had kept the wheels turning in hard times and provided work for many good Norwegians. Who didn't remember the grief and indignation that arose in the town when the shop was exposed to sabotage and several hundred men were left without work?

But the strongest argument in the ship owner's favour was his action in 1942, when he jeopardized his own well-being for the sake of a Jewish woman and her little son. For two and a half years he had kept them hidden in his house, protecting them from the horrors of the war. Such a coura-geous action bore witness to a high morality, and it would be a poor reward to summon him before a court of law. The case was dismissed, and before the year of liberation was over it was forgotten, and Andreas Sand came out of the ordeal even more respected and revered than he had been before the war, if that were possible. He donated large sums of money to charitable and public ends, and nobody offered any objections any more on the ground that the money had been earned in concert with the occupying power.

After the war, Andreas Sand made the most of his talents and expanded his empire in several directions. He invested in fresh enterprises, bought up firms that had declined during the war, and lent money to ailing companies against mortgage of real estate. If it was difficult to pay the interest and instalments on time, he was always willing to talk, and it usually ended with the debtor being granted a postponement. But sooner or later he had to draw the line somewhere, to show that business transactions were not the same as acts of friendship. He had a great sympathy for the losing party, listened patiently to the bankrupt's laments, and always tried to find an arrangement that was not excessively humiliating. This mild and Christian disposition was to stand him in good stead at a later time, and was remembered longer than his merciless last turn of the screw in his business transactions.

One day in the spring of 1948 he had a visit from an old friend who was the owner of the city's other large shipping firm. The man belonged to a family that had been in shipping for over a hundred years and was far above the upstart Andreas Sand in terms of culture and education. Now the firm was on the brink of ruin, and the old ship owner sought out his competi-tor in order to be granted a postponement on a large loan. It was not the first time that he had come to plead for mercy, and when the usual commonplaces had been reeled off, Andreas Sand made it quite clear that his patience could not be stretched any further. An instalment had to be put on the table, or he must at least ask for the thirteen thousand kroner that was owed in interest by his counterpart.

The latter hesitated a little, as if he knew a way out but couldn't quite decide to make use of it. But a moment later he had made up his mind and pulled an old sterling piece of jewellery from his pocket. It was the necklace set with rubies that has already been mentioned in these pages and that this summer completed its circulation by vanishing into the great nothingness.

"Then accept this as a pawn until I can raise the money," the debtor sighed, spreading the piece of jewellery on the table between them. "I'm sorry to have to use it as security, but I see no other way. I know you are a decent man who will take care of it until things improve and I can settle up. As you may know, this is an heirloom that has been handed down in my family from mother to daughter for several generations. My grandmother wore it during the festivities in 1872, when Oscar the Second was crowned King of Norway. My mother wore it at the ball in the royal palace in 1905, when King Håkon made his entry into Kristiania, and if my sister hadn't died of the Spanish flu in 1919, it would also have added lustre to her life. Now it has come into my possession, and I hope it won't be long before I can have it back."

Andreas Sand was silent a long while, as he weighed the gem in his hand in a businesslike manner.

"What do you suppose the ornament is worth?" he asked when he had finished his appraisal.

The old ship owner winced and was about to say something, but let it pass and got up to say goodbye.

"I can see you aren't very pleased with the arrangement," he said as he approached the door. "But I count on its being quite temporary. If everything goes well, it won't be long before I can redeem the gem. But let it go no further, please. My family know nothing, and they would never forgive me if they found out what I've done today."

Five months later the shipping firm went bankrupt, and before the year was over the owner had died in unfortunate circumstances. Andreas Sand kept the jewellery and maintained silence, even after the relatives of the deceased inserted an advertisement in the paper to retrieve the ancient heirloom.

Twelve years were to pass, by which time my grandfather lay at death's door, before a secret drawer in his writing table was unlocked and the gem brought to light.

"Take this for your faithfulness," he said, "and for all the harm I once did to you."

4

The milliner's shop, *Hundred & One Hats*, was situated in a side street to Strand Street, not far from the place where the Jew Baumann had had his stationery store before he was apprehended and sent away.

To help the business get started, Andreas Sand had put in a modest sum, which in his heart he regarded as money thrown away. But to his great surprise he was to discover that his two sisters had a flair for business that rivalled his own. After just a year Theodora and Severina had created a flourishing enterprise, which became a must for the town's ladies and attracted clients from the entire surrounding area.

Showing considerable knowledge of human nature, the sisters had specialized in two different types of hat, both of which had terrific sales. One was the traditional married woman's hat, with dent and pin, which every well-dressed housewife past a certain age barricaded herself behind when she set out on her day's shopping. It had existed since the beginning of time, and it was vain to think that it could ever be done away with. The novelty was that in *Hundred & One Hats* it could be had in several variants, with certain elements bordering on the imaginative. The prototype was made from a rather fleecy felt, brown or grey, with a good-sized pearl in the hat-pin. But depending on the season it could also be had in different fabrics, like fur, straw, *peau de pèche* or tartan wool. On this solid foundation, the two milliners operated with a light touch, making the result a bit more daring. They equipped the hats with a bright clasp or a single bird's feather and replaced the pearl with an eye which, in all innocence, peered sideways, keeping a watch on the passersby. All of them cautious and perfectly respectable ideas, which no one had any reason to be ashamed of.

The second hat was of an extravagant type, mostly coming in black and as voluminous as a magpie's nest. But it could also be worked out in strong, almost loud colours, such as cyclamen, turquoise, crimson or orange. The brims were usually arranged asymmetrically, so that one was turned up and the other down, and on the drooping side were placed all sorts of ginger-bread and gewgaws – amulets, bundles of beads and charms, bunches of flowers, cherry clusters, multicoloured feathers, even entire bird's wings.

The first time one of these chimeras was displayed in the shop windows, there was a regular disturbance on the pavement outside. Ladies of all ages huddled together, discussing in loud voices what this might signify, whether it was meant as a joke or as a rather unusual way of angling for customers. Who could see herself appearing with such a fright on her head, unless the place was the Wild West, but in a respectable Norwegian coastal town in the year 1952? Phew! It's for the birds – a hat as ugly as death, with a veil like a spider's web and a brim like spread-out bat's wings. No, thank God, it must be simply a Shrovetide joke, a pure eyecatcher that nobody need take seriously.

But one Tuesday morning, in the middle of Holy Week, the incredible happened. A youngish lady from the higher bourgeoisie stepped out of a cab and strolled calmly and coolly down Main Street with the unfortunate hat on her head. True, the lady did have eccentric proclivities and was already a subject of gossip, but she was not a through-and-through coquette, that nobody could say about her. She sauntered cockily along without any hurry, as though blithely unaware of the commotion she caused. The older gener-ation showered her with hard looks, which also devolved upon her husband, an attorney with rather too liberal views. But the town's young girls were gaga over it and followed her with avid eyes, ready to throw themselves on the horror and make it their own should a gust of wind blow it off her head.

Shortly after Easter there was a fresh model in the display window, if possible even more imaginative than the previous one. Before closing time it had disappeared, and the little doorbell at *Hundred & One Hats* kept ringing without a break for the rest of the week. Nobody understood how this milliner's business could be reconciled with the sisters' strict religion and their membership in the Ark. But the Sand family had never been easy to figure out. Perhaps the sisters needed to allow themselves this bit of frivolity in order to be able to wrinkle their noses and purse their lips all the more in other connections.

During the 1950s, *Hundred & One Hats* became a rendezvous not only for women shoppers, but for everyone who liked to hear the latest news and to tell a good story. If anybody had dared to call the shop a headquarters for gossip, the ladies would have been extremely surprised, because nobody peddled trumped-up stories or was crude enough to use heavy guns. The art of insinuation was popular, and why say things straight out when one could deliver an equally crushing judgement by hints and brief remarks?

One of the customs that Dora and Rina had brought with them from the States was to observe a siesta in the middle of the day. The sign in the window called attention to the fact that the shop was closed between twelve and half-past one, and everyone knew that tea was being served in the back room Monday and Friday, and coffee Tuesday and Thursday. With that it was wisely seen to that ladies of good society would never collide with dreary wives when they felt like dropping by for a chat. It soon became an unwritten law that the tea parties were reserved for the upper crust, and that all the rest had to be content with slurping coffee on the odd days of the week. If it happened from time to time that someone was unlucky enough to steal in the back door on the wrong day, she was met by an eloquent silence, which at once reminded her that she was very busy and had to go.

It was on one of these tea days that the truth came to light concerning the black hat with bat's wings.

"Well, have I got something to tell you!" said the ship broker's wife, lowering her voice to a dramatic whisper. "Don't you believe that Mrs X bought that hat because she thought it was becoming! Oh no, far from it. She bought it out of sheer devilry, that's a fact. And she strolled through town with it just to make fun of *Hundred & One Hats* and put us all to shame. Oh yes, I have it from her own lips. She was dying with laughter after her walk, because of all the stupid people she had managed to fool. She simply thought that the hat was terrible, and called the shop a chamber of horrors and a temple to bad taste. She had done her part and rid the town of this one hat, and it was going to be fun to watch who would take pity on the remaining hundred."

The ship broker's wife was well underway, forgetting all about the art of innuendo, when she suddenly caught an ominous glance from one of the sisters. Theodora resembled Andreas, her brother, in having the same kindly blue eyes, whose glance could harden and go frigid from one minute to the next.

"Oh, pardon me, I must be out of my mind talking so much," the woman hastened to say, with a little confused laugh. "But honestly, I do think it's a bit thick, and everyone is better off by having the truth come out."

Silence settled on the back room, and for a while the clatter of the teacups was the only sound to be heard. Only after the matrons had rallied round morality and promised it their full endorsement, did the mood pick up again. It was read out and passed that Mrs X had gone too far, and that when all was said and done her crude joke would backfire on her. And she was not alone in being brazen and revelling in impudence. Times had grown shameless, and the town was full of dubious individuals who needed to be taught a lesson.

Theodora nodded and found a pretext for going into the adjoining room to open the shop, although it was nearly half an hour too early. When she came back she seemed strangely remote and took a seat on the edge of the group. There she remained, pensively chewing her lower lip, as if she were considering a confession in the Ark or just pondering a design for a new hat.

5

Throughout his adult years Andreas Sand had been a diligent votary of the art of poetry; he never said no when a missionary magazine or local newspaper asked him for a contribution. Prologues, occasional songs, odes, moral pamphlets, endless verses on Biblical themes flowed from his hand, and his sole problem was to stop once he'd started.

In the mid-1950s the pile of clippings filled a whole drawer of his writing table, divided among folders, loose-leaf books, big and small envelopes. At regular intervals he spread them out on the tabletop, read them aloud and arranged them in categories according to secular punch and Christian pathos.

It had always been his secret dream to publish a collection of poems, and once, just before the war, he had selected the soundest of his verses and had them printed at his own expense. The copies were piled high in one of the cabinets in his office, and he handed them out generously left and right, without petty regard to whether the recipients were worthy of them or not. In the course of the years, he reaped many words of praise from the like-minded, but it had also happened that his gesture was rewarded by embarrassing silence. Then he became despondent and brooded over what the ingratitude might be due to, whether the recipient didn't know anything about poetry, whether he was jealous of his poetic vein, or whether . . . The last thought he was never able to think to the end, but consoled himself by deciding he had overestimated his reader and thrown pearls before swine.

But one day in August 1954 it looked as though his fortune was finally made. He had received a letter from the capital, a superb piece of writing that gave him back all the self-confidence he needed. He had the letter on him when he came to dinner, seating himself at the big oval dining table with an air at once triumphant and secretive. He waited until it was quiet around him and said grace as usual, though he may not have bowed his head quite as low over his plate as was otherwise his custom.

At that point the household had been shrunk by two people, so that a hole had arisen in the circle at the end of the table. The two quarrelsome cousins had been caught red-handed in an excessively warm friendship and sent off in different directions, one to the University of Oslo, the other to the School of Commerce in Bergen. Vidar, who now called himself Nicce, or on more solemn occasions Nicolai, had repented at once and eaten humble-pie, from which he profited by each month receiving an ample amount of money to live on. But that pighead Gore refused to understand what he'd done wrong and had to keep body and soul together doing odd jobs.

When Ruth, the housekeeper, appeared with the soup tureen, the master of the house raised his arm and made her understand that he had something to tell the family before the first course was served. She quickly disappeared into the serving area, setting the door ajar in readiness to reappear. Andreas Sand took his time, but he struck his breast pocket promisingly and proposed they sing a hymn before he let them in on his secret.

When the expectation could be stretched no further, he took out the letter, weighed it in his hand a moment and spread it out with deliberate gestures. Before he read it aloud he explained that it had come from Ansgar Publishers in Oslo, in other words from the country's most venerable Christian publisher. To dispel all doubt, he held the sheet of paper up across the table so that everybody could see the name of the firm at the top. Then he began to read, in an unusually loud voice and with long, expressive pauses, while the family listened and stared.

It said that the publisher had noticed the abundance of good, Christian poetry that flowed from the ship owner's pen, and that the name Andreas Sand had established itself in literary circles as a name that inspired respect. Now the question was whether the creator of all this edifying poetry would permit his best poems to be collected and placed on the publisher's autumn list. An advance would be paid out as soon as the poems were received and the editor had made a selection, in consultation with the author. It would be an honour for the firm to publish the book, and they could only hope that no other publishers had stolen a march on Ansgar's.

"There you see!" Theodora cried when her brother had finished his reading. "Haven't I always told you that nobody writes such moving poems as you? It's certainly about time you were discovered, it should have happened long ago!"

"But my dear Andreas, you don't have any doubt that your answer will be yes, do you?" asked Severina, who had a more observant eye for her brother's ambivalence. "You're much too modest, that's for sure."

What she had picked up with her special intuition was a genuine surprise in her brother's manner, a doubt that made him perplexed and had a disturbing effect on his happpiness. Andreas Sand was a naive and gullible man, who was ready to interpret everything to his own advantage. But he was also a clear and scrupulous rationalist who always asked himself whether the return was in keeping with the investment.

"Don't sit there down in the mouth like that, as if you were jinxed," Theodora said, patting her brother's hand encouragingly. "You're losing your good humour, that's what's wrong with you. Be glad that you have two sisters who wish you well and haven't lost faith in your lucky star."

She went on rejoicing in her brother's luck for the remainder of the meal, until she noted that it was taking effect. When they got up from the table, Andreas Sand was more lighthearted and the day was saved. He had folded his hands and thanked God for all his good gifts with a conviction that could only mean he had made up his mind and was all right.

What had caused him to be surprised by the letter for a moment was a certain clumsiness in the language and the somewhat excessive praise of his creations. It was well deserved, as he well knew, but his good sense told him that a publisher ought to express himself in more sober terms. But there was no mistaking the letterhead with the name of the firm, so he was obliged to believe his own eyes. Despite everything, he was a simple, ordinary man, and his experiences didn't extend beyond shipping and similar mundane enterprises. In reality, he knew very little about the literary world and with what flowery speech a publishing house decorated its letters.

That same evening he sat down to write an answer to Ansgar Publishers, in which he briefly and without the least bending of the knee confirmed that he accepted the offer. He would very soon mail the publisher a selection of his best poems and wait to be summoned for an interview. If the editor was of the opinion that some of the poems should be left out, he would be open to good advice; he had an abundance of material to choose from if the publisher's evaluation was contrary to his own. In any case, he didn't worry about the size of the advance, a token payment would be all right for the time being. He had what he needed for his earthly sustenance and had no intention of turning his writing into a livelihood.

For the remainder of that week Andreas Sand seemed rejuvenated, looking like himself as he was in the distant past, when he went in for big ventures and stood on the springboard of his happiness. He was restless, went early to town, and caught himself whistling in the streets, just like the young sailor more than forty years ago. He chatted with friends and acquaintances, even with people he scarcely knew, and in the course of the conversation he always found a pretext for taking out the letter and letting the other in on his good fortune. And when he sat in his office in the evening busying himself with the manuscript, a faint sound of singing was heard from in there, as if he were setting his verses to music as well. Anyone who at such moments opened the door and peeked in would see him deeply engrossed in the agonies of selection. Sitting with the clippings in front of him, he nodded or shook his head, changed the word order, expanded and condensed, tossed whole sheets into the waste-paper basket, and picked the curled leaves up again and carefully smoothed them out.

At last, when he was all set, he took out the writing pad with the printed monogram, which was only used on rare occasions, and made a clean copy of all the verses in his clear, almost calligraphic handwriting.

Three weeks went by, and the poet was about to jump out of his skin with impatience when the answer finally came. It was so disheartening that, at first, he recoiled and refused to accept it. He tore off his glasses, quickly replaced the letter in the envelope and hid it under a mound of legal documents that were lying on the writing table. Shutting himself up in his office all day, he restlessly paced the floor, drawn towards the hiding place as though by a magnetic field. He let out loud groans, clutched his head, clenched his fist in the air and gave vent to a number of whispered expletives, or he fell to his knees on the floor and humbly prayed that this cup pass from him.

Only at dusk, after dinner was over, did he find the strength to attend to the letter and take a closer look at what it said.

"Mr Andreas Sand, Author," it said, and the sheet was confusingly like the one he had received at the beginning of the month.

> Thank you for your letter of 8 August and for the enclosed manuscript. We have read your poems with interest; they reveal in some places a genuine lyrical vein as well as great ingenuity in regard to rhyme and imagery. All the same our editor thinks that they are not suitable for publication in book form. But do not lose courage, Christian friend, there are good and pithy verses here and there which may be enjoyed within a narrow circle, among family and friends.
>
> Your statement that our publishing firm has approached you with an offer for publication must be due to a misunderstanding. Nobody here knows of any such proposal, and we are sorry to have to admit that none of us has ever read a poem of yours before. To all appearance, someone wanted to play a practical joke on you and used our stationery to carry out this heartless jest.
>
> Regretfully,
> N. N., Editor
> Ansgar Publishers.
>
> The mansucript is being returned to you today.

After staring at the letter for a while, as though paralyzed, Andreas Sand jumped up, crumpled the paper and flung it with all his might in the waste-paper basket. His first thought was to go to the police and demand that an investigation be made. By Jove, he would never put up with it! He was certainly going to pursue the matter, and not rest until the culprit had been punished as he deserved. Quick, quick, not a moment to lose! He would lead the criminal investigation himself, and promise a huge reward to anyone who could throw light on this shameful forgery.

But, after regaining his composure, he realized that it would only aggravate the situation and proclaim his disgrace in every street and alley.

He visualized all the spiteful sneers behind his back, and could already hear the jokes and malicious innuendoes that would result from reporting it to the police. The culprit was no doubt some enemy or other he had made during the war, someone who looked at his success with a jaundiced eye and was annoyed that he had escaped being dragged into the judicial purge at its end.

If he had taken the trouble to take out the first letter again and read it with a keener eye, he would most likely have picked up a clue to the identity of the culprit. But that, too, was doomed to disappear when he tidied up around him and made a clean sweep. He had ransacked cupboards and cabinets, and everything that might remind him of his disgrace had been collected and emptied into the waste-paper basket. Even his dearest keepsakes were doomed, and before he managed to check himself he had ripped a yellowed picture off the wall and let it go the same way.

The following day he began to have regrets and went on an errand to the rubbish dump to retrieve his treasure. But to no avail, the container had already been emptied. The spirit of extermination that possessed him had had its will, the world was without form and void, and his poetry had been carried off to be turned to dust and ashes.

6

Towards the end of August the extended family in Strand Street had been reduced by an additional person. Nearly nineteen-year-old Aaron Baumann had left his childhood refuge and gone to the capital to prepare himself for a future that had yet to be clearly defined. For the time being he was to enrol at the university and take the preliminary examination in philosophy and Hebrew, after which time would tell where providence was going to lead him.

It was with a sorrowful heart that Andreas Sand let go of him. The boy had sweetened his life for nearly twelve years and brought out his total sum of tender feelings. It was a miracle of the heart that the old man never ceased to wonder about. For he really didn't like Jews and had never made a secret of it when he gave his thundering speeches in the Ark. He regarded them as off-shoots from the offence of the Cross and mistrusted them all, as if each and every one of them had nailed the Saviour to the Cross.

But little Aaron had entered his life at a time when the shadows were falling and he found nothing but emptiness everywhere. He became a very angel of light, hovering over his roof and settling in secret in that small attic room. During the last years of the war it was as if the child shed his earthly shell and changed in the old man's eyes into a purely symbolic figure. He became a mascot and a pledge of survival, a promise that the darkness would recede and that the large house behind the blackout curtains would ride safely through the period of occupation and foreign domination.

But the near things were not forgotten. Every evening the little cave dweller was brought down into the living room, where his lively spirit sparkled in competition with the lights of the crystal chandelier.

"Call me Grandpa," the old man said one evening, clasping the child to him as if he'd never before had a grandchild. He delighted in the boy's brightness, and in two and a half years he brought his pupil far beyond the level to which ordinary schooling would have taken him.

Andreas Sand was a self-taught man, with imagination as his foremost guide, and his instruction was in keeping with that. He had nothing but contempt for textbooks, since all the world's wisdom was to be found in the Book of Books. Night after night the two friends put their heads together under the lamp and trusted in the old family Bible they had on the table in front of them. They always opened the book at random, so that the divine spirit could guide their thirst for knowledge. And the sacred book unfolded itself and became an encyclopaedia of all the insights and skills that lived their secret life between heaven and earth. Now it was a textbook in reading and arithmetic, now it opened to a complex study of history, geography, religious faith and knowledge of human nature. The book was printed in the old style, and the boy learned to read by following the grandfather's index finger from one line to the next, from verse to verse, chapter to chapter. For a long time he believed that the Gothic letters were the only ones that could tell a story, and he was greatly amazed the day his master opened a book of fairy tales to show him that there were also other, less venerable type styles. The boy gave a loud laugh and revealed what he had up to then thought about the newspapers and magazines in his father's stationery store. He had believed they were aids intended for purely external use, something like the chart the doctor had hanging on the wall to find out whether people needed eyeglasses. His captivity in the attic had turned him into a guardian of secrecy, and its script was the quaint and crooked one that crawled along the lines of Grandpa's Bible. No other script could tell how it felt to sit under the roof expecting anything to happen: a bomb to fall and smash the Cuddy to smithereens; Maren popping up with some extra good food on her tray; the NS troopers to come storming up the stairs, forcing him to say those terrible words "*Heil & sæl*"; peace suddenly to come some day, so that Mousedaddy could venture out of his hole and shed his animal skin.

Since school under the crystal chandelier was in every respect a Bible school, a lesson in arithmetic could be roughly like this:

"Aaron," the grandfather says, "you remember, don't you, that yesterday we read about the seven plagues that the obstinate Pharaoh called down on Egypt? One of them was the swarm of grasshoppers, which you saw so vividly before you that you had to shade your eyes with your hand. Let's say that it poured into the country for three days. The first day there came 9,336 grasshoppers, the second day 6,428 and the third day 4,512. Now pay careful attention: how many grasshoppers were there altogether which afflicted the country of the Pharaoh?"

"Should I do the sum in my head?" Aaron asks, scratching the nape of his neck.

"Really now. Grasshoppers come in multitudes and can never be figured by ready reckoning. Write the numbers on the paper, and you'll have a whole minute to figure it out."

It takes Aaron a mere eighteen seconds to find out that the plague sent 20,276 grasshoppers into ancient Egypt.

"Good that they came in three heats," the boy says, giving a sigh of relief. "Otherwise the swarm would've been so thick there might be a solar eclipse."

"In the course of those three days they stripped trees and plants of all greenery," the grandfather goes on. "Then most of them went away. But before the swarm rose to fly on to other lands, one fourth of the grasshoppers had died."

"Had they eaten too much grass and leaves?" Aaron asks, wanting to get beyond dry numbers.

"That may be. But as I've already told you, that sort of speculation has nothing to do with arithmetic. Figuring is about being able to imagine things, and the numbers are always floating in the sky."

"Just like the grasshoppers."

"Careful now, you pighead, you know what I've told you."

"I'm sorry, Grandpa. Numbers don't have wings, but I forgot. And they don't eat grass, not even when they come in large swarms."

"Shhh. Instead, hurry up and figure out how many grasshoppers died, and how large the swarm was when it continued on through the land of Africa."

The following evening the turn has come for ready reckoning, and the teacher manages to guide God's hand so that the book opens on The New Testament.

"Aaron, listen, today we'll forget all the cock-and-bull stories in the Old Testament and deal with the twelve apostles. How many arms and legs and fingers and toes they have together, we won't worry about, that's much too easy to add up for an eight-year-old with your clever head for figures. But as you know, the body has seven openings, and we might as well begin with that. How many openings does that make for all the twelve apostles?"

"Isn't Jesus going to be part of it? He's also a sort of human being, isn't he?"

"Quiet, and mind your tongue, boy! Jesus Christ is God's only begotten son, and we don't do arithmetic with the sacred."

"Well, no. All right, then I can use the twelve table. But wait a moment, you've forgotten something. The body has more than the seven openings which are in the head."

"Quiet, I've told you. How dare you!"

"Don't get angry, Grandpa, but I come out with eight openings. You forgot the opening the disciples had behind, just like other people. And if we count Martha and Mary as disciples, then there's still another opening. Because women have a secret place from which blood flows once a month. Sometimes so much blood comes that there's a deluge, and Maren has to change the sheets."

"For shame, boy! What kind of talk is that? If you continue that way I'll send you up to the attic again. Now let's find another place in the Bible and try something else. Look, there is the story of Jesus as a twelve-year-old child in the temple!"

"But we aren't going to do sums with him, are we?"

"Certainly not, I never meant to. But we could measure how far it is from

Nazareth to Jerusalem and calculate how long it takes to make the trip on foot."

He gets up, walks into the office and comes back with the world atlas and a ruler to measure with. They're both equally eager, and by joint efforts they discover that the distance between Nazareth and Jerusalem, as the crow flies, is one hundred and five kilometres.

"Let's assume that they manage to walk fifteen kilometres a day," the grandfather says, slamming the atlas shut. "How many . . ."

"Shouldn't we rather say thirty-five, that's also a number that goes into one hundred and five?"

"Shhh, boy, no objections now."

"But I don't think they will walk that slow. I'm only eight years old and I can walk five kilometres in half an hour. And Jesus can't be any poorer, can he, he who'll soon walk on water?"

"Here's one thing you should know, you little snooper. The climate in Palestine is not like ours. In the middle of the day it's so hot that they have to take cover in an olive grove."

"Well, that alters the case. And maybe they drop by Shechem and Bethel to say hello to friends and family. Perhaps they feel like visiting Elisabeth, you know, who also had a son by the Holy Ghost. Then Jesus and John could talk about what they want to be when they grow up."

"Tut, what are you saying, you little rascal?"

"Well, you know, Jesus hadn't meant to be a carpenter, like Joseph. And John was to be a baptist, after all, so he had to start early on to get used to eating locusts and wild honey. I hope there came a swarm of locusts over Judea now and then, so he didn't have to die of starvation."

"I'm sending you up to the attic this minute, now you know!"

"No, don't, Grandpa, let's just say they walk fifteen kilometres a day, then it takes exactly a week to get to Jerusalem. The rest of the problem is quickly done. They stay in Jerusalem for five days and sacrifice a few small birds, for they are poor folk, Joseph and Mary. Then they begin their journey home, but after a day of travel they discover that Jesus isn't with them. Then they have used thirteen days in all. Back to Jerusalem and a desperate search for Jesus for three days before they find him. Then off once more and the whole trip home without stopping. Thirteen plus one plus three plus seven, that adds up to twenty-four days in all. It's a long time to be on the go, just for a sacrifice. But Grandpa, we must remember something. Without all this running back and forth the Bible wouldn't have had the story of Jesus as a twelve-year-old child in the temple."

"O, Aaron, Aaron, you certainly have a way of saying things! What would we have known about the Saviour's childhood if we hadn't had that story?"

Because of the boy's knowledge of the Bible it had long been the grandfather's dream that Aaron should be a missionary. Could there be any greater task for a son of Jewish parents than to expiate his ancestors' sins by bringing his people the light of the gospel? As the boy grew up, it happened more and more often that the old man mentioned the matter, saying that the Israel Mission must be the right place for him. As a child, Aaron nodded agreeably, and the old man hardly noticed that the boy's docility diminished as he grew older, until it was nearly gone.

Aaron had too much affection for the grandfather to wish to cause him sorrow, and when he had graduated from the *gymnasium* with a major in Latin and the old man proposed that he go to Oslo to prepare for his preliminary examination in Hebrew, he had no objection. Perhaps he was already at a crossroads, his eyes turned toward entirely different prospects. But no final plan had been made, and when he departed in August 1954 it was to enrol at the University of Oslo and begin the first part of the curriculum in divinity.

The only thing that could have made Andreas Sand suspicious was the boy's political alertness and his association with a group of adult men who were avowed adherents of socialism. But, as always, Aaron watched his step. He had a long way to go, and he was still so uncertain and confused about what he wanted that he confided his dreams of the future only to one person.

7

After the war there had also taken place great changes on Sandane farm, located at the mouth of the fjord.

Andreas Sand had spent the summer in town during the last two years of the Occupation, contenting himself with making flying visits out to his childhood home. The place bordered on a military area, and an anti-aircraft station had been built only a few kilometres from the farm. When the Allies escalated the air war in the late winter of 1945, a bomb fell on the property and caused great destruction. The farmhouse was razed to the ground, the fields were torn up, cliffs shattered, and most of the brushwood scorched.

As soon as Andreas Sand had been paid the war indemnity, he intended to rebuild the farm. But he had lost his appetite for the place and couldn't pull himself together to speed up matters. He postponed the reconstruction from one month to the next and hadn't yet made his decision when his sisters arrived from the States in the spring of 1948.

After Theodora and Severina had been out to the old homestead and seen the sad remainders of their childhood home, they agreed with their brother that rebuilding was not the right solution. The farm would never be the same with the new buildings, it would only make matters worse and remind them all of what had been lost.

After another waiting period and joint consultations, suddenly one day Theodora had a good idea, or a revelation, as she preferred to call it. Sandane was to be built anew, not as a vacation spot for the family, *not at all*, but as a much larger and more richly blessed gathering place.

"*Listen to me, Andrew*," she said, as a blissful smile spread across her large horse face. "*I've got it!*"

"Well, I'm listening, but speak my language," Andreas said, annoyed by the linguistic mishmash to which his sisters switched when they were enthused and had something very important they wanted to say.

Theodora still waited a moment, then she straightened up and looked intently at her brother. "*Well*, we shall found a full-evangelical centre," she said, putting extra stress on the prefix "full" to make it quite clear that there would be no question of doing anything by halves.

Andreas promised to think it over and submit the matter to God in prayer, and when the family sat down to breakfast the following day the answer had already arrived. Sandane was to be rebuilt as a meeting place for all who in their hearts professed the evangelical-Lutheran faith. Of course, the Ark had to reserve for itself the two or three best weeks of the season. But during the rest of the summer the place could be leased at a nice profit to congregations that were capable of paying and whose faith was firmly grounded.

The only thing he was a bit doubtful of was whether the place ought to be called "full-evangelical". It did seem rather excessive, didn't it? He constantly choked on it and wondered whether simply "evangelical" would do.

Nor did he like the word "centre" and would sit uttering it to himself time and again while slowly shaking his head. Centre? Centre? Centre? By God's holy name, what sort of a word was that? It sounded like a blasphemy, and he couldn't help thinking that it would scare good Christian people away from the place.

But Theodora and Severina stuck together, and they simply pooh-poohed their brother's cautious suggestion of *Sandane Evangelical Summer Home*.

"*Dear brother*, I know you mean well," Theodora said, placing a forbearing hand on his shoulder. "But you should know how many *wonderful* centres they have over there. *Be sure*, soon we'll have them here with us too. Shopping centres and church centres, centres for the elderly and relief centres, even emergency centres for people who really *have got a hard time*. Listen to what your more experienced sisters are telling you, centre is *the real thing*! *You see*, it is a name that says something, is *up to date* and hits the mark, and isn't it just that which we want Sandane to be?"

It was all settled and the sisters had their will. After the project was finished in the summer of 1950 – main building, chapel and residential cottages – a portal was erected at the entrance with an inscription in large, rather gaudy lettering that read: *Sandane Full-Evangelical Centre*.

Already from the very first summer, the beach meetings at Sandane were a great success, and so eagerly coveted by congregations from all over the country that they had to be on a waiting list for months on the off chance of being accommodated in late August or September. Everybody knew that it was a place for conversion and the confession of sins, and associations that preferred preaching of a less heated character were forewarned and stayed away.

In June, July and August Andreas Sand was himself present, keeping an eye on the place from his small summer apartment, so that everything was done in the right spirit. A popular speaker with a knack for conducting meetings, he was glad to help out even when other congregations than the Ark filled the hall. Here, close to the ocean, his preaching was milder and more tolerant than it was known to be in the city. The sea air had an animating effect on him; he rediscovered his good humour and the almost merry Christian disposition that had been peculiar to him in his youth.

But the outcome of the meetings was given, and in this regard he was uncompromising. The penance bench was a fixture of the chapel, and a revival meeting always ended in the same way: the hall ceiling drew closer, the chorus of praise died down, the organ music renounced its polyphonic jubilation and became a monotonous and insistent repetition of one and the same motif. The leader of the meeting gave a brief prayer and urged the participants to be open and not to hold back. A sense of restlessness stole along the rows of seats and people became more and more fidgety, knowing that the hour was imminent. Soon they would be obliged to shed their camouflage and display their sin and shame for everyone to see. It would be heavy going to find their way up to the penance bench, with the breath of sensationalism in the back of their necks and the yoke of condemnation on their shoulders. But how glorious it would be to walk down again with their accounts settled and the deficiency made up.

As soon as the ordeal was over and the sins forgiven, the vital spirits picked up again and received a fresh impetus. After a hiatus of nearly forty years, Andreas Sand sat on the small hill below the flagpole, wistfully watching the hawk chasing the dove and the thief running with light feet over the turf. He didn't participate in the games himself anymore, his back had started to cause trouble and could no longer tolerate all the capers that had accompanied his journey through life. But his alert blue eyes never tired of keeping up, and every time a pretty thing was stolen and carried off, it happened by a kind of secret substitution, as if in reality it was he himself who stormed into the circle and brought off the great coup.

But while the lawn was open to free competition, the beach was the place for the strictest planning. The beach was divided in two by a long rocky ridge that extended some distance into the water, making it impossible for a bathing male angel to see a glimpse of a female one. If some depraved soul saw his chance to climb up and peek over at the other side, he came away with very little visual delight. The young women at Sandane lived under strict rules and begrudged air and sun the least peek at their nakedness. After smuggling into their bathing suits behind a cliff, they rushed off and plunged into the waves as if Old Nick were at their heels. Left on the beach were the matrons, sweating in their salmon-coloured slips, bulging with excess fat and happily protected from carnal temptations.

But if, despite everything, it happened that a couple in love managed to finagle a walk by moonlight, they let themselves in for it! Some distance down Lovers' Lane the director's sisters were waiting; they emerged from the scmi-darkness like two cherubs black as night, barring the entrance to the garden of pleasure.

"*Dear friends,*" said the taller and more authoritative of the two, "what are you doing here *so late in the night*? It's past eleven, didn't you hear *the bell*? If you wish to avoid *trouble*, take leave and say a nice good night. *Just so,* you go in this direction, and you go in that direction. *Sleep well, and God bless you.*"

Sandane Full-Evangelical Centre had from the very beginning been a private institution with its own rules and its own economy. The director had had the foresight to register the property and had seen to it that the legal formalities were in perfect order. But when he accepted rent from the congregations, it would happen now and then that he put the money in his own pocket, at times through sheer distraction, at other times purposely, out of contempt for what he called public extortion.

In the course of the years it amounted to rather large sums of money that in this way were lost to the municipal treasury. And as shipping started having financial difficulties, he also became more and more careless with the firm's accounts. He got hold of a smart business manager, and made use of all the tricks and remedies a large concern has at its disposal to conceal its assets and income. He deposited considerable amounts in Swiss banks, fixed himself up with figureheads, established fictitious companies and slowly began to register his fleet abroad.

But, gullible as he was at bottom, he somehow operated in a state of innocence, tacking his way ahead at random and never fully mastering the turbid waters of investment. Tricks that his grandson would one day perform with a practised hand were approached gropingly and in the dark, while he consulted the Saviour and consoled himself with the thought that the nooks and crannies of this world were beyond human ken.

8

When Idun and Urd (alias Finelotte and Thrinebeth) were reading for confirmation in the fall of 1952, they each received a memory book from their American great-aunts. Idun's was made of red artificial leather and Urd's of green, with *Memories* printed in gold letters on the cover and a flap with a lock and two tiny gold keys on one side.

In her speech at the festive table Aunt Dora explained that the books were not intended for verses and greetings from friends, male or female. The twin sisters themselves were to write in them when they felt they had something to say. But secretiveness was not a good thing, which couldn't be stressed enough. The older generation was concerned about the spiritual life of the young, and from time to time the aunts would be glad to hear what was written in the memory books.

Urd, who now refused to be called anything but Thrinebeth, played along with them, thinking it was a nice idea. She wrote the best essays in class and was also doing very well in foreign languages. Besides, she was the undisputed leader of the flock, as much courted by the girls as by the boys. In all the schools she had gone to she had managed to bring off the same feat: after a few weeks of scepticism, indifference and teasing by her class-mates, she inspired respect and ended by being the one who controlled the course of events. A slight wave of her hand was enough to hurl her peers into the abyss, or lift them up to the pinnacles of bliss.

Therefore her memory book had anything but trifles to report when it was opened in the evening for general instruction. In a light, witty style it related what was happening at school and in the town, noting not only her classmates' family circumstances and the teachers' shortcomings and peculiarities, but also intrigues and dramas that had partly been invented by herself. The family in the ship owner's house had many a good laugh, but also a good portion of worry; and once in a while they experienced emotions approaching shock and spiritual upheaval. Thrinebeth's reports soon outstripped the tea party gossip at the milliner's, being minted with great precision and constantly bringing new material in denunciation of the town's customs and morals.

It wasn't quite as plain sailing with Idun's memory book, and all indications were that the present was wasted. When Thrinebeth had finished her reading and the aunts turned toward her twin sister, she simply shook her head and looked embarrassed. After three months had passed and not a word had been set on paper, Aunt Dora lost her patience and wanted to take the book back. But Idun sweetly asked for mercy, and with tears rolling down her cheeks she insisted she was glad to have the memory book and would like to keep it. She just wasn't as good at telling things as Thrinebeth was and couldn't come up with anything to write in it. But there was no need to be in such a hurry to fill it up, was there, she would put it away until she grew up and had experienced something that was really worth remembering. The book had 250 pages, she had already counted them over. So if she began to write when she was twenty and continued till she was seventy, there would be only five pages for each year. After all, it was to be a memory book for life, Aunt Dora had said so in her talk. And then one couldn't just scribble away about this, that and everything, one had to save the book for experiences that were really important.

Aunt Dora sniffed and Aunt Rina sighed, but they left her alone. Once in a while they nosed about in the drawers to see whether Idun (Finelotte) really was as spiritually emaciated as she seemed, and when a year passed and the book had still only blank pages, they gave up and concluded that one of Mary's daughters not only had her appearance against her, but unfortunately was a vacuous and unimaginative young girl as well.

Finally, in January 1954, when Idun could feel confident that the aunts no longer expected anything from her, she took out the memory book and began to fill the first seventy-four pages with her small firm, neat hand-writing. As we shall see, she had more than one reason for choosing exactly New Year's Day for initiating the memory book. Barely seventeen years old, Idun was a timid though indomitable soul, full of hope and expectation but uncertain of everything and everybody. She had little faith in her own decisions and often put her trust in hints, magic numbers and strange coincidences.

1 January, 1954. Today, thirty-seven years ago, Father received an almanac as a birthday present from the parish pastor at Gjerpen, and already the next day he began writing in it. I don't labour under the delusion that I can write as well as he did, though I'm almost the same age as the young fugitive of 1917 and have had a far better schooling than he.

But wish me luck. Because it is New Year's Day I'm going to open the memory book by making a copy of the three almanacs that I was able to salvage from the rubbish truck. It will probably take a few days; I have to watch out and use the time when Urd is out with her girlfriends and Signe is waiting on customers over at the milliner's. But I expect to have finished the copying before school starts. I have no idea why these almanacs are so important to me, it has almost become a matter of life and death for me to preserve them. I read them over and over again and keep shifting them from one hiding place to another, so that nobody can find them and take them away from me.

To do a bit of magic, I have put aside seventy-four pages (the sum of the digits in 1917 and 1954 + 37) for all three of them; I have estimated that this should be all right if I use tiny little letters. Even so, they won't be as tiny as Father's, but I won't have to write straight across weekdays, church holidays, sunrises, moon phases, trinities and ascensions. I also have a clearer hand-writing than Father, though the young Vemund Hov writes quite a bit more legibly than the older one. In the almanac for the autumn of 1944 the scrawls are so awful in places that I have to search high and low to decipher them. Could Father possibly have had his first stroke already that autumn? Or did the times so weigh on him that it made his hand shake?

Then, on page seventy-five, I'll begin my own notes, and there I really have big news to relate. My fingers itch and can barely wait. But easy now, easy, Idun, let eveything come in due course. First copy the three almanacs for 1917, 1934 and 1944, then I've made certain that they won't disappear.

13 January. The twentieth day of Christmas. I prolong Christmas as far as I can, because this Christmas holiday has made me into a new person.

Aaron and I have become sweethearts, there I've got if off my chest! It took place New Year's Eve up in the Cuddy, after looking into each other's eyes and promising some big and serious things.

First of all, that we will be faithful to each other for better, for worse, till death us do part. It was as solemn as a wedding, and afterwards we kissed for the first time, and we managed to get it right. I've always dreaded this matter of kissing, something that others are doing all the time without turning it into a problem. I would become a laughingstock in class if they found out that I had to wait until I was almost seventeen before getting my first kiss.

I think there must be something the matter with my head, it tilts to the wrong side and always collides with other heads when someone wants to give me a hug. But this time it all went as it should, maybe he too tilts over to the wrong side. Anyway, there was no collision, our lips found each other as though they had never done anything else but meet in hot kisses. We nearly weren't able to stop, so it was good that we were wise enough to make the pledges first.

Beside the pledge to be faithful, we promised each other three other things, almost as in a fairy tale.

1   That we would always be truthful and not hide anything from each other. (That won't be easy, because I feel I have so many things to be ashamed of, both in the past and the present.)

2   That we would never be greedy for money or get tied down by material things, but be ready to move on when life summoned us. (That will be easier, I've never known what to use my money for and have always been something of a vagabond.)

3   That our sense of justice shall not only apply to ourselves, but that we will stand on the side of the weak against the strong, the poor against the rich, the oppressed against the oppressors.

In between all the kisses we talked about how difficult it is to be truthful and to live without lies and hypocrisy. I realized that something was weighing on him, and suddenly he said that he didn't believe in God.

"Oh, but aren't you going to Israel to be a missionary?" I said.

He shook his head, and after sitting a while in silence he told me that he had quite different plans. After going to the university for a semester and passing his Hebrew examination, he would leave for Israel and settle in a *kibbutz*, he said. He had already been studying Hebrew on the side for over a year and counted on celebrating the next New Year in Jerusalem. But there was one condition: he had to persuade his mother to join him, for without her he couldn't see himself emigrating.

"But what about me?" I asked, because it almost looked as if he had forgotten what we'd just promised each other.

"Don't worry," he said, "I'll come and pick you up as soon as it can be done. It may take some time, but I won't forget that we love each other and want to live our lives together."

22 January. The twenty-ninth day of Christmas. When I stop to think, it doesn't seem entirely surprising that Aaron and I became sweethearts. We've been stuck on each other for a long time, although we were terribly shy in the early days, after I moved into Grandpa's house. We stole past each other like two shadows, still no doubt remembering that day during the war when he chased me down from the attic.

Last summer we were both volunteers at Sandane. That is, we had to help out in the kitchen during the beach meetings, set tables, wait at meals, wash floors, and be available for any chores that came up. In return, we could count ourselves as participants, attend the meetings, take part in the games and go swimming at the beach as much as we wanted to when we had time off.

Actually, our efforts were not purely voluntary. Grandpa proposed it to us one day in the spring, saying that we could do as we wished. But it was difficult to find help, he said, so he would be very sad if we thought only of ourselves and said no.

Aaron told me later that he would do it for Grandpa's sake and take it as an instructive lesson in the school of life. There were always so many odd characters who came to Sandane, and he might need some knowledge of human nature before going out into the world for good. And Grandpa had saved his life after all, so it was only fair that he did something in return. But it wouldn't be an easy role to play. He didn't like the heated atmosphere at Sandane and felt quite alien to all the hullabaloo that went on out there.

As for myself, I didn't have a choice: Grandpa had said he would be sad and that decided the matter. I, too, cannot say I'm wildly enthusiastic about all those high jinks at Sandane, whether they take place in the chapel or out in the yard. But I'll bear up, I thought, and if it should get too bad I'll just close my eyes and think of something else.

There is, in particular, a disgusting man with sweaty hands who always wants to steal me when we play Thief, Thief! He's after me everywhere, touches me when I wait on tables and always tries to take a seat beside me in the chapel. He must be far into his thirties and doesn't realize that I regard him as an old fogey. At the after-Christmas party this winter he never missed a chance to walk next to me round the Christmas tree, squeezing into the circle and having his own way. So I was forced to hold that dank hand of his in mine, while he was stroking the back of my hand with his thumb.

But most unpleasant of all is the sight of him standing up to confess his sins. His voice fairly sobs, although what he has on his conscience are the most absurd trifles. It's almost as if he prides himself on his sins, turning his head to look round every so often to assure himself that nobody has missed anything. When he walks up to the penance bench, I quickly change my seat to where people are jammed so tight that he can't possibly squeeze in beside me.

Aaron must have understood my dilemma, for during the fortnight we were out there he always stayed close to me. When he was the thief and had saved me from my tormentor, he pulled me out of the circle and suggested we go for a walk instead. Soon we began to meet at night, after the bell had rung and sent people indoors. We weren't stupid enough to go down Lovers' Lane, where the aunts were lurking. We dived into the shrubbery and rediscovered nearly overgrown paths, from the time when Sandane had been a small farm surrounded by coppices on every side. All that happened was that we held each other's hands as we walked, but that was not so little. He has such a good hand, which clasps mine firmly and seems to tell me something in a mute, secret language. And suddenly strange shudders shoot through it, which transfer themselves to my hand and send a warm current through my body.

The last evening I suddenly couldn't restrain myself, asking him whether he remembered Mousedaddy and the piece of cheese. For a moment he seemed to go rigid, and his hand gave a jerk as if he wanted to pull it away. But then he began laughing, a strangely bright and ready laughter. I realized I had reminded him of something that made him both happy and sad. Sad because it made him think of his father, who died in a camp someplace in Germany. But happy because we two were here alive, sharing something that nobody could take away from us.

After shuffling about for a while it occurred to us that we should take a swim together. A real skinny-dip, which would wash us clean after a fortnight's voluntary compulsion at *Sandane Full-Evangelical Centre*. He was to go in on the men's side and I on the women's side, and then we would swim out beside the long headland until we met in deep water.

While I swam out something odd happened to me. I felt strangely suspended and weightless, time was no more, and it was as though I had been tossed into the great Pacific between before and after. At each stroke that I made it became more and more difficult to keep my body under the surface. I had to think of something our physics teacher at school had said, that a horizontal motion was capable of changing into an ascending force. I let myself be borne by the waves, and suddenly there was nothing that could keep me down anymore. I shook off the last drops of water and climbed a mysterious stairway, where he sat waiting on the top step.

19 February. I love him! I love him! I love him!

Yes, that's how it is. I love everything that's his, from head to foot, from outermost to inmost. His sparkling dark eyes, and that black mop of hair that keeps falling down over his eyes all the time. His nose, even though it's rather large, and curves like the beak of a good-sized eagle. His mouth, which is so firm and yet so soft. His broad shoulders, his chest that's so good to rest my head against, his fine narrow hips, his legs that some would say are too short in relation to his torso, his feet that occasionally smell with sweat, his arms that embrace me in such a strong, gentle way.

He is four centimetres shorter than me, but I love that too. Because I'm tall myself, I have enough of tallness and have never been on the lookout for a beanpole.

This is how our sum looks: $(180 + 176) \div 2 = 178$. That is to say, one metre and seventy-eight to each, if we are to share everything equally, and of course we are.

No doubt there are those who will refuse to accept the distribution, saying that stature is not something that can be shared. For example, I know very well what Aunt Dora would say, if she got wind of our secret. She has said it before about others and will say it again about us: Shame on you, shame on you, a tall wife and a short little husband.

28 February. The otherness. That's what I love in him and in all things. It tempts me and attracts me and almost feels like something sacred. All that's not me, but sort of moves upon the face of the waters, so that she who's called Idun shall finally come into being.

Perhaps that's why we human beings believe in God. Because he is otherness itself, which we can love and give ourselves over to without losing anything of that which is our own.

12 March. Last night he showed me his Hebrew textbooks, which he has borrowed from the parish pastor over in my old parsonage.

How queer life is. It's just as if it cannot think up anything new but goes on making stories, over and over, following the same recipe. Once upon a time there was a young boy called Vemund who had great plans and went to the parsonage to learn Latin. Now his name is Aaron and he has even greater plans, and goes to the parsonage to learn Hebrew.

To me Old Hebrew looks terribly complicated, or cryptic, as Aaron says when he opens the book and shows me a page.

Imagine a language without vowels. No wonder the Bible is an enigmatic book that can be interpreted in any number of ways.

"There it says JHVH," he says, pointing to the four letters of God's sacred name. It's pronounced Yah-weh."

"But how can one know that one must insert an *a* and an *e*?" I ask. "After all, one could just as well use other vowels."

"Exactly," he answers, "that's why the scribes can never agree on what God's name really is. Some claim that it's Yahweh, others that it is Jehovah, and there is a conflict of evidence. Learned quibblers will while away the time this way until all the vowels have been used up and the god disappears into the great nothingness."

"But how is it in Israel today?" I ask. "They can't be using such an ancient language, can they, one where the words may mean any number of things?"

"No, the vowels have fortunately been invented," he says. "And almost every day a new word is created that corresponds to a modern reality. The writers are taking the lead in inventing needed words, and then it doesn't take long before they're picked up by others. The cabby picks up an expression he has long been without, the businessman snaps up another and lets it jingle in the till, the doctor can make a better diagnosis and no longer needs to call all illnesses leprosy. Even the streetsweeper's eyes pop as he sees a new word floating in the dust he whirls up from the ground."

"What if I too could go to the university and take an examination in Hebrew?" I say, staring dreamily up at the hatch to the roof, where a lone star twinkles.

"You can, if you put some effort into it."

But I shake my head. "Grandpa has decided that I shall be a nurse. Then he'll have someone to tend him in his old age. He thinks so anyway."

"There you are," Aaron says with a little laugh. "The old man has found a way to arrange your life as well."

"Yes, I suppose he has. I was so good at tending Father, he says. So now I'd better educate myself and make nursing my vocation in life."

"Hm, that might not be such a bad idea," Aaron says after thinking a moment. "In Israel there is probably a greater need for nurses than for people who've read too much Hebrew."

25 March. Last Saturday I got so furious because of something Urd read to us from her memory book that I jumped out of my chair and left the room in protest.

It was a crude ridicule of our form-master, Nils Haugland, who is the best teacher we have but is despised by the snooty clique in class, who call him a clown and a peasant lout.

His appearance counts against him perhaps, though I don't think so. He is a man of medium height, on the heavy side, with lively movements and slightly greasy hair that he is constantly brushing back from his forehead. We have him in German and Norwegian, and for the two years I've known him he's been one of the few bright points in my life.

He is always dressed in the same rumpled suit, with chalk marks way up on both sleeves, because he likes examples and doesn't stop until he has covered the entire blackboard with them. To make us remember irregular declensions, he invents the funniest things to hammer them into our heads.

One day he writes in big letters straight across the blackboard: *Das Auge, das Ende, das Ohr, das Bett, das Hemd,* all nouns with an unusual inflection. "Ladies and gentlemen, wake up," he says, peering expectantly around the classroom. "Give me a suggestion of how to remember these five nouns, which gang up on us and refuse to behave as they should. No suggestions? That's sad, because then I have to think up something myself, and I always like to have some help. Now listen, we have to come up with something that can unite them, so that they stop being a curiosity and follow a rule.

"We all have a bed, right? *Das Bett,* that dear fleabag, which is so good to stretch out in when the night comes. What is it that we always have with us in bed every night, can you tell me that? Oh yes, *das Auge,* naturally, or *die Augen* – unless we are just as one-eyed as the Cyclops! And what more do we have with us? Oh yes, *das Ende.* Oh, I'm sorry, shhh, shhh, we don't talk aloud about that. But *das Ohr,* there is a part of the body that can be mentioned in good society. And what are we wearing when we crawl under the feather quilt? Make a bid! Of course, *das Hemd,* the nightshirt or the shift, unless we are shameless enough to sleep naked. See, there they are, all five of them lined up: *Das Auge, das Ende, das Ohr, das Bett, das Hemd.* Just remember that they follow the weak declension in the plural, which is usually not good form among neuter nouns."

When he has finished his lecture the class as a whole is amused, only the trend-setters groan and refuse to join in the fun. They are hypnotized by his rumpled suit and his greasy hair and hasten to send out signals on how the inner circle looks at things. One by one the insecure pupils desert, until I and a couple of other blockheads are the only ones who let themselves be seduced. But we still do not dare hold up our hands when he asks questions of the class, because then we would be class enemies and paragons of virtue currying favour with the peasant lout.

But the lout doesn't let on, he quickly distributes our exercise books and asks us to sharpen our pencils.

"A galloping little grammar quiz, ladies and gentlemen, what do you say to that? It may come at an inconvenient time, but we have to find out if the message has sunk in, you know."

Then he fills the blackboard with problems, turns around, wipes the chalk off his sleeves and rubs his hands.

"Get going, folks, you have exactly twenty minutes. Ready, steady, go! This is a race to beat all races, now you have a chance to go places!"

When he looks for something in the corner cabinet, he sometimes knocks on the door and calls "Come in" before opening. He's just being waggish and merry, but the snooty clique is a priggish sect that doesn't appreciate practical jokes. He's a clown, of course, there's no doubt of that! But he's an intelligent and conscious clown, and that's something altogether different than putting your foot in your mouth and being unintentionally funny.

Urd is offended with him because he doesn't cater to her, even though she's the best in class and writes altogether superb essays. By contrast to my essays, which he often reads in class and praises, but never can give a better mark than C+ or B−. They are too complicated and original, he says, rummaging in the bunch for Urd's essay, which has received a B+ and is such that every composition teacher has to fold his hands and chime in with hallelujas and amens.

When he calls out the names of Urd and me from his register, he cannot help teasing us because of the confusion surrounding our names. After the name change of 1951 we are called Sand, of course, but every once in a while I forget myself and write Idun Hov on my copy books. Urd calls me Finelotte and herself Thrinebeth, and I call her Urd, but in the register it says in black and white that our names are Kathrine Elisabeth and Josefine Charlotte Sand. *Punctum finale*, the cat's in the alley.

Quite a few puns and wisecracks can be got out of this mess, and Senior Master Haugland does not hold back. Lately he has started calling us Scylla and Charybdis, after the two sea monsters that were lying in wait for Odysseus in the Straits of Messina. If he managed to avoid one, he ended up in the jaws of the other, there was no getting around them. As far as I know, I'm the terrible Scylla with her six heads, whereas Urd manages very nicely with just one head. She's Charybdis, the insatiable gorge that devours learning three times every twenty-four hours and spews it out faultlessly in her essays and her German retellings.

When he really likes to tease us, he performs a regular ballet in the corridor to get past Scylla and Charybdis with life and limbs intact. It's nothing but playfulness and lively fancies, and I won't stand for Urd exposing him to derision in her memory book. Ridiculing him for his heavy-set figure, making fun of his clothes and mimicking his dialect, which betrays that he comes from some valley or other. After all, her own father also came from the country, he too was a peasant lout, has she forgotten that? Or perhaps she remembers it all too well and hasn't yet ceased being ashamed of him?

On Saturday she was truly infamous, and the aunts immediately began to put their heads together and whisper that our form-master has unnatural proclivities.

It's true that he is very physical and may take it into his head to put his arm round a pupil when the mood is right, or poke us with a playful forefinger to see if we are ticklish. But he does it in such a funny way that one has to have a pretty dirty mind to see anything wrong in it.

I surely wish that old codger over in the Ark would be just as pure and stop pursuing me in such a revolting fashion.

7 April. By the way, my friendship with Aunt Dora has improved lately, since I began to run errands for her. Mostly it is hats that have to be delivered, but once in a while there are also bills that I have to drop in people's letterboxes.

It always takes place in the late afternoon or in the evening when it's getting dark. Before I set out, she admonishes me to take good care of the letters and make sure they are delivered without anyone being aware of it.

I don't see why it has to be done so secretly, but there must be some reason. Perhaps they are people who have bought hats and refuse to pay, so it would be embarrassing for them to run into me. I don't know; I just do as she says, give a good look around, hurry over to the letterbox and drop the envelope through.

I don't get paid for going the rounds, nor do I expect to. But I do wonder what the point is of this delivery service, since she could just as well put the letters in the post. Maybe the answer is that she wants to save the postage. Aunt Dora is terribly greedy in little things, well, in big things too for that matter.

When I get back she questions me on how it went, and I tell her the truth – that the letter has been dropped in the right letterbox and no one saw me. Then she smiles a curious smile and says she hopes she can trust me.

"This is only between you and me," she says; nobody needs to know that I deliver bills for her.

"All right," I say, promising to keep mum. Aunt Dora has so many strange ideas, all about equally strange.

But what if she knew how scared I get when she gives me a bill to deliver! I have violent palpitations, and as I approach the letterbox I feel like fleeing, or tearing the letter to pieces. I know it's stupid, but I feel as if I've got into mischief and am about to commit a crime.

26 April. Something unexpected has happened, and I feel so elated that I'm all the time humming a song that's very unpopular in this house. Grandpa would probably not feel very kindly toward me if he heard what kind of song it was.

But let me explain. Wednesday last week Aaron and I were supposed to go to a meeting in the Ark, the usual Wednesday meeting that we had better not miss, though it's just as voluntary as the summer service at Sandane!

But the previous day Aaron came over to me in the school yard and told me he was going somewhere else. There would be someone there who was eager to meet me, he said, so it would be great if I could join him.

We left home separately to avoid arousing suspicion and met in front of a big grey apartment house in Skipper Street, as we had agreed beforehand. We went through the gate and across the courtyard, and entered a hall where the Workers' Association holds its meeting.

There was no meeting that evening, but a small group of seven or eight men get together there now and then when they want to discuss something. One of them is the janitor, and therefore they can let themselves in whenever they like without any interference.

The seven men (plus Aaron) belong to the left wing of the Workers' Association and hold a rather critical view of societal developments. They're not communists or revolutionaries, but something more like anarchists or utopian socialists. As far as I understand, it is their dream to strengthen the labour movement from within, holding on to the old ideals and ensuring that the idea of brotherhood won't be lost in the general urge to get ahead at the cost of others. They have a vision of a better and more beautiful world, but at the same time they are realists who do not believe it is possible to bring heaven down to earth.

They received me in a friendly way, almost gallantly in fact, and when I offered to go to the kitchen and make coffee, they pushed me down on a chair and said they didn't need a maid. I was a guest this evening, they said, and they would like to make a little fuss over me. I noticed that they had confidence in me and regarded me as one of their own. Everybody spoke his mind freely, and no one thought I would go straight back to the ship owner's house and report them to Grandpa.

Six of the men in the group are well up into their forties, and only the seventh one is relatively young. Not the same age as Aaron and me, but roughly ten years older, by my reckoning. He was the one who had said he would like to meet me, and as we said hello to each other I was rather curious to know what he had on his mind.

His name is Arne Langenes and he is an engineer with the National Railways, but in his salad days he was a worker at the Sandane Machine Shop. He is a quiet and taciturn fellow, so it took a while before he got going. But gradually he overcame his shyness and became almost eloquent. Well, he had been in the Resistance Movement during the war, he said, and was the fourth member of the covert group that blew up the machine works in the autumn of 1944. At that time he was barely eighteen, and thanks to his youth he was the only one who was pardoned. My uncle, Steingrim, and the other two were court-martialled and sentenced to death. They were executed a few days later.

He had much praise for Uncle Steingrim, whom he called a fearless, thoughtful and generous man. He was the one who remained in the shop till the last moment to light the fuses, and to make sure of the outcome he waited so long that he had a hand ripped off.

But all this I had no doubt heard, he said, so enough. It was something else he would like to tell me, something he'd had on his mind for so long that it had become a matter of conscience with him.

He had long thought that the brothers, Vemund and Steingrim, were direct opposites, both unyielding and uncompromising in their different camps. But gradually he'd come to understand that they were men of the same sort, eccentric and hard to figure out, but right-minded, genuine and true to themselves to the very end.

328

What he wanted me to know here and now was his overdue gratitude to my father for intervening and saving his life. During the trial of Vemund Hov he had still been so full of contempt for the pro-German pastor that he had been unable to do him justice. He had regarded him as a crackpot and an erudite numskull who couldn't make up his mind and didn't care whether he answered yes or no. Only long afterwards did he come to like this strange man, who didn't bother to defend himself but sat in the dock working against his own interests. And that was why, ten years after the action and eight years after the judicial purge, he wanted to shake hands with his daughter and beg her forgiveness for not having stood up for his rescuer in a more whole-hearted manner.

And one more thing, he said, after reaching across the table and giving my hand a good, hard squeeze. The first day in the courthouse something else happened that he would like to have cleared up. In the middle of the proceedings the door had suddenly opened and a little girl with her school-bag on her back had come rushing into the hall. She looked extremely upset and had something to say that was tearing her apart. But before she was able to speak, someone shushed her and led her out.

"You wouldn't know, would you, who that little girl was?" he asked, giving me a sidelong glance and laughing. "I imagine she's not completely unknown to you."

"Oh no, she's not," I replied, feeling my cheeks flush. "I had done something that sent me straight to the courthouse, something terribly wrong that I could no longer keep to myself. I hadn't done it on purpose and realized how wrong it was only when it was too late. I believed that Father would be punished for it, and that I was to blame if he was sent to prison. That's why I ran up to the men sitting at the judge's table and wanted to tell the truth. But I didn't get that far; someone stopped me before I got there and sent me away."

"Don't take it so hard," he said, making a curiously gentle gesture with his hand, as if he wanted to brush away the eight-year-old tears that filled my eyes. "Let me tell you, no court of law puts any weight on testimony coming from a child. Your statement wouldn't have had any effect on the sentence, take comfort in that."

A weight was lifted off me, and the sadness that had lain heavy upon me since the end of the trial in 1946 let go its hold on me. The miracle had occurred, Father was rehabilitated and had been raised from the dead. He had shed the traitor, and I could confront him without sinking knee-deep in guilt and shame.

The next couple of hours were spent planning the first of May celebration, an affair that didn't exactly take place in silence. The question was whether a real anarchist had any business walking in the mass procession, and what motto he should line up under in case he did. It would be a blunder to march under slogans that had long ago been taken over by the whole population, from the extreme left to the extreme right.

"Mark my words, friends," said a little skinny man with sparkling eyes in a rugged bird-like face. "In a couple of decades even the extreme right will join the procession, so they can dilute our message and divide our ranks, before going home to their villas to burn brush and hang up the dinner jacket and the mink for airing on the veranda."

The discussion was very lively, viewpoint clashed with viewpoint, one rejoinder followed hard upon another, while buckets of coffee were consumed, along with home-made waffles. Once in a while someone would crack a joke and everybody laughed, even if it was rather corny at times. "Don't tell us we don't have a heart," chuckled a hefty eater, stretching out his hand toward the cake dish. "For my own part I'm already good for eight hearts, and here you see the ninth," he said, holding up a golden heart-shaped waffle between two fingers.

Big applause and tumultuous hilarity all round. In good company one isn't that particular, laughing once too many rather than too little. One is always ready to burst out laughing, and it doesn't take much to have people rolling in the aisles.

Before the meeting was over and all went their separate ways, I had time to make yet another new acquaintance. When the discussion had died down and clouds of smoke were hovering over the table, one of the "old-timers" came up and asked if he could sit beside me for a moment. "Johannes Hegna," he said, giving me a rough, bronzed hand. Son of a smallholder from Lower Telemark, anarchist by conviction and in his daily business a locomotive engineer with the South Country Railway.

He had known Uncle Steingrim from the time they were reading for confirmation, he said, they had been friends and fellow conspirators for a quarter of a century. And what things they ever got up to together! At first it came to nothing much more than warm-ups and trial runs, but they rose to the occasion, until one day they were fully trained. In the autumn of 1938 came the cry of distress from the Iberian Peninsula, and they got it into their heads that they had to sign up as volunteers in the Spanish Civil War. They quickly scraped together what savings they had, and by New Year's day they had got as far as Marseille. But they hadn't provided themselves with the right contacts, and ran up against so many obstacles on the way that the battle was lost before they managed to set foot on Spanish soil. When they finally found a ship that was willing to take them across and had paid their passage, they got the sad message: the Falange had won, General Franco was marching into Madrid, and the second Spanish republic was no more. The skipper who was to take them across was a pirate who refused to return their money, and only after a violent brawl did he toss them a few coins. The upshot was that they had to head home, depressed and penniless, and what was worse: a great vision the poorer.

No, he and Steingrim hadn't exactly been lucky with their operations, you could hardly say that. Five years later, in the summer of 1944, they had got ready for a somewhat smaller action, but that didn't turn out well either. They were to have rescued Steingrim's sister from imprisonment in her tyrannical brother's house, and everything had been well arranged, with a place of refuge, horse and cart, and all. But unfortunately it didn't lead to anything, the poor woman put up a struggle; she was so cowed and frightened that she didn't have the courage to face freedom.

"I know that," I said. "I brought her a message once."

"But all good things come in threes," Johannes Hegna went on when he had filled his pipe. "The third time, there was to be a blast at the Sandane Machine Shop, and there was a blast, that's for sure. I guess you could say that this time I was lucky in a way. I had been tagged to be the fourth man in the action, but the day before we were to bring it off I dislocated my shoulder and they had to find someone else. And so I saved my life; it was Steingrim, that enthusiast, who took it upon himself to light the fuses. Alas, that's how it goes sometimes. Coincidences play their little game, and one bites the dust while the other escapes with life and limbs intact."

He maintained a long silence, staring into vacancy, as if he were directing his eyes at some faraway point beyond time and space. Then he roused himself with a start, took a harmonica from his coat pocket, put it to his lips and made some quick tentative runs up and down the scale. The harmonica was so tiny that it almost disappeared between his lips, and he didn't hold it really firmly but just used his fingertips to move it back and forth.

"It has a good sound, considering it's so tiny," one of the men said. "But be careful you don't swallow it."

"Oh, what the hell," someone else said with a hollow laugh. "A harmonica is nothing. It would've been worse if he'd been playing a grand piano."

Everyone laughed, and the musician continued to feel his way, until he hit the right note and began to play old battle songs. The pipes and the tobacco pouches were put away, and the whole flock joined in any old way. One was just humming, another sang out of tune, a third was trailing, but a couple of them had really fine voices and sang loud enough to raise the roof.

As for me, I neither knew the tunes nor the texts, so at first I was just listening. But I've always had a talent for picking up tunes, so that when we got to the second or third or fourth verse, I fully joined in and even managed to add an upper part. And when we got to the hymn itself, "Arise, ye prisoners of starvation", I was the one who led the way, even though I only knew the words of the first line. I didn't give a fig about metre and sang at the top of my voice with fine, rhythmic syncopation: "Ta, ta, ta-ta-ta-ta-ta-ta, ta – ta, ta, ta-ta-ta-ta-ta-ta!" In the end I was so carried away that I raised my hand and conducted with it to make the singers keep time.

I must have looked funny, for suddenly they all started laughing, and there was no more singing. I felt terribly embarrassed and quickly withdrew my hand. I sat looking from one to the other for a while, trying to tell them what there was about this song that made it mine.

And now I go about here singing it to myself every day, when I'm alone and nobody can hear me. I don't sing very loud, and apart from the first verse the wording is still just ta-ta-ta-ta-ta-ta.

But what if Grandpa suddenly popped up like a jack-in-the-box? Then it wouldn't feel so good to be a prisoner of starvation.

4 May. Mother has just come back from the hospital, and it hurts me to look at her. She has lost several kilos, her face has become notably sharp, and the blond hair she always was so proud of has acquired streaks of grey. It's almost incredible that she's only thirty-nine years old, she looks as old as the aunts, who are past fifty.

She has been ill for a long time, ever since last autumn, but Grandpa didn't allow her to go to the doctor. If you have placed your life in God's hand, he says, you must be patient and wait until His hour is come. Then you should commend yourself to His mercy, and it's a sin and unbelief to turn elsewhere.

Every other Wednesday there is a day of healing in the Ark; then all the sick come to the podium so that the director can lay his hand on them and pray God to deliver them from the evil spirit that has caused the illness. Grandpa stands up there like a high priest, praying in a loud voice, reciting passages from the Bible and making conjuring gestures over the spot where the disease is located. The gathering pays close attention, and at regular intervals it gives its response by calling hallelujah and praise God.

I sit in a sort of torpor, and suddenly something happens to me. All the near things become strangely faraway, I'm carried up on a wave of unreality and can hear myself calling out words of praise louder than anybody else. Grandpa says I've got the feel for it, and that the day will soon come when the divine spirit will fill me entirely.

But afterwards, when I get out into the open air, a sudden change occurs. I become angry with myself for catching fire that easily and agree with Aaron when he calls the healing a swindle and a juggling trick. Mother came to grief after all, and got to the hospital just in the nick of time. Grandpa is a bit more subdued, but he goes on as before with his laying on of hands, and there are plenty of sick people who put their trust in him.

But I feel sorry for Mother, who once was so full of life and now looks so pinched and grey. She tries to hide what they have done to her in the hospital, but the aunts buzz and whisper loud enough to make us all well informed. When she was admitted, she had a malignant tumour in the uterus, and now she's been "stripped of her femininity" and hasn't even kept her ovaries.

One day when I had an errand into the entrance hall, I could see her through the chink in the door; she was standing before the large mirror crying, she who never was able to go past a mirror without turning round and smiling with satisfaction to herself. The tears were trickling down her cheeks, and her body was shaking like someone having convulsions. She stamped her foot, as if refusing to put up with what she saw, but a moment later she leaned her forehead against the mirror and sobbed quietly.

Suddenly it looked like our roles had been reversed: she was the helpless child who was in need of comforting, I the maternal arms in which she could seek refuge. I stole quietly up and put my arm round her neck, trying as best I could to tell her a few soothing words. It would soon be better, I

333

said, she shouldn't lose courage; summer was approaching, and then she would regain her strength and everything would be as before.

She turned her head with a start and gave me an almost hateful look. "You lie in wait for me," she cried. "Yes, you do, don't try to deny it! You steal about with your eyes popping out of your head, it's just like having a spy in the house. But look out, I won't put up with it!"

I tried to tell her that I was only going down into the hall to fetch my schoolbag, but she refused to listen to me. For a moment we were screaming and yelling at each other, she about my spying, me about her being unjust. Then I slammed the door and fled up the stairs, without the bag.

But I have pondered it since – she's not completely wrong in her accusation against me. It's true what she says about my being a stranger in this house, I trust no one and give the family circle the once-over with watchful eyes. (The eyes of a spy.)

Aaron is the only one I feel I can trust, but he is also a stranger and already on his way out. What will happen to me when he goes to Oslo to study in the autumn, I really don't know.

9 May. The class has a reading period, and a few hours every day I sit in the graveyard solving equations and turning the pages of my textbooks to see if there is something I haven't covered. I'll be taking my *artium* examination in mathematics in three days, to be followed by one end-of-year written exam after another in the other main subjects.

I'm not worried about the maths, it comes to me by way of the Holy Spirit; the teacher says it's really too bad that I'm not majoring in the sciences. Geometry has always been my star turn; I can see the constructions before me, as in a vision, and get angles and circles down on paper almost without knowing how it's done.

But Master Holm isn't right at all in saying I ought to major in science. What you have the greatest aptitude for isn't always what makes you wiser, you comprehend it too easily and finish too quickly with it. I solve equations roughly the way Grandpa cures sicknesses, as a test of strength or a higher kind of pastime.

But as soon as I get my hands on a text by Goethe or Shakespeare, things get serious. I become lost in thought, forget my surroundings and enter a world where everything is fugitive and changing. It's not like having solved a problem in mathematics, knowing that the result is correct. I'm all wonder and uncertainty, noticing that I've set foot on unknown territory. A process has got started in me that spreads in all directions and can never be completed.

For example: Is Shylock in *The Merchant of Venice* a comic or a tragic figure, I ask myself. Most people no doubt feel he's comic, but I don't quite know what to think. Of course, he's so greedy that he isn't far from being a cannibal, and he deserves what he gets when he's led by the nose in the last act. All the same I feel sorry for him in the end, when Portia reads the sentence and he has to throw up the game. There is a heart-rending air about him as he stands there caught in his own trap, his hair falling over the nape of his neck. His defeat causes him to grow into a great character, while all the rest come to seem like indifferent puppets.

And how about that magician, Faust, who buys happiness and success for himself for twenty-four years, until Mephistopheles comes to get him? If we think of Mephisto as death – and I always do – then, after all, it's the same contract that all human beings enter into. So and so many years of life and happiness, until the time runs out and the price must be paid. Some are granted a longer time and some a shorter, but the conditions are always the same. Even Aaron and I, who have just barely begun to live, won't escape. When we are together, I sometimes feel that a shadow falls upon us, as if someone were standing on the fringes of our happiness, counting the hours.

I've tried to tell him about it, but he just laughs and thinks I've got too lively an imagination. Aaron is the most sunny and trusting human being I know, perhaps because he lived in hiding for so long. When the war was over he stepped out of the darkness and found a place for himself where nothing bad can happen to him.

22 May. I've discovered something about Grandpa, something secret that I wish I had never found out. I almost had a shock last night when the truth suddenly dawned on me. But when I think back I realize it's something I must have known for a long time.

Because I lie in the crack of the double bed or have difficulty going to sleep, or both, I lie awake for quite long at night, listening to the breathing of Signe and Urd, who have grabbed the best places in bed and shut me in from both sides. Last night it was especially bad, and I heard the clock downstairs strike twelve before I had managed to fall asleep.

Finally I decided to go down into the kitchen and make myself a cup of warm milk with honey, it's usually a good medicine for insomnia. I was able to get out of bed without the others noticing, sneaked out the door and down the middle stairway on tiptoe. It's quite difficult to get to the kitchen after Grandpa closed the door between the bedrooms, and it doesn't make it any easier that all lights in the house are turned off at bedtime, which is half-past ten. The middle stairway is like a precipice in the pitch-darkness, and once you're safely down you have to grope your way through three night-dark rooms before you finally get there.

The door between the dining room and the kitchen was ajar, and I was about to push it open when I heard someone on the kitchen stairs. I withdrew a few steps, but not so far that I couldn't keep a lookout through the chink in the door. The small light over the stove was on, so it wasn't difficult to see who it was. Still I was startled, and could barely believe my eyes. It was Grandpa, sneaking along in nothing but his nightshirt – he doesn't use pyjamas, but has white nightshirts, with tails and red edging, sewn for himself by an old seamstress in town. It was strange to see him so undressed, being always so bundled up, even when he is on a full-evangelical holiday at Sandane.

Quiet as a mouse, I saw him cross the floor and through the door to Ruth's room. I was so embarrassed that I wished myself far away, but felt paralyzed and couldn't budge. The clock in the dining room struck the half hour and the quarter hour, and I was still listening to the sounds coming from in there. The mumbling and the groaning from Grandpa, the thin, whimpering voice of Ruth, and the creaking of the bed boards which went on and on and would never end.

At long last I seemed to wake up and come to my senses. Grandpa and Ruth are sweethearts, I said softly to myself, as if it was something I had only arrived at after long deliberations. Or perhaps not exactly sweethearts, after all. Perhaps it's only Grandpa who insists and has his will, while Ruth gives in and lets it happen.

I didn't get round to making myself any warm milk with honey, nor could I get any sleep for the rest of the night. I lay there thinking back, remembering all the signs that ought to have told me what the situation was between Grandpa and Aaron's young, attractive mother. The locked door between the bedrooms, Grandpa's many quick visits to the kitchen, his hand that chanced to brush her in passing, the glances he gave her from the corner of his eye, or that suddenly flashed at her. And Ruth's bashful behaviour in the house, her self-effacing chores, her small cautious smile, her sudden blushes, her flinching eyes that looked elsewhere.

I don't think I'll say anything to Aaron about what I discovered last night. Either he knows and doesn't need to be reminded of it. Or he doesn't know and will be at least as horrified as I am.

I'm almost certain he knows about it. That's the reason he wants to emigrate to Israel and tries to persuade her to go with him.

11 June. The exams are over, and I don't care a fig anymore about the requirements, whether they're called obligatory or general readings.

But I've become so used to sitting in the graveyard in the afternoon that my feet take me there of themselves. Sometimes I bring books with me that I've borrowed at the library and do not dare show anybody at home. At other times I take along the memory book, for I never tire of reading what is written on the first seventy-four pages. I'm constantly discovering new things, as if a great number of unknown persons are hidden in the gaps between 1917, 1934 and 1944.

I sit under the old oak on the small hill, where Father and I used to tend the grave of the Moluccan Princess at one time. The stone where it said *Emigravit* has been removed, and the little coffin of my namesake sister has been moved over to the family plot at the other end of the grounds. The burial plot of the Sand family is the largest and grandest in the entire cemetery, fenced off in the most approved fashion and with a tall, polished marble stone where for the time being there are only two names: *Augusta Sand, born 1882, died 1919*, and *Josefine Charlotte (surname unknown), born 1935, died 1935*. But just wait, the tombstone looks greedy, it's nearly two metres tall and sizes itself up in preparation for devouring us all.

I can't help giving a thought to Father, lying quietly and meekly under his tombstone in Our Saviour's Cemetery in Oslo. Now everyone must be satisfied, I think to myself, he has made himself invisible and sunk into the ground for good. He can no longer get angry or go against the crowd, annoy the parish council, sing solo before the altar or give odd sermons; and above all, he cannot associate himself with the enemy and turn into a traitor.

But once in a while I just cannot restrain myself and whisper his name in an especially urgent way, to raise him from the dead. The place is Our Saviour's Cemetery, but I can see him coming sort of from nowhere and stop before the grave, like his own *Doppelgänger*.

One-time parish pastor, he reads on the gravestone, and though he has his back turned toward me, I can see that a humorous expression crosses his face. "Hm, 'one-time'," I can hear him mumble, and the chuckle that I know so well blends with his mumbling. "Well, well, old friend, it's all right," he says forgivingly. "Where you're now lying you can hardly be anything but one-time."

What has happened to the other inscription, the one his little daughter daubed with blue paint at one time, I have no idea. It must have been erased long ago, either by the gravedigger or by wind and weather. There is no longer any gravestone where it says *Emigravit*, apart from the monument to Albrecht Dürer, somewhere in Germany.

But I take a sacred vow at this very moment, more precisely on 11 June, 1954, at 3.22 p.m: When I come of age some day I'll give Father a new gravestone, where he's no longer "one-time" but has found a means of escape.

16 June. Today the examination results for the *artium* degree were announced. Aaron received A in three written subjects and the rest all B's, even in New Norwegian, where he had expected a C at most.

Lively discussions and much patting on the back before the bulletin board. Aaron is well liked in school and so superior in all subjects that no one begrudges him the fine results. Even Vidar (Nicce) came over and slapped his shoulder and congratulated him, though his own marks were plainly below average. Vidar is bright, there's no question of that. But because of "systematic bad luck", as he says, he managed to garner only four B's and one C. (Unsystematic bad luck, I would call it, for despite everything he got only that one C.)

I must not forget to mention that I got an A in maths, when the results for fourth-year students were put up later in the day. As I stood slightly apart, waiting for the crush before the bulletin board to thin out, I had a distinct sense of my loneliness in the class. Nobody came up to congratulate me, or even just to tell me what marks I had received. I was nothing to them, and nobody saw any reason to envy me or even to compare herself with me. While the others were embracing one another, crying, comforting or exulting, I stood in my corner completely unnoticed, a spectator to it all.

I have no idea what they think of me in class, if they think anything at all. Today they probably felt that I was supercilious, because I was in no hurry to get to the bulletin board and see the result. They do not know how natural I find my place on the fringes, from where I've always watched people going about their lives.

What's the matter with me, since I've never had any friends? I ask myself. Well, no enemies either, for that matter. The girls in class talk over my head and past me, even if I am so close that they could stretch out their hands and touch me. Only when they need to solve an equation or translate a German poem, do I emerge from invisibility. Then they gather round me in a circle and lean on me with their many-headed attention. For a brief moment I feel the whiff of their breaths and the sheltering warmth of their bodies; then the problem is solved and I vanish into thin air, like one of those gases that are lighter than H_2O.

It's my own fault, I know that very well. I'm an aerial spirit, a living vanishing act that cannot be grasped. I move away and erase my tracks almost without my own knowledge.

It began already in the lower grades of elementary school, when I was the scapegoat of the Hov family, the chubby little Nazi kid who had to endure all the words of abuse that no one dared throw at Vidar and Urd. Oddly enough they managed to go free, though they too had Hov for their surname and a father who was a traitor. As if by a secret law of nature, they rose in the terrain, while I was their shadow, trampled by all who dared enter their circle of light.

And later, when the teasing stopped, something else came in-between. When the school bell rang it jarred on my ears like an ominous alarm, and I hadn't a minute to lose if I was to get back to my father's sickbed (or deathbed) in time. I must've been something of a phenomenon as I rushed out of the school gate and straight through the flock of pupils. I never said where I was going, nor was it necessary. There was an odour about me that cried "out of my way" and quite automatically caused the flock to scatter. Not an odour of youth and freshness and freedom from care, oh no, but of sense of duty, sadness, sickness and death.

And if there is one smell that isolates and that nobody wants to get to them, that must be it. Out of the way – a thirteen-year-old girl rushes home from school, her back hunched and her hair flying, as if the speed and anxiety could by themselves keep the angel of death away. But no, the end result was that she lost the race and got there too late anyhow. One day when she was delayed on the way home, her father was dead when she arrived, and the smell of grief and negligence stuck to her for good.

22 June. Great to-do in the house: Gore and Nicce have been "unmasked" and "caught red-handed", as Aunt Dora says.

Her tongue didn't rest for a second while we sat at the dinner table yesterday, and Grandpa was so worried that he forgot to say grace. The two offenders had to get by without food, being locked up in separate rooms so they could ponder their deeds. Nicce in Grandpa's office downstairs, Gore in the boys' room upstairs.

Aunt Dora had suspected them for a long time, she said. It wasn't as it should be that two young men who had previously looked askance at each other had suddenly become such great friends. Nor did she like the way they dressed, their silly hairstyles, or the jewellery they were wearing round their necks. One had to be deaf and blind not to figure out what was going on between them. The lustful glances they gave each other, their flippant talk, a body language from which any decent person would turn away.

But now, as stated, they had been unmasked and caught red-handed. In the middle of the morning, in broad daylight, she had seen them walk hand in hand in the town park just like a pair of sweethearts. And when she followed them at a considerable distance, all her misgivings were confirmed. The shameless fellows had stopped three times to give each other a hug, under the very noses of respectable people walking by. What they did in more shady places, nobody could know of course. But, but – it wasn't hard to guess.

Grandpa bowed his head over his plate and didn't say a word for a long time. For once he appeared completely perplexed; indeed, he was so strangely subdued that one could almost believe it was *he* who had been exposed and caught red-handed.

Aunt Dora continued, slowly and pedagogically, to work on him in faultless language, and in the long run he couldn't act as though nothing had happened. Suddenly he got up from the table, threw his napkin down and said he would give the hotheads a grilling on the spot. Just wait! Take it from him, there would be no more strolls in the park with fingers interlaced. He would take them by the scruff of the neck, he would, and send them so far away from one another that they couldn't give each other as much as a little finger!

Now the storm has subsided, the two friends are no longer roommates, and Grandpa has already taken care of the matter. Vidar (Nicce) is leaving for Bergen in a few days to take a preparatory course before applying for admission to the School of Commerce. Gore is going to Oslo on more of a gamble, but the idea seems to be that he will begin the study of law in the autumn. Grandpa has provided lodgings for them both, but only Nicce will receive a monthly allowance.

"That pighead Gore will have to support himself," Grandpa said angrily when he was done with "lambasting" him.

I haven't been the fly on the wall, of course, so I cannot say for sure what the lambasting was. But from various hints and leaks from the three who were involved, I work out that it went roughly like this:

Nicce, that sly fox, tried at first to play the innocent victim and put the blame on Gore and his American immorality. When that didn't lead anywhere, he promised to mend his ways and went down on his knees to show how sorry he was.

Gore, on the other hand, held his own and refused to be cowed. He drew himself up and protested, and was so adamant that Grandpa didn't get anywhere with him. He could manage very well without that rented room in Oslo, and he didn't need any financial assistance. He would find a place to stay by himself, and as soon as possible get a job that made him independent of the family.

30 July. Back in the graveyard again, where I'm breathing a sigh of relief that the month of July is ending. It has been the saddest summer I can remember, next to the one three years ago, when I was prowling about on the gravelled paths in Our Saviour's Cemetery.

Worst of all, I've been missing Aaron, who left for Oslo right after Midsummer Day and will be home for the holidays on 8 August. The parish pastor got a summer job for him at the University Library, where he's now been padding about for more than five weeks, wiping the dust off old folios (as he calls them).

I haven't heard anything more from him than what was in the collective letter received by the family about the middle of the month. It has been hard being without a word of love from him, but that was our agreement before he left. We wanted to see if we could stand being separated, for that is just what we shall have to be during the next couple of years after he goes to Israel.

Some wise person or other has said that absence extinguishes a small glow but makes a great one leap into flame. So, time will tell whether it is a great or a small glow that we carry in our hearts. For my own part there's no doubt. If I didn't know it before, I do know it now, that for me it's Aaron and no one else, for life. And I'm not anxious about seeing him again. I think that his glow, too, has used those six weeks to grow big and strong.

Because of Aaron's absence I've been all alone at Sandane this year. Yes, I do say all alone, despite the fact that there have been bigger crowds out there than ever before.

First, the Ark had its annual celebration, and that was the worst of all. Ånon Sakariassen was constantly after me, though I tried to give him a wide berth by taking myself off when the games began. One might almost suspect that Grandpa plans to make a couple of us. He constantly takes me aside to tell me what a solid and enterprising fellow the young Sakariassen is.

Young Sakariassen, he said. Ha-ha, I really must laugh! He is thirty-six years old and nearly bald, and besides he smells bad and has a potbelly and a sickeningly limp handshake, so it is like taking a piece of raw beef into your hand when he comes to say hello.

But he is a good businessman, Grandpa says, and a faithful servant in the vineyard of the Lord. He has worked up the small family hotel he inherited from his parents into a first-class mission hotel.

All right, he has made good and can call himself a hotel proprietor. But what do I care about Central Hotel? That's the last place I would set foot if I didn't have a roof over my head.

"You and I together will fly," he whispered into my ear once last summer, when he was hawk enough to catch me. Ugh, the very idea makes me shudder! What if I should lose my courage? What if my path in life should be so grey and mean that he were able to catch me for good?

The man is no doubt completely harmless, in any case for external use. But when I see him flailing his way up to the penance bench, I feel like pinning a note to his back which says, as it did on the parcels of rat poison: "WARNING! Must not be taken in!" (At home in the parsonage when I was small, I didn't understand what was intended by saying that the pack mustn't be "taken in"; I thought it meant that it mustn't be kept inside the house. Father had a good laugh when I came rushing into his office to tell him about the dangerous poison that was lying in the kitchen cabinet and would soon exterminate us all.)

While I'm touching on this affair of the good laugh, I mustn't forget to tell how "young Sakariassen" made a fool of himself at one of the revival meetings this year. I had to hold my hand before my mouth to check a loud fit of laughter, and when I peeped between my fingers I could see that there were also others who found it hard to restrain themselves.

When he gets up to testify, he's so puffed up with sanctimoniousness that he almost breaks in the middle. He pants like an over-worked nag, gasps for air, and is in such a hurry to spread the glad tidings that he trips over his own words, forgets what he wanted to say and occasionally produces a Spoonerism. He has said many weird things before, but at the beach meeting this year he surpassed himself.

At the outset he stuck to the usual jargon, and everything went as it should. It was suffocatingly hot in the chapel, the atmosphere was drowsy, and I could see that some of the older people were about to doze off. But suddenly he became inspired, worked himself up and spoke faster and faster, until passages of Scripture were gushing from every buttonhole.

"Paul, my friends," he said, brandishing his arm like a conjurer. "Paul, my friends, was a great man who had to tolerate both being snobbed and mucked. No, no, what am I saying? I mean mucked and snobbed, mucked and snobbed!"

It stands to reason that I can control my enthusiasm for the man; the only thing he can tempt me to is hysterical laughter. But I'm very careful not to say anything nasty about him in Grandpa's hearing. When he praises young Sakariassen, I just answer "hm" and "uh-huh", nod piously and act as if I'm playing along.

I don't like to deceive Grandpa, but I do it in sheer self-defence, in order to divert his attention from the love of Aaron and myself. I don't dare to imagine what would happen if someone over in Strand Street got wind of our plans for the future. We wouldn't get off as easily as those two sinners Gore and Nicce. Grandpa would have to invent entirely new compass points if he were to succeed in sending us as far away from one another as his holy wrath desired.

5 August. The countdown has begun. It's at this moment three days, two hours and twenty-four minutes until Aaron will get off the train and be home again. (Assuming the train is on time!)

I'm sitting on the little hill, under the oak, as usual. We've had a dry, hot summer, the leaves on the tree are already brown at the edges. It has also been hot inside me, but there has been no drought and no sign of autumn.

Today I brought along the little notebook I was writing in during Father's illness, just a few days before I returned from school to find him dead. Because one side of his face was paralyzed, his speech was very unclear, and since he wasn't quite clear-headed all the time, it was difficult to understand what he was saying. For long spells he would fall back into a semi-slumber, before awakening with a start and picking up the thread with a presence of mind that astounded me.

He must have known that the time was short, because he urged himself on, and his mind jumped from one conclusion to another without taking the time to include the middle terms. When I look at my handwriting, I find it to be nearly as incoherent, with half sentences, missing words and scrawls that are almost undecipherable.

I don't understand much of what is written there, even when I'm able to make out the writing. All the same it gets something started inside me and gives me something to think about. When the text becomes too difficult I read it slowly once more, taking comfort in what Father said on one of our walks, while he was still quite lucid:

"It's what we do not understand that makes us wiser," he said, "because it challenges our thirst for knowledge and forces us to go deeper. We live in a grey zone of ignorance, where we are constantly learning something new by drawing elements that are alien to our self into it. What we understand we're already finished with, and it's no longer a source of intellectual growth." (I wrote it down on a slip of paper as soon as we got home and put it away in a secret place, together with some of the rusty nails that were to be kept for a hundred years.)

This thin notebook with twenty-nine pages of riddling talk is the only thing that is left of Father's thought. It was supposed to be the final chapter of the work that he called the *Apology*, and I just barely managed to copy it in the book before it disappeared into the rubbish truck. While he was dictating and I taking things down, I was constantly dying to ask him about something but never got round to it.

I wanted to ask him why he called his book an apology, when it didn't at all resemble a defence. Quite the contrary, he was all along attacking himself, pursuing his own trial further and further and sparing no pains to break down his self-defence. It was as though he were omniscient, soaring above his own life history and seeing through every error and aberration that had led him into an impasse.

What he says about guilt and shame has made such a strong impression on me that I've read it over and over again until I know it by heart. And since I have just as much of an aptitude for shame as for guilt, it does me good to see how he sheds light upon them and brings them together at last.

To feel shame, he says somewhere, is to see oneself from the outside, with the eyes of others; shame is a sense of honour rooted in pagan thought. Our ancestors could grieve and waste away with shame if they didn't receive satisfaction through blood revenge. Their lives were bound by unbreakable laws; they were in every respect what the clan, the tribe, the family doomed them to be. To be expelled from the community was the same as being an outlaw; it implied utter condemnation and meant nothing less than death for an individual.

The feeling of guilt, on the other hand, is a matter of conscience; it is an inner acceptance of the laws that prevail in a Christian society. The eye that sees has become your own eye. Man has become his own judge and, what's more, has assumed a responsibility and an obligation that reaches beyond the circle of those closest to him. We are guilty of everything for everyone, as Dostoyevsky writes.

After making this clear, he admits to himself that he has been outside society during his whole adult life, or that he has "moved upon the waters", as he calls it. He has been a nihilist who prescribed his own laws, able to say like the God Yahweh in The Old Testament, "I am that I am". And because his creed was "existence" and he was himself "purely", he had been bothered neither by guilt nor by shame.

Most of the *Apology* was written in prison, and toward the end of the five years of imprisonment something must have happened that caused him to look at himself with different eyes. He who had never wanted to submit to any other laws than his own, gave his assent and shouldered the sentence. He who had always gone his own way saw the error of his ways and realized that there existed a society with common obligations. I have no idea what struggles and temptations had shaken him while the Apology was in progress, slowly expanding into a self-examination. Perhaps it was the association with the other prisoners that in the end broke down his isolation and made him take the step from "I am that I am" to "We are guilty of everything for everybody".

345

I believe it was this new insight that finally set him at rest and made his death as peaceful as it turned out to be. The last day I sat with him he was singing almost all the time, with a deep, warm voice, the way I remember it from my very first childhood. And when I returned home the following day and found him dead, I could scarcely believe what I saw: his face was transfigured in a smile, a wonderfully mild and mysterious smile that made his features shine. His hands were joined on top of the bedspread in a brotherly shake, as if they had at last settled something that had long been in doubt.

I have drawn a picture of them here in my memory book, and though it may be superfluous I have written Guilt on one hand and Shame on the other. Lying so close together, they seem to be making peace, as when a plus and a minus in mathematics cancel each other out and make a clean sweep.

7 August. One day, three hours and eleven minutes until Aaron will come (and while I'm writing this, the eleven minutes are dwindling to ten, nine, eight, seven . . .). Our meeting races towards us at a speed that fairly makes me dizzy.

"Happiness has no songs," says a poem I was reading in the library yesterday. It's a fine poem Edith Södergran has written, but this bit about happiness and song isn't true as far as I'm concerned.

Because I've had two parents with great singing voices, I've always been bashful about singing, and only when I'm overcome with enthusiasm do I let loose the joy of singing that must dwell somewhere deep inside my breast. I would rather say: Dejection has no songs; but happiness is full of song, and it cannot be held back.

I'm taking organ lessons with the church organist; he used to know both my parents and remembers their voices from that memorable Easter of 1934, when they sang themselves into one another's soul. He knows about my inhibition, but refuses to take it seriously. Music chooses many paths to get out in the open, he says, but it's always one and the same. Some sing, others whistle, dance, play jazz, make music, or keep time by clapping their hands. Actually, human beings are full of music, and the body selects only a few of all the strings it has to play on.

"Your voice is rather weak perhaps," he says, "and I don't think I'll advise you to go to the opera. On the other hand, you have perfect pitch, and that's no small gift. You can find every note on the keyboard and sight-read any tune, transpose from major to minor and add a second part on the spur of the moment."

I've told him that I sing only when I'm happy, and he says that this is quite natural. Like all music, song is a religious expression, and its true voice is praise. Thank the Lord, he says, that life has gifts for us that make us burst out in exultation.

And here I sit on the hill under the oak tree, exulting in the gift that life has for me, the one that will step out of the train in one day, two hours and thirty-three minutes. I race to meet him at greater speed than the express train of the South Country Railway, and sing our signature tune at the top of my voice, the one that Aaron is in the habit of whistling down the stairway from the attic when the path is clear and I can steal up to him in his Cuddy: Ta, ta, ta-ta-ta-ta-ta-ta, ta, I sing in major and minor, while twirling the little medallion I carry in a chain about my neck, round and round.

The medallion is an old silver two krone piece with a picture of Mother Norway on it, and it has a special history. I got it from Father exactly ten years ago as a reward for something I said one day we had been in the woods picking berries.

The berry-picking at Hov was no pleasure, it was the summer's "villein service", which the little ones went to with hanging heads and heavy hearts. Because Father had been forced to make himself useful from the time he worked in the field as a five-year-old, he didn't want his children to grow up to become sluggards and freeloaders on earth. As soon as the blueberries were ripe we were sent to the woods with a four-litre pail each, and weren't allowed to return home until the pails were full. We roamed about in the wilds for hours on end, devoured by mosquitoes and on the verge of tears from exhaustion, until the sun finally went down behind the hill and the hour of deliverance struck.

Father used to come with us to the woods in the morning to show us the best blueberry patches, but went home again as soon as he had set us to work. One day as he was striding off as usual, stepping over bog holes and pointing here and there in the underbrush, came that historical moment which was rewarded by a silver two krone piece.

"Listen, brats," he said in that special voice of his I could never make up my mind about, whether it was playful or threatening. "Now everybody pick berries into the pail, and nobody into his mouth!"

And as he said it, he bent down and snatched a handful of berries from a blueberry bush in passing and put them in his mouth.

In the evening, as we were sitting at the kitchen table cleaning the berries and scratching our mosquito bites, I glanced at him and said, "Dad, do you know who I am?"

Well, he didn't know exactly, but he would like to hear.

"Okay. I'm the daughter of Nobody."

"What's that?" he said of a sudden; it almost looked as if he was losing his temper.

"Sure," I said. "Today in the woods you said that Nobody picks berries into his mouth, and then you bent down and did it."

I saw some ominous twitches pass across his face and was almost certain that now it was all up with me. But suddenly he burst out laughing, patted my head appreciatively and promised me a two krone piece as a reward.

"This is for Nobody's daughter, as a reward for her sense of logic and her consistency," he laughed, and later, when he was in the humour for it, he often used the name Nobody for himself. "What can Nobody come up with to say in the pulpit today? I wonder if Nobody will be able to take the low G? Here comes Nobody to say good night. Won't Nobody get a kiss on the cheek?"

I'm not sure whether I think the name is amusing or threatening, it all depends upon how I feel. Sometimes I shudder, noticing that an emptiness is spreading inside me. But when I feel like today, nothing can cloud my bright, happy mood. For now the daughter of Nobody has become the sweetheart of Somebody, and I sing ta-ta-ta in all keys while twirling the medallion round and round.

Here end Idun's diary notes, and they were never resumed, apart from a few lines written on 8 June 1955, the same day she returned home from a nearly six-month stay in Denmark: "Grandpa has deceived me, I shall never forgive him! Nor do I forgive myself after what has happened. What is to become of me?"

VII

What Is to Become of Me?

1

When Aaron came home on holiday on 8 August, the house had been turned topsy-turvy. Andreas Sand had just received the promising letter from Ansgar Publishers and was all fired up.

He sat shut away in his office all morning picking and choosing from his big pile of poetic creations. Anyone putting his ear to the door could hear him mumble and hum in there, and every once in a while he would take a turn round the room while reciting a particularly precious stanza in a loud voice.

When he entered the dining room for the meals, he always brought along some hand-picked poems which he read aloud after grace, asking the family members to express their opinion of them.

"*Marvellous!*" cried Aunt Dora, barely waiting till he had finished reading the verse. "*Wonderful, dear Andrew, not bad, pretty good,*" she rejoiced, being so entranced that she used her superlatives in reverse order.

The poet cleared his throat and turned to his other sister, who he knew was more sober and therefore more trustworthy.

"And what do you say, Rina?"

Aunt Rina was in a quandary. She always used to have some words of praise at hand, but after the "unmasking" of her son Gore there had been a tiff between her and the two older siblings. And so she didn't join in the chorus of acclaim and contented herself with staring pensively into vacancy and nodding slightly.

During the reading, Aaron sat in his accustomed place at the foot of the table, listening with an indefinable expression on his face. Idun was keeping an eye on him and felt that something was wrong, but couldn't figure out what it was. Now a smile seemed to brush his lips, now he knitted his brows, or his mouth became twisted with what looked like an involuntary grimace. When Grandfather wanted to hear his opinion, he answered evasively but hastened to add that he didn't know anything about poetry. During the three weeks he was at home on holiday, his attitude to the old man was strained, and when they bid farewell on 29

August, they were never to see one another again.

When Andreas Sand realized that he had been fooled, he went to bed with "the flu" and didn't get on his legs again until well into September. He was inconsolable, complaining loudly that he was a defeated man who would soon follow his life's work to the grave. Before he lay down, he had tossed everything that reminded him of his disgrace into the waste-paper basket, and when he changed his mind and wanted to take back his treasures, the garbage can had already been emptied.

What he didn't know was that most of the papers were still intact. According to the domestic discipline in 24 Strand Street, it was Idun who was charged with emptying the waste-paper baskets and taking out the rubbish, and this time she left the job only half done. Out of concern or sheer curiosity, she had rescued part of the contents of grandfather's basket and hidden it in one of the many secret places she had around the house. One evening she took the papers with her up to Aaron in the Cuddy, so they could look through them together and decide if there was anything that ought to be kept.

"Who do you think could have written that first letter from Ansgar Publishers?" Idun asked, searching through the bundle till she found the crumpled envelope.

"Hm, who knows?" Aaron replied, putting on an inscrutable face.

"Grandpa thinks it must be an enemy he acquired during the war, when he collaborated with the Germans and made good money."

"And what do you think?"

"Me?" Idun said, with a shrug. "What can I think? The only person I know in Oslo who is Grandpa's enemy is my cousin Gore."

"Precisely," Aaron said, smiling slyly. "You said it! Gore has got a job as delivery boy at Ansgar Publishers, didn't you know?"

Idun shook her head and looked completely thunder-struck.

"Yes, it's true. Quite a coincidence, eh? I met him on the street once this summer, and then he told me about the job. By the way, let me see the letter, I would like to take a closer look at it."

He smoothed out the crumpled sheet and started reading it, scratching his head and nodding meaningfully now and then.

"Hm, Grandfather can't have been very sharp," he said, moving closer so that Idun could read too. "Look here, do you think that expression is right? And what about the word order in that sentence there, doesn't it give the impression of being imported directly from the other side of the Atlantic? The spelling is all right on the whole, give the devil his due. But I would like to see a publisher who addresses a mere rhymester in such exaggerated words and phrases. If at all, it would have to be a full-evangelical publisher at its very fullest."

"Anyway, what is your opinion of Grandpa's poems?" Idun asked a little later. "You looked so weird as he was reading them at the table."

"Who wouldn't look weird?" Aaron laughed. "I got out of it by saying I didn't know anything about poetry. I didn't want to be a killjoy. But one doesn't have to understand poetry to figure out that the old man's versifying is sheer nonsense. Poor fellow, he hasn't made the least progress since the time he stood in the Seamen's Church in Brooklyn reading his poem about Peter's fishing."

"But he says it was a hit and that he got a loud round of applause," Idun objected.

"Of course he got applause. Sailors are known to be generous and stand in awe of anything in rhyme. They think of poetry as something that must be highflown, as something soaring in the clouds. The further removed from reality, the better it is."

"But look, there is the 'Ode to *Quietude*' itself," he cried, dipping into the bundle. "A real treasure, the frame must be priceless."

"Too bad the glass is cracked," Idun said, passing her hand over the shipwrecked steamer, which had strayed off course and showed the effects of forty years of lyrical spindrift.

"Go down and tell him the *Quietude* has been rescued," Aaron said. "It might cheer him up and get him on his feet again."

Before sneaking down from the attic, they still rummaged in the bundle for a while, reading a few lines aloud, laughing a little in-between, pulling out fresh clippings and subjecting them to a two-part declamation.

"Good heavens!" Aaron said, dropping the last sheet. "It's so inept that it's almost touching. Just look, here I sit with real human tears in my eyes."

"You don't mean to say that Grandpa is stupid, do you?" Idun said. "He did manage to found an entire shipping firm, you know."

"Who has said he's stupid? He simply bites off more than he can chew and offers convincing proof that poetry requires something besides a smart head."

The last week in August Andreas Sand was to have directed one of the beach meetings at Sandane, but had to call it off on account of his sickness. Since no equally strong leader could be found at such short notice, the meeting was cancelled at the last moment, and the centre remained empty for the rest of the month. Before the janitor went on holiday, he assured himself that all windows were closed and all doors securely locked. In any case, the furniture in the buildings was so modest that there was no reason to be afraid of burglary.

Nevertheless, when he returned it appeared that someone must have got into one of the cottages and stayed there overnight. The bunks had been made, and one of the sheets was soiled in an unseemly way. The window was ajar, the shower was dripping, and a comb with long, blond hairs had been forgotten on the shelf below the mirror.

The uninvited guests had also left some traces in the kitchen and the chapel; in the latter, the penance bench had been removed and the candles on the altar were burned down to the grease-guards. The extra set of keys that used to hang behind the firewood in the shed, was gone, the doors of the main building were unlocked, and the entrance to the chapel was wide open, as if a squall had swept through the room.

While the janitor went round putting everything in order, he wondered whether he should report the matter to the director. But when he found the penance bench on the beach with a bathing towel on it, he made up his mind to wait until he had consulted with the sisters, Dora and Rina. The guests were most likely a shameless young couple who had found the place empty and taken the law into their own hands. There were bicycle tracks in the grass, and an issue of the evangelical magazine *The Spiritual Friend* had been hoisted to the top of the flagpole, where the edifying meditations fluttered wildly in the wind.

No wanton destruction was to be seen neither inside nor out, and the janitor heaved a sigh of relief that things were no worse. Soon he found the keys on one of the benches in the chapel and put them back on the hook in the shed for the time being, while looking about for a safer hiding place.

But the open doors gave him no peace, and he long wondered how the uninvited guests could know where the keys were to be found. Could it possibly have been local people up to some mischief? The times were depraved and wantonness was lurking about, even in the most devout families. Sometimes children didn't take after their parents at all, no, they certainly didn't.

A few days into September, new congregations moved in everywhere and erased all traces. The janitor pushed aside his August visions, and gradually he started doubting whether he remembered correctly when he saw himself come panting up the knolls with the profaned penance bench on his back. As the only witness to the sacrilege, he folded his hands on the quiet and prayed that the Almighty take action and punish the evildoers.

When he raised his eyes to the clouds, he occasionally thought he saw something up there, a big, all-knowing eye that dwelled on *Sandane Full-Evangelical Centre* and observed every little thing that took place down there. It lasted just a moment, then it was gone. He had a question on his lips, but that too was gone before he could formulate it in words.

But the riddle had been solved on a higher level and was no longer altogether mysterious. The big eye had looked down upon this particular spot in the universe and seen what took place there during the three weekdays of 26–28 August. It had seen who went bathing in the nude on the beach, swam a race out to the farthest skerry, and afterwards threw themselves in the sand to fulfil the divine commandment to be fruitful and replenish the earth; seen who it was that raised the penance bench up from sighs and laments and carried it to a place where it got to hear two-part inventions and resounding odes to joy; who turned on the lights in the chapel, kneeled at the altar, exchanged genuine brass rings, and repeated the solemn pledge to stay together and remain faithful unto death.

It had seen who suddenly jumped up from the altar, stood still and listened, stole on tiptoe towards the exit, opened the door and saw the parked car of the janitor by the portal far over at the other end of the grounds; seen who scanned the area in all directions, gave each other inquiring looks, grasped each other's hands and fled in such a hurry that the door of the chapel was left wide open behind them.

3

The autumn of 1954 came, and it proved an agonizing time.

The evening before Aaron went back to Oslo he called Idun up to the Cuddy with the familiar whistle and told her something that was so difficult to say that he wasn't able to come out with it until the very last moment.

He wouldn't remain in the country late enough into the autumn to be able to take his Hebrew examination. His plans had been speeded up, and his departure for Israel was imminent. Already in June he had applied for a visa for himself and his mother, and he assumed that they would be set to go sometime in October. Ruth had been persuaded and was ready to break up after her twelve-year captivity in 24 Strand Street. But shhh, shhh, that was something which had to be kept strictly confidential. If her master and deliverer learned about what she had in mind to do, he would see it as gross ingratitude and move heaven and earth to prevent her from escaping.

Next day he said goodbye without giving himself away, and went off to the railway station with a suitcase in each hand to start the first leg of his long journey. Idun had promised to be patient and wait until she would have a possibility of joining him. People couldn't emigrate on their own until they had turned eighteen, he had told her. And if the family was opposed to it, as many as three years might pass before she could make herself free.

While they were still sitting in the Cuddy that last night, she suddenly burst into tears and was barely able to stop. She wasn't sure whether she could endure such a long wait, so he might just as well break it off now. She was not an altogether reliable person, as he'd better know before he left. It was as though she belonged to another world, was much too suscep-tible and not always capable of separating dream and reality. She would often go about in a trance, conjuring up visions out of nothing and being so absent that she gave a start when she suddenly heard someone speaking to her. How could he possibly trust her, when she didn't know who she was herself and kept the door open to another reality all the time?

She pushed him away and was completely inconsolable, but he just laughed and didn't look at all alarmed. It was not a bad thing to have imagination, he said, and went on to develop the point: "What we picture to ourselves is more genuinely our own than what has really happened to us, just as what we forget runs deeper in us than what we remember and have a clear idea of."

"I'll never forget you," she cried. "I'm only warning you while there's still time. If we ever become a couple, you will be solving riddles and equations with one unknown."

"That's all right," he said, giving her one last embrace. "I'm quite good at solving equations, and this time it may be one with two unknowns."

4

Towards the end of September, when Andreas Sand was sufficiently recovered from his poetic shipwreck to begin to be up, he received an unexpected visit. The visitor was X, an attorney, the town's most sought-after lawyer, a notorious *roué* and man about town. When the housekeeper opened the door, he assumed a commanding posture and demanded to speak with the ship owner. He had an extremely important matter to present and refused to be content with being told that the master of the house was ill. If Andreas Sand declined to see him and the matter couldn't be settled in a friendly way, he would be forced to take legal action.

After some negotiation back and forth the visitor was shown into the living room, where he sat waiting for a long time. Andreas Sand was annoyed by the man's intrusiveness and took his time getting washed and dressed. He felt debilitated after his long confinement in bed and tried to the very end to find a pretext for sending the visitor away. But as he was descending the mid-stairway he perceived to his surprise that he walked with firm steps and that his agitation acted as a tonic.

The attorney was a brisk gentleman in his forties, affable in his manner and dressed with conspicuous elegance. An experienced tactician, he didn't state his business immediately but asked politely about the ship owner's health and gave him a few good pieces of advice for stress and physical wear and tear. Andreas Sand refused to be diverted, and when the overture began to drag on he asked straight out what the visitor had on his mind.

After still a few minutes of idle talk, the attorney at last produced an envelope from his inside pocket, pulled out a folded sheet and handed it across the table to the ship owner.

"Read this," he said, with a wily smile. "I think it will interest you."

While Andreas Sand was reading the letter, the visitor echoed the play of his features, frowned when the other did so, raised his eyebrows, bit his lips and opened his eyes wide in the right places.

"Well, what do you think?" he asked at last, when the ship owner had finished reading the letter and had had plenty of time to digest it.

"This is an awkward business," the ship owner said at last, lowering his hand with the sheet of paper. "I quite understand your indignation, anonymous letters are always a bad thing. I just don't see what it has to do with me and my house."

"You've been ill a long time," the attorney said to smooth things over, "so you probably haven't heard the sort of rumours that are all over town. This letter, I can assure you, is not an isolated instance. I've already been visited by a number of people who have received similar letters and want to have the matter cleared up. Someone or other has morality on the brain and is engaging in systematic extortion. The letters are not mailed in the customary way but carried by an unknown person and placed in people's letterboxes. No one has so far been able to solve the mystery, but yesterday I just happened to be standing by the window and saw who the messenger was."

Andreas Sand was silent, he didn't say anything for a while. He was still as much in the dark as ever, but there was something ominous in the situation that didn't escape his attention. The letter-writer pledged discretion in return for a certain amount being paid to the Israel Mission, and it was common knowledge in town that precisely this mission had his special favour.

"You're not insinuating, are you, that *I* am behind this letter-writing business?" he shouted furiously.

"Not at all, Mr Sand, not at all. But it may be a good idea to go and fetch your granddaughter, the one with the eyes, you know. I would like to have a few words with her in private."

5

While the ship owner goes upstairs and the attorney is taking notes on the back of the notorious letter, the narrative will use the pause to turn back the calendar one day.

On Saturday 19 September, when the family had just left the dinner table, Aunt Dora made a sign to Idun to come with her over to the shop. Here she led her into the back room and put on water for tea while she began repeating the same old story of the low level to which the town's morals had sunk. Idun knew it already by heart and used to listen with only half an ear. But suddenly it struck her as strange that this lament was invariably the introduction to the errands she ran for her aunt.

There was always a hectic air about Aunt Dora when she took her along to the shop after closing time. She paced the floor restlessly and tore her hair, and denunciations that otherwise emerged merely as hints and brief remarks here degenerated to the wildest exaggerations. At such times Idun wondered whether her aunt could be in her right mind, but decided that she was probably just eccentric and a bit too zealous, and left it at that.

But today Aunt Dora was so excited that it almost made her scared. Her manner was eerily electric: her hair stood on end, she never stopped talking, and her eyes gave off sparks. Idun was beginning to fear the time had come to send out fresh bills, when the aunt opened a drawer and took out two light-blue envelopes.

Business envelopes aren't light blue, flashed through her mind as her aunt handed them to her, and all at once she knew for certain that the letters she was carrying around could have nothing to do with business.

"*My sweet girl,*" her aunt began, switching as usual to her own tongue when she wanted to ingratiate herself. "*Here are two letters I wish you to bring round for me. Yes, be sure, it is only bills as usual. Bills of right,*" she added, winking at her messenger in a conspiratorial manner.

Idun measured the distance to the door, having a good mind to run away, but her courage faltered and she held out her hand for the envelopes. While she was shifting from one foot to the other, impatient to get going, her aunt showered her with the customary admonitions: she must make sure to drop the letters in the correct letterboxes, not dawdle at the door, and by all means watch out that nobody caught sight of her.

When they parted outside the shop, darkness had already fallen, and she had to stop under a street lamp to read the names and addresses on the letters. One address didn't mean anything in particular to her; she knew who the addressee was, and it was not entirely improbable that someone or other in his household could have bought something in her aunt's hat shop. But when she brought the other envelope into the light, she gave a start and became so doubtful that she considered tearing the letter to pieces. *Senior Master Nils Haugland*, it read in the somewhat outlandish letters of her aunt's portable typewriter, which she had brought with her from the USA six years earlier.

As soon as she had delivered the first letter, she made a bold decision: she made up her mind to go and ring the bell at her form-master's house and put the letter into his hand. When all was said and done, it was perhaps a completely innocent letter, which he with his highly developed sense of humour would simply be amused by. In any case, she couldn't see herself going behind his back and slipping the envelope through his letter-box on the sly. Besides, he rented an apartment in a villa and shared the letterbox with his landlord, so she had better make sure that the letter didn't go astray.

Master Haugland opened the door himself, and his round benevolent face lit up as he invited her in. He refused to listen when she said she was just delivering a letter, being his student after all; she hadn't become a complete man-hater lately, had she? He was just reading her last essay, he said, and it was not at all to be despised. She had always written interesting essays, although they had so far been a bit chaotic. But now she was beginning to get her material into shape, the assignment she had handed in this time was tip-top, and he wouldn't hesitate giving it an A^+. Just imagine, to conclude an essay with a poem about parting! None of his students had ever brought off anything like that before.

Idun blushed and was dying with embarrassment, but felt that she couldn't refuse his invitation to step inside and have a cup of coffee. While he was rummaging in the kitchen, she stole a look round the little room and was truly touched by how modestly he lived and how messy the place was. She had always assumed that he had a wife, though there was a lonely and neglected air about him in the midst of all his jokes and merry caprices. But after a few quick glances about the room, it was not difficult to figure out that he was an old bachelor. There were clothes and newspapers and textbooks strewn all over, a prehistoric vacuum cleaner stuck its saurian head from under the writing table, leftovers from some dinner were still on the table, and a suitcase sat in lonely majesty in the middle of the carpet, its lid thrown open and displaying an incredible content of tools, shoe-shining paraphernalia, tin cans, light bulbs and electrical wires. The pictures on the wall were good, that she could see with half an eye, but the windows lacked curtains, the shade of the ceiling lamp was cracked, and the furniture was sadly worn and looked as though it had been brought together from several homes.

"Speak of bad luck," he exclaimed as he realized Idun's quandary on entering with the coffee tray. "Here Odysseus uses every conceivable stratagem to avoid the terrible Scylla only to find her suddenly standing at his door. Ooh, he doesn't even dare think about what awaits him! *Abyssus abyssum invocat*," he mumbled cheerily, starting to clear away the leftovers from dinner to make space for the cups. "Oh, wait a moment, I forgot, you're not taking Latin. Anyway, cheer up, let's take a more optimistic view of the situation and say that a joy comes seldom alone."

"I have this letter for you," Idun began, her hand in her shoulder bag, but the master warded her off and said there was no hurry. He poured the coffee, pushed the tray with the layer cake over to her side of the table and apologized for the big inroads that had already been made in it. Some would no doubt call it *gefundenes Fressen* to serve a layer cake from the day before yesterday, he laughed, but there was a natural explanation for it. He had had a visit from some old-time fellow villagers, and according to good rural custom they had to be urged to help themselves seven times before they dared set their teeth in a piece of cake. But then they really pitched in and tucked it away, so that what was left was nothing to boast about.

He hailed from a small hamlet called Iveland, he told her, an attractive and innocent place that only had the drawback that there was a religious meeting house at every turn of the road. If she had paid attention in her Norwegian classes, she would remember that one of the country's tempestuous poets had written a magnificent poem about just this place. Enough said, he had been brought up in the nurture and admonition of the Lord, but for some reason or other it hadn't made any impact on him. He had been lucky enough to escape before being properly chastened, even though his luck had the disadvantage that it drew the maledictions of his family down upon him. It had cost him twenty-seven years of exile to shake the dust of the prayer meeting off his feet and get to where he was today. Whether it was a promotion or a humiliation was perhaps a moot point, he said, giving a quick look about the room. Who knows, perhaps it hadn't been worth the trouble to undergo so many hardships, to end up as a rather dubious pedagogue at an old-fangled Latin school.

"You mustn't say that!" Idun cried. "You're not some dubious pedagogue.

You're the best teacher in the whole school, though there are some who don't understand and try to catch you out."

"But Idun Hov has understood, the only one in Class 5B to do so," he said, glancing at her with a roguish gleam in his eye.

"Don't make fun of me," she said, turning away. "I wouldn't have understood either if I hadn't had a father who – . Well, a father who – "

"No need to explain," he said. "I know the background history, though it took place a few years before I myself got stranded in this merciless coastal town. It has been instructive to me to observe how differently the same circumstances have affected three siblings of nearly the same age. Your brother, Vidar, alias Nikolai, has denied everything and will shortly achieve amnesia. Your sister has chosen the oblivion of perfection and will go far on the path of infallibility. You alone carry your stigmas around with you and do nothing to hide them."

"That's not quite true," Idun said with a faint smile. "I do try to hide them, but they are so obvious that nobody can avoid noticing them."

The moment she said this she felt a wave of nausea coming on, and she realized that she was starting to feel sick. It must be the cake from the day before yesterday, she thought, and to get a better taste in her mouth she swallowed a big gulp of coffee. But she felt that her insides continued to be upset, as if the indisposition sat deeper and was due to some still unknown cause.

"Oh, by the way, there was that letter," he said a moment later, seeing that she again had her hand in her bag. "Perhaps I'd better see what it has to say, though I have my misgivings. It's probably just another complaint about my teaching methods and my lack of dignity and authority.

"Hm, what? My, that's really something," he mumbled to himself as he ran his eyes over the paper. "Ouch, my good reputation, it's no trifles this time, that's for sure. By Jove, it says in black and white that I behave offensively toward my students."

"It's probably just because you sometimes tickle us," Idun said cautiously.

"Oh, you think so?" he laughed, making himself more comfortable in his chair. "Yes, there's something to that, the letter-writer isn't entirely wrong there. Alas, my unmanageable index finger, sometimes it just cannot restrain itself."

"If you think it's me who . . . ," Idun began, but came to a dead stop and said no more.

"It says that the letter-writer is someone who wants my own good, so it

362

could easily be you," he hinted in the same playful tone. "No, no, don't look so scared. If we undertook the sort of textual analysis we now and then do in class, it would certainly become evident that this product cannot have come from the same person who writes wistful poems about parting."

"I only distribute the letters," Idun said evasively. "So I can't say anything about who has written them."

"No, I understand," he said, giving her a thoughtful glance. "But you must be wrapped up in your own dream-world if you don't know what the townspeople have been whispering for the last six months."

"I've heard some hints here and there and understood that there was something. But it was only today that I realized there was something wrong with the letters I had been dropping through people's letterboxes."

"You're certainly no sissy," he laughed, with an appreciative look at her. "Something dawns on you, and you dare to walk straight into the lion's den!"

"At first I thought of tearing up the letter," she cried, a lump in her throat. "But I changed my mind and didn't do it."

"Let me tell you something," he said all of a sudden, after a long silence. "I know perfectly well who is writing these letters, it's what is usually called an open secret. But you have nothing to worry about as far as I'm concerned. I'm not turning a hair and do not feel insulted."

"You don't feel insulted?" she asked, looking at him in surprise.

"No. To tell the truth, I rather feel that the reproof is merited. Because there is some truth in the accusation against me, that cannot be denied."

He got up from his chair and began walking about the room, while mumbling in a low voice and running his hand through his grizzled hair. Suddenly he stopped and clapped his hand to his forehead, as if he'd just had a higher inspiration.

"No, it cannot be denied," he repeated. "The gods know, I've behaved offensively toward my pupils in more than one way!"

"What are you saying?" she cried, opening her eyes wide.

"Listen to me," he said, getting back to himself. "It's not so unheard of, is it, that some old Adam forces himself on a young goddess and abandons himself to profane dreams about her? With his common sense he knows that it's not seemly, that it's both too late and too early. Still, his naughty index finger is itching, and he cannot rest until he's heard those squeals and shrieks that tell him that he can still make an impression – though in a somewhat awkward way."

"Does that mean you'll have to stop tickling us from now on and be just as boring as the other teachers? You won't ever again dance ballet in the hallway to escape Scylla and Charybdis?"

"Oh no, I'll probably have to walk on a tighter rope now, lest the temptation should become too strong for me. But you're gasping for breath, I see, you need a mouthful of fresh air. Go home and tell the letter-writer that she's been detected and should stop her activities before worse things happen than have happened today."

"And one more thing," he said mirthfully as he saw her to the door and helped her with her jacket. "I cannot agree to the deal she proposes at the end of the letter. I'm not a special friend of the Israel Mission, tell her that, nor do I have the five hundred kroner she demands in ransom."

Idun nodded and hurried off, and the last he saw of her was her hunched figure rushing down the stairs, her hand pressed against her mouth.

What he did not see was that she bent over a gooseberry bush at the very bottom of the garden path and vomited profusely.

6

Attorney X. Well, look, there's the carrier pigeon. The Holy Ghost itself, if I may say so.

Idun knits her brows but says nothing.

X. Are you dissatisfied with something?

I. You shouldn't blaspheme. Grandpa would get angry if he heard it.

X. Oh, pardon me, I forgot that we are on sacred ground. But don't worry, no one is eavesdropping. Your grandfather will remain in the upper regions until our conversation is over.

I. I know very well what you want to ask me about, but I won't say anything. You'll have to clear up the matter yourself.

X. It's already been cleared up, nothing more is needed.

I. Then I don't see what you want to talk with me about.

X. (*ingratiatingly*). You run errands for your aunt, isn't that so?

I. Yes, that's true. I'm a kind of messenger in the shop. I deliver new hats and pick up old ones that are to be altered. Now and then I go around with bills, and sometimes also with other letters. If there are any.

X. And you haven't known anything about what the letters contained?

I. How could I? The envelopes are sealed.

X. But don't you think it's a bit strange that your aunt doesn't post them in the customary way?

I. Yes, I have wondered about that several times. It must be for the sake of the excitement.

X. For the sake of the excitement?

I. Well, it's quite unnerving while it lasts, you know. Mostly for me, of course, but also for Aunt. You go with your heart in your mouth and are afraid to be discovered.

X. Your aunt is slightly eccentric, isn't she, to put it mildly?

I. I think she's bored in this country. She's used to places where lots of things are going on.

X. Maybe you would be interested to know how we cleared up the matter?

I. Grandpa said you had seen me yesterday when I put the letter through your letterbox.

X. Certainly. But that simply confirmed what I already knew in advance.

I. How's that? Are there also others who have seen me?

X. No, not at all. You've done an incredibly good job as the Holy Ghost. Pardon me, I meant as carrier pigeon.

I. So how did you know?

X. Oh, we have many methods of clearing things up, and they rarely fail. Tell me, by the way, have you seen your aunt's typewriter?

I. Do you mean the old one from before the Flood which she refuses to part with? Which is as noisy as a threshing machine and lacks several letters?

X. Precisely, that's the one I mean. I imagine there is something wrong with the key for the question mark, for curiously enough every interrogative sentence ends with %.

I. Yes, it's quite funny. We have had many laughs over it in the family.

X. Then you will understand that it hasn't been very difficult for us to find the letter-writer. There are also other peculiarities in the letters that have put us on the trail.

I. I know. Aunt is in the habit of writing "&" instead of "and," it seems to be something they do in the States. And sometimes she changes the word order, or writes *w* where there should be a *v*. But you should ask her instead.

X. I would have, of course. But it looks as though she doesn't feel quite

365

well at the moment. She has had a minor breakdown, according to what the maid says.

I. Yes, she became completely beside herself last night, when I warned her after getting home. So I guess I'll have to answer for both of us.

X. Hm, strictly speaking, you haven't done anything wrong. At least not anything you can be held responsible for.

I. I did say earlier on that I had been wondering. That I had palpitations and felt like a sneak when I was carrying the letters around. Even though I didn't know what was in them.

X. I understand. Your conscience is a bit uneasy, isn't it, you feel as if you were privy to her design?

I. Yes, perhaps, to be quite honest.

X. Take it easy, young lady. Your conscience is your own affair, we don't stick our noses into that.

I. What do you intend to do with Aunt Dora? She won't go to prison, will she?

X. No, we don't plan to deal that severely with her, even though she has engaged in extortion and placed some ugly blots on many people's reputation. But she has to recognize that she has gone too far, and to promise that what she has done will never be repeated.

I. I think you can rely on that. You should have seen her when Grandpa came up and told her who sat waiting downstairs. She has always been a bit queer, but now she's gone clean off her head.

X. Good, she's been taught a lesson, and we won't be pursuing the matter any further. Thanks for the conversation, you may go now. Ask your grandfather to come down for a moment so we can wind up the matter. Tell him we will let ourselves be pacified and that nobody in this house has anything to be afraid of.

7

When Aunt Theodora had confessed and the attorney had promised to show mercy, she shut herself up in the Cuddy and didn't show her face in town even once before returning to the USA, eleven months later.

After recovering somewhat from her shock, she descended from her prison in the attic and began to walk freely about on the lower floor. But she had become so wary that she fled as soon as the doorbell rang, or she heard strange voices on the stairway. The family left her alone and never reminded her of her misdemeanour. Everybody realized that she had succumbed to a fixed idea and was no longer quite sane.

On the face of it she weathered the storm. She even gave a hand in running the house, taking over the management of the kitchen when the family came to lack a housekeeper later in the autumn. But she had become a shadow of her former self, her eyes staring into vacancy and her emaciated body moving stiffly through the rooms; and when someone spoke to her she pretended not to hear, or she answered with a vague shake of her head.

Only Severina, her sister, was able to pierce her armour every once in a while. In the middle of the night footsteps would sometimes be heard on the stairs to the attic, and a moment later the door creaked in the bedroom where Rina was now sleeping quite alone, and the silence of the large, sleeping house was broken by a soft whispering that occasionally increased to sobs and choked screams.

Such nights Idun didn't sleep either, but lay with her ear to the wall listening to how one of her aunts was pouring out her troubles, while the other did what she could to shush her and calm her down. Severina had grown strong now, that was clear, she had the upper hand and was getting even after a lifetime of neglect.

Tomorrow I'll go up to the attic and try to comfort her, Idun thought. What's done is done, I'll tell her; right now things look pretty bleak, but we're here all of us and the world hasn't come to an end. We have both been stupid, I'll tell her. I knew all along there was something wrong with those letters, and the receiver is no better than the thief.

These were Idun's thoughts as she lay half asleep, while time was passing and the voices in the next room rose and fell. What the two of us have been doing was obviously on the borderline, I'll tell her, and wrong, of course. But it was adventurous too, and not something that just anybody would come up with. Maybe we simply wanted to stir up some excitement in this tired and unimaginative small town. And we succeeded – we surpassed ourselves, hitting on something that won't be forgotten very soon. Now every gossip has acquired a good household remedy for boredom. Every time they feel that life is a little drab, all they have to do is to put their heads together and say, Do you remember the letters of the hat lady?

367

Yes, that's what I'll tell her, Idun mumbled one more time, before she turned on her other side and fell asleep.

But when she came down for breakfast the following morning and saw her aunt's stony face, she lost her courage. If she succeeded in catching the other's eye every once in a while, she drew back and quickly turned away. The look in her aunt's eyes was at once suffering and accusing, as though she were saying, You could have stopped me. You should have torn up the letters, or refused to deliver them. Stupid and spiteful child that you are, you may as well admit that you are to blame for the whole thing. You saw that I wasn't myself and that the devil was tempting me. But you carried my shame around and saw to it that the whole town could thumb their noses at me.

8

The month of September was coming to an end and, after a lull of a few days, October came rushing along on the wind, turning the big chestnut tree behind the ship owner's house into a blaze of colour. The autumn was pregnant with new, nerve-racking experiences, and soon something happened that gave the family in Strand Street entirely different things to think about.

During the first half of the month it was Idun's turn to help with the dishwashing after dinner. She would give loud groans at the dinner table, letting on that it was an irksome duty, while privately she looked forward to being alone with Aaron's mother. Neither was particularly talkative, but they got along very well. While plates, knives and forks passed from hand to hand, there arose a secret intimacy between them that was worth more than many words.

On Friday the 9th of October, as Idun was drying the pots, she noticed that Ruth had something special on her mind. This woman, who was otherwise so quiet, appeared strangely agitated and rattled the dinnerware in a way that wasn't like her. She started saying something several times but checked herself and just gave a little cough behind her hand. Idun had already hung the dish cloth on the rack and made ready to go, when the housekeeper shook the water from her hands, dried them quickly on her apron and took an envelope from her pocket.

"Would you be kind enough to do me a favour?" she said, holding out a trembling hand. "Put this letter on your grandfather's plate tomorrow morning when you come down for breakfast. You know, he sleeps late in the morning now and only eats after you've left for school."

Idun hesitated a moment before accepting the envelope. Then she glanced quickly at the superscription, which read ANDREAS SAND in big block letters.

"There's nothing wrong, is there?" she asked, looking anxiously at Aaron's mother.

"No, nothing except that I won't be here in the morning when he asks for me. I'm taking the early train to Oslo at ten to seven.

"Well, Aaron has probably told you," she went on when she noticed that Idun was taken aback. "We're going to Israel at the end of the month, as soon as we get our visas and he's through with his job at the University Library. An old friend of ours has promised to give me a room until we leave. But shhh," she whispered, putting a finger to her lips, "no one in this house must know about it. I'm only telling you, because I know I can trust you."

"Grandpa is going to be . . . ," Idun began, but got no further.

"Yes, I know, I've thought about that, believe me. He's going to be both angry and sad, perhaps mostly angry, if I understand him correctly. But there's nothing to be done about it, this cannot go on any longer."

"You probably have a lot of luggage, since you're moving," Idun said, seeing that Ruth was on the verge of tears and quickly starting to talk about something else. "I could go with you to the station tomorrow morning and help you carry. You know I'm always up before any of the others."

Ruth nodded, and it was agreed. They slipped away early next morning, each with a large suitcase and a good many small items. They had already said goodbye on the platform and Aaron's mother was getting into the train, when Idun raised her voice and said, "Ruth, wait a little, there's something . . ."

"Yes, what is it?" the other asked, turning around.

Idun swallowed and couldn't utter a word. For a moment she was moistening her lips, trying to overcome the nausea stuck in her throat during this period, mostly in the morning. "Ruth, there's something . . . ," she repeated, letting her eyes glide helplessly along the train, which curved and seemed to get lost in the infinite distance.

"Well, say it then!" cried Ruth, who hadn't had a quiet moment until the train started moving. "What's the matter with you, you've become so strange lately."

"Oh, it's nothing," Idun said at last, shielding herself with a smile. "I just wanted to say that you must remember to give my regards to Aaron."

She kept waving long after the car with Ruth's extended hand had disappeared at the bend. Then she shuffled home lost in thought, and managed as usual to be the first to sit down for breakfast.

"What kind of letter is *that*?" her mother asked suspiciously when she saw the envelope lying on the old man's plate.

"Who knows?" Idun replied, putting on her most innocent face. "It was lying there when I sat down at the table. It's probably just some message or other to Grandpa."

9

Andreas Sand took it hard, but in a different way than expected. There was no holy wrath, and the sighs and jeremiads that had been heard while he was confined to his bed were nearly gone. He had become curiously quiet and thoughtful and would stop in the middle of the room as if fallen into a trance, before rousing with a start and hurrying off on some urgent business or other.

On the morning of 12 October he threw off the dressing gown he had practically lived in that autumn and got his best suit out of the closet. At nine o'clock sharp he stepped into the main office on the first floor, where he hadn't set foot in nearly two months. He summoned the manager and asked him to produce all the firm's papers, together with a rough estimate of the total of securities and real estate that the house had at its disposal.

During the next two weeks he shut himself up in his office to pore over these documents, from time to time making notes on a piece of paper. The manager was the only one who was allowed in, and when he came out again his lips were sealed. All sorts of conflicting rumours began to circulate concerning what was in the wind. Now it was whispered that the firm was in financial difficulty and was forced to liquidate, now it was said that the company was riding on the crest of a wave and planning to buy out a competing shipping firm in the neighbouring town. There were even those who maintained that Andreas Sand had taken to shady transactions and was gambling in foreign shipping shares.

None of this had any basis in reality. Andreas Sand had had his fill of devouring ailing companies, and the speculations that were prophetically attributed to him would only be realized by his grandson twenty years later.

What he was brooding over in private were exclusively personal deliberations. His grief at Ruth's departure had gone deeper than anyone might have realized, stripping him of all initiative and reminding him that the time had come for winding up his estate. His activities had taken on a spectral quality, as if his true self had died that morning when he found the farewell letter on his plate, and only his ghost was keeping upright and taking its precautions.

The result of his solitary meditations was the draft of a will, where he named his successor and divided what he owned in shares, bank accounts, bonds and real estate. It wasn't executed until the fall of 1960 when he was on his deathbed, but it was well considered and well conceived in every detail. The manager was to administer the firm after his death, with Nikolai, his grandson, as his right-hand man. But the order of succession was placed within strict limits: the young man would have to go through every step from the bottom up and only take command after an apprenticeship of ten years. The document was transcribed in his neatest handwriting, with his signature and stamp, and concluded with a self-effacing quotation from the Book of Job: "Naked came I out of my mother's womb, and naked shall I return thither."

Aside from one single decision, no step was taken at this time to distribute his assets. But after nine days had gone by, more exactly on 21 October 1954, the business manager was charged with dispatching a six-digit amount to a farmer in Georgia, USA, who was said to be in great pecuniary distress. No letter or explanation was enclosed with the dispatch, and only those closest to him knew that with this action the ship owner was repaying a debt of honour to his elder brother, the freeholder at Sandane, whom he had ruined almost a generation ago and driven from the farm.

When the financial affairs had been put in order, the turn came for the Ark, where he made a clean sweep in the same resolute manner. On one of the last days in October he summoned that untiring confessor of sins, Ånon Sakariassen, and had a long conversation with him in his small private office on the third floor. No one knows what they talked about during the hour and a quarter they were together, for she who stole up the kitchen stairway

371

to eavesdrop could only hear a faint mumbling behind the double door. But when "young Sakariassen" stepped out on the street he was visibly exalted, looking about him with the same gratified air he displayed when, having unburdened himself of his sins in the Ark, he was on his way to the penance bench. The observer behind the curtain in the dining room felt a nausea rising within her, and a shudder went through her when she saw his fleshy posterior wriggle its way down the many steps of the main stairs.

Only three days later, on Saturday 31 October, did Andreas Sand stand forth on the rostrum in the Ark and drop the bombshell. Owing to his age and failing health he had decided to retire as director and hand over the leadership to someone younger and more vigorous. No, no, the congregation had no cause to feel uneasy, he had found a worthy successor, whom he now had the pleasure to install as their shepherd.

At that moment he closed his eyes and, without any perceptible transition, slipped into prayer and carried on an intimate conversation with the beyond for several minutes, as if the gathering below the speaker's platform didn't mean a thing to him. He asked the Almighty to bless his choice of successor and to help and strenghthen the Chosen One to remain faithful and follow the call.

After taking up plenty of time negotiating with the Most High, ending by veritably challenging the deity to do its part, he turned toward the bay window to the left of the penance bench and waved forth the new director who had been hiding there, biding his time as if in the wings of some theatre.

Brother Ånon Sakariassen strode onto the platform on such stiff legs, and with his head held so high, that he was barely able to stop himself and avoid falling over the edge, onto the front row of seats. Andreas Sand caught him by the arm at the last moment and held on to him, until he composed himself and realized his natural limits.

After they had shaken hands on it, and another blessing had been called down on him, he straightened up and gave his inaugural address. He loudly lamented the fact that the Ark's heaven-inspired founder was retiring, it would be no easy matter to follow in his footsteps. But God worked in mysterious ways, and it had happened before that He had shown his mercy and filled a frail vessel with spirit and power.

The Saturday meetings would continue as before with song and music, spiritual guidance, testimony and praise from faithful brothers and sisters. As far as the Wednesday meetings were concerned, the situation was slightly more uncertain; the healings might have to wait until he had familiarized himself with how to handle them and received the right spirit.

"These tools are still full of sin and uncleanness," he declared in a loud voice as he raised his hands, turning them this way and that so that everybody could see how unclean they were. "But God is good, and He will provide and fill them with curative powers. Be cheerful, my friends, do not forget that there is someone who looks after us and makes everything turn out for the best.

"Oh, what is this?" he cried of a sudden, opening his eyes wide. "Praise God! Already I feel something happening: a current of grace is flowing through these hands, making sin and sickness go away. Verily, a miracle has taken place! God is good, he has whispered in my ear that we can begin the laying-on of hands already next Wednesday. Praise God, friends, halleluja and thank the Lord! Come on Wednesday, every soul among you, dear brothers and sisters, do not hold back. Remember the Master's words, 'Come unto me, all ye that labour and are heavy laden, and I will give you rest.'"

While the newly hatched director was commending himself to the meeting, Andreas Sand stood loyally beside him without moving a muscle. His hands folded, he was staring into vacancy, and it was impossible to decide whether he was satisfied with what he heard, or whether the man's bombast appeared excessive, even to an evangelical ear. The one time he made as if to interrupt, it just came to a faint twitch of his shoulder. Maybe he remembered his own religious exercises on the ridge of the roof while the Ark was still young, and it was important to recruit new members and overshadow the other places of worship.

When "young Sakariassen" lowered his voice and finally took time to breathe, Andreas Sand hastened to propose that the meeting be concluded with the song "The promises shall not fail". The next moment the organ began intoning, the accordions inhaled deeply, and lively fingers took to running over the guitar strings.

Idun sat in a funk in the last row. It was getting dark around her and she had a feeling that Doomsday was near. Half asleep, she was waiting for that terrible refrain, which was invariably sung triumphantly and with a will:

Heaven and earth shall burn, heights and rocks vanish,
but he who believes shall find, the promises never fail.

373

10

A few days later, on Friday 6 November, three family members are waiting for her in the entry when she returns from school. They look so much in agreement that they resemble a veritable Trinity, and that's never a good sign. The usual thing is that they plot against and stir up one another, and when two of them put their heads together it's mostly to keep a third party out of it.

"Josefine Charlotte," they say as if with one mouth, nor does the over-careful pronunciation of the two Victorian names bode well. "Put your schoolbag away and come with us into the living room, there's something we want to talk to you about. But hurry up, please, before we are disturbed."

The three women march into the living room and settle on the sofa below the large picture of *The Last Supper*. Idun follows reluctantly, full of anxiety and misgivings. She sees that tea and sandwiches have been set out on the coffee table, but nobody asks her to sit down, and a quick glance tells her that there are only three teacups.

"You must have eaten your snack at school," Aunt Dora began, "so we thought you wouldn't want anything. Anyway, you don't have much of an appetite these days, do you?"

Idun withdraws into herself, knowing what is coming. It had to come of course, she thinks dully. After all, the secret she is harbouring cannot remain hidden; it's constantly growing and will sooner or later betray itself.

"As you know, I'm the one who sorts the laundry after Ruth abandoned us," Aunt Dora goes on, drumming on her plate with her index finger and making it clink softly. "Why do I mention that? Well, just guess."

"Dear Dora, stop beating about the bush," Mary begs. "You'd better speak plainly."

"*Very well*," says the aunt, trying to catch Idun's glance. "I've noticed something lately that has made me wonder a little. You haven't had your period since the middle of August. Well, you probably know that I keep accounts and have the dates written down."

Idun is silent, a hopelessness steals over her. She keeps standing in an oddly twisted position, staring at the old picture over the sofa, where there are thirteen at table and the shadow of the traitor falls ominously across the tabletop. "That thou doest, do quickly," it flashed through her mind. "That thou doest, do quickly!"

"And then there is the fact that you've become so skinny this autumn and hardly eat anything at all. Can you explain that to us?"

Still no answer, only a deep sigh that may mean anything, rebelliousness or a first sign of admission.

"And what's the reason you rush to the bathroom and vomit in the morning? We've heard you, all of us, and wonder why. Can't you take the food in this house any more, or what?"

"Dora, let's get it over with," says her mother. "Keep in mind who will be coming in a few minutes."

"Right you are. We've sent for the family doctor, and he may be here any moment. Your grandfather is informed and he's extremely worried, I can tell you. As if he didn't have enough trouble already."

"Do with me what you like," Idun suddenly cries, her voice breaking. "I'll be going away soon, and you'll never see me again."

"Well, listen to that!" Aunt Rina says, sticking her nose into the matter. "Where would you go, in your condition?"

"Aaron has promised to come and fetch me," Idun cries, a lump in her throat. "It was the last thing he promised me before he left."

"We-e-ll, there we got an admission out of you anyway," Aunt Dora remarks. "You think, perhaps, we don't know how you were carrying on at Sandane during the summer?"

"A fine state of affairs," Aunt Rina chimes in. "We know everything there is to know, you can be sure. Our janitor has kept his eyes open, and what he has to tell is anything but trifles."

"If I were you I wouldn't rely too much on Aaron's promise," her mother says dryly. "He's a liar and a swindler and has been deceiving us for a long time. And gratitude is unknown to him. I dare say he has completely forgotten who saved his life."

"May I go now?" Idun asks, looking imploringly from one to the other.

"Yes, come to think. Run to the bathroom and wash and lie down on the bed. Doctor Hansen may be here any moment. He's coming to examine you, and if it is as we fear, we'll have to hold a family council as soon as possible."

11

It was as they feared, and in the following days Idun goes about in a strangely wavering state of mind, which oscillates between apathy and rebellion, despair and happiness.

Her refuge is the graveyard, where she can rest and remove the mask of calm and courage behind which she hides. At this time of year the grounds are deserted, and she rarely meets anyone when she rambles about the gravelled paths or drags her feet through the fallen leaves.

Occasionally she leans her head against a tree trunk and breaks into loud sobs, or sits hunched up on a bench rocking her body back and forth. What's to become of me? a voice inside her whimpers. God in heaven, what's to become of me?

But a moment later she jumps up and walks about the paths in a resolute manner, clenching her fists and instilling courage in herself. Don't give in, Idun, stick it out and don't let yourself be cowed. Easy now, easy, we'll soon be out of the woods, you shall see.

Or she happens to remember something and laughs softly, while stroking her midriff with one hand.

"How are you doing in there, my little baby-Jesus?" she whispers in tender blasphemy. "Should I tell you who you are? Well, you're the Saviour himself, you're the Lamb of God who bore the sins of the world."

If there is no one in the vicinity, she sometimes cups her hands into a megaphone and sends out a police bulletin in the direction of the Middle East.

"Aaron, are you there? *Shalom*, beloved, have you found a place for us to live? What kind of *kibbutz* have you settled in? Are you clearing new land and harvesting oranges, or are you breeding fish? Why aren't you writing as you promised, what's wrong, have you broken up with me as I was once stupid enough to suggest?

"We are going to have a child together!" she cries, on the verge of laughter, "what do you say to that? A little 'Idunaaron' or 'Aaronidun', if you see what I mean, one who is both of us and yet neither of us. An entirely new invention that has never been seen before, a mean proportional, a pendulum, an unknown quantity to the highest power.

"Aaron, you don't say anything, you won't let me down, will you? Don't, please, I beg you so sweetly. You're the only thing I have, and if I lose you I don't know what I'll do. Then I'll really be the daughter of Nobody, as it says on the medallion."

The morning hours are the hardest to get through. Then she sits alone behind her double desk at the bottom of the class, staring out of the window as *Travel Recollections* by Vinje, the massacre of St Bartholomew, the *Mayflower* and "*faire la liaison*" pass over her head like a remote hum. If a teacher speaks to her she gives a start and answers at random, mostly so senselessly that she makes everyone laugh. She never eats the packed lunch she has brought, for fear nausea will slide its invisible hand down her throat and turn her inside out. She is still holding her own because of her quick mind, and her first-term marks were only slightly below what she is capable of. But it is obvious that something is wrong, and one day the form-master detains her after the last class.

"Idun, you aren't very happy, are you?" he says, with a worried look in his eyes. "Do you have problems at home, or is there something here at school that bothers you?"

Idun looks away and faintly shakes her head. She has ensconced herself in her loneliness, with walls so thick that a friendly voice cannot reach her.

"Idun, are you there, don't you hear that I'm talking to you? If you are in trouble, maybe I can help you."

She again shakes her head, ready to deny everything, but changes her mind and lifts her eyes. "I'll probably be going away," she says in a faltering voice. "I may not stick around long enough to graduate in the spring."

"That would be very sad," he says, knitting his brows. "In heaven's name, girl, you aren't ill, are you? You do look rather thin, and green about the gills."

Idun answers with a slight shrug, before shouldering her schoolbag and making ready to go. The teacher takes a step forward and makes a gesture to stop her, but gives up and lowers his hands.

"All right," he says, resigned, "if you don't want to tell me, I'm not going to press you.

"But wait a moment," he calls after her when she's already some way down the hall. "If you should be prevented from graduating in the spring, remember that there is something called a make-up examination. If you let me know and provide me with a doctor's certificate, I'll take care of it for you."

12

The family council at 24 Strand Street has lasted for nearly an hour and increasingly takes on the character of a legal proceeding. The accused is Idun, seventeen and a half years old and in the third month of pregnancy; the judge's bench is occupied by her six relatives, one man and five women.

The session was opened with prayer and hymn singing, while she was waiting in the hallway. When she is finally called in, the members of the family are sitting in a circle at the head of the big dining table, merging before her eyes into one huge, many-headed monster.

Andreas Sand has been on the move for several days and has made his preparations, and since the question of guilt is clear and the accused looks suitably contrite, the only thing that remains is to read the sentence. But as is meet and proper, he rounds it off with a summing up, in which he reviews whatever extenuating circumstances can be found. For the last several months the family has been undergoing a crisis, he says, domestic discipline has been lax, and the forces of destruction have had a free rein. And since the accused is a minor and has never previously shown any signs of disobedience, she will not suffer any punishment. Quite the contrary, with God's help he has found a solution that can be a blessing to those closest to her as well.

After he amplifies what he has in mind, his granddaughter looks thunderstruck. Her eyes pop open as though she had heard something totally insane, a dreary tale that's neither here nor there. She looks about her in bewilderment for a moment, before opening her mouth and laughing artificially.

"Now, my child, what do you say?" Andreas Sand asks, pretending not to have heard his granddaughter's derision. "I realize that you are surprised and need time to think it over. But let me assure you that we wish you well and have arranged everything in your own best interest."

"What do I say?" Idun suddenly shouts in a piercing voice. "I'll tell you. You can take the disgusting fellow by the scruff of the neck and send him to the back of beyond!"

"What's that?" the grandfather says, refusing to believe his ears. "You refuse to take a good Christian man who's willing to spare you the shame?"

"I'm not at all ashamed, I assure you. I would've been happy if I just had another family! Aaron and I love each other, and we have kneeled by the altar out at Sandane and promised to be true to one another till death us do part."

"Now, that's a bit thick!" her mother says sharply. "Do you imagine we'll tolerate letting you stay in this town and bring shame on us all?"

She bends over the table and says something to her fellow sisters, and the next moment all of the five women get in on it and shout at the same time.

"Quiet!" Andreas Sand cries, slamming the table with the palm of his hand. "It's all been decided and there's nothing more to discuss. Tomorrow night young Sakariassen will bring the rings and we'll have an engagement party. The banns will be read on the second Sunday of Advent, and the wedding will take place on the quiet between Christmas and New Year."

"I won't have him, I've told you!" Idun cries, sounding desperate. "If you force me, I'll answer 'no' before the altar, tell the pastor so to his face!"

"Doesn't it seem to you that this is a poor way of repaying our Christian brother?" asks the grandfather, affecting a mortified tone. "When he's willing to take up the cross and risk his reputation?"

"He can take up all the crosses he wants," Idun shouts, laughing through her tears. "As long as he doesn't try to pretend there has been something between him and me."

"Quiet, child, it will be as I've said," Andreas Sand says, his face showing signs of holy wrath.

"Mama, please, I beg you," Idun says in a thin voice. "You were yourself once . . ."

"Shhh, we won't talk about that," the mother says, putting on an injured face.

"Help me!" Idun cries, looking searchingly round the table; but the figures appear dim, their contours strangely blurred. To keep them apart from one another she mentions each and every one by name and appeals to them all in the same urgent, heart-rending way. "Mama, I beg you once more, please. Urd – no, I mean Kathrine Elisabeth, you who are my twin sister. Aunt Dora, you who just . . . Aunt Rina, you who always . . . Signe, you who . . ."

When none of the five holds out a helping hand, she turns to her grandfather and dissolves in tears.

"I won't do it, Grandpa, I'll never put that engagement ring on my finger. And if you try to force me, I'll just disappear. I'd rather die than marry that horrid fellow!"

"Well, I had expected you to make difficulties," Andreas Sand says at the end, heaving a deep sigh. "But I warn you, there are limits to my patience. If you don't come back to your senses, you leave me no choice but to send you away."

13

At night she has a terrifying dream that makes her start from sleep with a long scream. For several days she is so upset that she sees blood everywhere, and only much later does it dawn on her that it was a dream of suicide.

It's late one autumn evening, so full of darkness and desolation that it feels as if she is the only living soul under the vault of heaven. She's taking a walk somewhere on the outskirts of town when a thought strikes her like a bolt from the blue and splits her into two parts.

One part is her familiar self fleeing along the country road out to Sandane, just as blindly and recklessly as that time long ago when she was fleeing the same way with Uncle Balder, the bogeyman, at her heels.

The other part is her reflection or shadow, an angel of darkness that streaks near her head and again and again whispers the same words in her ear, "That thou doest, do quickly".

As she rushes along, the borderline between the two dissolves and she doesn't know who she is, the unrelenting angel that almost brushes her with his wings or the material fugitive hastening towards some urgent action.

Suddenly, without any transition, she finds herself in the woodshed at Sandane, where she once sat curled-up, whimpering, until the search crew discovered her. She places her hand over her eyes, noticing how reality and unreality become interwoven and indistinguishable. The terrible angel has stolen all her power of resistance, he has grown big and mighty from her terror and forces her to kneel down and put her head on the chopping block. There she lies in a curiously distorted position, counting the seconds, while the other slowly raises the axe to separate her head from her body. She lets out a piercing scream, at that instant being both executioner and victim, the still-warm body that suffers a violent death and the ice-cold decision that has sentenced her to death and carries out the act with merciless precision.

14

Three weeks later she stands on the deck of the small Danish boat, *The Dove*, looking towards a flat spit of land that can slowly be distinguished from the darkness.

The ship is a medium-sized steamer that has been carrying miscellaneous goods from the Norwegian coast to Zealand Point for a generation. Mostly lumber, saltpetre and aluminium, but also hides, ironware, rock-wool and canned fish. Though the run has shown no profit for many years, Andreas Sand has been reluctant to put the ship out of commission. *The Dove* is the shipping firm's oldest ship, and the owner has held a belief verging on superstition that it holds a sort of magic, or blessing, as he prefers to call it. As long as it chugs its way across the Skagerrak, it means good luck for himself and success for all his enterprises.

It happens more and more seldom that the ship takes passengers, the four spacious cabins amidships are usually vacant or serve as storerooms. On this trip Idun is the only passenger, which in her present mood feels like a relief. Having got up early, she has been looking towards land for over an hour. She knows that somewhere out there an unknown woman is getting ready to meet her, she may already be awaiting her lodger on the pier. She is the sixty-year-old midwife and nurse Ida Andersen, who will take care of her during her pregnancy and deliver the baby when the time comes.

The Danish woman has the best references; Andreas Sand lost no time exploring the terrain around the Sejerø Bay and consulting with his business contacts in Nykøbing and Fårevejle. He didn't mention, most likely, that it was his own granddaughter who had to go into hiding in a Danish village to bear a child clandestinely. With his gift of the gab, he no doubt managed to pass it off as a good deed he was doing for the daughter of one of his employees. Only the midwife and the authorities have been informed, and they are bound by professional secrecy.

Idun least of all knows what awaits her there when spring comes around. As she sails unsuspectingly into her own destiny, she thinks there is almost a homelike air about the narrow point of land that is gradually coming into sight. After the terrible heartbreak that has lacerated her during the last few weeks, she feels relieved that the matter is done with and all storms have died down. She has almost forgotten the documents she put her name to;

they were placed on the table before her, and signed when she was in a state of apathy and despair. Her grandfather, having assured her that they were merely a formality, had pointed to the line where she should put her name, and she accepted the fountain pen and wrote what was required.

She's now gazing towards the open curve of the bay and feels almost cheerful. She doesn't know that a scant six months from now she will stand here on the same deck, undermined as only someone can be who has committed an unforgivable mistake and knows there's no longer any hope. All the plans she made last night while lying awake in her cabin will come to nothing, all the gentleness in which she has wrapped her happiness will be put to shame. Her wanderings across the windswept sand banks will be wanderings with a dead end, the ode to joy will fall silent, all the poems and lullabies she has written to the Lamb of God will be torn up and spread to the four winds.

She will be left with a dark despair and with an outcry, to be found in big, trembling letters on page 116 of the memory book: "Grandpa has fooled me, I shall never forgive him! Nor will I ever forgive myself after what has happened. What is going to become of me?"

15

The reconciliation came, but only in the late fall of 1960, when Andreas Sand hadn't seen his granddaughter in five years. A nurse at Bispebjerg Hospital in Copenhagen at the time, Idun was called home by a telegram, informing her that her grandfather was gravely ill and at the point of death.

A number of embarrassing and dramatic events had knocked him off his feet and strapped him to his sickbed. The previous year there had been a lawsuit involving the revenue service, from which he finally managed to extricate himself with the help of shrewd attorneys, but which attracted great attention and permanently stained his reputation. He began to show signs of poor health and had a pain in his abdomen, but true to his own precepts in similar cases, he omitted consulting a doctor before it was too late. Nor could he benefit from Ånon Sakariassen's heaven-inspired hands, because the malady was located in a place that was difficult of access if it was to be done before the eyes of a congregation as curious as it was godfearing.

The diagnosis "cancer of the testicles" was only made when the disease had reached its last stage and spread to his whole abdominal cavity.

It didn't take Idun long to make up her mind when she was called. She arranged a leave of absence for an indefinite period, packed a suitcase with clothes and nursing requisites and boarded *Princess Margrethe*, which was still enjoying its uncrowned days before *Queen* and *Crown* and *Scandinavia* appeared, catching the travellers in a gigantic trap, like mice and rats. A cry of distress had reached her from afar, a patient needed her, and she shed her hard feelings and indignation like a set of worn-out clothes.

When she got home it was as a stranger and outsider, who knew nothing of the hair-raising confession her grandfather had made in the Ark, before returning home and taking to his bed for good. At a Saturday meeting in mid-October he had asked for the floor, stepped up to the speaker's platform and exposed himself so thoroughly to general condemnation that it was inconceivable he would ever again show his face at the meetings.

To begin with he offered up a prayer in an overwrought, broken voice, before he pulled himself together and began, calmly and systematically, to enumerate all the big and small sins he had had on his conscience from his first youth up to that very day. First, all of his cuss words and strong language, from the rather innocent "By George!" to "Damn it!" and "Go to hell!" and even worse. Then all his shady financial transactions with strawmen, hidden bank deposits, dubious investments and tax evasion. And finally the sin beyond all sins: the lust of the flesh, with names, time and place, and every detail.

While it was going on, Ånon Sakariassen got up from his seat several times to intervene, but hesitated, shook his head uncomprehendingly and sat down again. Only when all was accomplished did he hurry up on the platform to lead the sinner to the penance bench, probably not without a certain sense of triumph. Andreas Sand ducked his head and went along, with Sakariassen's paternal arm resting heavily on his shoulder. But as he stood before the ignominious bench where he had so often forced others to their knees, something happened to him. He took a step back, shook off the other's clinging arm, turned around and sent the gathering an indescribable look, before leaving the temple with such rapid steps that he appeared to be fleeing. He collapsed on the doorstep, where he sat motionless clutching his head until a merciful individual lent a hand and took him home.

Now he's been in bed for over four weeks, yellow and shrunken, most of the time delirious and with his skinny hands curved like claws on the coverlet. Idun gives him an injection against the pain every four hours, but sometime in the third hour, when the effect decreases, he starts tossing and getting restless. If he has the strength to do so, he edges his way towards the headboard until he sits half-upright in the bed; then he fumbles at his forehead and blinks his eyes, as if rousing to a clearer and sharper consciousness.

Idun helps him into a sitting position and shakes his pillow so he can lean on it. She already knows what is coming and tries as best she can to say a few words to calm him down. But he keeps harping on one thing: picking up the thread, he continues his long self-accusation, which allows for no solace or extenuating circumstances. At first his words come in brief gusts, then develop into long, continuous jeremiads that fade away in deep groans of pain, before a new shot brings relief and forgetfulness.

"Just look! Here lies Andreas Sand at last, his insides rotting," he begins in an almost gloating tone of voice. "It serves him right, he lies in the bed he's made for himself."

Idun bends forward and adjusts the top sheet but can't think of anything to say.

"Oh yes, it serves him right, it does. The wages of sin is death, and my stinking sins will have a long and painful death. My soul has been depraved from the very first moment. And now the corruption has spread to my whole body, and I'm finished."

"No, Grandpa, you mustn't talk like that," Idun says, stroking one of the skinny hands resting on top of the coverlet.

"Oh yes, that's exactly the way I must talk. The moment of truth has arrived and soon I'll stand face to face with my judge."

"Please, Grandpa, try to calm yourself. You probably haven't always been the way you should, but who has? You have also done much good in the world."

"Have I? I have no knowledge of that. Tell me, Idun, what it is, so I can have some hope."

"You saved two human lives, Grandpa. You remember Ruth and little Aaron, don't you, whom you kept hidden in the attic during the war?"

"Oh, *that*," the old man sighs, turning away. "That was nothing but selfishness and carnal desire. I lusted after another man's wife, that's how it was. So that rescue mission doesn't count."

"But you *did* it, Grandpa, you saved the lives of Ruth and Aaron. A good deed is a good deed, and it doesn't make any difference what the ulterior motives were."

"Oh, no, and again no, it does make a difference! And I took my commission, I assure you. I bound her to me by a debt of gratitude that she had to pay off with her youth and beauty. I was crazy about her and could never have enough. No wonder the illness that's eating me up started exactly where it did."

"Oh Grandpa," Idun tries, but checks herself and says no more.

"And I forced her to do something that was so hideous that I can never get rid of it. She wept and asked for mercy, but I made certain it was done. After all, she was someone else's wife, so there was no way to get around it. I forced her to . . ."

"You may as well say it, perhaps you'll feel easier," Idun says when she sees he can't come out with it, however hard he tries.

"I won't feel easier, but I'd better get it out. She became pregnant the second year she lived in the attic, and I forced her to have an abortion. She almost died and refused to have anything more to do with me. But I had my will with her as before."

"Stop torturing yourself, Grandpa, it won't help. What's done is done, and it can't be done over again."

"And that from *you*, to whom I've done even worse things."

His voice is diminishing already, and she knows that shortly he will writhe in pain and try to wheedle her into giving him another shot. But a glance at her watch tells her that it's still three quarters of an hour before she can give him relief.

"What are you thinking of?" she asks, leaning forward over the sick man to hear better. She has violent palpitations, she knows she has raised a question she ought to have left alone.

"Oh, little Idun, they're such foul things that I can barely make myself utter them." He tosses his head back and forth on the pillow. And she can see that his body under the bedclothes is writhing in pain.

What if I stopped giving him more shots? it flashes through her mind. Then he could just lie there on top of his misdeeds and get a foretaste of eternal torment.

385

"Well, I'll soon stand face to face with my judge, so I'd better confess. You remember, don't you, that I had your child adopted without telling you beforehand?"

"Don't remind me of that, Grandpa, I cannot stand to hear it. I'll start feeling restless and have to go on a search when I get back to Denmark."

"No, no, I won't say anything more. But can you forgive an old man who is so wretched lying here that he cannot even ask his God to forgive him?"

"I *have* forgiven you, or I wouldn't be sitting here. It's much harder for me to forgive myself. You have no idea how I have tormented myself during the last six years. If and if and if and if. If I hadn't been so relieved that I got out of marrying Ånon Sakariassen. If I hadn't been so apathetic and weak-willed. If only I had refused to go away. If I had read what was in those papers before I signed them."

"There is also something else," he says moments later, after lying with closed eyes for so long that she thinks he has fallen asleep.

"Yes, Grandpa, I'm listening."

"Wait a moment, what was it I wanted to say? Oh yes, it was I who managed to get it over between you and Aaron."

"But he never wrote me from Israel as he had promised. Finally I stopped waiting, I thought he had forgotten me."

"Oh no, little Idun, he had not forgotten you. He wrote two letters, which I snapped up and made sure you didn't receive. I burned the first one when I saw what was in it. But when the second one arrived I had made my decision and sent him a reply."

"And what did you write?" Idun cries, a six-year-old lump in her throat. "Please, tell me, or I don't know what will become of me!"

"I wrote him something that I knew would quench his desire to send you any more love letters. I told him straight out that we didn't want to have any Jews in the family. You had just become engaged to someone else, I wrote, and he would only make it difficult for you if he persisted."

"Oh, but Grandpa, how could you do it, when you knew what was between Aaron and me?"

"I was at the mercy of Mammon, my child, that's how it was. I needed a large sum of money at short notice, and the banks didn't want anything to do with it. But Sakariassen was bursting with money, as everyone knew. And seeing how smitten he was with you, I knew he would go to great lengths to get you."

"And so you sold me to the highest bidder and killed Aaron's and my love in cold blood."

"Yes, I suppose I did, if the truth be told. Let me tell you one thing, little Idun, something I understood only when everything was lost. It's money that has been my god in life, the investments that have been my worship, and the banks that have been my temples. My Christianity has merely been a way of protecting myself, one among many others."

"A way of protecting yourself?"

"Yes, I know now why people of my sort are so preoccupied with salvation through Jesus Christ. We want to be on the safe side, in the big things as well as in the small. Salvation is a kind of higher insurance policy, which delivers us from uncertainty and guarantees us eternal life."

"Grandpa . . ."

"Now let me tell you one thing I had almost forgotten. While your father was parish pastor in this town I went to church to listen to him once in a while. Not to hear the word of God, don't you believe it, but to spy on him and catch him out in interpretations I could use against him in the parish council. One Sunday he said something from the pulpit that was just what I was after. He called Jesus a transforming spirit and took the Gospel to witness that we should not aspire to salvation. It was a very beautiful and thought-provoking sermon, that I see only now. It was a proclamation of the mystery of transformation, and I can remember that he repeated the words, 'For whosoever will save his life shall lose it', over and over again, almost like a refrain. I carefully took them down while sitting in my pew, and later brought the matter up at the next meeting of the parish council. And if I remember correctly, I also wrote a letter to the bishop in which I charged your father with heresy and accused him of denying the salvation through Jesus Christ as the foundation of faith."

"Grandpa, I'm preparing the injection, so you can rest a little."

"No, no, away with it, I don't want it! I know what I have thrown away, and no soothing injection can make up for it. 'Become new,' the Master said, 'drop what you have in your hands and commit yourself to being transformed.' And here I lie rotting, chained to the old Adam."

The last hours of his life were terrible; he yelled and screamed, resisting to the very end and refusing to be comforted. When Ånon Sakariassen was called in to offer spiritual solace, he was turned away with bitter words and the most implacable gestures.

He died divided against himself and lay there in a grotesque position, his limbs contorted and his face totally disfigured by grimaces. When she tried to stretch him on his deathbed, the body couldn't be straightened, having stiffened in a final convulsion, the hands clenched in the air as if, at the last moment, they had hit upon some profit they didn't want to miss out on.

Before Idun went downstairs to announce that the old man was at peace, she stood a long while looking at him with a pity she had never felt before at a deathbed. It was almost incomprehensible that so much goal-oriented energy could mistake its goal and come to a dead stop in such a desperate way.

She couldn't help thinking of her father's peacefully folded deathbed hands, which she had made a drawing of in her memory book, rescuing them for eternity by calling them Guilt and Shame.

She stood for a moment and listened, her ears trained on the lower floor where the family was gathered, with visitors from as far as the other side of the Atlantic. Then she bent over the deceased and whispered, almost inaudibly: "Sleep soundly, little Grandpa with the light-blue eyes, you closed them just in the nick of time. The race is run, old knight of the main chance. Your reckonings became too simple, your dodges too familiar, your tricks too transparent, even for your own time. Can you hear them beginning to stir down there? Shortly they will jump out of their chairs, and more hardened hands than yours will be raised to fight over the inheritance."

VIII

Shall – shall not, shall not –

1

Although I dread it and have been postponing it from one day to the next, I can no longer put off relating the nightmarish visit I had here in the ward on 31 October, the day before I received the letter from Jerusalem and four weeks before the letter-writer himself appeared.

As I've already mentioned, my fantastic tale of 1979, *The Papessa*, was reissued in June, and in August, while I was away on my latest adventure, two of my other books came out in paperback. The books had practically no sales when they were originally published and would probably not have attracted any attention this time either if it hadn't been for the rumour of my disappearance. The papers had carried more or less extensive notices of my escape from the hospital, and I had been reported missing by both radio and TV when I was discovered by a canal in Amsterdam and sent home.

In the meantime the three books had been selling like hot cakes and the print-runs were virtually exhausted. There had even been fresh reviews in several newspapers in the capital, which hardly ever happens with reissued books. Critics that at one time had dismissed the books as myths divorced from reality, had suddenly put on a new pair of glasses and read the books in a more open and sympathetic manner.

As soon as I returned from my stint of dissipation and was installed in the six-bed ward, the editor had approached the hospital in order to invite me to dinner, but had been turned down on the grounds that I was subject to curfew. A few days later I received a big parcel from the publisher with complimentary copies of my three books, newspaper clippings of reviews, and a letter of congratulation from Chirpety-Chirp in which he regretted not being permitted to see me.

The parcel and the letter did me more good than I can express in words and removed the uncertainty that had been knocking about in my head: Could I trust my own recollection during the last confusing months, and could I be certain that my books would again see the light of day? Had my two visits to the publisher's actually taken place, or were they just pipe dreams and pure invention? I had been gnawed by doubts all summer, when I was on the road, leading my precarious existence on drugs. What if it were all just a mirage, I said to myself, nothing but self-preservation and tilting at windmills? Suppose I had once and for all disappeared into the fiction and lost the ability to distinguish between reality and unreality? How long could I keep it up in that borderland between being and non-being? Couldn't a human being sink so deep into degradation that she caught at every fancy to retrieve a wasted life?

We were now well into the month of October and I gradually began to feel on firm ground. Then one day unreality disguised itself as reality and came knocking at my door: a journalist from one of the morning papers succeeded in passing himself off as a clinical psychologist and behaved so convincingly that he was admitted to the ward without any fuss. It was late in the day, the evening chores were done already, and the nurses were relaxing in their lounge as usual, waiting to be relieved.

Suddenly, while my roommates were floundering about in the ward and I myself was trying to collect my thoughts behind the screen, there he stood in the middle of the room giving the menagerie the once-over. I could see him through a chink in my parapet as he pulled his photographic equipment out of the attaché case, scouting about for the object he was after. Before I knew what was happening, the room was illuminated by a number of quick flashes, and my vigilant ear picked up the hissing sound of a camera in operation. My fellow patients were running about on the floor, laughing and hollering, but through all the noise I could hear a male voice asking where Idun Hov, the author, was hiding.

The name didn't seem to tell the patients anything, for they continued with their racket, and the one expecting a visit from the Holy Ghost every night became so frightened that she collapsed on her bed amid loud laments. Under different circumstances the nurses would long ago have understood that something was wrong, but their lounge is located some way down the hall, and Ward No. 6 is not exactly one of the quietest in this wing.

For a while it was completely still, and I began to wonder whether the visitor might not have left, when I suddenly heard furtive steps in the room and saw a head peek round the edge of the screen. I was sitting in my usual writing posture, my memory book on my knees and the ball-point pen wedged tight between three fingers, when a blinding light hurt my eyes. The photographer had reason to be satisfied. What more could he wish for? He had gained entry into the holy of holies and seen his chance to immortalize the author in the moment of creation. I let out a scream and shielded my face with my arm, whereupon a star shell swooped down on me, followed by a number of sounds that to my panic-stricken imagination sounded like the faraway crackle of machine gun fire. When the attack was over I heard a voice asking if I was writing another novel, and if the central figure might not be a psychiatric patient this time around. After all, Idun Hov was known for writing about weird and shady characters, and it would be exciting to see what she had cooked up this time.

That was all he managed to say, for at that moment the head nurse stood in the doorway, asking in a commanding voice what this was supposed to mean. The journalist backed away a step, but didn't lose his composure. He quickly packed his things, turned on his biggest smile, bowed politely to us all, and disappeared in a hurry without deigning to give anybody an explanation.

Five days later the photograph was published in the most shameless and aggressive morning paper, framed by an article that could rightfully be labelled *paparazzo* journalism. Far from forgetting me, the originator showed himself a true friend by posting me the entire Saturday issue. "COMMITTED PATIENT SITS BEHIND A SCREEN WRITING AN AUTO-BIOGRAPHICAL NOVEL (SEE PAGE 4)," it said on the front page, and when I finally took courage and looked up the right place, it felt like a slap in the face. A whole page was devoted to a meeting between two people that had lasted just a few seconds and had come about through an encroachment of the rights of one of them.

The photograph, which filled up most of the page, was a grotesque study in light and shadow, using every trick to increase the drama. A shapeless figure sits hunched at the head of her bed, trying to hide her face behind a raised arm. The eyes looking out from under the arm radiate a wild terror, and the lower part of the face is exposed to a dazzling light, showing the mouth distorted in a permanent scream. A book has slid from her raised knees, and her writing tool is still wedged between the fingers of a claw-like hand. As the situation has been manipulated, nobody can be in doubt that the patient is anxious and ought to be detained in a closed section. The uprights of her bed look like the bars of a prison, and the figure's violent resistance speaks such a clear language that any further comments are superfluous.

When I had read and digested the sparse text around the picture, my eyes fell on the signature, and it suddenly occurred to me that there was something familiar about it. "O. D. Hunter," I repeated to myself over and over again, picking up a distinct flavor of game. By rummaging in my skull for a while I finally found the solution. Yes, of course, the signature was identical to the one that had once appeared under a discussion of *The Papessa* in the weekly magazine *Farmand*. The review was an ingenious production of elegant jokes which left the novel open to cheap sneers from the less discriminating segment of the reading public. "The author Idun Hov has her own tone of voice," it said, "and it sounds confusingly like the dialling tone."

In 1979 the review had made me profoundly unhappy; I was so depressed that more than a year passed before I dared write another word. In November 1994 I was better off and could even summon up a little laugh when I had recovered from my initial shock. I had stopped believing that I could achieve any kind of success as a writer and had thus become invulnerable. And, above all, I had received a surprising letter from Jerusalem that occupied all my dreams about the past and the future.

2

Aaron flew to the USA on 19 December to celebrate Christmas with relatives and with friends of his parents, and will lecture on socialized medicine at Princeton, Yale and Columbia University throughout January. At the same time he will try to collect money for a Jewish-Palestinian hospital which he plans to establish on the West Bank. It is conceived as a bridge of reconciliation between two fighting peoples, both of which claim the territories and have used every means to drive each other out.

His plans are not yet official, and he doesn't know if they can be realized. He is still associated with the Jewish hospital in West Jerusalem, where he has been medical director during the last six years, but he is considering resigning from his position, because he sees the hospital as a fortress of Zionist thinking. During his years of service there he has never seen the shadow of a Palestinian, even in times of riot when people were lying in the street and needed instant help. The hospital is situated so close to the border of the occupied territories that it is also the nearest hospital for many of the inhabitants of East Jerusalem. He has witnessed the most flagrant examples of would-be patients being turned away, and in the course of the years he has come to feel increasingly uncomfortable and compromised as a physician.

During his stay in the USA he will address himself to well-to-do liberal Jews and other reasonable people who realize that reconciliation is the only way to go in the war-ravaged Middle East. If everything works out, his hospital will be an emergency clinic for everybody, without petty regard to whether the injured parties are Arabs or Jews. It will obviously be a hospital for the poor segment of the population, the mentality of the higher strata obviating a more mixed clientele. But I believe it will suit him fine to settle in the slums. According to the Hippocratic oath he has sworn to treat everyone, without fear or favour, and true to the ideals of his youth he doesn't make a secret of where his heart is.

It was strange to see Aaron again after being apart for forty years. At first glance I could barely recognize him. The person we harbour in our memory is eternal and untouched by the ravages of time, and when I read his letter I constantly saw before me the radiant young man I had so passionately loved during the faraway summer of 1954.

Then he suddenly stood before me in the flesh, and I found it almost incomprehensible that he would look so old, much older than his fifty-nine years. His back was no longer straight, nor were his motions light or resilient; and his features were not unfinished and softly drawn. Still, most amazing of all was his hair, which was no longer coal-black but bristled around his head like a white halo. The only thing that was unchanged were his eyes, which looked just as dark and beaming as I remembered them, with a glow and a drive that contradicted the weariness of his stooped figure.

He had seen the review of *The Papessa* in a Norwegian paper he came across by sheer chance during a visit to a compatriot. It was one of those good reviews that rehabilitated the book, and it made him so glad that he quite spontaneously wrote a letter to my publisher and asked for my address. The reply was long in coming, and when it finally arrived the message was disheartening. The editor, the loveable Chirpety-Chirp (who on this occasion no doubt signed his other name), informed him that I did have an address in Oslo, but that it would be useless to write there. The sad truth was that the author was an inmate of such and such a psychiatric hospital, with small prospects of ever being released and leading a normal life again.

"It was then I made my decision," Aaron told me when we saw each other again on 29 November. "At first I was to leave for the USA around Christmas, but I discovered that I could extend my leave of absence and have a go at seeing the old country before taking off across the Atlantic."

And quite a go at it he had, and he also managed to set many things going during the scant six weeks he was here. As I've already related, there was a thorough shake-up, which turned him into a feared but highly respected person in our wing. The medical director tried at first to go into hiding, but when Aaron threatened him with testing the case before a court of law he had to come out in the open. Two weeks later the diagnosis had been invalidated and the declaration of incompetence found null and void; and the patient was no longer to be committed.

Before we said goodbye, he even managed to persuade me to do some-thing I at first vehemently refused. Already in his letter from Jerusalem he had proposed that we get married, and that I accompany him to Israel on 31 January, when his leave of absence expired. Just imagine, he was willing to take me back after a lapse of forty years, without first inspecting the article to assure himself that it hadn't received too many scratches in the meantime. Aaron Baumann was no coward, that I knew, and had never been afraid of taking a chance. But I still retained a modicum of pride and refused to offer him just a piece of wreckage.

Therefore, when he suggested that we ask the banns I protested for the good reason that I still hadn't made up my mind. After all, the agreement was that we would both be free to think it over while he was away.

"Exactly," he replied, "you will have six weeks to consider the matter, and I'll humbly withdraw if you come to the conclusion that you won't have me."

"But why ask the banns when I haven't made up my mind?" I asked.

"Listen," he said, putting things right with his sovereign logic. "If we ask the banns, we are free to marry when I get back from the States. Are you with me? But if we do not ask the banns, it means that we have already made up our minds. Because then we cannot have our wedding at the end of January, and the unsuccessful suitor will have to go back to Israel alone."

3

Yesterday morning I had a visit that left me in a truly celestial state, though the three individuals came on very earthly business. The incident appeared to me in a dreamy haze all last night, and I've had my doubts whether it actually took place. Time and again, I've had to turn on the light and get my copy of the agreement from the drawer of my night table, so as to assure myself that I remember correctly and am not a prey to fresh illusions.

On Monday 9 January at 11.15 they came marching into the ward in a body, as if it were an altogether everyday occurrence. Fortunately they didn't have to set foot in Ward 6, where I dragged out my existence throughout the autumn, until the rehabilitation took place in mid-December. I now have a peaceful and quiet single room where I can relax and regain my strength before being discharged at the end of January. (And who knows, perhaps I can also manage to get discharged in another sense by then, by finishing my writing.)

The visitors were my sister and my brother, with the family attorney as a bodyguard and financial ventriloquist. At first I thought they had come up with another trick to outmanoeuvre me, so I made myself as small as possible waiting for the triple oracle to find its voice. Off and on I threw a quick glance at my brother, Nicce, whom I hadn't seen since Grandpa's funeral in 1960. He had then come rushing home from his position in an English shipping firm, convinced that he was to take over the company. But he cut his trip short when the old man's will was opened, sentencing him to a ten-year-long apprenticeship. The only thing about him that made an impression on me at the time were his shiny eyes, which I believed were due to tears at Grandpa's passing. I didn't know then that there was something called contact lenses, a trick that prosperous men have recourse to when they need something as ordinary as glasses. By now he had had to resign himself, and since he was constantly putting his glasses on and off, I could see that his previously starry eyes were shot through with a network of burst veins.

"Miss Hov, we have a happy announcement for you," the lawyer said at last; it was the same lawyer who had looked me up fourteen months ago to tell me I had been disinherited. I took note of the fact that he no longer was on a first name basis with the patient, but made every conceivable effort to show her respect.

"Since you are no longer declared incompetent," he went on, "you will in the very near future receive your part of the inheritance from the dear milady your mother." (Yes, I heard it correctly, he really said "the dear milady your mother", and his voice was just as pompously bourgeois as his language.)

He put a paper on the table before me and pointed with an omniscient finger to the seven-digit sum that would come to me. I made a gasp, looking inquiringly at my two siblings to assure myself that this was not just a delayed New Year's prank.

"Take it easy," said my mercantile brother with the bloodshot eyes. "You're not seeing visions. The money will very shortly be made available from the share capital and deposited in a separate account. Unless you prefer to have the capital remain in the shipping firm and to live from the interest?"

"No, thank you," I said, when I had recovered somewhat and felt confident that the whole thing wasn't just a practical joke. "I may go away and start a new life somewhere abroad, and then it will be nice to have some initial capital."

"That's quite all right," Nicce said grandly. "You can do as you like, so you will only have yourself to blame if you are foolish and squander your money."

The attorney unfolded a document on the table and showed me with the same excessive clarity as last time where I was to put my name in order for the transaction to be valid. I couldn't help smiling to myself at the thought of our previous meeting, when he wanted me to sign a statement to the effect that I was of unsound mind and had to be declared incompetent.

Thrinebeth hadn't said a word until now, but she looked visibly relieved when she heard that I might leave the country. Finally she would be rid of that bothersome twin sister who was stealing her identity, threatening her infallibility and being a haunting presence, her evil genius.

"Oh, by the way, congratulations on your books," she said all of a sudden. "Several of my colleagues have read them, and they are impressed by your psychological insight. It seems to run in the family, they say."

"Oh, do they?" I replied without much enthusiasm. "Anyway, I didn't think that psychologists operated with hereditary characteristics."

"But Finelotte, I'm congratulating you," she said, heaving a deep sigh.

"Ever so many thanks, my gracious sister, but aren't you a little late? It's ages since the books were first published, and then your congratulation would really have done me some good."

"There, there, little girls," Nicce said, trying to mediate. "No bickering, please. This is a day of happiness for us all. Our poetess has appeared in a new edition in more ways than one, and she seems to have big plans for the future. Too bad I didn't meet Aaron when he was here, it might have been amusing to catch up on old memories. He'll be getting back from the USA on 27 January, won't he? Oh, shucks, the very day I have some important business over there ."

"The paths of the two planes might cross, you know," I said teasingly. "Then you could stretch out your famous long arm and wave to him."

"My famous long arm, what do you mean by that?" Nicce asked in a slightly hurt tone.

"Well, you know, the arm that just needs to make a flourish in the air to get control of an East European tank fleet."

"Oh no, please, don't remind me of that miserable affair," my brother said, smarting. "It sent me into exile and is of little credit to Norway, the tutelage state. Fortunately the matter was over and done with a long time ago."

"Well, then I think everything should be shipshape," the attorney hastened to say and began to collect his papers. "Miss Hov, we'll send you further instructions when the money has been deposited, and give you the account number. One million three hundred and eighty-seven thousand, eight hundred kroner is quite a tidy sum of money, don't you think? With a profitable investment it should give a good yield. And in addition, of course, you have your shares in the shipping firm, which are not to be despised either, though sailing under a foreign flag causes certain problems."

"If you intend to set out on a long journey again, I hope you will provide yourself with a passport," Thrinebeth remarked acidly. "This time, I'm afraid, I cannot put mine at your disposal."

"You don't need to worry on that account," I said, "I was at the police station only yesterday and picked it up. So there should be no danger that your dubious twin will be able to misuse your good name."

"Don't try to be funny," Thrinebeth said, rising and preparing to leave. "As a matter of fact, I've had a lot of trouble because of the stolen passport. And in case it should interest you, I won't be doing my Friday programmes for TV for a while. I've had enough problems with twins, if you see what I mean."

"Oh, by the way, one final point," the attorney said on leaving, as the delegation was waiting to depart. "Miss Hov, I suppose I ought to point out to you that you have the right to file a complaint, both concerning the commitment and the ensuing declaration of incompetence. But take a good piece of advice: let the thing rest. A psychiatric grievance is a slow process, it can take several months, if not years. And besides I think you ought to drop the matter out of consideration for your family."

"That's all right," I said magnanimously, "one should always listen to good advice, especially when it has to do with something as rare as showing consideration. Anyway, I can't see that I have anything to complain about. I have been staying in a first-class hotel, with full pension and an orchestra seat, watching the human drama, which in this place surpasses itself and gives performances around the clock. Don't worry, I've taken it all in, missing nothing. I've had a bed all to myself, and I didn't even lack a screen when I needed a little privacy now and then."

We said a quiet and friendly goodbye, with all the customary kisses and hugs. After escorting them to the door, I followed them with my eyes as they walked confidently down the long corridor, where usually a flock of bizarre figures wander about in search of their lost lives. People weighed down by anxiety, led astray by visions, chased by delusions and pursued by inner voices.

As I stood there watching the visitors leave, they appeared to me like creatures from a faraway planet, like demigods who had descended for a brief moment to us mortals, until they disengaged themselves and returned to their proper element. The fashionable clothes fluttered about them like celestial draperies, and it seemed to me they rose just a bit from the floor as they approached the revolving door to take flight for higher spheres.

4

Another postcard from Aaron, the fourth since he left. We have agreed we won't write letters as long as everything is up in the air between us, but content ourselves with sending one another brief signs of life.

He relates that his lectures are going far better than expected and have aroused lively debate. On the other hand, the collection of money has been something of a disappointment. Everyone thinks the project is promising, even orthodox Jews are enthusiastic and blow their ram's horns. But when the chips are down and the bank account is to be opened, they change their tune. So far he has only received pledges for $42,000, about one eighth of the capital that he needs.

He has obtained premises in Jerusalem at a reasonable rent, and a number of physicians and nurses have offered to take on watches without pay, alongside other practice. But the hospital has to be renovated and furnished, equipment and costly instruments must be procured, so the expenses will most likely be close to two million Norwegian kroner. Is there any point in going on with the collection, he asks, or is the plan stillborn and all efforts doomed to fail?

I have written back, urging him to keep his spirits up. Perhaps the money can be found somewhere else, I told him. Who knows whether there might not be a newly rich soul here in Norway, someone who feels weighed down by abundance and is on the lookout for a good project?

5

Since I'm no longer committed, I can come and go wherever I please, and during the last few weeks I've been constantly on the move. I've been well on the way to see my publisher and say hello to Chirpety-Chirp as many as three times, but at the last moment my courage faltered. The traces of my flight through the corridors nine months ago, as well as of the spooky night I spent in the publishing house half a year previously, keep frightening me.

After all, each and everyone knows my history, it runs ahead of me wherever I go and takes the words out of my mouth. Strictly speaking, it's probably no more hair-raising than the literature a publisher lives on and accepts with open arms. It's just that fiction can take liberties that life had better refrain from. It's commendable to write adventurous books, the wilder the better, judging by the taste of our time. It's something else to carry out one's fantasies and go astray on the continents of reality.

In any case, I got cold feet and turned back on the stairs, before the corridors managed to swallow me up. Instead I've made a few trips to my apartment in Homansbyen, where I tidied up and packed my sparse possessions. Whatever my immediate future will look like, the place is dead for me. I've used it up – shadows fall and emptiness re-echoes from the ceiling and the walls. It is unthinkable that I shall ever return, though my contract says I can live there rent-free for the rest of my life.

It was there that, during some good years in the 1980s, I was writing two of my best and most interesting books. But it was also there that I succumbed to my old demon and again became dependent on drugs.

I had said in an interview that I was trained as a nurse and was looking for a place to stay after living abroad for many years. Two days later I received a letter from a friendly lady who offered me a studio apartment with separate entrance, on condition that I become her nurse and give her the injections she needed for her diabetes.

This business with the diabetes proved to be a blind, she was simply a morphine addict and far gone in her abuse of the drug. She had a good friend who was a hospital doctor, and they had both been bitten by the snake. He called on her at regular intervals and supplied her with all the pain relievers she might desire. My task was limited to disinfecting the syringe and being available when she summoned me by the intercom.

When she called the poison "insulin", she always winked at me, knowing full well that I couldn't be fooled. By a tacit agreement we didn't refer to the illness by its real name but pretended that we were acting in full accordance with the law. I returned the wink and played along, her condition being so far advanced that I couldn't see any hope for her.

As I sat in my room writing my fantastic stories, suddenly the intercom would ring, and I knew what it was about. I lifted the receiver and announced that I was ready, changed into my nurse's dress and hurried over to her wing of the apartment to prepare the shot. My place was at that time the maid's room in a large residence; it was situated at the end of the hallway, by the back stairs, and was partitioned off by a solid wall only after my landlady's death in 1987.

By the time I entered the living room, she was expecting me eagerly, experiencing pain; often she was writhing in her chair, suffering all the agonies of abstinence. Then I came floating through the room like an angel of light and once more brought heaven down to earth for her. As the years passed it became more and more difficult to carry out the operation, her poor body being in the end so full of scars and wounds that I had to look for quite a while before finding a spot where I could insert the syringe.

The effect was instantaneous, almost before I had managed to empty the syringe. It was like a small miracle. I've never known anyone who absorbed the dope so quickly. Her last moan was prolonged in a cry of joy, with no perceptible transition. She smiled blissfully and sank into an indefinable state in which dreamlike silence alternated with loud bursts of laughter.

When she had received her euphoria-inducing shot, she ordered tea and sandwiches from the kitchen and asked me to show myself as a true friend and share the ecstasy with her. Mostly I excused myself, but once in a while I gave in and took a smaller dose, roughly one or two centigrams, as against her four or five. But since I was still a kind of novice in our sisterly order, the effect was about the same, and I could follow her in her flight through the many stages of bliss.

And thus we were able, for a few hours, to attain a state of perfect mutual understanding, in which our beings took off and became part of a great harmony. She was a musical and creative person, formerly a prima donna at one of the city theatres. When she was inspired she would recite parts of her great roles, scenes that I too loved and largely knew by heart. As our intoxication increased, gravity was suspended and, holding each other, we soared into worlds of infinite peace and happiness. But our celestial flight did not last forever; sooner or later the rebound came, for my part with nausea and dizziness, for hers more drastically, with convulsions, vomiting and total loss of memory.

Before it came that far, she asked me one day to open a drawer in her writing desk and take out a document that had already been registered and was stamped and affixed with a seal. It was her will, and she wanted to show me that my name was mentioned and that she hadn't forgotten me. She had no heirs, she gave me to know, so after her death her many nephews and nieces would fight over who was going to have the apartment. "Just let them scratch each other's eyes out," she laughed, "they won't get their hands on your little poet's den." It had already been decided that it was to be turned into a separate dwelling, with shower and a small kitchen, and entrance by way of the back stairs. It wasn't exactly a royal palace, but it would suffice, and it matched her ideas of how a poet's abode ought to look.

During the first seven years I managed to keep within reasonable limits and have everything under control. For most of the 1980s I rode on a crest of inspiration and was able to complete two of my strongest books: *The Angel and the Monster* in 1983 and *Jocasta's Revenge* in 1986. Then came stagnation, emptiness, paralysis, which called for their opposites, break-up, flight, dissipation. Imperceptibly, the fiction sneaked in on me, and before I realized what was happening it had stolen my life.

Afterwards I haven't been able to live quietly for very long at a time, but have always been ready to make off, my foot put forward. Instead of setting words down on paper I have given myself up to the dubious desire of being creative with my body, the upshot being a slew of queer stories. I have wandered aimlessly around the world for months and years on end, getting back to myself only at the last moment, before everything was lost. When I sneaked up the back stairs to my apartment, I was so peaked that I no longer cast a shadow; I had become my own shadow, which had emerged and detached itself from its material source.

As the years went by I noticed more and more how unwelcome I was on the property. The neighbours stopped greeting me, following me with suspicious glances when I sneaked through the gate, hurried across the courtyard and onto the back stairs. I know there have been actions to collect signatures and have me evicted, but so far they haven't led to anything. My long absences have caused the matter to be shelved, but I'll hardly be missed by anyone when I now move out of the house voluntarily.

When I had locked up after me and was on the stairs, I suddenly remembered the small exercise book with the last chapter of the Apology left in its hiding place behind the wall. I put down my luggage and stood still for a moment, considering whether I should let the book remain where it was and permit oblivion to close over my father's last chaotic thoughts. Then I rushed back in a hurry, as if it was a matter of life and death, stuck my hand into the hole and pulled out the small yellow book. Before depositing it in my suitcase, I sat down on the stairs, turned a few pages and read a paragraph here and there, without finding any order or coherence. A strange awe came over me, as if I were collecting the last remnants of a brain that had aspired to the impossible and blown itself to fragments.

As I closed the book my eyes fell upon a quotation or motto that was written at the top of the wrapper. It was a couple of lines of verse by the German poet Rilke, taken down from dictation in the childish handwriting of the thirteen-year-old: "*Weil es niemand meistert, bleibt das Leben rein*"

(Because nobody masters it, life remains pure), it read, and I continued to sit there as if in a trance, repeating the words to myself until I noticed that something became clear to me.

It was as though those two lines became the solution to the riddle, giving my father the acquittal that the court had denied him.

6

I have just had a conversation with Sister Sigrid that has heartened and strengthened me in my struggle against despair. I'm staying in a room on her aisle again, and she drops by every day to check on how I feel and what my future plans are. She thinks it is a good sign that I get by without methadone and have been off drugs for nearly five weeks.

"You must have found a better way of kicking the habit," she says, checking my record and giving me a mischievous look. She knows about the possibility that Aaron has opened up for me but doesn't try to influence me, though she no longer makes a secret of her great liking for the man.

This time she came to say goodbye and to hand over the big bundle of manuscript she has been keeping for me. Tomorrow morning she goes away to take a short course, and by the time she gets back to the ward on the 6th of February, the bird will have flown.

She came to my room about half-past six, after her watch was over, and had already managed to get out of her uniform. It was so strange to see her in ordinary clothes that for a moment I was completely at sea. I have always had difficulty recognizing people if they appear in disguise or show themselves outside their accustomed surroundings. To me, Sister Sigrid is the epitome of the good nurse; she has become a kind of symbol, and I find it hard to envisage her any other way. When she suddenly stood in the doorway dressed in slacks and sweater, I was startled, holding an arm before my face as if another "hunter" was coming, stripping me of my skin and reveling in my vulnerability.

But recognition liberated me, and when the danger was past we both had a good laugh. After all, she knows I'm one of those primitive people who succumb to magic spells. In this respect I'll never grow beyond the age of four; I believe firmly in Santa Claus, dragons, demons, angels and Puss in Boots.

At first we talked a little about this and that; I told her I had finished tidying up the apartment in Incognito Street and would never again set foot on those inhospitable grounds. We laughed a bit over the curious coincidence that I had lived like someone unknown in just that street, and I explained how I had envisaged remedying the estrangement. One day very soon I would insert an advertisement in the capital's most Christian newspaper in which I offered to lend the apartment for an indefinite period to a person with perfect house manners, perhaps for many years. What was to become of me was still uncertain, I said, giving her a mysterious glance. But there was no need to worry, she would hear from me when I had found a place to live and had a permanent address to boast of.

While we were chatting, I had all along a question on the tip of my tongue, which had to be cleared up before I could make any decision about my future. When a pause occurred I took courage and asked if she could tell me a little about the rules for being committed. How could it be, I asked, that suddenly, as if by magic, I had now received my freedom, after being locked up like a prisoner for months and years?

It took a while before she answered, hesitantly and with great misgivings. It was a matter of confidential material, which she couldn't bring to light then and there. As a nurse she was bound by her professional secrecy and couldn't cast doubt on the doctors' decisions. I had been allowed to see the medical record, of course, but considering how faulty it was, it probably hadn't made me much wiser. Except for what I had seen, my case was classified, and she could only express herself in general terms.

A commitment was always problematic, she said, being based on an estimate and often open to great mistakes. The law stated rather vaguely that a patient could be committed if he presented a danger to himself or his surroundings. Insanity had to be demonstrated, but that was always a broad concept, of course. Beside outright lunacy, there was a grey zone of mental ailments that could be interpreted in any number of ways. Some physicians would place normality within wide limits, while others were inclined to restrict them. If a patient belonged to the doubtful cases, he was in fact worse off than a criminal. The criminal had the right to confront a judge twenty-four hours after the arrest, a provision lacking in psychiatry. Once a patient had put up with being committed, it was seen as an acceptance, and he was locked into his situation and at the mercy of the more or less precise diagnosis of the medical director. He could choose to file a complaint, but the possibility of getting anywhere with it was minimal. One of the parties to the case knew the terminology and was experienced in speaking, while the other had to present her case sitting on the edge of her bed in a depressed state of mind. If the committed person lost her patience and showed some fight, it was all up. Then she had offered proof that she really was crazy and was rightly kept in custody.

"Thanks for the lecture," I said. "It deserves to be remembered, and as soon as I'm alone I'll quickly write it down in *my* report."

"Your report?" she said, giving me a quizzical look. "What's that?"

"You know," I said, laughing. "The one you've been taking care of for me and are right now holding on your lap."

"Oh, this one here," she said, taking the big pile of manuscript out of the box and weighing it in her hand. "I've read a bit here and there, and if you ask me I would say it's a novel."

"Novel or report or something quite different, it's all the same. I suppose it's not really a good old-fashioned novel, with all the different voices that get to speak. And the experts will probably say that it isn't a completely reliable report either."

"Here it is anyway," she said, handing me the manuscript, which had a bulk and a weight that were truly alarming. I almost wished I had put it all in the waste-paper basket and contented myself with keeping those parts that I had entered in the memory book.

"Quite a loaf," she said, as if she had read my thoughts. "Three hundred and sixty-five pages in fifteen months, or let us say a year, deducting the summer months you were out having a good time. That comes to one page a day, even without the Sabbath being kept holy."

I admitted that I had worked away and used my time, but couldn't help smiling a little at her time table and the fine-spun manner in which she computed my scribblings in terms of days, months and years.

"Wait a bit," I called after her, when she had wished me good luck and was already leaving. "There's one thing I should like to know. How was he able to turn the magic trick? I mean Aaron, Dr Baumann. How did he manage to make the diagnosis disappear up his sleeve and to rescue me from the grey zone and into the land of the living?"

"You'd better ask him that," she said, half turning, her hand on the doorknob.

"I have asked him," I said, "but I'm not sure I understood him correctly."

"Then ask him again, and don't give up until you've got the whole story."

She opened the door but still lingered a moment, as if she had remembered something.

"Come to think, I can tell you this," she said all of a sudden. "Dr Baumann has written a report about the matter which is highly respected around here. I'll make a xerox of it and drop it off before I leave."

7

I hadn't thought it would come to anything, but now Father will get the new gravestone I promised him over forty years ago. Today I was again over in the stonecutter's workshop, seeing it rise and come into being.

It is an unhewn granite stone that shades into grey or brown or black tints depending on how the light falls on it. With its broad lower part and the fine *rondure* at the top, it looks like a miniature of the Hov Mountain. The only thing it will lack when put up next spring is the double sunset that casts its magic light over the yard at Nether Hov. First the sun went down behind the sparse spruce wood on the Hov summit, and the shadows fell as though it was already late in the evening. But wait, soon it begins to flash and gleam over in the gap, the sky revives and becomes increasingly lighter and more golden, and there, there, there the sun sticks its flaming face out a second time, giving the day a respite.

This time I didn't ask the family's permission, but took the initiative and arranged everything on my own. I had made a firm decision that the time had come and was careful not to tell anyone what I had in mind. It would be unfortunate if it turned out as it did in 1960, when I was stupid enough to ask the others' advice. At first they just thought it was one of my crazy ideas and exchanged meaningful glances. But when they realized that I was in earnest they vetoed it, putting me to shame like Antigone.

They probably wouldn't be particularly kindly this time either, if they knew what I am about to do. My lips were sealed when they visited me here, and there is no risk that my stepping out of line will be discovered. Since Father's funeral in 1951 my siblings have never set foot in Our Saviour's Cemetery, nor will they ever do so. Vemund Hov is dead and buried in every sense of the word and cannot in their eyes become any more "one-time" than he already is. He is and will remain the blot on the family, which cannot be erased by any other means than oblivion. To commemorate him is tantamount to an embarrassing silence, to mention his name is like uttering an ugly and indecent word.

The stonecutter is an elderly man about my age, and we've become very good friends during his work on the engraving. At first he didn't see what was wrong with the old stone, and I had to explain to him this matter of "one-time." He broke into a smile when he got the point and confessed it was an inscription that he often chiselled on gravestones without his ever having thought about it.

"Yes, you're right, it is a bit odd," he chuckled, "but you know how we mortals are. We don't want to lose anything, even when we have turned up our toes. We scrape together things with arms and legs and want to take it all with us into eternity."

He was a little surprised when I asked him to put *Emigravit* at the bottom of the stone, and seemed none the wiser after I told him what it meant.

"All right, no problem," he finally said, and promised to be very careful to get the nine letters in the correct sequence.

"Speaking about emigration," he said, "I have two cousins who emigrated, but no farther than to Canada."

Then I had to tell him the story of the little grave of my namesake sister and of the inscription that had become homeless when the stone was removed and the coffin taken to the family burial place. And since Father had originally intended to use it for his own gravestone, I had promised myself to carry out his wish.

He has done a remarkably fine job of the inscription, in deep, almost luminous letters on the coarse surface. It's a special technique that only stonecutters know about, he says, making the lettering stand out and shine, even on a rough surface.

I have visited him in his workshop almost every day since he began working on the stone, and we have gradually become so well acquainted that I catch myself thinking aloud while listening to the ringing sound of his chisel.

Today, 18 January, I said something to him that made him turn round and give me a terrified look. "In not too long, I may have *emigravit* myself," I said, unaware that it might be misunderstood.

When it dawned on me what he was thinking, I couldn't let him remain in uncertainty, but set his mind at rest by saying I had no yearning for the land of the dead.

"I'm just wondering if I should emigrate to Jerusalem," I said, "and I've just ten days to make up my mind."

8

Four days until Aaron will be back from the USA.

I have become strangely alert and sharp of hearing lately, about the same as what happened in 1954 after he had gone to Israel and I was waiting to hear from him. I prowl about like a beast in the jungle, scouting about for signs and omens that can tell me something about the near future. I know it's absurd, but I don't even shun black magic to find out about the powers that rule our lives.

Sometimes I get the idea that I have to turn around three times before daring to sit down on a chair. It's an exorcism I have to execute very discreetly and cautiously in this place, with nobody watching, lest a new diagnosis be fished out of some desk drawer. When I go for a walk in the city, the sidewalk sometimes turns into a regular minefield, where I have to plant my feet in the right places not to miss my footing and topple into the abyss. Standing at a crossroads, I may take it into my head to say to myself, If you walk in the direction you had really meant to, you will end up going astray and all is lost. But if you take the opposite way, which seems to be a cul-de-sac, you come to a bridge that will lead you out of the labyrinth of doubt and over to the other side.

During the five weeks since Aaron and I said goodbye, I've been carrying on a virtually non-stop conversation with him about all that has been and will be. It is an imagined conversation, undisturbed by any physical presence, and I'm the one who both answers and asks the questions. But what is said is not pulled out of thin air. It is a paraphrase of our dreams and fantasies, and of all the tender, serious and clarifying words we told each other while we sat talking together behind the screen in Ward 6.

IDUN. Aaron, please tell me who you are, I mean who you have become during all those years we have been away from one another. Because you don't want me to believe, do you, that you are the same as the person I said goodbye to some day in August more than forty years ago?

AARON. Easy now, my friend, I'm not a seducer or wizard who wants you to take on faith something that you cannot experience with your own senses. So tell me instead what you see.

IDUN. I see a sympathetic but rather outlandish man around sixty, who both attracts me and frightens me a little. How shall I explain it? Well, I feel as if I'm floating in a vacuum, unable to find the connection between before and now. You cannot possibly drop a person by the roadside and hope she can be picked up again undamaged after ages have gone by, can you?

AARON. You're right, the connection between us was broken and cannot be re-established as it once was. But that doesn't worry me. All human relationships are changeable and must constantly be started afresh.

IDUN. How is that? Try to tell me. You know, I'm somewhat of a sceptic and have never shared your view of life.

AARON. In the first place, I never imagined I would pick you up undamaged, as you put it. I'm not plagued by any tactile phobias and don't mind associating with people who've got scratches and wounds.

IDUN. And in the second place?

AARON. In the second place, it isn't true that we dropped each other by the roadside. We were separated from one another by outside interference. You've told me yourself how Grandfather snapped up my letters and saw to it that you didn't get them.

IDUN. All right, let's say that we make a fresh start and that I join you when you leave for Israel in six days. But what about our child? Can we really find it in our hearts to abandon it, leaving it behind all alone?

AARON. Pardon me, now I can't follow you. What child are you talking about?

IDUN. Oh dear, you know very well, don't you, that we were going to have a child together when we parted in 1954?

AARON. What are you saying! How could I know about that?

IDUN. Well, now you know. We have a child walking around in Denmark somewhere, waiting to be found. I've been looking for it for ever so many years and won't stop until I find it.

AARON. (*after a long pause for reflection*) Idun, pardon me for saying so, but now you're wandering. The child you're talking about is a child no more, but a grown-up man or woman around forty. It is living its own life and has no wish to be found, I dare say.

IDUN. But I won't have any peace until I find it. I just have to know what has become of our child. If I go with you to Israel, it means that I've given up and must live with my neglect for the rest of my life.

AARON. Your neglect? What exactly do you mean?

IDUN. Well, you see, I was so apathetic and weak-willed at the time. Grandpa got me to sign some papers, and I had no idea that they were adoption papers. When I was sent to Denmark, I thought I would take the child with me back home.

AARON. Tell me what happened while you were down there.

IDUN. A married couple came to the midwife's place for coffee, I just thought they were some friends of hers. They were so brimful of friendliness toward me that I ought to have become suspicious. But I was stupid and understood absolutely nothing, not even when they quizzed me about my family, whether they were well and what they had accomplished in life. I was so in need of some human warmth, and it did me a lot of good that somebody showed concern for me. I had roamed about the beach at Sejerø Bay all winter and felt all alone in the world.

AARON. And what then? What happened when the winter was over and spring came?

IDUN. It was a difficult birth, suddenly it all stopped, and the child was drawn with forceps. A doctor came and administered anaesthesia, and when I woke up I was running a fever. The midwife managed to hoodwink me for almost a week, telling me that I had to grow a little stronger before learning anything about my child. She even refused to tell me whether it was a boy or a girl.

AARON. Dry your tears, my friend, they won't do you any good. That was forty years ago, and you will have to resign yourself to it.

IDUN. But I can hear the child crying when I lie awake at night. I can hear it call me from somewhere far away, and I get to feel that I have to go out and look for it.

AARON. (*after another pause for reflection lasting for several days*) I've been thinking, Idun, maybe that was the reason you began to roam.

IDUN. I don't know. You see, already as a little girl I had a tendency to run away, when I'd done something wrong and life became too threatening. Once I sat in the outhouse at Sandane a whole night, waiting for the world to come to an end. That was during the war, I was only seven years old and had accidentally given you and your mother away.

AARON. I know that, you told me about it. It was your inner judge who drove you away, and who knows, perhaps it is the same accuser who is persecuting you today.

IDUN. And then there was that time two years later, when I came stumbling into the courthouse and was turned out. I was completely inconsolable, running about the streets all day and shouting all kinds of bad words at myself. I should have confessed, you see, so that Father could've got off scot-free, but I didn't get that far. It still persecutes me in my dreams, in ever-changing variations. I stand before a counter and have something essential to relate, I open and close my mouth, making the utmost effort to get it out. The judge looks at me more and more sternly, and the entire room is buzzing with impatience. But not a single word escapes my lips. When I wake up I feel like an outlaw, a homeless person, someone who is an outcast and doesn't belong anywhere. I can no longer remain where I am, but have to get away before being caught by retribution.

AARON. Hm . . .

IDUN. Did you say something?

AARON. No, just go on, I'm listening.

IDUN. I suspect we'll have to talk a little about that diagnosis; you know. Or the persecution monster Paranoia, as I call her sometimes.

AARON. Yes, let me hear.

IDUN. Basically, of course, it's nothing but a paper tiger that is dozing between the pages of the medical record. There it is well protected and can't hurt a fly. But some day when you are particularly vulnerable it gets up and takes wing. It tracks you down with its omniscient eyes and stands waiting for you round the corner. Wherever you turn it's right at your heels, you feel its breath in the nape of your neck, and before you know it you are rushing away in headlong flight.

AARON. Wait a bit. Now you're too light of foot in more than one sense. Let's look at that time in 1944 when you were seven years old and ran away the first time. You had really done something wrong, though not intentionally. You had given away a secret and knew that some terrible

413

things might happen. Away, away, little Idun, before someone catches you.

IDUN. Exactly. But the one who wanted to catch me was not Paranoia, is that it?

AARON. No, not by any means. You simply obeyed a natural instinct and ran away from a real danger.

IDUN. And what about all my breakups later in life? I've read your report, but can't quite figure it out.

AARON. I try to prove that they all have a natural cause and have nothing to do with imaginary persecutors.

IDUN. Like, for example?

AARON. Like, for example, the two times you ran away from the place where we are right now. You were committed – that is, you were locked up within regulations which deprived you of the freedom to come and go as you pleased. There are many ways one can use to resist being committed. Some protest with attacks of rage, others with apathy and despair. You protested by disappearing, that's all.

IDUN. Are you so sure of that? It almost sounds too simple. I've been very low, and many times I've been so weak that I've come close to thinking of this place as home. And I can assure you that I've had moments of apathy and despair.

AARON. That may be, but one thing I can say with certainty. You do not suffer from paranoia, as it says in the medical record. You have none of the well-known symptoms that accompany schizophrenia. No hallucinations, no blunting of emotional life, no mental disturbances or delusions. You are a focused intellect that shows no signs of disintegration, and knows perfectly well how to distinguish between fiction and reality.

IDUN. So what do you think I'm suffering from?

AARON. Putting it a bit too simply, you suffer from an excess of imagination. You are a dreamer and a rebel against heaven, someone who cannot be satisfied with life as it generally presents itself.

IDUN. And what do you want me to do about it, Mr. Peeping Tom of the soul?

AARON. Listen, you have for a number of years found an outlet for your imagination by writing strong and original books. So I don't believe I need prescribe any cure for you, it seems you've already found it.

IDUN. Do you mean those three little poems to joy that I wrote in December and copied on the last page of the memory book?

AARON. Yes, my friend. I mean them and I mean *The Papessa* and *Jocasta's Revenge* and *The Angel and the Monster* and the other books you've written. I've read every one of them, and they tell me that you are a poet, heart and soul.

IDUN. Heart and soul, no trifle that. (*Starts giggling shyly.*) Ha-ha, pardon me, but I can't help laughing. Perhaps you can tell me what a poet is, you who know so much about the heart and the soul?

AARON. I'm just a poor grubber before the Lord, but all right, I'll take you at your word and try. A poet is a human being who has suffered a loss like all the rest of us, but who cannot resign himself to God being dead and the gates of paradise closed. He must create another reality that can explain, restore and outshine his wasted life. In his search for perfection he moves about in a borderland, where he's constantly expanding his world and constantly running the risk of taking a false step and plunging to perdition. To carry out his work he has to divide himself into a number of dissimilar characters, all of whom relate to him like shadows of some kind, or *Doppelgängers*. It may very well look like split personality, but, mind you, this is a perfectly conscious splitting of the personality. I call it a self-healing activity, a manifestation of exuberance that pertains to art and has no place in the psychiatric ward.

IDUN. But what about my drug addiction? That can hardly be called a manifestation of exuberance, can it?

AARON. I won't try to figure that one out, for I've never seen you when you were high. But let us say it is a desire for adventure that has gone astray. Something your creative imagination takes to when it is in the doldrums and won't wait until the right stuff turns up.

IDUN. But what's going to happen to me the day I have no more adventures to relate? The day I'm discharged, not only from the madhouse, but also in the other sense of the word, empty and written out?

AARON. I do not believe that day to be imminent, if my opinion means anything to you. There are no signs that your creative imagination has outlived its day.

IDUN. But what if it should?

AARON. (*with a little smile in the corner of his mouth*) Well, then I can only suggest that you realize your idea of being creative with the body, as you call it in the memory book. That you resume your old work as a nurse and give me a hand in my hospital.

9

Another postcard from Aaron, one of those double ones in giant size, to make quite sure! It runs like this, if I can decipher his hieroglyphics, which spread across all three sides and haven't even let the side with the picture alone:

Manhattan, Saturday 21 January, 1995

Shalom Idun,

Yes, greetings, my love, this time from Columbia University, where I'm going to give my last lectures before boarding the plane and heading home.

Pardon this whopping "sign of life", which you will probably see as a breach of our agreement. The double card is by itself a bit of trickery, as I know very well, and there's even a danger of my going after the goddess of liberty on the front, disfiguring her with my scrawls. But my dear, I have something important to tell you, so for once I'm going to act as a sophist incarnate and insist that a postcard is a postcard.

Enough of that and to the matter in hand. While we were talking behind the screen in Ward 6, you asked me several times who I am, and you did it so urgently that I went away with a sense that I owed you an answer. Usually a question like that is superfluous between people who are close to each other and know the art of reading what's unspoken. But forty years of separation has brought us to a situation where everything is up in the air, and your question has become a matter of conscience to me.

You know most of it from our conversations, but here is an outline of my path in life from the autumn of 1954 to today. It is tortuous and full of dead ends, but I'll try to trace it briefly and not wander too freely.

I arrived in the young state of Israel as a true pioneer, full of enthusiasm and hope for the future. Mother and I settled in a *kibbutz* in the vicinity of Tel Aviv, where we soon acquired good friends and came to feel at home. The change of air was particularly beneficial for Mother, who blossomed and rediscovered her natural *joie de vivre* after her twelve years of shadowy existence in 24 Strand Street. Today, forty years later, she still lives in the same collective, happily remarried and mother to my two half-siblings, thirty-six and thirty-four years old.

For a few months I picked oranges on the slopes around Tel Aviv, studied Hebrew in the evening and participated eagerly in the communal life of the *kibbutz*, which as far as ends and means were concerned differed little from my anarchist circle in the old country. Then came military service, where I was enrolled as a paratrooper and managed to become a sergeant. At one time I considered staying in the army and having a military career; it agreed well with the ideals I then had of building the country and securing its existence. But after some vacillation I ended up at the university, more specifically in the Department of Sociology. Medicine hadn't yet entered my thoughts; it was the body politic, Society, that called on me and monopolized my ardour and passion.

I finished my studies and was given a university appointment in Jerusalem; then came the six-day war and everything changed. I do not exaggerate when I say that this blitzkrieg was the turning point, my Damascus experience, as Grandfather would have called it. It was the disaster that gave my life a new direction, the nightmare that swallowed me whole and spewed me out again as another person.

I was a member of the elite unit that conquered Jerusalem, a specially equipped troop that led the way, operating in the front rank. We fought our way from street to street and from house to house, detonated fire bombs, threw hand grenades into entrance-ways, and mowed down every living soul that got in our way. At the end the city was an inferno of blood and fire, and we ourselves were just as infernal as we clambered over ruins, desecrated the holy places and trampled on the bodies of dead men, women and children. The god of war had become my lord and master, I acted as though I were deaf and blind, a killing machine on two legs, a living machine-gun that stormed forward, shunning no obstacle.

When I came back to my senses, I was sitting on a doorstep by the Damascus Gate, stripped of everything: patriotism, Zionist phrases, the whole myth of God's chosen people. The victory was ours, but to me it seemed more like a defeat. My spiritual armour fell off me like an empty shell: I was a murderer without Bible verses on my lips, a clear-sighted eye that realized the absurdity of turning the clock back and laying claim to territories that had belonged to other peoples for two thousand years.

It was then I decided on medicine, where I could preserve life and do penance for all the innocent people whose lives I had taken during those six days the conquest of the Holy City was going on. (I call it the Holy City on purpose, because it is full of laughing and suffering and hoping human beings, that is, of the living life which I have learned to regard as holy.)

Unfortunately I was to learn in the course of the years that not all physicians see it the same way. I was shocked to the depths of my soul last winter when I learned that one of my previous colleagues at the Augusta Victoria Hospital had broken into the mosque in Hebron and shot down twenty-nine Palestinians who were kneeling at prayer. Heaven only knows what lightning bolt had struck the perpetrator of this act. I knew Baruch Goldstein as a conscientious and perfectly normal man, without any conspicuous religious fanaticism. Today he has been proclaimed a martyr, and on his tombstone in the settlement Kirjat Arba it says that he sacrificed his life for a sacred cause.

It was after this last disaster that there arose in me a vision of a new state of things, one in which Palestinians and Israelis have made peace and live side by side as good neighbours in the Holy Land. Yes, dear Idun, it may be just a beautiful dream, or a utopia, as it has become customary to call ideas that cannot be realized. Heaven cannot be brought down to earth, I know that well enough; the wolf cannot live with the lamb without the strongest and the most voracious of them consuming the other.

Even so I cannot let go of the thought of utopia, that creative dream that is so little appreciated at the moment. In my view it is the incentive behind our noblest actions, our most humane impulses, our guiding star that we reach for without ever catching it.

Take care of yourself, my love, see you in six days.
Your Aaron

P.S. My dear friend, bear with me if you feel that the words "love" and "your Aaron" are too demanding in our present situation. But make no mistake, you *are* my love, regardless what you decide. And I am *your* Aaron, now and for the rest of my life, even if you discover that you cannot be mine. Our Oslo agreement may not be entirely mutual, but it exists and can be expanded!

P.P.S. Let me own up to another thing: Before I left Oslo I was brash enough to look up the editor at your publishing house and ask him if he would be my best man, should the wedding come off on Saturday, 28 January. He immediately declared himself willing to do so and promised to be available at short notice, if necessary. All other formalities are taken care of and arranged. Halleluja.

P.P.P.S. The reason I am proceeding so boldly is that I have had so many good, beautiful dreams lately. And usually my dreams come true!

P.P.P.P.S. The collection of money for my hospital has turned into a minor fiasco, as I've already told you. But I'm terribly curious who that newly rich person you think I can put my trust in might be!!??

10

How strange, almost like an omen. Last night I too had a happy dream, though usually I'm haunted by all kinds of terrors and nightmares during my sleeping hours.

I was standing on a path at the edge of a wood that was so overgrown that it looked more like a thicket. As always happens in dreams, the place was indeterminate and yet oddly familiar, and it took a while before I realized that I found myself at the approximate midpoint of Lovers' Lane at Sandane. The moon shone above the tree tops, and I seemed to be on the look-out, as if I were waiting for something special to happen. In the thicket I could make out a dark figure that was also on the look-out, and it occurred to me that it must be Aunt Dora at her post, waiting for a pair of sweethearts to pass by.

Suddenly I catch sight of two solitary individuals who step into my field of vision from opposite ends of the path. They are a young man and a young woman; the distance between them is about one hundred metres, and they come sneaking along from different directions, as if they know they are running a risk. Anxiety grips me, and I want to call to them to watch out for Aunt Dora, who is lying in wait for them in the thicket. But I don't see how I can warn them without alerting her, causing her to rush out of hiding and to separate them.

Suddenly a wind comes up, the moon scuds between the clouds, and the lovers hurry up and breeze toward each other. I see them approach one another at breakneck speed, shrinking from no danger, and no power on earth can keep them away from each other.

But what is this? Time too is speeding up, and as they hurry off, summer, autumn, winter and spring slip by over their heads. Now the trees sway with fresh foliage, now the leaves fall to the ground and snow settles on the naked branches, which a moment later shake off the layer of snow and turn green once again. When the young man briefly enters my field of vision, I notice that he is of medium height, with black hair and an athletic build. And now the moonlight falls upon the young woman who rushes off to her tryst, the long, blond tresses fluttering wildly about her head. I see them wave to one another and increase their speed, until their bodies fairly float along the path.

But while they are on their way, the earth turns at a dizzying rate, the seasons can no longer be kept apart; there is an eternal "springwinter" with a tinge of late summer in the air, and I can see that their figures find themselves at a kind of flying standstill. But heedless of everything, they wave anew and fly towards one another with open arms. The shadow in the thicket imperceptibly withdraws, melting into the many half-rotten tree trunks that are hidden in the darkness. The two lovers have just a few steps to go, they are out of danger, no one can interfere and separate them anymore. But as they arrive and throw themselves into each other's arms, I see to my surprise that in their wild race they have put their youth behind them, the man's hair being completely white and the woman's falling over her shoulders in long, grey-gold tangles.

I woke up from hearing myself shout, not in my usual meek and slightly faltering voice but in the young, exultant and bright voice that was once so certain it was right: "I love him! I love him! I love him!"

I wish to express my gratitude to Eléonore Zimmermann for her patience, support and encouragement during the period I was working on this translation, and for reading the entire manuscript. My thanks go also to the author, Bergljot Hobæk Haff, whose answers to my queries were prompt, gracious and informative.

S. L.